Savior on the Zenith

(Fragmented Fates Duology, #2)

Nancy Foster

ISBN-13: 978-607-29-5333-8

TABLE OF CONTENTS

ACKNOWLEDGMENTS

I wholeheartedly thank my cover artist Armd for exceeding my expectations once again and created a cover that beautifully balances the vibe from Fragmented Fates. This sequel is much darker than the first half, and I found the symbolism quite fitting. Miriam, thanks for helping me with the back cover!

Since my cat Ardilla sadly passed away several years ago, I guess I should maintain the tradition and thank my cat Mika that I rescued during the pandemic. She always seems happy when I see her. Yuri too, but I suspect he's only happy because he expects me to feed him even though he just ate.

And finally, I thank you, the reader who is holding this book and probably very curious to know how the story ends. I hope you enjoy the sequel!

THE STORY SO FAR...

Approximately 150 years ago, an elf named Lord Jamarnid was given the death penalty for impregnating a woman with human and harlequin ancestry. Sentenced to die by having his limbs crushed with hammers in the Elf King's palace, a group of harlequins infiltrate the palace, kill hundreds of spectators, and rescue Jamarnid.

Humiliated in front of everyone, Master Lord Salman ordered his royal Äimite guard to exterminate every member of Jamarnid's birth clan. Pinned to a wall without any hopes for salvation, the Grey Clan's new leader Hormandra fights the guard to the death within the walls of Teryoura Palace.

A badly wounded Jamarnid, his newborn son Jarahad, his nephew Sharad, alongside a small contingent of male elves escape the Elf Kingdom. They soon seek refuge in the harlequin city of Orsenmuray. Jarahad always felt like an outcast by both elf and harlequin society. Raised by his disabled father, Jarahad spends his childhood alongside his lover, a fellow harlequin hybrid elf named Talgel.

Not much is known about Talgel during the time she lived in Orsenmuray alongside her parents. Hints are sprinkled regarding her once wholesome persona and hopes to someday wed Jarahad when the human invasions stopped. A few days before the city fell and her parents died, Talgel awakened powerful clairvoyance magic at the price of losing her eyesight. Crushed by this loss, Talgel's personality changed forever, and she has staunchly rejected Jarahad's hand in marriage for unclear reasons.

Upon the fall of Orsenmuray, both the elf and harlequin survivors were forced to embark on a dreadful voyage through human lands that lasted several years. Steadfast in never settling down in lands occupied by humans, the refugees found the new city of Almjarhad next to an impassable bay in the desert. Disappointed about suffering endless traumatic experiences his whole life, Lord Sharad flees the city and his whereabouts are unknown.

This is where the main story commences.

After Talgel ended up wounded killing a vagrant, Jarahad assigns a female harlequin named Henrietta to tend to her personal needs. Skeptical about her true motives, Talgel treats the kind woman with scorn during most of the story. Early in the story, Talgel summons her phantom beast and discovers an important future prediction that won't happen unless Sharad returns to the city.

With some difficulty, Jarahad wounds an Äimite guard commander named Senior Lord Froylan and helps return Sharad to Almjarhad unscathed. Now that Sharad has returned, Talgel summons her phantom beast a second time by accident. She discovers a certain inhabitant of the city must elope with the exiled harlequin ruler named Hurrujat.

Jarahad is granted permission from Hurrujat to become initiated in the combative harlequin arts despite his mixed ancestry. Winning Talgel's love motivates Jarahad during his long training. Much to his chagrin, the final test involved killing a human child. Disgusted due to preferring to pass the initiation at the expense of his morals, Jarahad keeps these feelings of self-hatred to himself. Things become more complicated when Hurrujat's new lover named Hamara entices the harlequins to leave Almjarhad. Jarahad tries to maintain a neutral position against the wishes of his father and hopes the harlequins become happy in their new home.

Just like Jarahad and Talgel, Tioja is a young elf with mixed harlequin and elf ancestry, which are colloquially named halflings. With dazzling reddish-green eyes and a perky smile, Tioja's simple life is turned upside down when his parents commence having nonstop marital problems. Filled with frustration and self-loathing, Tioja assumes Talgel's unannounced visit to speak to his mother Hamara meant his life would return to normal. Much to his chagrin, Hamara's true fortune lies in founding an underground harlequin city alongside her new husband Hurrujat.

Jamarnid's life has changed in many ways after his botched execution. Due to his disability, Jamarnid is forced to relay most governing functions to his son Jarahad. Little does he know, Talgel has been manipulating every important event of the city behind the curtains the whole time. For what reason? This has been left unanswered. The only thing Jamarnid knows is that his trusted close friend, a fellow elf named

Priest Soremin believes in Talgel.

Dismayed by seeing his mother abandon Almjarhad forever, Tioja tries to make life easier for his alcoholic father named Jamad to little avail. Worse, Tioja soon discovers he has awakened an uncontrollable magic ability that can destroy anything with his mind. Despite Jarahad's best attempts to train him, Tioja ends up fleeing Almjarhad. He is currently traveling to the harlequin city alongside his mother, where his destiny awaits…

CHAPTER 1 ♦ TIOJA

There was one thought piercing through Tioja's mind: he wanted to murder his mother. And he hated himself for it. It was true he felt resentment when Hamara abandoned her home to elope with a geriatric harlequin. That didn't justify these vile desires that flashed into his subconscious the instant they departed Almjarhad a few hours ago.

Ever since Tioja awakened his demonic beast, he no longer felt like his mind was his own. Shrouded by the initial pain of his new wings that appeared on his back out of nowhere, these feelings became stronger over time.

This wasn't the only thing that disturbed him. Exposed bones, limbs dangling in unnatural angles, and so much blood that stained the sand. Inappropriate thoughts about seeing Talgel's corpse were frequent whenever he rested.

As the two halflings rode on Hamara's steed in the unforgiving desert, their voyage was characterized by silence. Was she angry at him? Hamara wasn't displaying fear like everyone else, so perhaps that was the problem.

Before Tioja knew it, Hamara's back lurched forward, and her body teetered against the saddle. "Mom!" With a rapid hand motion, Tioja used harlequin air magic to straighten her in the nick of time. As the horse stopped, thunderous beats pounded Tioja's heart, and Hamara soon stirred.

"Huh?" For unexplained reasons, Hamara's red eyes seemed puffy. Disorientation imbued her beautiful face. Soon enough, Hamara snapped awake, and she returned to her regular self. "Oh, my. Did something happen, little Tio?"

Unsure about the strange sequence of events, Tioja shook his head. "I… The sun is… Can we hide somewhere? I'm terrified of harming you."

Instead of showing concern, Hamara's face remained unreadable as she stared at their surroundings. Towering mountains dotted every direction, with a vast landscape devoid of life except for errant thorn bushes and weeds. It took Hamara a few minutes to spot something in the distance. "We'll take a detour over yonder to rest."

The horse plodded with an uncertain gait over rocky formations while Hamara remained focused on her task. Initially uncertain about her plan, Tioja's heart jumped when they encountered several rock formations looming ahead that offered sufficient shade.

Hamara dismounted first and removed the hood from her travel cloak. Dressed in elegant robes, Tioja only felt increased intrigue about Hamara's life in her new home. "Let me help you dismount, Tio."

Tioja's unsteady legs trembled from the exhaustion of sharing the same saddle and stumbled a few steps when his feet touched the ground. He would have probably fallen if it hadn't been for his air magic. Hamara, meanwhile, was rubbing her eyes as she fastened the horse to a stone and sat down.

His mother's unsettling demureness only made him want to study her even more. A gasp escaped his lips upon spotting something dangling on her hip. "Is that a sword? Since when can you use one?"

Aan odd twitch escaped Hamara's lip, leaving her both flustered and somewhat annoyed. Was his mother always so callous? Did something happen to her? Tioja soon sat next to his mother. His mind focused on Hamara, who seemed so close, yet so distant.

"Are you all right, mom?"

Hamara's eyes fluttered from somnolence, and a barely audible murmur echoed. "I must rest, my child. And you should too." Upon finishing that sentence, Hamara entered a state that seemed far too lifeless to be sleep. The only hints of life came from the rhythmic movements of her chest.

Even though Tioja was very much sleep-deprived, the senseless thoughts trying to grab hold of his mind made it impossible to fall asleep. So Tioja spent the better part of the day wallowing in sorrow.

When the seer announced the legend of the Cursed One, he

assumed it was an event that would never happen during his lifetime. Something that was not important or worthwhile. His life was ruined when his grandfather Jamen told him to summon his beast on the beach alongside his uncle Nurran.

That horrible, wretched desire to rip everything into pieces was now a part of him. It accompanied him during the day as he trained, ate, bathed, and even dreamt. No matter how hard Lord Jarahad tried to teach him to ignore it, there was no turning back. Did the seer Talgel feel something similar when she awakened her phantom beast and lost her eyesight? Utter nonsense! As far as Tioja knew, Jarahad never lost something when he first summoned his phantom beast which resembled a detachable green armor. Maybe he truly was cursed, and everyone would fear him from now on…

No, that couldn't be true. So far, Hamara had not shown any degree of fear of his uncontrollable magic and was risking her own life to bring him somewhere. Yes, maybe he can be happy for a change. Hopes for a better future were the only thing that maintained Tioja's last string of sanity.

As the sun raised into the sky, Tioja's heart raced with increased ferocity as the heat became more intolerable and his shadow crept on the ground.

"Something troubles you, my fair child." Hamara's grasp on Tioja's chest was comforting as she woke up.

"Mother, I fear hurting you. I learned how to summon a phantom beast."

A sinister laugh escaped Hamara's chapped lips. "Congratulations! I thought Talgel and Jarahad were the only lucky halflings."

"That isn't true! Several halflings can summon beasts. Your siblings are working hard as well. Maybe you can use sorcery too!"

"Oh, perhaps I can." A cunning grin invaded Hamara's lips. "You don't look happy being one of the chosen."

"That is because my beast is evil! I have these thoughts when I summon it. Every time I use it, I can't control the desire to destroy everything I touch."

"Talgel warned me not to return until you were ready."

"When did that happen? Talgel has never left the city."

"She talked to me when you were sequestered in Soremin's temple. I was instructed to visit the pagoda the night I found you. If it hadn't been for Talgel's insistence, I would have visited you sooner. Would you know the reason why?"

Tioja blinked in disbelief upon discovering why Hamara had not visited him before. A sense of warmth filled his heart, knowing his mother's love was genuine. He spoke with a firmer voice. "Jarahad tried his best. When everyone discovered I destroyed the palm trees on the beach that fateful day, they agreed I was the Cursed One from Talgel's premonition. Almost everyone wanted to oust me from Almjarhad. Jarahad is one of the few elves that still believes I could be saved and let me live with him. We trained almost every evening in the desert, so I didn't hurt anyone. His efforts were useless. I can't control it and feel scared of hurting innocent people."

"Don't be angry. I might not have agreed with Jarahad, but he is a good leader. If he hadn't remained so blindly faithful to the customs of the elves and embraced his true harlequin ancestry like me, Hurrujat would have recognized him as his heir."

"You are acting like Lord Sharad doesn't even exist."

Hamara's lips twitched at the sheer thought. "Given I have nothing tying me to the kingdom, I can speak my thoughts. Just because Sharad has a true blood claim to lead the Grey Clan doesn't mean he is a worthy leader. I wouldn't be surprised if he still acts like a belligerent child catching butterflies with a net instead of assuming his birthright."

Tioja sighed without showing insult. Hamara was always an opinionated woman from his scant memories of her as a child. Even though he realized it would be pointless, he still wanted to satiate his curiosity. "Jamad misses you."

"Oh, I am certain he does. He will never meet a woman quite like me ever again. I could never love him but never forget he will always be your father. How many years have passed since I last saw him?"

"It has been 18 years, mother."

"Well, I guess Jamad wishes to embrace the nonsense elvish custom of remaining alone for a century. At least it seems like your father has treated you well."

"Actually… I have been disowned."

Hamara sat up straight. Her stern yet gorgeous face was staring at Tioja with fierceness. "That bastard… abandoned you? When you needed his support the most?"

"Please don't take revenge! He is just scared. I can make things explode with my mind, and I can't seem to control it! I beg you to run away from me and hide because I might kill you!"

"Foolish little boy. I can absorb your mana. You will never feel afraid or alone if you stay by my side. Your new home awaits you."

"Home? But I am no longer welcome in Almjarhad."

"How convenient. It means you have severed the chains that always hindered you. I know you are afraid of your harlequin blood due to Jamad's ignorance, and I am here to make amends. Please be patient and try to rest. You are safe with me."

When the sun reached its zenith in the sky, Hamara remained pensive as she ate some of the food Tioja stole from the castle's pantry.

This odd behavior didn't seem too insulting to him. It was only natural Hamara would be thinking about the unfairness of his eviction from the city. Even his grandparents were hesitant to approach him after that fateful day. Only Jarahad and his uncle Nurran dared to be nice to him.

And so, Tioja nibbled on his meal and took advantage of these moments of silence to study his mother further. Hamara had aged very little from the last time he saw her. Her wavy grey hair was shoulder-length and fastened in a ponytail. A pair of crimson eyes glistened ever so brightly against the battering sun. Hamara's sienna skin seemed quite pale, almost to the verge of being sickly. Her travel robes were unusually thick and unsuitable for this climate. Made from fine fabric, he felt increased curiosity about Hamara's new life. Tioja wondered if his mother's inherent beauty was why Hurrujat fell in love with her. A pang of disgust at the idea of Hurrujat's infidelity shook Tioja to stop thinking about that.

What was more confounding was that Hamara hid her face beneath her cloak and constantly rubbed her eyes as she ate her meal. And so Tioja quenched his curiosity. "Are you infirm?"

"I am used to living underground. My eyes irritate me."

"Underground? Weren't you born in a depressing and miserable prison? Why would you like to live in a dungeon? I don't know if I should go."

Hamara shook her head and smiled as the traces of her face were visible beneath the cloak. "I am certain you will feel quite comfortable in Murdorhiolan."

"That is the name of your city?"

"Correct, and we should arrive within a few weeks. Try to rest, and we shall reach it soon."

As promised, both halflings crossed the desert and eventually reached a dense forest. Whereas Hamara seemed relatively unmoved from the change of scenery, Tioja would often stare in every direction to admire the unfamiliar sights. "Everything is so green!"

Hamara chuckled with politeness as the horse cleverly dodged rogue branches and rocks on uneven ground. "I find it quite amusing you would feel awed by such an ordinary thing."

"Not at all! I have seen the olive trees on the city's outskirts grow over time. Not even the fields turn into this radiant color during the wet season!"

"Orsenmuray was close to the southern border of the Elf Kingdom. I recall playing in the snow quite a handful of times as a child."

"Amazing! I have never been allowed to fly to the mountaintops near Almjarhad to see the snow. What is it like?"

"Cold, wet, and fluffy when it is fresh. You might see it for yourself in Murdorhiolan if you are lucky. Your sheltered life has made me think about my own upbringing. I initially felt the same way when we first reached Almjarhad and saw the ocean for the first time. Until the hardships began due to the relentless food shortages." A venomous hiss escaped Hamara's lips upon saying this final statement.

"Why didn't you stay in Almjarhad and say hello to everyone?"

Any tint of emotion vanished from Hamara's face. "While I harbor no ill towards Jarahad, my home is in Murdorhiolan. If you stay there long enough, you will no longer miss the city that abandoned you."

Hamara's disconcerting warning prompted Tioja to observe her sword better. The hilt was decorated with gold leaves, which struck him as odd. Hamara never learned to fence when she lived in Almjarhad and dedicated her life to being a simple housewife. Part of him wanted to satiate his curiosity, but his mother's current sodden mood was a hint to avoid any touchy topics. He had plenty of time to ask once they arrived.

As the steed marched on, the forest slowly thinned into a series of mountains intertwined with rivers. Awed from this display of color and freshwater, Tioja marveled from these new sights and the sounds of birds he had never heard before.

Insects sometimes zoomed past his face, and the tenacity of mosquitos living so far away from his birth city felt marvelous in an unusual way. Not that Hamara seemed to care about his joy. Hamara seldom bothered to speak to her son, and only focused on reaching their destination. Whether it was because Hamara was always this unapproachable or she was concerned about miscreants, Tioja never addressed these concerns.

For the first time in ages, their horse ceased trampling on ferns and bushes to throttle on a paved stone road. Before Tioja could inquire about this unexpected work of masonry, Hamara spoke for the first time that day. "We are getting closer to the first human settlements that surround Murdorhiolan."

"That is nice to hear, mum. Did the humans build this?"

"Of course not, silly! We did… with magic."

While Tioja didn't find it odd that an earth mage built this road, it perplexed him Hamara's kin would assist humans. During the years Tioja lived in Almjarhad, Jarahad never bothered to help improve the neighboring human settlements. The paved road to Almjarhad vanished a few miles after the uninhabited mountain chain that separated the city from the peninsula ended. "Mother, did the humans ask for your help?"

"Not exactly. We protect these lands from criminals, and the humans help us doing various things. Such as grow livestock, or deal with that human king," Hamara's eyes sharpened without revealing the true meaning around her second statement.

Tioja considered it best to avoid prodding her mother about that topic further. Doing so was wise because Hamara's mood continued souring as they reached an area where the paved road stopped out of nowhere. Hamara clutched him closer to her embrace. "Stay alert and don't let go. I promise to protect you." With a swift jerk, Hamara commanded her steed, and it whisked them across the path in a frantic gallop. Concerned about this odd turn of events, Tioja heard a shrill sound fast approaching them.

Hamara growled at once. "Bloody cowards." Her right hand fumbled for something while her left continued guiding the horse at full speed. More shrill sounds echoed from afar, forcing her to draw her sword and slice passing arrows heading their way.

Realizing the humans in this area were hostile, Tioja hid his face in Hamara's chest and prayed they would escape unharmed. After a few desperate minutes, the horse decelerated and was now walking at a relaxed pace while heaving from exhaustion.

Knowing the danger had passed, Hamara spoke the instant the horse was now pacing on a paved road. "Sorry about that scare. The humans in the village continue to be hostile to us and they recognized my horse. From this point on, our voyage will be uneventful."

True to her word, Tioja eventually regained his confidence and peered from Hamara's cloak. They were now crossing a medium sized human city with unusual wooden log dwellings. An unfamiliar human language was spoken and most of the humans had the same skin color as his father Jamad. It never even occurred to Tioja humans could have pale skin. What gawked him further was the odd sight of humans with red air. "Look mom! I see a woman with fire in her hair!"

Hamara had recovered her joviality and spoke. "Elves and harlequins cannot have red hair. It is not a common hair color, but you will occasionally see it in this region. You will soon get used to seeing humans with blue eyes as well. Everything will become normal the longer you live with us."

As the sun began to set, they finally reached a towering stone wall that was carved from one of the hills. This stone had intricate statues of humans and harlequins in various poses. Some of the fields had livestock that were being guided beyond fearsome gigantic wooden doors.

Before Tioja could ask further, Hamara confirmed his suspicions. "Humans farm some of our food because we don't like living in the sun. Cows supply our city with ample amounts of blood to keep us alive, and we have developed our own blood wine recipes that cater more to our taste. I am certain you will enjoy drinking our wine very much. Let us go inside."

Crowds saluted Hamara and a few halflings bowed in her presence. Mindful of Hamara's political position, Tioja avoided saluting anyone and let her do everything. Their horse took a different detour from the main tunnel the livestock were going as the last rays of sunlight became replaced by odd green lights. The shift in light made Tioja furrow his eyebrows. "Mother, where are the animals going?"

Hamara remained adamant as they ambled past stone ramps inside tunnels large enough to carry dozens of armed carriages at once.

"Almjarhad has defenses, too, you know."

This was a strange response. "Earth mages did community service by moving the rocks on the bay further into the sea so enemy ships couldn't dock without permission. But I don't understand. Cows are not rocks!"

"Silly child. Murdorhiolan needs a lot of food to feed all of us. The main gate has many hidden layers of reinforced steel that will be difficult to destroy even with harlequin magic. The tunnels are, in fact, a complex maze with hidden traps. Enemies that try to invade our city risk bumping into hidden guard posts and getting ambushed."

"So, if we are attacked, we won't starve?"

"Yes, Tio. We also have underground fish reservoirs along with freshwater shrimp farms. Most of our meat comes from seafood. With time, you will learn the design of our city without feeling lost. For the time being, you should travel with a chaperone to avoid falling into a trap and hurting yourself."

They passed through a series of dizzying tunnels with the ever-constant presence of guard posts watching them with keen eyes. With each minute, Hamara's demeanor became haughtier, and it was little surprise why. Murdorhiolan was a vast cavernous city constructed in a maze of caves of varying shapes and sizes. There were dozens of ponds imbued with colorful fish that dazzled Tioja's eyes with their fluorescent exoskeletons. Unusual flat plants peppered the walls in ethereal greenish lights and countless lamps offered subdued greenish visibility to their surroundings. After a while, Tioja's initial fears of the outdoors during the day were soon forgotten as he gawked at the shapes and sizes of the city's dwellings, perfectly manicured streets that offered a large berth for Hamara's steed and inhabitants that saluted them with overt enthusiasm. The air had a spicy odor Tioja was incapable of pinpointing. He was soon convinced Jamad's stories about the filthiness of harlequin cities were more a reflection of his intolerance than something based in truth. So, his heart jumped a beat from excitement as the horse approached the castle at the heart of the city.

Murdorhiolan Palace was three times larger than Almjarhad Castle, with an octagonal star shaped structure of dark stone with pillars that glittered in the artificial lighting of the city. Balconies with large windows adorned every wall. Unlike the modest patio of Almjarhad Palace, this castle boasted large fields in every direction covered in more fluorescent lichen and fishponds. Servants were alerted long ago about Hamara's arrival and stood side by side in a seemingly endless row to salute their queen. Soon enough, the steed reached the entrance where Hurrujat was awaiting with glee.

While Tioja expected the harlequin to have aged over the years, it was startling to see the facial tumor covering Hurrujat's entire right eye, which had to be enucleated.

Hurrujat now walked with a cane that jittered from instability and pain. Despite the discomfort, his unpleasing face was imbued with the smile Tioja had always remembered growing up. "My love! Blessed the gods that the seer's prediction had come true! You've finally brought my son home!"

"My... son?" Clamminess covered Tioja's hands as Hamara set him down, and he tried his best to kowtow before the city's ruler. Assuming the greeting was due to a linguistic mistake, Tioja spoke in the Almjarhad pidgin language with stoic politeness. "I am honored to be granted refuge in your city, Lord Hurrujat. I am pleased to meet you after so many years and hope my company is not a hindrance to your hospitality."

"Nonsense, my boy! I always felt terrible when you rejected my wife's offer to accompany us to our home. The only reason I didn't pressure you at the time was due to Lord Jarahad's command regarding the underage citizens. I am proud to announce in front of my people that I officially recognize you as my adoptive son. From now on, you will be treated like my own blood and will someday govern this city alongside your brother."

Upon hearing such an outrageous speech, Tioja lifted his head and gawked at the sight. Before his mind could process anything, Hamara hugged him with all her might. "Yes, Tioja. The little guy standing next to my husband is your younger brother Gulraj."

Screeches echoed in the vast stone hallways that morning. Taking advantage there weren't any planned meetings in the throne room today, a grin imbued Jamarnid's face as a servant pushed his wheelchair.

Soon enough, the chair reached a metallic device installed on the wall beneath the dim glow of a ceiling sphere. The servant removed the hatch with deftness, and a glass tube emitting pure green energy was now visible in the middle of the crevice.

Mana imbued Jamarnid's body, and the stone bracelet dangling on his left wrist made a tiny phantom beast appear on the servant's hand. Jamarnid's Lusenia possessed a humanoid face, wolf torso, paws, and lizard hind legs. The miniature variant of his summoned beast was devoid of spikes on its tail and seemed almost like a cute, albeit odd, pet. Its eyes were a dull black because Jamarnid was not in meditation.

Even though the temptation to steal mana was great, the servant would never risk insulting the vassal Grey Clan Leader and current ruler of Almjarhad. With care, the servant placed the phantom beast next to the glass device, and mana energy was soon lured inside by an electromagnetic attraction.

As the device absorbed more mana, their surroundings became brighter. Within a few moments, the passage was almost as brilliant as walking outside during the day.

Jamarnid cleared his voice as his beast vanished. "Let's reach the third level."

With a polite bow, the servant locked the hatch, grasped the chair's handles, and turned it around. To make Almjarhad Castle wheelchair accessible, it possessed a unique architectural design akin to harlequin tastes. The circular-shaped building had the entire middle as the colossal throne room, which could be occasionally observed below from a few scant windows. The portion of the building facing outside contained the common rooms. Nestled in between had beige stone hallways wide enough to accommodate Jamarnid's wheelchair and passersby.

Only the highest levels of the castle had windows in the hallways, which meant artificial lighting was needed to maintain proper visibility in the lower levels. When the castle was first built, they used regular torches. This was no longer the case. Ever since the dock was inaugurated more than 10 years ago, commerce with the Elf Kingdom was now possible.

Every few weeks, Jamarnid visited each lamp in the palace to reignite the mana lamps as part of his self-professed community service duty. Doing so always gave him a sense of satisfaction he seldom felt.

Among designing a castle that felt appealing to their harlequin allies, architects devised building interlocking wheelchair-accessible ramps and regular staircases to reach each level. A visitor had to walk to the other side of the building to make everything fit. Ramps and staircases were built right next to the hallways facing the lateral rooms. These cramped crannies ended up being converted into storage rooms.

Thanks to Jamarnid's mana, this ramp was well illuminated, albeit the brightness of the lights diminished with each step towards the third level, whose lighting device was running low on mana.

After donating mana to the third-level lighting device, Jamarnid turned around. His face became imbued with a slight frown. Jarahad, the son he illegally procreated with a human-harlequin noblewoman 100 years ago, was rushing off with a stumbling stride and a forlorn expression.

Usually, Jarahad was very mindful of saluting his father and only ignored him whenever there were urgent matters in the city he helped rule. Jarahad's facial expression hinted at an overt of aloofness. Was it possible Jarahad was thinking about the lover that rejected his hand in marriage?

Jamarnid shook his head. His son was an adult halfling elf with an exceptional sense of morals. There was no way he was off to beg the seer once again for her hand in marriage. Perhaps it was something else…

Soon enough, a male elf dressed in elegant blue silk sleeping robes was prancing on the hallways while brushing his blond hair. Under normal circumstances, Jamarnid would have felt compelled to berate the passerby for waking up so late. As the true heir to the Grey Clan, Sharad enjoyed a myriad of privileges, including being exempt from Jamarnid's ire.

"Good afternoon, Lord Sharad."

Like usual, Sharad's freckled face had a mist of dreaminess. His bright blue eyes glistened upon recollection, and both pureblood elves stared at each other: Sharad with curiosity and Jamarnid with intrigue. "Oh, hi, Uncle Jamarnid. Hey, did you notice my cousin is acting strange today?"

For some odd reason, whatever Sharad lacked in common sense was compensated with a keenness about people's inner feelings. Taking advantage he had free time, Jamarnid spoke. "Would you like to have a chat in my office? A merchant brought a bottle of high-quality rice wine from the kingdom."

Upon hearing the invitation, Sharad nodded with overt enthusiasm.

As it was, Jamarnid's office was located on his level, so the servant didn't have to waste much time pushing the wheelchair in the right direction. Now that the new dock made it cheaper to buy wood from abroad, Sharad had spent the better portion of the past 15 years building doors for the entire castle.

Jamarnid tended to be prickly about many things. Any design that reminded Jamarnid of the Äimite guard he betrayed or his deceased lover Chandrice was out of the question.

Left with few sensible options, Sharad carved a rather abstract motif of the kingdom's capital for his office. The nondescript shapes from his scant childhood memories had Master Lord Salman's palace looming on top of a towering mountain in the distance.

The door creaked open, prompting a smirk on Sharad's face as he stormed in front of Jamarnid without caring about being impolite. "I think someone needs to put oil in that door."

Jamarnid nodded without showing insult. "The weather has been very humid these past few months. Rust must have affected the handles in the entire castle. I'll order servants to assess the damage and make appropriate repairs to satisfy you, my Lord."

Sharad barely batted an eye at the strange politeness coming from Jamarnid, who usually barked orders and insults at everyone. Rummaging through the wooden shelf filled with books, Sharad first compulsively tapped on the wood and then spent more than a minute studying it. A smile covered his face upon spotting one random book with leather binding. "Oh wow! I can't believe a merchant sold you this book!"

Jamarnid smiled as the servant placed his wheelchair on the other side of the desk and fetched for the wine bottle without uttering a word. "Merchants sold me a few books in the sacred Elvish tongue. Most of the books are complete rubbish. Some illiterate idiot must have bought whatever they could find in a trash bin, assuming I should feel grateful to finally read books in my birth tongue. That book is special. It is a first edition of the Elven Priestess novel series. I cannot sense anything, but my son Jarahad told me there are still scant traces of magic on the pages to preserve the paper."

With resolute eagerness, Sharad fumbled through the pages and gawked at the elegant cursive Elvish script with archaic words that were no longer in everyday use. He then plopped on an adjacent chair with red leather cushions. "How old is this book anyways? Several words in it seem sort of old fashioned."

"I wouldn't be certain either. Soremin believes it is at least 2000 years old. Perhaps mages used a spell to preserve the paper so it didn't get ruined. I presume this is why the pages seem almost brand new. I still can't believe the merchants sold it to me for such a puny fee. It took every fiber of my being to maintain a blank expression while I fumbled through the pages."

Sharad soon felt bored and returned the book to the shelf. There was plenty of time to read it when most of his mind was too allured by the tempting offer to enjoy some rice wine.

The instant Sharad held the cup of the transparent liquid in his hand, he spent a few minutes smelling it, and tears welled from his eyes upon recalling painful memories he tried to suppress. After savoring a sip, a whimper escaped his lips until he swallowed it in one huge gulp. "Thank you so much for this, Uncle. I…"

Jamarnid smiled with kindness. "You know better than anyone I am not allowed to drink alcohol. Yes, you will tell me I am no longer a guard and can break the rules. But it has become a crucial part of my self-identity, and I still cannot fathom wearing clothing with any color. Feel free to share the wine with Jarahad."

Sharad's blue eyes blinked upon hearing the name.

Taking advantage of the flurry of emotions, Jamarnid approached this delicate subject. "You have become closer to my son over the past few years. My servants have told me you drink in the privacy of his bedroom and talk about all sorts of topics. And no, I do not feel insulted you are doing those things." Jamarnid's face became sterner. "My son has been acting strange. This isn't like the times he fawns over that useless woman Talgel. Has he shared some clues with you?"

"Um… well… I am glad you have wanted to talk to me about this, Uncle Jamarnid. I can feel his vibes sometimes, and they are just, well… Jarahad is crawling into a dark crevice of self-hatred, and I don't think it's because he's jealous I sometimes flirt with his girlfriend."

Jamarnid's black eyebrows twitched in an unconscious reaction. Knowing the answer depended on not getting angry at Sharad, Jamarnid took advantage of his military training to remain impassive during the interrogation. "Yes, it is certainly something else. What do you think?"

After having another sip of wine, Sharad's head compulsively tilted both ways. "Maybe he feels angry about the way you treated Tioja. I told you he is awesome, and his magic was not harming anyone. Talgel keeps assuring me that Tioja is doing fine in the harlequin city. I want to visit him and apologize for not being supportive enough."

"What?! You want to risk your life by leaving the protection of this city?! The Äimite guard could ambush you! If you believe you have the right to abuse your power and risk your life, I am sorry to inform you that Äimite guards are authorized to tie up their masters and keep them under lockdown if their lives are in danger!"

"Ugh, you just never listen! This is why Jarahad has such a hard time being honest with you! I don't have a death wish and have always left the city accompanied by bodyguards, just like all the pureblood elves. Maybe if you weren't so hot-headed and miserable, Tioja would have stayed in the castle until he mastered his magic."

"What? Master his magic? Maybe you were too busy doing carpentry in your private quarters to have paid any attention, but his phantom beast destroyed several palm trees! At least half of the city's inhabitants were present when it happened!"

"Well, why didn't you train him? You always blabber to everyone about your glory days as a member of Salman's guard. Yet you never did anything to help Tio! If you had even the smallest modicum of decency, you would have taken advantage of your training and helped him!"

"How do you expect me to teach a mage when I no longer have legs and hands?"

Jamarnid's latest tirade made the temple veins on Sharad's frustrated face to pulsate while he tensed his fists. Knowing it would be pointless to continue arguing with his uncle, Sharad shook his head and marched away without even bothering to finish his wine.

Relentless pounding filled Jamarnid's chest from the realization he had just insulted the only inhabitant of the city he truly respected. It filled his heart with shame. His dark green eyes stared at the cup of wine on his desk and muttered to himself. "He didn't even bother to finish my gift."

Countered with the conundrum, the servant knelt before Jamarnid and spoke in formal Elvish without staring at his face. "Do you have any orders regarding this beverage, my Lord?"

Usually, Jamarnid would have felt tempted to swat the servant. Today would be different. After the shame wore off, Jamarnid relaxed his hands. "I'll drink it and order you to not divulge what happened to anyone."

****

Several days passed by, and Sharad soon regained his usual carefree demeanor. While Jamarnid drew a sigh of relief because Sharad forgave him, this didn't solve the issue regarding his son's elusive behavior.

Given that he would never beg Talgel for help, Jamarnid had no choice but to visit the city's only inhabitant he trusted. Now that Almjarhad's worst food and water shortages had been solved, even the streets reaching the city's outskirts on top of the hillsides were pavemented, so the servant didn't suffer too much pushing his wheelchair to Almjarhad Temple.

While Soremin's residence was small compared to most temples of the Elf Kingdom, the recent bout of prosperity in the city made it possible to build several more structures with the architectural techniques of the kingdom that were interconnected with wooden ramps.

After pushing the wheelchair on a ramp, the servant changed into indoor walking slippers, and they continued venturing inside. "Head Priest Soremin might be in his living quarters right now, my Lord."

Jamarnid nodded. "Fine, let's go there first."

Whether it was coincidence or fate, Jarahad was departing the room. Like the other day, he wandered off without even noticing his father was there.

A male pureblood elf with wavy chestnut brown hair and white priestly robes was standing by the doorway. "Good day, my friend. Need a hand?"

A timid smile imbued Jamarnid's face. "Always. Mind if I come inside for a private conversation?"

Soremin's room reflected his simple outward persona: square, clean, and bright. As the only building emulating authentic Elvish architecture in the city, the three straw mat floor panels had an asymmetric shape: a long one engulfing half of the room and two square ones sharing the other half. Harlequins believed the elves were superstitious regarding their aversion toward symmetrical flooring panels, and Jamarnid couldn't care less. He felt such a rudimentary decoration in his closest friend's otherwise empty living quarters was proof the priest knew the most righteous path.

The instant the servant left both elves alone, Jamarnid spoke sternly. "Do you know what is bothering my son?"

Soremin's eyes sharpened as he stared at Jamarnid's face. "Yes, he confessed the truth. I have offered him forgiveness for his sin. No, I am under no moral obligation to share anything with you because I risk breaking my oath to the gods."

"Huh? What…" Jamarnid shook his head at once. "Why can't he tell me? I'm his father and would do anything for him!"

"Jarahad knows this, but he cannot tell you. He is honor bound to keep it a secret for the rest of his life."

Unlike most people, Soremin tended to get to the point with a relaxed demeanor when he spoke to Jamarnid. Whether it was because they had known each other their entire lives or his priestly training, Soremin's riddles were designed to make the person guess the correct one so that he didn't have to lie.

The last figment of anger evaporated from Jamarnid, and his shoulders slumped against his chair. "This must be related to Jarahad's sword training. Those disgusting harlequins did something to him, and he is honor-bound to suffer alone. I told him he didn't have to get initiated!"

Soremin strutted a few steps forward and his arms embraced his friend in a soft hug. "Talgel is the reason why Jarahad became initiated."

"What? That horrid woman did this?" Waves of emotions churned deep inside as Jamarnid's arms longed for release, only to feel the priest's firm embrace enveloping his body until the last inch of anger melted away into tired defeat and tears covered his face.

Soremin's voice faltered for a few moments as he spoke. "I urge you to forgive Talgel for this one offense. There must be a reason why she begged Hurrujat to lend the sword to your son instead of taking it away when they left. If our city ends up attacked, Jarahad might be our only hope. Have some faith in her predictions, my dearest friend."

Gulraj enchanted and mesmerized Tioja the instant he saw his younger half-brother for the first time. The scrawny bald child with lanky knees and a handsome angular face smiled effusively as he stared at Tioja's strange eyes. "Mother is correct! We are brothers!"

"Huh?"

Hamara knelt before Gulraj and caressed his face. "Gulraj, my dear, your brother cannot speak our sacred tongue. Why don't you speak to him in Elvish?"

"I am sorry, older brother. Can you understand me now?"

"You speak Elvish with a strange accent. It sounds, um... like the slithering of a serpent," Tioja pondered out loud.

Hamara beamed even more. "Harlequin is less guttural than Elvish with stronger intonations of specific consonants. Some sounds are prolonged, and the tongue position causes a rather stuttered effect when native Harlequin speakers switch to Elvish."

This strange confession confused Tioja even more as he stared at the handful of eager harlequins in every direction. "Is that how you communicate in this city? Doesn't everyone use the Elvish of Almjarhad?"

Gulraj's strikingly sharp teeth became visible as he smiled, prompting Tioja to squeak in fear. "His Lordship Hurrujat wants us to know how to speak ancient Elvish so that the tongue is not lost. I sometimes hear the adult half-bloods speak in a strange tongue from your birth city, and I don't understand them."

Hoping for answers, Hamara smiled with endearment. "The Almjarhad tongue has no value to us. Human merchants from this region can't understand the strange words, and we want our children to primarily speak Harlequin. The adult halflings speak Elvish, and we encourage them to use it with their children because they have the right to embrace their mixed ancestry. Gulraj speaks Elvish very well, so feel free to ask him questions and start learning Harlequin. I can guarantee he is a great teacher."

"Why are you wasting your time talking in the street? Please come to your home," Hurrujat commanded.

Servants pushed the towering dark wooden gates open and Tioja was bombarded by a dazzling sight. The entrance of this palace eagerly welcomed him with polished dark stone floors that glowed in an array of green and violet hues.

Empty arched windows decorated with glowing vegetation in the ridges were intertwined with gigantic Corinthian pillars. Circular steel supporting beams that were covered in small threaded green lights that seemed to shimmer and dance in the ceiling above.

Speaking of which, the entrance had a ceiling covered in glowing paint depicting intricate geometric shapes intertwined with shiny mosaics jewels that displayed a beautiful rainbow far above. This entrance was met by two identical staircases characterized by more dark stone masonry, odd green lights that granted perfect visibility and sharp turns as both staircases met on a second floor that vanished into several hallways.

Hurrujat limped ahead as Hamara held him in a tight embrace. Gulraj was meanwhile walking backwards while he stared at his face nonstop with a huge smile. Unlike Tioja, Gulraj was dressed in a beautiful velvet robe that covered most of his body while his blue sash belt shimmered wherever he went. Gulraj couldn't resist the temptation much longer. "Tioja, you will accompany me to the bathhouse of my home so that you are ready for dinner."

"I… uhh…" Flummoxed, Tioja tugged his modest shirt that was now covered in grime and sweat. "I apologize for arriving to your home with dirty robes. I could use my water magic to clean this."

"Ho, ho, ho, ho! Nonsense, my boy! You will never wear those filthy rags ever again! For tonight, I ordered my servants to give you some robes that might not fit you perfectly. My servants will take your measurements, and you will have a brand-new wardrobe in no time!"

Embarrassed by Hurrujat's offer, Tioja whimpered even thinking about it. "Please don't spend your money on me, my Lord. I would be glad to work somewhere and pay my keep."

Gulraj raised his thin eyebrows from the comment. Confused, he rushed to his mom's side. "My brother wants to be a servant. Is that what he said?"

Hamara stood in front of another staircase and looked upwards. "I will bathe in my bedroom. Your brother will show you the rest of the way. From now on, your life as a pathetic peasant is old history. Tomorrow, you will have a free day to spend alongside Gulraj. Once you have settled down, tutors will give you much-needed lessons. You will be so busy learning about your new duties that you will forget you were an elf in the first place. Now, go on and we'll see you at the dinner table."

The bath was not all that different from the months Tioja spent in Almjarhad Palace. He first scrubbed himself clean while a few servants observed him with overt curiosity. Gulraj watched everything he did and laughed for odd reasons. After tossing a bucket of perfumed water on his head, Tioja was about to return to the dressing room when Gulraj grabbed his wrist. "Now enter the bath!"

"I already washed myself and am ready for dinner."

"No, you are not! Elves taught my father how to relax in warm water, and now you will too!"

Tioja's pleas went unheard, and servants let Gulraj pull Tioja who tried covering his body with a towel to a large octagonal bathtub that glowed in the dark. Concerned this was a potion that would kill him, Tioja tried to resist Gulraj's constant pulling. Only to end up tossed unceremoniously in the water at the very end. What stroke Tioja to be odd was how warm and soothing this water was. It glowed and the walls were covered in even more jewel mosaic paintings in every direction. Some servants remained at a safe distance and the soothing sound of a flute reverberated in every direction. Whether this was magic or not, the combination of exhaustion from the voyage, the new city and the emotional first meeting with his younger half-brother prompted Tioja to relax his shoulders.

An ever-inquisitive Gulraj sat nearby, careful not to get his own robes wet. "I already had my bath today, so you'll have to enjoy this alone."

"Why are you wasting so much water?"

Gulraj didn't understand what Tioja meant with that. "We have plenty of water in this city. Isn't there an ocean next to Almjarhad?"

"Well, yes. But you can't drink or bathe in saltwater. Freshwater is precious and we only bathe with limited amounts of it. This is sinful."

Flustered about Tioja's odd comment, Gulraj stomped outside at once, leaving him alone to his inner thoughts.

By the time Tioja was dressed in a loose suit that resembled Gulraj's attire at the dining room, Gulraj had already forgotten about his rude comment. Chances are Hamara talked to him in private. Feeling shy, Tioja sat next to Gulraj in the large rectangular dark stone table while his mother and Hurrujat were already slurping a strange soup. "What is that?"

Hamara lifted her face and stared at Tioja with incredulity. "The servants prepared mushroom soup. Eat it."

Taken aback by Hamara's rudeness, Tioja complied and marveled at the spicy earthiness of this unusual new dish. There was something else that was hard to pinpoint at first. Soon enough, Tioja's suspicions were confirmed when he started munching on something that reminded him of the ocean he was already missing. "Shrimp?"

Hurrujat cocked his head and set his silver spoon to the side. "Yes, my son. Do you like it?"

"It's… different. I only eat shrimp stew when I visit my grandfather's place."

"Silence. I don't want you to continue whining about that dreadful city. You hear me?"

Tioja's heart sunk seeing his mother angry. Uncertain about why

Hamara was acting this way, Tioja surmised it was because she was tired from the voyage. Servants served him other dishes, mostly carnivorous ones such as slices of venison combined with steamed vegetable roots. Chances are, the pureblood elves taught Hurrujat some of their favorite vegan cuisine, and he had grown attached to the blended culture over time.

Mindful of Hamara's ill mood, Tioja spent his evening speaking to Hurrujat and Gulraj about their voyage, his feelings seeing pine trees for the first time, and the dangerous village that nearly killed them.

This part of the story intrigued Gulraj as he stared at his parents. "We must do something about that village. Those humans are a threat."

Hurrujat nodded in agreement as servants cleared his table. "Yes, yes. That village must be subdued soon."

Hamara seemed ambivalent. "With the neighboring town under our control, they are now fully surrounded by our allies."

"Are you going to starve them into submission?" Gulraj asked with giddy eagerness.

Hamara shook her head. "No violence. I want to rest for a while and my son to adjust to his new home. When the time is right, all three of us will visit them and they will sign the treaty."

With that said, the conversation was over, and the dining room once again became silent except for the pleasant sounds of string music from a group of musicians. Despite the tense conversation, listening to the melancholic tunes with vivid crescendos made Tioja smile. On occasion, Hurrujat spoke to Gulraj in Harlequin. Tioja could only understand a few words here and there and didn't know what they shared with each other. Hamara was too immersed in her inner thoughts to speak.

Servants soon arrived with a mouth-watering meat dish Tioja had never seen before, and his plate became covered with slices of a reddish meat covered in a mushroom gravy. After cutting the slice and placing it in his mouth, Tioja was marveled at the juicy flavor, and intrigued because he had never tried it before. Tioja had eaten meat dishes very often in Svetlana's tent, but they were usually seafood or mutton stew. In comparison, this was no peasant dish. Its texture melted in the mouth and the fungi had a uniqueness that remained on the tongue long after he swallowed it. Intrigued by this new experience, Tioja asked his mother. "Mom, is this beef? It is delicious!"

A sinister giggle escaped her lips as she sliced pieces of meat and served them in Hurrujat's eager mouth in between passionate kisses. Gulraj was so amused by Tioja's ignorance that he could barely contains his laughter. Realizing Tioja was truly clueless, Hamara wiped her mouth with a napkin and spoke with confidence. "The servants only make this dish on very special occasions. I feel glad that you enjoyed it. He was a human that was condemned to death the other day for breaking our laws. I'll tell the cooks you liked it and hope we get to eat this again sometime soon."

Upon hearing this haunting confession, Tioja grasped his stomach. Without asking for permission, he rushed away from the dinner table. He was heading for the bathroom and wanted to vomit at once.

***

"Wake up, wake up, wake up!"

"Huh?" Tioja opened his eye the following morning and stared at a strange lamp that emitted a bright green hue among the endless darkness. "It's still nighttime."

"No, it's daytime!"

Before Tioja could snuggle under the blanket to continue resting, he felt someone bouncing on the bed. A snarl imbued his face after getting stomped on far too many times. "Ouch! What is wrong with you?!"

The jumping abruptly stopped. Gulraj sat cross-legged on the bed and sulked from the blight. "I am sorry. Hamara told me stories about my big brother, and I always wanted to meet you. Hurrujat believed you would remain in the elf enclave forever, and I felt so excited when you arrived last evening. Perhaps you are still tired from the long trip."

Trying to ignore the haunting experience during dinner, Tioja studied his surroundings. Tioja had gotten so used to sleeping in the soft beds of Jarahad's palace that he initially assumed he was still there. His new bedroom was brighter than when he went to bed a few hours ago. The lighting was strong enough to almost give a sense it was daylight. Exhaustion prevented him from noticing the extent of the luxurious bedroom. His blanket was made of soft silk that shimmered a bright violet against the lamps on the walls and ceiling, his bed had an unusual oval shape, and the walls were covered by endless jewels that sprinkled a dazzling array of colors.

Due to Gulraj's present age, the floors were covered in huge chests with toys. Curiously enough, Tioja recognized a few dolls made by Daedoman resembling Hurrujat, Hamara, and even himself when he was a child. After studying his surroundings, Tioja took his time to get a better glimpse of Gulraj for the first time. At first sight, Gulraj didn't seem all that impressive. He was ridiculously skinny with prominent knees, his eyes glowed in an array between red and pink. Had it not been for the excessive youth and gaunt cheeks, his face would have been rather handsome. Perhaps when he grew up, Gulraj would look almost as attractive as his mother. "You know, you almost completely look like a harlequin."

Gulraj giggled at once without showing insult. "Silly brother! Our mother is a half-blood, and my father is a pureblood. We are more alike than you think! We are 75% opposite and half the same thing as well!"

Upon realizing Gulraj was three-fourths harlequin, whereas he was almost a pureblood elf, Tioja found the comparison undeniably funny. "I never met a harlequin without wings before. Nobody would suspect you had any elf blood if you grew a pair of them during the change!"

"In the dark, you could almost pass as a harlequin too. Maybe if we are lucky, we will grow a pair of wings at the same time and have an artisan paint us."

Tioja blushed as he thought about Gulraj's proposal. "Well, it is rare for halflings to grow wings during the change. I suppose I could grow mine the next time you have them."

This strange comment took Gulraj by surprise, and he crossed his arms. "Um… You can't exactly choose to grow wings when you shed,

Tioja."

"You don't have to be so formal with me. Call me Tio. And yes, I can grow wings anytime!"

The oddness of Tioja's comment only piqued Gulraj's attention further, and he sat closer. "Nobody can do that!"

"Well…" Tioja blushed and averted his gaze. "When I summon my Lehart, a pair of black wings grow on my back."

"Really? The mages from my clan can't do that!"

"Well, I believe it is sort of rare. Out of the few halflings in Almjarhad that summon demonic beasts, at least two suffer a change of appearance for a few days. Jarahad believes it has something to do with our harlequin blood."

"That is very interesting. I heard from Hamara the only halflings with a phantom beast were Jarahad and the seer."

"Oh… well, Jarahad can summon a magical armor called Rashid. It can float in the air and reassemble itself into different shapes. He sometimes uses it as a mode of transportation because it is so fast. And the seer is named Talgel. She…" Tioja sighed when he thought about her.

"Is there something wrong?"

After wiping a tear from his eyes, Tioja shook his head and smiled. "She is a very strange woman, and I don't know anything about her. Her predictions are always correct. The night before I left Almjarhad, she told me to be good to someone I would meet. It must be you!"

"Well, we have an entire life to become one big, happy family. I promise I will make you love your new home so much that you will never want to return to Almjarhad again!" Gulraj offered his hands in a cupped shape. Feeling flustered with this specific harlequin social custom, Tioja frowned without knowing what to do.

"Silly brother! Don't the elves offer their hands as a means of making a promise?"

"Well, elves just bow at each other. My papa Jamad did tell me they sometimes copy a human tradition." Without waiting for his little brother to ask, Tioja offered his pinky finger.

Following his cue, Gulraj interlocked his pinky finger and shook it. "Is this correct?"

"Why yes! How did you know that?"

Gulraj grinned with glee. "Hamara will pay a special visit to a nearby human enclave for an important meeting in a few days. I sometimes go with her to learn more about diplomacy. Someday, all these lands will become mine, and you will rule with me!"

Before they knew it, both brothers laughed nonstop as they shook each other's fingers. Tioja barely even knew his little brother and loved him already.

CHAPTER 4 ◆ TALGEL

With each passing day, Talgel's impatience increased even further. Over the years, Henrietta occasionally left Almjarhad to tend to her private affairs. Whatever these were, Talgel was never allowed to discover Henrietta's past. In fact, her phantom beast seemed to avoid revealing anything about the woman to irritate her.

At first, Talgel surmised Henrietta had to visit various harlequin enclaves to obtain more blood wine. That was until Jarahad accompanied her on one such trip and obtained the secret recipe to preserve animal blood in wine. Now that the harlequins departed Almjarhad, there was little need to raise livestock since most of the remaining inhabitants were vegetarians. With their blood storage problem solved, livestock was raised in Almjarhad for their blood, and the meat was later dehydrated and sold to harlequin merchants.

Henrietta was usually chosen as the middleman, which rejoiced Talgel. Having a few weeks of solitude was always quite pleasant. Even though Henrietta had proven her worth as a trusted assistant, there were some predictions Talgel felt were unsuitable even for her. This created a new problem for Talgel: how could she write predictions to the correct person if she was blind?

Mindful of her needs, Jarahad used earth magic to create a shelf with alphabetically organized braille indentations so that Talgel could deposit secret predictions to the correct person. Some predictions were harmless and could be shared with Henrietta. Others were so secretive that Talgel sprayed them with various perfumes that meant different things. Henrietta was well-versed on recognizing the meaning of each scent. Even though Talgel's phantom beast allowed her to see the future, one obnoxious defect of her gift was being unable to know when a specific prediction would happen.

Talgel was finishing one such secretive prediction when writhing, agonizing pain heaved into her veins. It deprived her of much-needed oxygen for a few minutes. If Henrietta had been here, she would have offered her some blood wine to avert the same disease that afflicted every harlequin elf. Left with no choice, Talgel closed her ink canister and heaved deep breaths until the pain receded.

When she felt more like herself, Talgel stood up, grabbed her walking stick, and approached the pantry. After gulping some blood wine from the bottle, the pain receded, and she was allowed to return to her task. There was one problem. Even though Talgel was careful not to let the ink spill on her prediction, there was no way to know if any ink splotches fell from the quiver. Knowing the importance of this prediction, Talgel opted to lift the paper in the air and activate her harlequin fire magic. Warmth wafted against her face, and the fire vanished the instant there was no longer any paper left to consume. Talgel grabbed a rag and wiped the table from any errant pieces of ashes. A grin invaded her face. "Jarahad would have a fit if he saw this mess."

And then this idea was followed by sadness. Jarahad was always in her thoughts, the halfling she loved so dearly who would never become her husband. It was strange how Henrietta's company was so unwanted, yet she helped maintain Talgel's loneliness at bay. Could it be she considered the harlequin a friend?

No, that wouldn't be it. More like a useful servant that followed her commands. Talgel soon recalled the prediction she had to write and started it from scratch. This prediction was of the odder sort and filled with half-truths like so many other predictions she shared.

Knowing nobody would be present to hear it, Talgel recited the prediction out loud.

Dearest Priest Tanato.

"If you read this letter, then it means you have become disabled. I confess this was my fault, and you are free to hate me forever. Given what you will obtain in return, I am certain you will enjoy a fulfilling life.

You have worked hard to summon your demonic beast, and I am proud of you. I don't believe in the afterlife, but our people need something to believe in. Contrary to your suspicions, your beast will only be awakened using söma. Therefore, I hope you

*read this prediction to give you a sense of free will to expiate my
tainted conscience.*

*I want you to use your beast nonstop. Ignore everyone's
warnings and use your beast to its full potential. The price you will
pay for attaining your heart's true desire is an early death.*

*If you decide against drinking söma, you will have
regrets on your deathbed. Knowing you, I am certain you will accept
it. Feel free to share this knowledge with Priest Soremin and enjoy
your gift."*

Your timeless friend,

Talgel

Knowing Tanato, the brute might run off right now to obtain söma
from a human. Doing so ahead of time could ruin Talgel's plans. Under
normal circumstances, she would have let Henrietta deliver the missive.
Concerned about Tanato's impatience to reach his self-destruction too
soon, Talgel applied a few sprays of cinnamon perfume. She then placed
the letter in Soremin's box on the shelf. There was still plenty of time to tell
Soremin when to deliver the prediction to its rightful owner.

"Your ladyship! I'm home!" Henrietta charged inside and her feet
were already stomping the rugs like a dratted boar.

"I don't want dirty boots in my home, Henrietta! If you make a
mess, you're cleaning it!"

From the awkward squeak escaping the harlequin's lips, it was
obvious Henrietta had just made a mess, prompting a grin to appear on
Talgel's face. As obnoxious as the woman was, Talgel loved making her feel
discomfort. A suitable punishment for staying away from Almjarhad for so
long.

"Sorry about that, your ladyship. I'll start cleaning your home
immed… Oh my! Your arms are full of black lines! Are you going to shed?"

"Of course, I am about to shed. I shed every five years. How could you forget this?"

"I uhh… Sorry about taking so long to return. My family misses me, and I wanted to spend time with them."

This confession piqued Talgel's interest and made her lift her eyebrow. Maybe she could finally discover the woman's secret identity. "Oh, and will they come to Almjarhad anytime soon?"

Henrietta sighed. "It is… complicated. There's been some problems. Oh, don't worry, nobody is dying or…" Henrietta stumbled a bit, and Talgel quickly placed her ink vial in a safe place before Henrietta made even more messes.

Unable to see her roommate, Talgel listened to some clackety noises and wondered what the woman was carrying. A sharp noise echoed from the table, and Henrietta screeched momentarily until she sat down. "I apologize for that. My arm has a bruise, and it is still healing."

"Oh really? Were you having sex with a man while chained to a bed or something?"

"Of course not! How could you even think of such an inappropriate thing?!" From the nervous giggles escaping Henrietta's mouth, she injured herself doing something else.

It increased Talgel's suspicions. "Was your city attacked?"

"Don't worry, your ladyship. Everything is solved, and I want to show you something!"

"Huh?" Before Talgel knew it, Henrietta grabbed her wrist and let her touch the mysterious object on the table. Four wooden supporting beams were interlocked without requiring the need for nails. A sturdy kind of fabric was fastened to the beams. With some prodding, Henrietta shoved the fabric open like a tent, and Talgel soon realized there were two strips of fabric on both edges of the thin wooden beams. "Is this a kite?"

"You guessed it on the first try! Did you see this in a vision?"

Talgel grumbled as her hands continued fumbling over the box-shaped kite, and she flapped the taut cord. "I am about to shed my skin and could die from starvation during the process, and you were busy playing with a toy? You're the worst servant I've ever had."

Nervous heaves escaped Henrietta's mouth as she stood up and began sweeping the floor. "I apologize for that. My siblings miss me, and I couldn't say no to their company. When I talked to them about you, they encouraged me to let you use it."

"I'm blind! Why would I find this stupid thing to be fun?"

"Please try it! You won't regret it."

***

The following day, Talgel was standing in a remote field far away from the city alongside an eager Henrietta and Sharad, who spotted both women walking across the city while carrying the obnoxious object and couldn't resist the temptation to tag along.

Like usual, Sharad took advantage of Jarahad's absence to hold Talgel's hand as they walked together. It was obvious Sharad was planning on flirting with her, but Talgel feigned ignorance. It was fun to manipulate the stooge every now and then. Sharad was one of the few inhabitants of the city she not only tolerated but enjoyed spending her free time with.

Henrietta's sugary voice was audible nearby along with the sound of wood scratching against the dirt. "Give me a second, my ladyship. I just need to finish assembling the parts and we're good to go!"

Talgel grumbled. "What is the point of all of this? I have never seen this event happen in a vision and will not enjoy myself. It's a waste of time."

Sharad's hand pressed her fingers for a moment, and he let go to admire the object. "Hey, don't be a sourpuss, Talgel. Henrietta came all the way from her home to do something fun. You've been spending far too much time locked in your home. I miss seeing you wear your swimming clothes and go to the beach!"

Ugh, Sharad was such a voyeuristic creep. No wonder he was still single. Henrietta found Sharad's inappropriate comment to be funny and was giggling nonstop. It was times like this Talgel wished Henrietta had stayed away for just a few more days. That way she could continue writing her predictions and speak to clients in peace.

Worse, it seemed like Henrietta agreed with Sharad. "The weather is getting very warm. If my ladyship recovers from the shedding before the rains start, we should all visit the beach together! She bought a new red water dress that is stunning!"

"Oh, golly! You got to see her wear it? Really?"

Talgel grumbled when she heard that.

Henrietta beamed even more. "Talgel would never buy clothes that don't fit her. It was a good thing I am always around to approve of her purchases. Ever since I have moved in, her sense of style is the best in the city. Countless clients have commended me afterwards about her spotless appearance. Talgel is very wealthy!"

There was no limit to the degree Henrietta would blabber her heart away. Talgel only tolerated it because she knew Sharad would forget about this conversation by tomorrow. As annoying as he was, Sharad still had the innocence of a child and never harbored any true malice.

Before Henrietta could continue embarrassing her any further, she placed the thick cord on Talgel's hands and clasped her fingers. It felt odd to touch Henrietta's skin for the briefest of instances. Talgel never realized her roommate's hands were so soft and strong at the same time. Most disquieting indeed.

"I am going to help you get this kite into the air. Hold on tight!"

With a few flaps of the bat-like wings on her back, Henrietta soon jettisoned into the air holding the kite. With Sharad's help, Talgel felt the cord flap a handful of times in various directions that was hard to control at first. This was the reason why Talgel would have preferred to wait for this event to be seen in a prediction. The sense of disorientation due to not knowing where or how the kite would go meant she had to bend her knees and yank the kite whenever it felt like veering too far away.

Sharad was so immersed in his private thoughts that they barely even spoke during these moments of solitude. Meanwhile, Henrietta's wings batted far in the air. It was possible she was keeping an eye on the kite. Which seemed like a fruitless endeavor given the wind howled rather noisily today. If Talgel still had eyes in her sockets, she would have spent half of the time rubbing sand from her face.

Before long, she got a hang of holding onto the kite. For the first time in decades, Talgel felt something. It was neither the disdain she usually harbored towards her peers, or the negative emotions of jealousy or anger. This feeling even made her forget about her unfettered love for Jarahad. No, it was a sensation that she had forgotten long ago. Her mother and father, a couple that didn't quite love each other but formed an amicable friendship for her sake.

Talgel had long ceased to fret over their deaths in the second purge. In fact, they had died at such a young age, she never quite cared about them at all. And yet today, a memory of the time she went fishing with her parents in an underground lake resurfaced. Laughter, the funny gurgling sounds her father made, they were experiences that had been left buried through the passage of time. Neither parent would make a dent in the history of her people. Their lives came and went without much fanfare. But this hidden feeling lingered, and something new bubbled deep inside of Talgel's chest as her hands pulled and twisted the rope with Sharad's assistance.

Before Talgel knew it, gurgling laughter spasmed through her body as she released the anguish and hatred brewing deep inside for the greater portion of her unfortunate life. Some ailments were most contagious, and thus Sharad's shrill laughter coordinated with her own and it was the most joyous thing she could have ever experienced. Upon hearing the unexpected noise, Henrietta landed with a thud. "Oh, I am so happy to know you are enjoying yourself, my ladyship! Isn't this fun? My younger siblings thought you might enjoy this gift. Next time, I'll invite Jarahad so that we all take turns using it."

And then, as if by magic, something changed inside Talgel. A sinister echo that resided into her chest burned deep inside and her body writhed from a heavy weight. This was not an impending blood attack; it was much worse. A burden only she could carry that would haunt her forever. The demon that bonded to her soul so many years ago would never allow her to experience joy. Without realizing it, Talgel's hands opened loose, and she could hear Sharad stumble on the ground.

"Ow!"

Henrietta flapped her wings as the wind blew with increased ferocity. "Oh dear! The kite is flying away!"

By the time Henrietta and Sharad fetched the kite that flew a great distance, Talgel was walking back towards the direction of the setting sun, where Almjarhad stood. The demon would never let her free from its grasp. Not even for one day.

CHAPTER 5 ♦ TIOJA

Tioja was encouraged by his mother to spend as much time as possible with Gulraj. This plan made him feel more welcome in Murdorhiolan and less disgusted that she was now happily married to Hurrujat.

Gulraj was excessively hyperactive and occasionally said unfamiliar Harlequin words whenever he forgot a particular Elvish word. Tioja didn't mind, of course. It helped him pick up Harlequin words from context, and he was beginning to understand at least a few of the most common gratitude phrases which tended to carry considerable weight within their heavily stratified society.

As the two siblings continued pacing around the wide streets filled with impressive multistory apartments, Tioja became curious about two things. "The lights are so bright. It is almost as if we were outside, but everything is green."

"When you combine the sorcery of the four elements, harlequin mages can create a material resembling precious jewels. They plant a sort of lichen that cannot survive in the sunlight. All the lights in the city are connected to a single source downtown. Mages can feed different energy into this system, and the lichens become alerted. After feeding from this energy, the light they produce is the digestion of magical nutrients. The elves have something similar, right?"

"Jarahad recently had special lamps installed in his palace. They work with mana, but they aren't living things. My home always used ordinary candles because the clan needed to build wells and grow crops during most of my childhood."

Gulraj seemed rather pensive as they continued pacing through the streets. "Hamara told me about her life in the city. She didn't have any time for leisure because everyone was starving. It must have been very hard for you."

Tioja smiled as he continued walking. "That is all right. I had a very happy childhood growing up with my friends and family. Everyone worked a few days each month to make the city sustainable. The earth mages also moved the rocks from the beach to deter pirates from harming us. Now everyone can swim on the beach in the summer! You would have a lot of fun!"

Gulraj smirked at the comment. "I will think about it. This city only has a few lagoons for swimming. There is a nice waterfall a day away from here on foot. I want to take you to the forest and get to know it better."

"Hamara says it sometimes snows here."

"We are too far south, and you will feel disappointed. Perhaps two days at the most each year has snow. You should never try to walk on the lakes when they freeze because you can fall inside and drown. You might be lucky and see real snow on the rare occasions we get pummeled by blizzards. I think you will enjoy it very much."

"You don't wish to visit Almjarhad, do you?"

"Not really. It only seems to give bad memories to my parents. I like it here and don't wish to live anywhere else."

***

A few days later, Hamara was busy dressing in travel robes in front of the mirror while Tioja and Gulraj were watching her. She didn't even stare at her children while braiding her long hair. "I am very pleased to see your smile, Tioja."

"I never knew I would love having a little brother so much!"

"You truly belong here with Gulraj, the city inhabitants, and both of us. I know you might feel uncomfortable eating alongside my husband. Hurrujat wants to recognize you as his son."

Upon being reminded again of Hurrujat's statement, Tioja stared at his boots. "I don't think I can see him as my father. He is more like a mentor to me."

"You just need more time. Hurrujat wants you to continue learning the language and customs of our people. He believes it is important for you to accompany me to the human villages we protect. You must learn about your future responsibilities when it becomes your turn to rule this city alongside Gulraj."

"We are so young! I don't think I can be like Jarahad!"

Hamara seemed amused as her hands cleverly assembled strands of her wavy hair. "I believe it was good for you to begin your training in Jarahad's palace. Perhaps you weren't allowed to be seated in a prominent place during his meetings, but I am glad he started teaching you the basics of fencing."

This comment perked Gulraj's curiosity, and he eagerly stared at Tioja. "You never told me you could use the sword! I can't wait to see your technique!"

Tioja blushed once again. "I don't think I am any good. I always felt very nervous staring at Jarahad and could never attack him. He is the city's ruler, and I might get arrested if I harmed him."

Gulraj beamed at once. "I took fencing lessons with several talented teachers the second I could walk! I even know how to wield two swords at the same time!"

"Wow! But you are so young!"

Hamara finished fastening her hair and turned around. "We have formed alliances with other harlequin cities because they are impressed with the efficiency of our city. In exchange for our knowledge, they have been training us."

Tioja soon noticed Hamara was again wielding a sword on her hips and couldn't resist the temptation. "Is it true? Can you use the sword?"

While Gulraj was cackling nonstop, Hamara decided to prove a point. She grabbed an apple from the table and threw it a few feet in the air. Before the apple fell to the ground, a rapid blade that emitted a pale green hue sliced it into dozens of pieces. Tioja was dumbfounded.

Hamara cleansed the unusually sharp blade with her handkerchief. "My teacher says I am quite a prodigy. Even though I began learning fencing as an adult, I learned the basics ridiculously fast. Most common criminals can be defeated with ease. Hurrujat constantly complains he wished he was younger to fight me to his full potential."

"You would still defeat my father even if he were young!"

Hamara smiled at Gulraj and picked up the sliced pieces from the floor. "Now, now, I would never insult my beloved Hurrujat. Let's go."

Tioja was surprised by the steepness of the climb from the northeastern exit. The closer they were to the surface, the more often the green lamps became intermixed with regular fire torches until they were replaced by them completely. The stairs were glossy and almost slippery. Had it not been for the handrails, Tioja would have stumbled into the ground more than once. Hamara meanwhile remained focused as the stairways winded around until they reached a small hidden exit and quickly unlocked the door.

A lock clicking noise preceded trace amounts of light to the ground, prompting Tioja to step backwards and huddle behind his brother. While Gulraj was taken aback from this, Hamara caressed his head. "Dearest Tioja. I already told you I am perfectly capable of stealing your mana. Do not fear going outside."

Gulraj seemed even more enthusiastic than before. He grabbed Tioja's hands and clasped them. "I will protect you, Tio."

Warmth exalted Tioja's mind, and he regained a tiny slither of bravery. He would have never been able to go outside during the day alone. With his family nearby, he would take the first step towards conquering his inner demons.

Hamara then turned around. "Close your eyes, children."

They were soon bombarded by the dizzying burst of sunlight. After focusing for a few minutes, Hamara was already acclimated. It took Gulraj a couple more minutes to stop rubbing his own eyes. This was the first time Tioja had a full view of his younger brother under normal light. To his surprise, Gulraj's skin was only a few shades darker than his own. Aside from the luminescent eyes and sharp teeth, the harlequin still had visible traces of his faint elf ancestry.

Hamara looked even more beautiful under the beating sun in her current attire, which was far more elegant than the robes she wore during the trip to Almjarhad. After accommodating her braid, she covered her head with a red hood. She then approached Gulraj and put his hood on. "You are not as used to the sun as Tio. Please cover yourself."

The group began walking together on a small dirt road through the forest. Tioja looked back to see the door and gasped. It had seemingly vanished.

Gulraj stared at him with a glimmer of his own mixed-colored eyes. "The doors are not hidden by sorcery. It is an optical illusion. We use paints to make the door harder to see in the forest. In the winter, artisans paint the doors a different color."

"Wow! You guys have things pretty much planned out! Why do you lock the door anyways?"

Before Gulraj could explain, Hamara spoke while she treaded a few steps ahead. "Murdorhiolan has five exits. We are using the northwestern one, which is supposed to be off-limits from visitors. It is also the smallest doorway, and every citizen owns a key. The other exits have winding outdoor roads and a few guard posts. Furthermore, the main entrance isn't as steep."

Gulraj interjected at once. "That is where farmers bring the food we eat!"

While his family seemed rather excited about those facts, Tioja still felt squeamish. "I don't know if I can get used to eating human meat. It feels... wrong."

His relatives chuckled at once, finding Tioja's complaints to be amusing. After around an hour, the group soon reached a medium-sized human village that appeared out of nowhere. Tioja felt surprised and perhaps even a bit disappointed. While Almjarhad was an impoverished city by elvish standards, it was still clean. In comparison, this town was characterized by excessive filth covering almost every inch and cranny. His boots were soon covered in thick mud, and he had to swat a few sprawling insects buzzing by.

Gulraj found everything he did to be beyond amusing. "You don't like Senhort?"

Tioja screeched when he found an annoying mosquito sucking his blood and swatted it. "Why is everything so dirty?"

"This is the first time you visit a human city?"

Tioja stared at his little brother with a frown while he rubbed his itchy arm. "Almjarhad was not nearly as filthy as this place. Are they dumping sewage next to a well?"

Hamara sighed. "We are trying to convince these human enclaves to accept our protection in exchange for their mana. Gulraj is already used to dealing with them. You must be careful, Tioja. Humans do not value honor and care more about exploiting the weak. The second they realize you are a newcomer, they will try to kidnap you or worse."

Hamara's worrisome warning caused Tioja to grimace as they continued passing through endless cabins. They soon reached a larger wooden structure with dilapidated roof tiles and a rotting stench. A portly man with large muscles and a sinister grin blocked her way. "Ah, you've returned to MY town to blackmail us into paying tribute for unwanted protection."

Hamara brushed him aside as she squeezed through. "Your mother is still alive, Didier."

Gulraj whispered into Tioja's ear as they followed Hamara inside. "More like his name is Didiot."

As the three halflings passed the narrow hallways imbued with a foul stench, Tioja studied his mother. Hamara was busy arguing with Didier in the local human tongue. "What is mom planning to do? Isn't she afraid of that man?"

"Silly Tio! Our mum could kill him in one blow. Just that doing so will ruin our plan to expand the influence of our city."

"Do the human mana donors come from this place?"

Both siblings took a sharp turn to the right in a path Gulraj seemed to know by heart. "Nah, Senhort doesn't have any mages. Our city's knights have come a few times to fend off attacks without being able to convince them to sign the treaty. Hamara hopes that Mayor Abilene will be more open to the pact if Hamara speaks to her. Abilene is dying, you know."

"Uh… that sounds terrible."

"Get used to outliving humans, Tio. Our mom believes Abilene will agree to sign it because her son will lose the elections once she is gone."

"Elections? These people choose their leader?"

"I know! The strongest warriors tend to become harlequin clan leaders, whereas I heard stories that the founders of the 36 elf clans used to be a great warrior… albeit I doubt Jamarnid really counts."

Tioja bit his tongue to avoid starting a recurrent argument with his brother regarding Jamarnid. Even though Jamarnid treated him horribly, Gulraj had no right to ridicule him.

They reached a bedroom where Hamara dragged a stool and caressed a human woman's frail hand as they continued speaking in the strange dialect. The wrinkled face, cyanotic lips, and labored breathing were sights that Tioja had seldom seen because most of Almjarhad's inhabitants were young. It caused a lasting impression on him to see how Hamara successfully coerced the fragile old woman to sign her scroll. As Hamara gloated from the success of her feat, Abilene and Didier exchanged endless shouts and cussing, which amused Gulraj to no end.

Soon enough, Didier stormed outside while hollering unmentionable words. Hamara apologized to the woman, fastened the scroll, and approached her children. "Time to go. Abilene needs to rest."

Gulraj twiddled his thumbs as they returned through the same pathway from where they first entered. "Why is her idiot son making such a huge fuss over the pact? His mother has just gifted him a guaranteed reelection."

"Because humans tend to be dim-witted and shortsighted. If he does something stupid, the scroll grants us the authority to enact swift justice against the city's inhabitants for rebellion. It's one of the main reasons why Didier was so stubbornly against the agreement."

"Why would he get angry about that?" When Tioja finished his question, they stepped outside and saw dozens of humans armed with pitchforks, swords, and axes.

This act of hostility made Tioja huddle behind his mother for comfort and pray to the elf and harlequin gods they would make it out alive.

Hamara remained undeterred, along with the ever-confident Gulraj. "The pact has been signed, Didier. We are now authorized to seize your assets if one of you attacks us without a justifiable reason."

"Hogwash! You took advantage of my mama on her deathbed to fill her mind with poison and got away with it! The king will side with me!"

Hamara smiled even more. "Oh yeah? Didn't you hear Murdorhiolan has been granted autonomous status? We are our own separate country, and any human enclaves that join our state cease to become subjects of the king of Kinau. One false move and…."

Before Hamara could even finish her sentence, a blast of fire was aimed at her head. "Mother, watch out!"

With incredible dexterity, Tioja nudged Gulraj to the ground and used air magic to deflect the cannonball into the upstairs floor with the subsequent crash of glass, falling debris, and singed wood.

"Mother!" Didier's howls echoed in every direction as the embers were intertwined with screams.

"I have to save them!" Tioja was about to help when Gulraj grabbed his wrist and yanked him to the ground.

"Stay down, Tio! You're going to get yourself killed if you put yourself in danger."

"But…"

Meanwhile, Hamara was alert as she turned in every direction to pinpoint the origin of the cannonball that almost killed her. Tioja and Gulraj did the same in the fray and saw several portable trebuchets hauled by Didier's angered friends. Hamara clenched her pommel and breathed with fury. "You dithering idiot! Did you realize what you have just done, Didier?!"

Not that it mattered. After coming to grips with his mother's death, Didier's face swirled in a flurry of confusing thoughts, with anger being shifted to blaming the wrong culprit. His eyes darted left and right. "You disgusting whore. You killed my momma with your treachery!" With increased bravado, Didier snatched someone's crossbow and loaded the weapon.

The snap of tightened rope being cut was followed by swooshes of more ignited cannonballs heading in their direction. While Tioja was full of anguish, Gulraj's eyes sharpened as he nodded with his mother.

An ever-determined Hamara guarded her weapon, and lyrical words in Harlequin spewed from her mouth. "I summon thee my phantom beast, the Demonic Doll Pirrum!" A shadow beneath Tioja's mother lifted into the air and enveloped Hamara's body into a cocoon. It soon hardened into a layer of darkness that seemed more reminiscent of a clay doll with detachable prehensile limbs. The hairless dark clay that covered Hamara's skin opened its frightful bright red eyes, and a sinister grin invaded its face.

Hamara tossed her red cape to the ground and stood in a defensive stance with clenched fists. Soon enough, a voice that seemed all too wretched to be Hamara's echoed from inside the creature. "As punishment for breaking the truce, I shall claim Senhort as mine!"

Hamara stretched her insanely long arms. Earthly dark goo shot against the two cannonballs with ridiculous ease, crushing the metal into pieces. Didier was meanwhile too busy loading the weapon to have noticed Hamara's frightful transformation that enticed plenty of marauders to start running for their lives. Aiming the weapon at Hamara's face, Didier squealed like a pig and didn't have much time to process his thoughts as Hamara charged in his direction with delirious bloodlust. He barely had enough time to soil his pants when her elbow pierced a hole in his skull, splattering encephalic tissue and gore on the grass.

Horrified, Tioja remained on top of his little brother as he watched his mother smash Didier's men to death using melee combat. Worse, the smile on her face exerted exuberance as she enjoyed the thrill of murdering humans, which filled his heart with absolute terror. Was this Hamara's true nature? Could he ever love such a hideous abomination of nature?

One of Didier's men approached Hamara with a drawn ax, prompting Tioja to holler. "Mother, watch out!"

"Don't worry, Tioja. She can take care of everything." Gulraj grinned as he shoved his brother to the side to watch with a glee that only increased Tioja's fear. Was everyone in his family a raging group of murderous lunatics?

Hamara drew her sword in a flash, causing blue sparks to flicker in the air when it entered contact with her opponent's weapon. While Tioja felt awed, Gulraj seemed slightly concerned. "Why aren't you destroying him, mother?"

Incredulous, Tioja hoped Gulraj would offer him much-needed answers. "What is all of his? What happened to our mom?"

"Oh, this must be the first time you've seen Hamara use her phantom beast. The Pirrum is like a magical clay that covers our mom's body. It grants her superb speed and strength. You can try to cut her apart with a sword, and the clay just reattaches itself without harming her real body. If you're lucky, she might even twist her head backward. Oh, look! We're in good luck! She's doing it right now!"

If the baffling behavior of his relatives didn't concern him enough, Tioja's mind ceased to process logic upon seeing the disturbing sight ahead. Hamara's bald head had turned 180 degrees backward while her torso was slashing humans with the sword. Her knees were bending at an impossible back angle while they kicked other enemies to death.

After killing off most of the horde, Hamara lifted her sword into the air, and it became imbued with blue and green magic. While Tioja was dazzled by the gorgeous colors, it was Gulraj's turn to drag him to safety. "Huddle to the ground, Tio! Hamara is going to flatten the whole town!"

Before Tioja could argue, the sounds of an explosion were followed by the fall of debris everywhere that knocked the air from his lungs. Knowing he was otherwise unharmed, it still took Tioja a few moments to garner the confidence to lift himself up. Not that it would be necessary, for Gulraj was the one that yanked his arm and helped him stand up. "Are you okay?"

"What…" The buzzing in Tioja's ears made him delirious as the surroundings buzzed in circles for a few moments.

Gulraj seemed amused as he enjoyed seeing the ruined village with delight. "Well, it seems like mom just got rid of another rogue village. Good to know Abilene signed it on time, which will grant our city political immunity."

The acrid smell of wood and cadavers burning, falling dust, and animals running in fear was pretty much all that was left. Chances are a few survivors would scamper off to safety and alert other people. It made Tioja feel sick to the stomach seeing this deviant new aspect of his once peace-abiding mother. "Our mom… she killed them."

Gulraj didn't seem to care much about Tioja's concerns as he wiped the dust from his face with a handkerchief. "I believe this is the second time a human enclave has tried to dispose of us with brute force. The first time being sent by the king. Our clan's mages did a good job taking over Kinau's only water reservoir and threatened to starve the entire country if we didn't get our independence."

"What? My tutors said Hurrujat was gifted those caverns!"

"The tutor lied to you. Unlike the peaceful elves that suffered in Almjarhad, we learned quickly that you must show a little force to get what you need. As a part of our peace agreement, the king will let us govern these lands and do whatever we want with the human enclaves as long as we never use starvation as a weapon against his nation ever again. To sweeten the deal, we sometimes pay a small tariff on merchandise that passes through our lands, so it isn't like the king is getting nothing. Oh look, the dust has settled, and I just spotted our mom!"

Both halflings ran towards Hamara, whose phantom beast had vanished. While she looked unharmed, she rubbed her eyes nonstop. "Did I get everyone?"

Gulraj nodded with glee. "Senhort has just been flattened. We might need to send a few knights to threaten any stragglers that remain, but we will soon rebuild this town and fill it with loyal humans that obey our laws."

"Then our mission was a success." As Hamara was increasingly lured by somnolence, she caressed Tioja's face. "Don't worry, my dear. I am unharmed. Help your brother carry me home because I need to sleep for a while." As sweat covered Hamara's weary face, she eagerly smiled at Gulraj and dropped the sword. "You know what to do."

Upon collapsing into a deep slumber, Gulraj tried pulling her prone body, to no avail. He soon wiped some sweat. "Ah, drat! We should have brought a horse with us."

Concerned about his mother, Tioja knelt and heard her chest. Hamara's heart continued beating with normality. He touched her skin and used some of his harlequin water magic in search of injuries. Much to his surprise, Hamara was completely unscathed.

Gulraj patted his shoulder. "This always happens when mom summons her demonic beast. She needs to sleep for a while and then wakes up. Her beast is very nifty, but she depends on traveling with a loyal friend to drag her to safety."

"Does that mean someone could kill her?"

Gulraj nodded as his eyes studied his surroundings. "All the horses seem to be dead or gone. And yes, mom risks getting herself killed while she sleeps. Good thing we are here to save the day," Gulraj added with a wink.

This comment intrigued and concerned Tioja as he tried thinking about a solution. "How long will she stay asleep? A few minutes?"

"Mom will probably wake up by nighttime. She used quite a lot of mana. Let's drag her behind those bushes and find something we can use to take her home!"

Even though Tioja would have preferred to wait it out until Hamara regained consciousness, the chances a straggler might return meant it was too risky. Tioja could summon his wings and return to Murdorhiolan, but that entailed risking the lives of his brother and mother. If anything happened to either one of them, Hurrujat would execute him.

This meant Tioja would have to protect Hamara with his harlequin air magic. He could defend everyone with air magic in a pinch, but evacuating Hamara seemed like a wiser idea. "Gulraj. I'll watch over mom and stop any assailants with magic. Can you fetch two logs and very thick fabric?"

"What for?"

"I know how to sew because my dad needed me to mend his shirts. If you can find those items, some strong thread and needles or nails, I could build a stretcher. Mom is too heavy for us to carry."

With a nod, Gulraj scampered off while whistling a song. Tioja wanted to swat the kid for making so much noise when their lives were in danger. Every few minutes, Gulraj would run back and show Tioja various items he found. Despite his weak body and inactive magic, Gulraj was very resourceful and enjoyed this mission. Watching his mother murdering a bunch of foolish humans and then performing these mundane tasks didn't feel troubling to Gulraj at all.

While the halfling was endearing, Tioja wished Gulraj wasn't so… well, sadistic. Better yet, he wished his brother harbored greater respect for human life. These thoughts pained Tioja as he avoided looking at his mother who continued snoring peacefully. Using air magic, Tioja cut the leather tent covering, stitched rope together and helped Gulraj pound nails on wooden lateral beams for extra tensile strength.

Both siblings did these tasks under the beating sun and stench of death for the better portion of the day in silence. By the time they had placed Hamara on top, something unexpected happened. Instead of an enemy charging their way, Hamara yawned, stretched her arms, and opened her crimson eyes. Overjoyed from seeing her sons, Hamara beamed with joy. "Good afternoon, boys. Did you have fun today?"

CHAPTER 6 ♦ TALGEL

Tioja's departure should have garnered something akin to emotions. An average person would feel pleased they protected their people from a potential threat or sorrow after they ruined an impressionable teenager's life. Neither feeling seemed to stir in the blind halfling.

"Your ladyship? Can you hear me?"

Of course, Talgel couldn't hear her assistant. Her body was ravaged by agonizing pain intermixed with the helplessness of losing two senses. Shedding your skin is a painful process and the first few days are always the worst. Both bandaged arms felt the bed. Judging from the size and shape of the border of the bed frame, Talgel was in Jarahad's palace. Typical of Jarahad to always concern himself with trivialities. Henrietta couldn't care less. Talgel's obnoxious assistant enjoyed staying there.

"Your ladyship, I have some food. Please eat."

Once again, Talgel couldn't hear her assistant's voice. The only hint it was Henrietta was from her distinctive body odor intermixed with something pungent that made Talgel's mouth salivate. Harlequins were unique because they shed their skin every few years to protect themselves from sun rot and scars. While the shedding was seamless for pureblood harlequins, hybrids like herself suffered from an unusually agonizing variant of the process, which lasted six weeks.

As Talgel willingly opened her bandaged mouth and chewed on her meal, she realized the shedding offered her a unique opportunity to think about her life goals. Now that Tioja was gone, Talgel's path was set in stone.

"Just more time, please." A rampant tear fell from her eye socket and moistened the bandage. Not that it mattered. The fateful event was about to happen.

***

It had almost been three weeks, and Talgel was starting to recover her hearing. Thick curtains ruffled against the soothing wind and Talgel ceased feeling any pain. Henrietta's characteristic smell was ever present as she dabbled water on Talgel's chapped lips. Footsteps followed by the creaking of wood indicated someone came to visit her.

"Has she consumed water?" Jarahad asked.

Henrietta continued dabbling droplets without turning around. "She is still deaf. I fed her a little bit of soup before sunrise. She will speak soon."

Disappointing news, albeit fully expected. Nonetheless, this didn't deter Jarahad's mood. "I will ask some servants to tend to her needs for the rest of the day."

"Is something wrong?"

"You haven't rested for several days. The worst of the shedding has already passed, and her life isn't in danger. I need you to visit my private office so we can talk."

Henrietta's voice became squeakier with devilish delight. "So, the time has arrived that we reach the pinnacle of our deal? I am quite pleased."

As the two left, a sneer embellished Talgel's lips.

A few years had passed, and the lingering thoughts of returning to Almjarhad vanished from Tioja's mind. Hamara was truthful when she claimed they would become one big and happy family. He even began to tolerate his elevated social status as the second heir to the clan and soon became fluent in Harlequin.

Over the years, Gulraj's rambunctiousness slowly delved into quite a sight. His lanky body filled up with muscle, and he became increasingly handsome with each passing day.

To apologize for the traumatizing incident when Hamara killed the stray kitten, Tioja was gifted a beautiful purebred cat with a pudgy face, soft white fur, and piercing bicolored eyes. Gulraj insisted on calling the cat Fluff, which became his name. It became common to see Fluff padding his paws behind both siblings all over the castle.

When Tioja discovered his mother could use the sword, he was awestruck by her gallantry whenever she trained with Gulraj. Hamara embraced everything about harlequin culture and was the most appreciative host when pureblood harlequins from allied clans visited the city. Tioja would spend countless hours watching his mother and brother duel each other using blunted swords. Much to everyone's chagrin, Tioja's mind would go blank the instant he held a sword and never seemed to learn how to do anything with it.

It soon became apparent he was a lost cause when it came to fencing, and a mental barrier slowly formed. Gulraj was constantly reviled by Tioja's poor attempts to overcome his handicap, but Hamara understood it would be preferable to let Tioja figure things out alone.

One day, they were seated in an outdoor garden of the palace, and Gulraj blurted something out loud. "Mother! I want to awaken my phantom beast too!"

Hamara was admiring her sword and smirked. "You haven't awakened your second element yet. It is too soon."

. "That isn't fair!" Gulraj's tirade became accompanied by jumping on the bench with a pouted face.

Surprisingly, Tioja sided with his brother for once. "Mother, please say yes. Gulraj is ready."

"But…"

"Ho, ho, ho, ho, ho! My dearest boy, I agree with you!"

"My love!" Hamara stood up to assist her ailing husband with so much speed, Gulraj stumbled on the ground with a loud thump. The tumor on Hurrujat's face had grown large enough to turn into a hardened prominence that spewed reddish ichor and had deformed his once symmetrical face to the side. Hurrujat knew his life would soon end and spent most of his time bedridden. On occasion, he still had enough vivacity to wander outside and spend his final moments with his family without ever losing his usual joyfulness.

Tioja's relationship with Hurrujat was a complex dance. He always viewed the old man as a revered leader instead of a father. Despite his shortcomings, Jamad would always be the only father Tioja ever knew. Even so, Tioja always treated Hurrujat with overt respect.

After endless discussions, Hamara conceded defeat, and they sat on a carpet a few days later in Tioja's bedroom. Hamara passed a stone pipe, and both siblings inhaled a strong whiff of the dangerous potion. Soon enough, Tioja's mind entered a dream like the previous times. Unlike his first voyages, he was no longer floating against the ocean. An open field with darkness in every direction was intertwined with abstract geometric shapes of varying bright colors. Tioja soon galvanized into utter fear upon the frightful realization he was alone. "Mom? Hurrujat? Brother? Where are you?"

Anxious, he flew around this place with no exit in sight. And then, a blob of grey viscous material bubbled from the ground. His foot stepped back in an automatic reflex and gawked as a clay figurine materialized into the familiar shape of the person he least expected to see. It was Talgel.

The masked figure stared at him with her usual blank expression.

"Little child, why do you hide?"

"I… I am… happy."

"Yes, I see. But why haven't you used your gift?"

"My gift?"

"Your Lehart, the most marvelous phantom beast to have ever existed."

Terror made Tioja cower as he tried to crawl away from Talgel's ghostly figure in vain. "No! I can't! That cursed beast wants to destroy me!"

His answer didn't stir any emotion from the figure. "Gulraj hasn't awakened his beast yet. What a waste."

"Huh?"

And with that, the apparition fizzled away, and Tioja was returned to the carpet alongside an ever-attentive Hamara. His mother was busy consoling a sobbing Gulraj. "Why? Why can't I do it?!"

"Huh?" Tioja realized something was wrong. Both he and his mother exerted trace amounts of mana from their bodies. And yet here he was: his endearing brother Gulraj seemed so out of place as he pitiably wailed in Hamara's warm embrace.

After Hamara left the room without saying a word, Tioja crawled towards his brother. "It is all right. You will summon mana."

"No, I won't! I'm jealous of you, Tioja! You have the most powerful demonic phantom beast I have ever heard of, but you never want to use it! My mama can also summon a beast that lets her fight against humans and maintain the peace!"

"But… I…" Tioja opted for a different tactic. "You just need more time. Maybe if you summon your second…"

And then, Gulraj lifted his hand, and demonic air magic scooted in his hand like a tiny tornado. While a feeling of joy enveloped Tioja because

Gulraj awakened both of his two elements, this did little to satiate Gulraj's dour mood.

Gulraj made the tornado vanish and pounded the carpet for an hour until he couldn't bear the pain. "You don't understand! My father is about to die from his disease, and I am not fit to rule the clan! I am weak! How can I protect any of you from the wicked Elf King if I can't use my magic to its full potential?"

***

As time went on, Gulraj became increasingly desperate. The innocence he once harbored was replaced with vivid jealousy that made Tioja question whether it was safe to even talk to him at times.

If there was one thing that amazed Tioja, it was the fact Gulraj was tenacious and harbored a profound love for his city and its inhabitants. Tioja suggested they should try drinking söma. This was an idea that Hurrujat agreed with, and it was relatively easy for him to request an allied clan to supply him with the potion.

Tioja was still too naïve to realize why Hurrujat spent so much time with a harlequin clan leader named Nemoraj. Hurrujat had invited plenty of nobledemons for business transactions over the years, but Nemoraj had been visiting his city constantly. The jovial man regarded Tioja with a small degree of antipathy.

Fed up with so much mystery regarding the visitor, Tioja spoke to Gulraj privately. "Brother, who is Nemoraj, and why is he visiting our city so often?"

Always adept regarding city gossip, Gulraj stopped brushing Fluff's fur and lifted his head. "Oh, come on! You don't know who he is?"

"Well, he speaks Harlequin with odd words, so I don't know."

"Ugh! You are such a lost cause, Tio. Remember our uncle Kashin?"

"Of course, I do! The last time I saw him, I was still a child in

Almjarhad. Wasn't he supposed to return to the city? I haven't seen him in ages!"

"Silly bloke! Kashin was sent to train in Nemoraj's city in the hopes he could awaken his phantom beast. After practicing for ages, he finally mastered it."

"Wow! Just like mom!"

"That is right. When Hamara awakened her demonic beast, she visited Kashin and threatened him to stop wasting his time. He was essentially barred from returning to our city until he summoned it."

"That is so cruel! I told you it was hard for me to awaken my beast!"

"And you continue to act like we are elves, Tio. Kashin swore an oath of servitude to my father. Without a phantom beast, he would be ill-equipped to protect our city from invaders. If he had taken any longer, my father would have been forced to behead him."

"What? But I know several warriors that returned to our city empty-handed without facing repercussions! Why would my uncle be treated differently?"

"Because if my mother could summon a phantom beast, then he had no excuse." Gulraj's glowing eyes rolled so profoundly inside his eyelids that the room darkened for an instant.

After processing his thoughts, Tioja furrowed his brow while Fluff musked his hands nonstop. "When did my uncle summon his beast?"

"Oh, about 3 years ago. My father only found out last year because Kashin didn't want to return home until he fully mastered it. That was when Nemoraj felt impressed with his tenacity and offered to initiate him."

Tioja's eyes perked at once. "Wow! Did my uncle get trained like our mother?"

"That's right. Albeit I believe Hamara was initiated by the Zusheroja Clan, which is further northwest. My father sends applicants to different cities, so they don't sabotage each other."

Feeling more relaxed than before, Tioja spoke with a firmer voice. "Kashin must have completed the initiation."

"Yup, and Nemoraj wants his arrival in our city to be a huge surprise. Kashin foolishly believes Nemoraj is busy doing a business trip and doesn't know he came here. Please don't spoil anything with your big mouth, understood?"

"Um… Yes."

After a surprising amount of preparation in the palace with a huge banquet and floral decorations, everyone was waiting for Kashin's arrival. Nemoraj spent most of his time gloating in the presence of harlequins from various cities, and the palace dining hall was a cacophony of voices engaged in amenable chatter.

Fingers pressed against Tioja's shoulder, prompting him to gasp at the sight of his young brother beaming in joy. "Hey, look! Kashin has just arrived!"

Kashin now exuded pompous dignity that made even Tioja flinch in reverie. His speech and mannerisms as he addressed nobledemons in the assembly room had lost any remaining hints of his past life as a peasant. When Kashin knelt in front of Hurrujat with the most extreme degree of respect, he lifted his head, and a discreet gasp escaped his lip.

Falsely assuming Kashin's reaction was due to Nemoraj's unexpected presence, Hurrujat spoke. "My dearest nephew, Kashin. You have proven beyond any reasonable doubt you deserve to be heralded as a hero. Not only did you master your demonic beast, but you also showed diligence and earned your harlequin sword. From this day forward, your home and the city that trained you shall be forged together by the strongest bond."

After finishing his odd speech, Hurrujat tied a thin gold rope on his wrist while Nemoraj fastened the other side to the wrist of a young female harlequin named Iora. The strange device glowed for an instant and sealed itself into a thick bracelet that forced Kashin to always stand close to this woman. The bracelet glowed whenever Kashin stepped too far away, forcing him to approach Iora like a magnet as she giggled with discretion.

Sweat beaded from Kashin's face when he realized the woman was dressed in elegant white attire with ruffled sleeves embroidered in her clan's pattern. Soon enough, his shoulders slumped in subdued defeat, and he no longer offered resistance.

This prompted Tioja to whisper to his younger brother while taking advantage Gulraj was in a good mood for once. "I don't understand. Why is my uncle Kashin behaving this way?"

A sinister grin invaded Gulraj's thin lips. "Lord Kashin is going to get married to that harlequin today whether he likes it or not. I thought he would feel excited because she has a high social standing."

Something felt off about this reunion as Tioja watched Hurrujat speak to Kashin and Nemoraj. While the woman gloated every time her hands touched Kashin's sword with reverie, something in Kashin's eyes seemed off.

Without wasting any time, Tioja whispered something in Gulraj's ear. "He doesn't look happy about any of this."

Not that Gulraj cared because the result of this reunion would further his goals. "You are the reason why he has to marry that woman."

"Huh? Why me?"

"Don't you realize we don't know how to make söma? Our clan will not give away the secrets to our engineering technology. Other clans won't readily initiate our clan members now that Charon died without leaving an heir. The only way to get initiated swordsmen to protect our family is to marry them to the highest bidder. Not only will Nemoraj's clan initiate plenty of our members, but they will also supply us with söma. Human mages have told us that söma might ensure I awaken my beast. I am so happy! We will be unstoppable if we master our magic!"

Contrary to Gulraj's optimism, Tioja watched Kashin's wedding with dread. As an honorary member of Hurrujat's family, he was forced to stand in Kashin's bedroom as he had sex with Iora in front of a cheering crowd. The rope that Hurrujat and Nemoraj fastened to their wrists was imbued with a magical spell that only worked on the initiated. As a fellow initiate, Iora's inked body glowed when she reached the pinnacle of ecstasy, and the rope that couldn't be removed made their tattoos glow in an iridescent gold hue that made them faint after reaching orgasm at the same time.

The moment they collapsed on the bed and fell into a deep slumber, the rope evaporated into thin air leaving behind a pair of identical gold bracelets on their wrists, and everyone clapped with joy. The female viewers, including Hamara, deposited bouquets as a celebratory offering. Males left incense canisters that imbued the room with a pungent odor before everyone left the room.

As they closed the door, Nemoraj clasped Hurrujat's shoulder and gave him a bottle. "This is the beginning of a great alliance, dear Hurrujat. Order Lord Kashin to sleep with my daughter several times each day until she becomes pregnant. I want a grandchild immediately."

"Ho, ho, ho, ho, ho! Kashin is young and in the prime of health! I've heard his demonic beast is most impressive, and your grandchild will be able to summon a demonic beast. Would you like to marry off more of your children to my knights? They are for sale right now!"

"You are quite a comedian, my Lord. Yes, we should do this. How about if, in the future, we ensure Kashin marries another nobledemon from my clan? Iora's second cousin Yurivia is most handsome, and she will give him plenty of children. I want his seed to infest my bloodline!"

"Yes, we shall agree to the stipulations, and he will have his four wives assigned. I guarantee he will become the most thoughtful and loving husband. Oh, Tioja! Please, run off to your brother and let me continue negotiations. Go on!"

A few days passed, and the visitors departed the city under the friendliest terms. Tioja didn't get to see Kashin much. From what little he saw, the poor halfling looked exhausted as Iora smothered him with kisses, and her wings embraced him wherever they went. They still wore the gold engraved bracelet, further reminding Tioja of his ignorance of harlequin society. Tioja decided it was safe to ask Gulraj. "Brother, why is my uncle acting so strange? Shouldn't he feel happiness?"

"Stupid Tio! Kashin can't disobey my father. Hurrujat is already planning to make him marry a second harlequin from the same clan. You will soon have dozens of cousins that will obey your commands and protect you from harm. I am so excited!"

Horror dawned on Tioja when he saw his uncle sigh whenever Iora's slender fingers caressed his bracelet. "My mother doesn't wear one of those."

"There is no need because Hamara wanted to marry Hurrujat. From now on, Kashin must wear that bracelet as a promise of fidelity to his father-in-law. He can't sleep with any woman that isn't approved by his wife for the time being."

"That… is terrible. I…" In the eyes of the Elf Kingdom, Tioja was a legal adult, so he shouldn't feel squeamish about sex. More like he felt horrified about Kashin being turned into Hurrujat's slave. Harlequins obviously didn't see any problem with this. They were at best, impervious to Kashin's misery.

Knowing it would be useless to talk any sense into his family, Tioja made a secret promise he would try to be nice to Kashin from now on. Maybe with time, Kashin will begin to love his wife, who seemed pleasant enough.

Now that the ruckus tending to the allied clan was over, Gulraj and Tioja began the 10-day fast, and he soon regretted his suggestion to use söma. The blood disease churned within as his higher elf blood purity made him far more sensitive than his brother, but he tried not to complain. If Kashin had to suffer for the clan, he would do the same.

Just like the occasion they smoked the harlequin drug alongside Hamara, the three family members were seated on the carpet in Tioja and Gulraj's shared bedroom. A conniving grin appeared on Hurrujat's disfigured face as he slumped on a chair to watch. "This is good! I want to see all three of you drink söma together!"

Even Hamara began sniffing the strange liquid with suspicion.

"You haven't tried this before, mom?" Tioja asked.

Hamara shook her head as she swirled her cup in circles and gawked at its oily texture. "I awakened my beast without using it. This should prove to be a fun experience."

Gulraj interceded when he saw the three bowls that contained water, dirt, and a candle. "I heard you must be exposed to the four elements to make söma work. Where is the final element? Where is an air source?"

Before they knew it, a whiff of air blew in their direction, and they realized Hurrujat was blowing a fan that made the candle flicker. "I suppose the two of you will be lured by air and water because those are your harlequin elements, but this is the tradition. Have fun!"

The three halflings drank the potion simultaneously, and Tioja was transported into a different world. This time, he didn't hallucinate in the same way as before. Söma's effects were more inward. He felt like time was set to a standstill, and the faces of Gulraj and Hamara ceased to carry any emotional importance. His sense of self-realization had been yanked away as well. Tioja was now reduced to a being that played the role of a mixed-blooded peasant elf and inhabitant of Murdorhiolan. If being a pawn of the gods for self-entertainment was his fate, then he should learn how to make the most of it. For now, his job was to stare at the elements and figure it out.

First, he watched the candle. Wax, red wax, thick, imbued flames. His hand touched it, hot, so hot. Dangerous fire. Not good.

Gulraj imitated him. As his sibling puppet, neither one of them was bonded by fire.

Hamara was also staring at the candle. Her facial features became imbued with pensive seriousness. And so, she touched the flame, which rejected her as well. For a brief instant, Tioja felt something disquieting. An eerie concern jittered his mind when the dancing flames reminded him of Talgel for no apparent reason. Initially concerned, the sensation became soothing, and maybe even magical. Tioja lifted his head and observed his two family members who seemingly ignored him. Assuming their disinterest was because none of them were destined to be fire mages, Tioja licked his fingers and rubbed the wick until the room became dark.

A gasp escaped the lips of the harlequin named Hurrujat, the man Tioja obeyed as his lord but would never become his true father. Old man, good man. A corpse clinging to life long enough to see his son Gulraj rise to his destined glory. Air, wonderful and soothing, blew in Tioja's direction. So, he crawled towards it and smiled. Yes, this was his element. Water soothed him, and he loved it, but his strongest element will always be air. Right now, Tioja felt safe in the confines of this dark bedroom as he started to feel something new about his beast. For the first time in his life, Tioja felt glad he possessed the Lehart even though he still couldn't entirely control it. Wings, he loved having wings. For now, he would resist the urge to summon his beast because it would ruin his silk shirt. The woman seated next to him would get very angry if he damaged it. Someday, Tioja will overcome his fear and embrace his inner demon if he can again feel the cold wind blast into his face.

After coming to this conclusion, Tioja smiled at Hurrujat. Tioja then stared at his mother. Hamara was an earth and water mage, and it was fun to see her smear dirt mixed with water on her face as if she were putting on a facemask. Low amounts of mana were detectable in her body. Just like him, Hamara resisted the urge to summon her demonic beast.

Finally, Tioja then observed Gulraj and his heart sank. Tears, terrible tears, spilled from his eyes. Gulraj wanted to summon his demonic beast because he would soon inherit Hurrujat's clan. Everyone counted on him. Kashin sacrificed his freedom to give him the söma that would awaken his mana. It was useless.

As the potion's effect simmered away and Tioja returned to his usual self, he ignored the bloodlust and spent the better portion of that evening hugging his distressed brother. Perhaps Gulraj was never destined to summon a demonic beast after all.

It was time to dig a hole in the ground. Well, more like it was time to gloat in pleasure as Talgel heard Henrietta digging under the battering heat for no logical reason at first. Soon enough, the woman removed some sweat from her head. "How much longer?"

"Dig, you brute! Dig until I tell you it is deep enough!" Harassing Henrietta was a great source of entertainment. What could entice a complete stranger to be so dastardly obedient? Henrietta was not a member of Hurrujat's clan, and she wasn't engaged to any inhabitants of Almjarhad either. Could it be…?

"Henrietta, that is deep enough. Put the metal box in the hole and bury it."

"Your orders are my command, your ladyship!" The metal scraping was soon intertwined with a soft pounding felt by Talgel's feet as Henrietta covered the clay soil and patted the top with her shovel. The woman sat next to Talgel, who quietly grumbled as she had to offer her roommate space on the boulder to accommodate her black wings. "Whew! This is indeed one of your most irreverent commands, your ladyship! Why did you order me to write such a strange letter to a guy named Damantin in the first place? There's nothing there!"

"As you promised when we first met, you will not interfere with my predictions. The relevance to Damantin's fortune is not your business. You will die centuries before he is born. For the record, he will have some fun alongside his older sister Jurhim."

"Uhhh… why are you so obsessed with my death? And who is Jurhim?"

A cruel grin invaded Talgel's lips for reasons Henrietta would never quite understand. "Just another halfling you will never meet, so their fortune isn't your problem. If it makes you feel any better, Damantin will not find anything except misery when he visits that place. I am only giving him this prediction ahead of time out of spite. He means nothing to me.

Satisfied?"

"Well… I guess there is no point in questioning your decisions, your ladyship. I just wished you could be more… well… nice?"

"Nonsense! Do you think just because I am blind, I should become a beacon of self-pity like that idiot Jamarnid? He can act proud of being mutilated if it makes him feel any better, but my life was ruined the day I summoned my beast. I will regret summoning it for the rest of my life!"

Expecting to hear Henrietta offering an unwanted pep talk, the harlequin surprisingly remained quiet as the wind caressed their faces that summer morning. "I am sorry. I should not have said such a hurtful thing, your ladyship. Please stop hating yourself. You never deserved to suffer, and I will always support you."

Taking advantage of letting her guard down, Talgel wanted to see if Henrietta fell for it. She grasped her hand, and Henrietta innocently clasped it, assuming it was an act of friendship. With a smile, Talgel approached Henrietta and their lips soon interlocked as she gave the woman a passionate kiss.

Much to Talgel's surprise, Henrietta froze at once and backed away. "Ah! Your ladyship! Please! I… I don't love you in that manner!"

Gotcha! A new piece of the puzzle behind Henrietta's true mission had just been revealed. Henrietta was not in love with her after all! The mystery behind Henrietta's presence in the city was only deepening. Talgel was forced to feign embarrassment so that Henrietta would not scamper off. With quality theatrics, she covered her face with her hands and turned away. "Sorry. I am so lonely, and you are always so kind. I will never do that ever again."

"Whew! That's a relief! I hope this doesn't ruin our friendship."

Once again, Talgel returned to her usual cruel self, realizing Henrietta would forgive this little prank. "Yes, we should forget this ever happened and visit him. I will show you the way."

Both women walked across the desert for a while until the sun was high up in the sky. Concerned about Henrietta's wellbeing, Talgel offered her roommate a parasol, and they soon found Jarahad seated in front of a giant cactus with a few violet flowers. Talgel had already seen this scene play out in one of her visions, and a sense of dread filled her heart for an ulterior reason. She would have to keep the truth to herself for a little longer. "Lord Jarahad, this is where you buried that boy, right?"

Jarahad didn't stand up and smother her with kisses and attention like usual. He remained seated as his hands rustled against the cactus's bristles. "Don't forget. We bury our dead and plant an edible plant on top of the tomb to feed the living. The child I murdered deserved at least this modicum of respect."

Henrietta sighed. "I am so sorry that we couldn't tell you anything. The child would have died soon anyways. You must forgive yourself."

"I suppose you are right, Henrietta. This plant will give us fruit in a few months. If you stay here for a while longer, I wish to give one to you as a token of my appreciation."

"Yes, I am elated."

***

That evening, Talgel summoned her phantom beast and encountered the demon, which seemed rather joyful for a change. "Your fate has been sealed. Still, you don't take him."

"What do you care? You only exist to punish me," Talgel snapped.

This didn't deter the demon as it floated in the air. "You know, we could be together. I could give you the eyes you lost and make your wildest dreams come true. Would you like to become initiated as well? I can arrange that."

"Shut up!"

The demon soon became bored and opened the portal. "I'll let you see something fun. Enjoy." Intrigued, Talgel entered the leyline realm. Some branches were cut off abruptly, suggesting a terrible battle looming ahead that would end the target's life. Other ones reached a lifespan surpassing a regular human, and very few branches extended vast offshoots into the future. This intrigued Talgel because it meant the target was potentially a halfling who might die very soon or remain as a bachelor until their expected lifespan ended. Under specific circumstances, they could have offspring.

A sense of wonder imbued Talgel, and she flew towards one of the branches where the target would live for a long time. The scenery was dark. Nighttime?

Talgel spotted two people. From the wings on their backs, it suggested they were both harlequins. Talgel couldn't properly view their faces or recognize their surroundings. Perhaps this event would take place in a harlequin city.

One of the two people knelt very low and offered a sword which Talgel found somewhat intriguing. It was shorter than an average harlequin sword with a slightly curved edge and a thin blade.

The instant the woman spoke, Talgel froze. "I am sorry for offending you, my dearest father. I forfeit my title and riches. May my sibling inherit the responsibilities of the blood that I am unfit to carry."

"Vile little bitch. You are a disgrace to your family! After everything we did to appease that worthless half-breed named Jarahad! We gave those elves the method to make blood wine, and Jarahad never let my men live in Almjarhad!" With each utterance of the man's words, the woman cowered lower. "I disown you, Henrietta. You were supposed to discover the secret to their technology, yet you only wasted your time working as a crippled woman's caretaker."

"Talgel isn't disabled. She's my friend!"

"Silence!"

Talgel shuddered when she heard a crack, followed by Henrietta collapsing on the ground as blood oozed from her broken nose.

As the vision became haunted by the man's tireless rant that accused Henrietta of every offense she had ever committed, Talgel felt both a sense of anger and satisfaction she had discovered part of Henrietta's secret after so long.

Talgel felt hurt as well. Why did Henrietta fret over keeping her secret identity for so long? It hardly surprised Talgel that harlequin clans wanted the engineering technology of the elves. But the degree Henrietta's father went towards his scheming and anger seemed somewhat overboard. What could have prompted this woman to betray her own family?

Soon enough, the vision faded, and Talgel could not continue spying on Henrietta's personal affairs anymore.

Worse still, she heard the one voice she never wanted to hear goading her like usual. "Your ladyship! You seem rather pale this evening. Was the vision terrible? Oh, please don't tell me you saw someone's death!"

"It was worse than that, Henrietta. We must see Jarahad and Jamarnid at once."

***

Jamarnid cleared his throat while they were inside Jarahad's office. "Very well, little tramp. What is the emergency? Has the Cursed One returned to murder Lord Sharad?"

Talgel felt disgusted even thinking about it. She then grabbed Henrietta's wrist and pinched her. The woman squealed and tugged her arm away, but Talgel never let go. "Jarahad knew Henrietta was a spy the whole time!"

"What?!" Jamarnid immediately began hurling vicious insults at Jarahad and Henrietta.

While Jarahad tried to reason with his father, Henrietta continued pulling her arm away. "Stop it! What are you talking about? I'm not your enemy!"

"Oh, but I saw you in some harlequin city. You were relinquishing your harlequin sword."

Everyone stopped talking. Jamarnid growled at one. "Do you mean this woman is not only a spy from an enemy of our city, but she owns harlequin steel as well? Jarahad, I order you to let me inspect it!"

Shoved to a corner, Jarahad's hands trembled as he unsheathed Henrietta's sword and offered the blade to his father. Talgel obviously couldn't see the weapon in her current state. From the way Jamarnid was taking his time and demanding Jarahad to reposition the weapon in search of its characteristic green fuller, it was indeed made from harlequin steel.

"Jarahad, I want this enemy to be arrested. Do it!"

"No! Please listen to me, dammit! Talgel, why are you accusing me of being your enemy? I never chose to become initiated!" Henrietta pleaded.

The room fell silent and Talgel let go of her hand. There seemed to be something else. "I saw your future, and my predictions are always true. You are a nobledemon of some harlequin clan and only offered us the recipe to produce blood wine to get something in return."

Jamarnid hissed at once. "Is it true? Are you only here to steal from us?"

"No! I..." Henrietta flapped her wings and spoke with a stutter. "Yes, I am a nobledemon, and Lord Jarahad knew everything from the start. And before you accuse me of treason Lord Jamarnid, you must understand. I never asked to be the firstborn daughter of a clan leader and become initiated. It is a miracle I have not been wedded off to someone."

"You are a liar!" Jamarnid scowled.

Henrietta's voice increased its staccato from her despair. "Look, my birth city is in shambles. We are under constant threat from human enclaves, and the city doesn't boast the defenses it needs to repeal more attacks. I was supposed to fulfill my mission ages ago, but I have continued to lie to my father. I guess it is too late to continue delaying the inevitable."

Jamarnid gasped at once. "Why are you in this city, Henrietta? What evil deed have you agreed with my son?"

"I…" It filled Henrietta with great sadness as she continued her speech. "I am supposed to be engaged to Jarahad!"

The instant Talgel heard this confession, a heat of ravaging vitriol spewed within the deepest recesses of her soul. She had constantly rejected Jarahad's romantic advances, which caused him undue suffering. Still, to discover Henrietta was pretending to be her selfless friend for so many years while she stabbed her back in such a way enticed her to require extreme measures.

With clenched fists, Talgel stomped towards Henrietta, grabbed her wings, and yanked them hard until the little twit whelped in pain. "Stop it! This hurts!"

"Good to know, you sniveling little cunt! Who gave you permission to betray me like that? You had plenty of chances to confess your true intentions to me, yet your silence further proves your guilt. I hate you and wish you'd just die!"

And then, acute, snarling pain was felt on Talgel's left cheek, making her crumble like a pile of hay. Who could have slapped her?

"Perhaps you are right, Talgel. I should have married Henrietta ages ago," Jarahad's voice was fuming from the contained rage he was finally allowed to externalize. Talgel remained too shocked to process the hurtful thing he had just said.

Akin to his gentle nature, Jarahad helped Henrietta sit on a chair. He spent a long time assessing the poor harlequin's wings while she occasionally moaned. "You're in good luck. Just a few pulled ligaments and no dislocations. It should heal within a few days, but I'll ask a medic to apply some numbing ointments to stop the inflammation. Give me a moment." Jarahad marched off without taking the annoyance to address either Talgel or his father. Not that Talgel could care at this point.

After watching the spectacle, Jamarnid remained quiet from the privy turn of events. Surely he would side with Talgel, right? What happened next only hurt Talgel's pride even further. "You know, I might dislike harlequins for many reasons, but I know when to spot one of the few redeemable ones. This is the first time I have ever heard of Jarahad's engagement with this woman. While I feel shocked from finding out in such a way, I believe Henrietta would make my son very happy. If you ever decide to marry my son, you have my fullest blessing."

"What? No!" Talgel tried to stand up, but her trembling legs gave up, and she collapsed on her lap from miserable defeat. "You can't do this to me, Jamarnid! Jarahad is mine!"

"Ha! You had your chance and continue to humiliate my beloved son for sheer entertainment. I might not fully trust Henrietta, but she has proven to care about my son."

"Can you guys please stop acting like I have no voice in this conversation???!!!" Everyone turned around and realized Henrietta was breathing heavily to avoid aggravating her injured wings. "My father bartered a deal with Jarahad in exchange for the blood wine, but Jarahad thought giving his people a one-time wine dowry was a poor offer. It isn't like halflings can be cured of their blood disease so easily. Jarahad stalled the ceremony after visiting my father in a neutral human enclave. I had a difficult time convincing my father to give him the recipe to make the halflings' lives easier. In exchange, Almjarhad would supply our city with dehydrated meat. The true reason why we got engaged was because my father wants to obtain the technology to build sewage systems. Both of you lived in a harlequin enclave and know about their sanitation problems."

Jamarnid seemed agreeable for once and spoke in a softer voice. "I see. I will presume you continued lying to your father by claiming my city's inhabitants were not sharing their secret knowledge on purpose."

"I swear I am not a traitor. Just an innocent person forced to do vile things because I am honor bound to obey my family. I only wanted to live a normal life. If I had married Jarahad, my father would have insisted we move to my birth city now that Sharad is safe."

The mystery began to unfurl, and now even Talgel began to understand Henrietta's motives. So that was the reason why the woman was so dodgy about her personal life! She just wanted to play devil's advocate and continue living the good life without any responsibility. In a way, Henrietta was no better than Sharad in Talgel's twisted point of view. Even so, the pain from her perceived betrayal didn't fully allay. It could have been forgivable if Henrietta had confessed she was engaged to Jarahad against her will when they first met. As it was, their phony friendship had been severed forever. No longer embarrassed to have been put in her place by Jarahad, Talgel stood up with her last figments of pride. "I am glad to have seen my vision. We are not friends, and I no longer feel ashamed to hate you. Remove your belongings from my home immediately. Goodbye."

As Talgel pattered away amid Jamarnid's insults and Henrietta's begging, she soon reached the main door and bumped into someone. Thanks to her walking stick and a whiff of fire magic, Talgel kept her footing. And then, she felt something deeply concerning. A sensation she had never sensed before in her lifetime had just activated upon entering contact with her magic, and she felt depleted of mana for unknown reasons.

A sultry voice with a heavy accent spoke in the common human tongue, sinking her heart into the deepest recesses of fear. "Why hello, my darling. I hope you didn't hurt yourself. My name is Anduvio, and I would like to meet the owner of this estate."

Talgel swallowed some saliva and whispered something that made the man smirk with disdain. If Tioja's demonic beast and the purges were terrible enough, the man standing in front of her was the worst threat of all. "I am going to someday kill you with my hands, Magician Anduvio."

His eyebrows lifted at once with brief incredulity. Before Talgel knew it, the strange man punched her in the stomach, rendering her unconscious.

CHAPTER 9 ♦ JAMARNID

Discovering Henrietta's true purpose in Almjarhad and Jarahad's private affairs was not even half as shocking in the greater scheme of things over meeting this human. Anduvio strode inside like he owned the palace, while carrying an unconscious Talgel in his arms.

Accustomed to human behavior, Jamarnid tolerated the man's almost comical showmanship. After tending to Henrietta and grudgingly allowing Talgel to rest in the palace, Jarahad was morally obliged to offer this man the chance to accompany him for a late-night dinner. Jarahad tried to hide the visible traces of exhaustion from being sleep deprived while the man became increasingly inebriated.

Kicking him out was tempting. Jamarnid's plans became foiled the instant a sleepy Sharad left his bedroom while staying up working on another one of his pet projects. Upon seeing the commotion, his energy levels shot through the roof. Sharad soon began singing alongside Anduvio a never-ending stream of obnoxious human tavern songs. Jamarnid remained perched on his wheelchair and watched the spectacle with utter disbelief.

For a moment, Jarahad seemed incommoded by Anduvio's closeness. At first, Jamarnid presumed it was because of the alcohol, and mishaps can sometimes happen. Jamarnid knew better than most the endless list of embarrassing incidents Sharad had done in front of him when he got drunk.

Every now and then, Anduvio goaded Jamarnid to enjoy a drink, but he outright refused. With a twitch on his lip, Anduvio stammered back to his side of the table and continued behaving like Jamarnid didn't exist.

By the time it was dawn, Anduvio was finally drunk enough to be yanked from the table and tossed into one of the palace's servant quarters. Given both Jarahad and Sharad were snoring on the table from inebriation, Jamarnid felt no guilt about not offering the human pest a far more redeeming treatment. On all accounts, Anduvio embodied many narcissistic traits that made Jamarnid dislike humans. He hoped Sharad would feel satisfied they offered him a safe lodging for the night so he could soon leave.

Alas, fate was unkind. The following afternoon, Anduvio strode right into Jamarnid's office while Tanato was brushing his long hair. His visitor today had huffed cheeks, a puffy face, and bloodshot eyes. The man's brightly colored mustard yellow shirt was an eyesore, along with his royal blue pants. With a trimmed beard and mustache, Anduvio wasn't physically repulsive, albeit his intolerable personality made Jamarnid hate the man even more than before. While Jamarnid smiled at the fuming man, Tanato gasped and ceased to brush his hair.

"You bastardo! I came here peacefully to enjoy a lovely evening, and you tossed me in a servant's room! How rude you are and a terrible host!"

This threat amused Jamarnid very much. "You don't say! I never recall ever letting you barge into MY palace so late at night and demand to abuse MY son's rule of hospitality to get inebriated at MY city's expense. The only reason I didn't kick you out of the castle once you vomited in my dining room was due to a sense of respect for Jarahad and Sharad. Now that you are well-fed and rested, I kindly request you to pack your belongings and find somewhere else to spend the night. You are not a nobleman or a wealthy merchant, so you offer my people nothing."

"Do you have any idea who I am??!!"

"Just a beggar dressed in a jester costume. A vile con artist with delusions of grandeur."

"Intolerante! My name is Anduvio, the great magician of the Partanio Valley! A powerful illusionist, and I will soon become the ruler of Almjarhad too!"

"Get out of my palace immediately! Guards!"

Before Jamarnid could react, Tanato tried to cover his body when the human vanished from his field of view. Horrified, Jamarnid sensed mana behind him and barely had enough time to turn around before he felt agonizing pain splitting into his skull and lost consciousness.

***

Pain, laughter, and more pain. Jamarnid's mind trailed between the realms of consciousness and death until he felt the grasp of the earthly plane once again. As he tried to moan, he felt some dabbles of potion in his mouth, which he eagerly accepted. Soon enough, the pain dropped to a tolerable level, allowing him to open his eyes.

Much to Jamarnid's surprise, seated alongside his bed was Soremin, his closest confidant and staunchest ally in the entire city. The priest's face was both a mixture of relief and dawning despair. His usually pristine robes were covered in a thin layer of blood, and Jamarnid deduced he had lost consciousness for at least a handful of hours from the darkness of their surroundings.

Speaking proved to be difficult, and thus Soremin grasped his shoulder. "The human visitor saved your life from a falling bookshelf. It seems like Sharad made a mistake when he built that thing. Tanato was also injured."

A sense of concern and glee seemed to compete for Jamarnid's emotions. He disliked Tanato, yet as the fog in his mind cleared from the concussion, he soon felt a pang of respect for the halfling after saving his life. "How is Tanato? I need to speak to him."

Soremin shook his head. "His head injury is far worse than yours. I simply cannot understand it. He is an adept air mage. Deflecting a falling bookshelf should have been easy. Medics are tending to him in an adjacent room."

Jamarnid began to process his thoughts as the pain medication exerted its effects. There was one thing that didn't add up. "Is that vile human gone?"

"About that…"

Much to Jamarnid's horror, Anduvio was gleefully seated on a chair while reading a book and strode his way without any care. The man shut the book right in front of Jamarnid's face and dumped it on his bed. "Quite a terrible head injury you suffered! Alas! It was fortunate I was there to rescue you from harm. I hope you enjoy my company in this palace now that I have been offered a hero's welcome thanks to my bravery! We'll be seeing each other a lot!" After gloating at the sight of Jamarnid's body and the bandage on his forehead, Anduvio stared at Soremin and caressed his wavy hair with a sigh. "Such a beautiful face shouldn't have short tresses. I suggest you should let it grow long, my dear." If disrespecting personal boundaries wasn't bad enough, Anduvio took a step forward and kissed a horrified Soremin on the cheek.

Soremin stood up immediately to protest. "Human! You should never commit such a vile act of disobedience to the preachers of the elf gods. I cannot allow anyone to behave in such a way."

"And do what? What can you do about it, mmm? Haven't you two heard? Lord Sharad has let me stay in the palace after your grandiose rescue. I think that means I can do whatever I want." With an accusatory grin and a wink, Anduvio totted away while laughing.

If Jamarnid disliked the man before, now he despised him. "Vile, disgusting bastard, I swear I…"

Soremin grasped his shoulder. "Don't counter violence with violence. It is what he wants us to do."

"He kissed you on the cheek and attacked me!"

"Huh? Attacked you? Impossible. You just hit yourself in the head by sheer accident."

***

As the days went by and Jamarnid's injury healed without significant consequences, the ambiance in the palace became bleak. Skittishness characterized everyone's behavior, and both the harlequins and halflings that knew magic jittered away from Anduvio whenever he approached them. This behavior perplexed Jamarnid. While Soremin felt annoyed by Anduvio's behavior, he believed the man only harbored the expected selfishness of an ambitious human. And so Soremin was unsupportive when Jamarnid pleaded to help him evict Anduvio.

Among the palace's inhabitants, Sharad was the worst of them all. He not only didn't sense anything wrong with the man, but he also liked him. Fortunately for everyone's peace of mind, Anduvio never behaved inappropriately in front of the elf outside of admiring his long glossy hair. Without Sharad's support, Jamarnid would be incapable of getting rid of this unwanted parasite from his home.

Henrietta vanished from her room the following day and moved into a house on the city's outskirts alongside some friends she had made over the years. Jamarnid presumed she continued to feel hurt by Talgel's behavior, and it would be best that he didn't get involved in such trivial matters.

While Jarahad clearly disliked Anduvio's presence and tried to avoid him at all costs, Jamarnid theorized it was due to the man's intrusive romantic advances. On all accounts, Jarahad was trying to maintain the peace by tolerating the man's presence in his home due to Sharad's authority and as a token of appreciation for rescuing Jamarnid. No, Jamarnid was really worried about Tanato, whose injuries had proven to be terrible. After a few days, Tanato slowly regained consciousness. While it was good news to hear, the poor halfling was incapable of speaking, and half of his body had become paralyzed. Whenever Jamarnid was in his room, Tanato tried to talk to him with all his might, only to give up from frustration as tears fell from his eyes. It was obvious he desperately wanted to say something important, but his brain injury made communication impossible.

If there was one thing Jamarnid detested, it was to owe a favor to someone. Whether it was Garlas, Hormandra, or Serumo, the elf would always hate himself for being unable to repay their sacrifice. Recalling his troubled past, Jamarnid spoke in a clear voice while taking advantage they were alone. "I apologize for mistreating you over the years, Priest Tanato. Thank you for your sacrifice and I will do everything I can to help you recover. I know you saw something amiss with that human. Is it something like harlequin magic? Something a pureblood elf such as me is incapable of detecting?"

Tanato's red eyes shimmered ever so brightly from Jamarnid's deduction, and his left hand gripped Jamarnid's forearm in agreement.

Realizing Tanato could understand him, Jamarnid decided to switch to a different plan. "I know you can't talk or write at this moment, but maybe there is something else we can do. Can you blink once?" Much to Jamarnid's glee, Tanato obeyed. "Can you blink twice if the answer is a no?" And so, Tanato replicated his command.

Feeling a sense of relief after discovering a way to share his knowledge, Tanato's eyes welled with tears.

Jamarnid spoke at a lower volume to ensure Anduvio couldn't hear in case he was standing outside. "Did you sense harlequin magic coming out of Anduvio the day we got injured?"

One blink with a determined expression on Tanato's face was all it took for Jamarnid to be certain Anduvio wasn't just a pitiable human mage. After bottling down the rage he felt deep inside, Jamarnid had to pry the injured halfling for more answers. "Do you believe Anduvio has harlequin blood?"

Tanato's face smirked as he tried to ponder for the correct response.

Jamarnid became concerned. "I was afraid of that. There is something wrong with this human. I have seen him parading around my palace over the past few days. While Lord Sharad and Soremin act like there isn't anything amiss, the halflings unconsciously avoid him. Can you sense something that I can't?"

Tanato blinked once without even thinking and pressed Jamarnid's forearm with increased firmness.

"I see," Jamarnid recalled the years he spent watching his son learn harlequin sorcery growing up. "Maybe this human didn't summon a demonic beast. Tanato, do you recall Anduvio muttering a summoning spell before he used mana?"

With a heaved sigh, Tanato blinked twice, which fully confirmed Jamarnid's suspicions this would prove to be a dead end. Instead of feeling disillusioned, it only enticed Jamarnid even further to get to the bottom of this mystery. "Maybe Anduvio does not have harlequin blood, so he summons his phantom beast the normal way. Did his magic feel like regular harlequin air magic?"

Tanato's two blinks and pensive face surprised Jamarnid. The halfling's red eyes darted to the left corner, possibly as a secondary effect of his brain injury as he pondered about Anduvio's strange magic.

This offered Jamarnid yet another idea. "Tanato, can you sense this man use his strange harlequin magic all the time? Or was it just before he appeared behind us?"

Once again, Tanato offered an interesting answer: he smirked without blinking once. Intrigued, Jamarnid knew there wouldn't be much more he could extract from the injured halfling in his current state. He patted Tanato's face with kindness and backed off. "I know you want to help me solve this riddle, and your help has proven invaluable. Jarahad has been avoiding me for some reason, and I suspect he has sensed the same thing as you. I order you to feign ignorance of Anduvio's ill intentions whenever he is nearby to ensure he doesn't have a reason to murder you. In exchange, I'll try to find a way to evict him before he harms someone else."

***

Much to Jamarnid's chagrin, talking to Jarahad was not nearly as fruitful. They were in Jamarnid's office as his son was busy patting off splinters from books and placing them in boxes. Jamarnid couldn't believe the degree of destruction upon seeing the severed bookshelf plastered all over the floor and ripped paper with dried blood. On all accounts, the crime scene was incriminating Anduvio even further.

"My son, you must agree there is no possible way Sharad's bookshelf could break apart like this. His carpentry skills are unparalleled!"

Jarahad didn't even lift his head as he continued packing books. "No, father. I am certain it was defective."

"If that is so, explain how Sharad could slice the wood with a saw and pound it with nails without breaking!"

"I… don't know."

It was beyond infuriating! Jarahad's confidence was usually indomitable. And yet here he was cowering into a corner like a scolded animal. Jamarnid had to get to the bottom of this immediately. "Has Anduvio raped you?"

"Huh? Not at all! Why would you say such a ridiculous accusation?" From the redness on Jarahad's face as they engaged in eye contact, Jamarnid felt relieved by the good news.

"Tanato has shown more bravery than you. Why are you so afraid of that human?"

"I… um…"

Jamarnid growled even further and deepened his breathing before he did something stupid. "I had a fascinating meeting with Tanato a while ago. He can't speak, but he understands me perfectly well. He will blink his eyes if you give him simple yes and no questions."

Changing the topic elicited Jarahad to return to his usual bold self once again. "Did you find any useful clues? Or are you going to slather imaginary crimes on this human?"

"Son, open your eyes! Don't forget I was an Äimite guard for several centuries and know when something is amiss. Neither me, Soremin, nor Sharad can sense strange magic coming from this human. The only unusual thing I could notice when he used his phantom beast was the excessive speed at which he seemingly teleported from the doorway to the windowsill. It only took him half a second to get there. Have you ever seen a human move this fast before?"

Jarahad froze, which only confirmed Jamarnid's method was working its magic. "I thought Anduvio ran towards you after you fell."

"Stupid brute! Look at the footsteps on the ground. Do you see any dust markings with the shape of his shoes going towards the window? Hrm?"

From the dumbstruck expression on Jarahad's face, it was apparent the plan worked. Now that the seed of doubt was planted inside of his son, it would be easier to convince Sharad to evict the human.

Jamarnid grinned even more. "Tanato's mind is sound. I bet he will agree the bastard can move at a superhuman speed and destroy the bookshelf using strange magic. Two reliable witnesses that agree to the crime should be more than enough proof this human is dangerous. Do you want him to kill Sharad next? Or maybe Talgel?"

"Shut up! I…"

Irritating his son was another classic tactic Jamarnid employed to manipulate him. Worked like a charm. "Son, I know you feel guilt-ridden to treat this human with respect because he claims to have rescued me, but this crime scene proves he is lying."

"Father… I…"

"Tanato told me this human doesn't seem to have harlequin blood, but he exerts some kind of undetectable magic. Tanato could not verify if it always happens or when mana is nearby."

"What are you getting with this?"

"Look, don't confront Anduvio for the time being. I want you to feel fully convinced Tanato's suspicions are correct before you make any false moves. As a pureblood elf, I can only sense normal magic, so I need your help. Get near this human and see if he uses harlequin magic all the time or only when he summons his phantom beast. I am good at spotting unusual patterns, and all halflings avoid him without being conscious of it. Don't you find that to be odd?"

From the consternation on Jarahad's eyes and bewildered face, Jamarnid caught him even further by surprise. "You're right! I… I always feel anxious when I sit close to him. I just can't explain what it is."

"Good to know I am not losing my mind. Is it harlequin air magic?"

"Not at all. It's… subtle, electric, like a sort of buzzing vibration. I have a hard time explaining it."

"I want you to do a little experiment. Use harlequin magic near this human for some menial reason. Maybe fix a chip in the wall or blow some dust from the table. Don't do anything that alerts the man. I want to test my theory the vibrations you sense change when he is exposed to magic. Can you do that for me?"

"Don't you think it's wrong for us to be doing things behind Lord Sharad's back?"

"If you want to avoid feeling guilty, this would be a viable excuse: Sharad can't sense harlequin magic, and he was never trained by an elite army like me. He is vulnerable to this human's treachery and could suffer Tanato's fate. As Sharad's serfs, we have the moral obligation to safeguard his life. Do you understand?"

With slumped shoulders of defeat, Jarahad sighed. "Are you sure of this?"

"Anduvio is an enemy of our city, and I want to get to the bottom of this before he kills someone."

Months came and gone, and Hurrujat continued to barter arranged marriages between his knights and a myriad of allied harlequin clans. Whenever Tioja saw a nobledemon spend a lot of time in the city, a sense of pity enveloped him. For the time being, Murdorhiolan had five fully trained knights who could all summon their own phantom beasts.

Due to the urgency of seeing Gulraj summon his beast before his death, Hurrujat was very eager to marry everyone off. Was forcing his loyal subjects into the bondage of marriage ethical? Hurrujat couldn't care less. The only thing that mattered was seeing Gulraj attain his demonic beast at all costs.

Tioja would later discover at least two marriages ended up as a waste because their home clans either broke the alliance or were exterminated due to infighting. Interestingly, this happened to Kashin's second wife, Golana. While she had proven to be a worthy initiate, her father was past his prime, and a peasant killed him during a mutiny to earn the throne. Out of all of Kashin's wives, Golana was the most grateful to live in the safety of Murdorhiolan. Not that she appeased her husband in any way, of course. More like she expressed her good fortune with increased cattiness and treated her servants with complete disregard.

Tioja felt numb whenever he had to see a betrothed knight have sex with their new spouse. While Kashin had grown used to Iora and treated her well, everyone could see the anguish in his eyes as his forearms became covered with more gold bracelets.

And all for what?

Gulraj attempted to use söma dozens of times, and nothing ever worked. After yet another failed attempt to awaken Gulraj's magic, Hurrujat lighted a pipe laden with powerful sedatives. With a whiff of the addictive smoke, Hurrujat's lips escaped a sigh and stared at Hamara. "Bring Kashin here."

A flutter of Hamara's eyes hinted she wasn't happy about this command. Without voicing her opinions out loud, she left the room without delay.

Tioja stared at Hurrujat. The creases of pain on his aged face softened as the drug exerted its soothing effects. Bloody droplets oozed from his emptied eye socket that spilled over his robes. Hurrujat had lost a lot of weight over the past 2 months, and death was eager to cover him within its embrace. After a few moments, Hurrujat stared at Tioja with a sinister grin. "When I am gone, Tioja, you will become the second ruler of this city. You are Gulraj's equal. Whatever happens, I wedded my knights to strengthen our clan. Become the bridge that keeps the means of communication open with Almjarhad. We might need each other. Do you promise?"

Uncertain about the implications, Tioja showed extreme humility by kneeling very low and offering his cupped hands. "I shall obey my king."

Soon enough, Kashin marched inside. Like their previous encounters, Kashin stared at Tioja with a slight tint of revulsion. Knowing the urgent call would be unpleasant, Kashin knelt before Hurrujat with clenched fists. Hamara meanwhile stood by the doorway with an inert expression.

"Knight Kashin, I know you have proven your worth beyond reasonable doubt. My son has once again failed to awaken his beast," Hurrujat said.

Deep exhalations escaped Kashin's lips. "Master, I beg of you to be merciful. I have married three nobledemons already. My worth in the battlefield has gone far beyond the demands you exerted on my peers."

"Yes, but you are my son's uncle. Which makes you a more precious asset."

"I beg for your mercy! Don't force me to marry a fourth wife!"

This time, Hamara spoke. "My love, please don't rush things. Kashin is the only knight that has married three women."

"You forgot about Kibito, my dear. Oh, and I am proud to

announce Kibito will get married to his fourth and final wife in a few days," Hurrujat snickered.

A gasp escaped Kashin and Hamara's lips. It seemed like Hurrujat was hiding these little affairs from everyone.

Hamara spoke once again. "Why didn't you tell me you would do this?"

"Kibito is the weakest of the five. So, he is easier to barter with lesser nobles. The great prize is Kashin."

Hamara shook her head. "Oshana has the same blood purity as me."

"Yes, and she is also our only female knight. As talented as she is with the sword, we were bending the laws when she married her second spouse. We don't have any other choice." Hurrujat exhaled more smoke and smiled.

The anguish on Kashin's face and Hamara's unexpected tirade against her husband enticed Tioja to speak in a tentative voice. "Maybe we must accept my brother isn't destined to summon a demonic beast. Gulraj doesn't need magic to defend this city. My magic should suffice."

The pipe crashed against the carpeting, and Hurrujat stood up. For a moment, Tioja shut his eyes, anticipating the man would swat him. Much to his chagrin, Hurrujat set his foot on Kashin's shoulder instead. He then forced the poor knight to kneel even lower. "You are using my son Tioja to skirt your duties. Shame on you, Kashin. You will be married off effective immediately. I want you to always keep those bracelets visible. You are forbidden to wear long sleeved clothes within my city's grounds. Someday, you will understand why I make these decisions, and you will appreciate your bracelets. If I had worn one in my youth, the second purge would have never happened. Get out."

Ashen death imbued on Kashin's face as his red eyes incensed in a final sign of defiance. As he marched outside while retaining some dignity, it was obvious to Tioja his uncle was no longer angry at him. Kashin now focused his bottled-up anger on Hurrujat instead. Gulraj's plight only served as an excuse for Hurrujat to inflict misery on his servants. The only person that showed a surprising loss of neutrality was Hamara. She tried to coax and goad Hurrujat to reconsider because they had sufficient söma. But Hurrujat was steadfast in marrying Kashin to his final wife out of spite. Tioja would discover many years later Hurrujat's odd behavior in his final days was due to drug abstinence combined with the relentless pain that gnawed at his skull.

Kashin was heartbroken when Hurrujat and another clan leader fastened the last gold rope to his fourth and final wife. She was small and pudgy with an unpronounceable name. With some effort, Tioja surmised the name sounded like Amarafghathia or something of the sort. While Hamara was usually congenial during weddings, she snapped at servants for no reason. Gulraj was meanwhile showing off his water magic in front of guests and found Kashin's problems to be an afterthought at best.

One day, Tioja ambled through the hallways of the castle while he carried his cat. For inexplicable reasons, Tioja approached a window and stared at a garden downstairs. Hamara and Kashin were arguing with each other. Curious, Tioja let the cat go, descended the stairs, reached the garden, and crawled behind a statue to overhear their conversation.

As expected, Kashin was furious. "I hate him! Hurrujat promised me I would be allowed to choose my fourth wife!"

"I know, dear brother. His drug addiction is making him lose any sense of reality. He… I am starting to no longer love him as much as before."

Concerned about Hamara's safety after hearing such a harrowing confession, Kashin turned in every direction hoping nobody was listening. He soon calmed down. "Don't even think about saying such a thing in front of the other knights. Hurrujat can turn you into a knight and marry you off to some brute as punishment. Do you want Gulraj to become homeless?"

"Of course not! I have tried to awaken my son's phantom beast. Why did Gulraj become so unlucky? Plenty of halflings with his blood purity awakened their beasts without too much effort. Even that pathetic knight Kibito has a beast."

"My life is pretty much ruined," Kashin growled with derision.

"Don't look at me like that, Kashin! I begged my husband not to wed you to that twit, but he went through with it out of spite."

"Then what do you plan to do?"

Hamara averted her gaze and caressed her sword. "I will request my husband for permission to visit the city where I was initiated. My teacher might know a method to awaken Gulraj's magic."

"That doesn't solve my marital conundrum, Hamara."

"And don't forget that I cannot harm your wives or dissolve your marriage, or you will die too. You will just have to wait until one of them dies from natural causes."

With that said, Hamara strode away, and Kashin paced around the garden with furious fervor. A bump on Tioja's thigh stirred his senses and almost made him squeak. Tioja sighed in relief when his unwanted visitor was his cat. "Silly Fluff. I thought you were Hurrujat."

***

Tensions were high when Hamara returned a few weeks later. Instead of visiting a bedridden Hurrujat, Hamara rushed to Kashin's palace with anguish. Tioja believed Hamara's odd behavior was because her mentor didn't have a solution to Gulraj's conundrum.

Tioja and Gulraj were seated on the outdoor bench while they took turns playing with Fluff. "Gulraj, do you still want to awaken your phantom beast?"

"Of course, I do! My life will never be complete without it. The fact that my father is about to die before seeing my beast is a fate worse than death!" Gulraj swooshed the stick, and Fluff pounced on the air in an impressive acrobatic display.

"I still don't understand all these honor rules in harlequin society.

My father Jamad… well… Maybe I should not judge Jamad after seeing his friends and family die.”

Gulraj's mind was busy with other thoughts as he continued swishing the toy around. “What were you thinking about when you first awakened your Lehart? You never told me.”

“Um… well… The mana was growing inside me, and I felt like I wanted something. Like, in the back of my head. Just that… well… I feel very ashamed to say it out loud.”

“Please tell me!”

A blush covered Tioja's cheeks as he scratched Fluff's ears. “I know it is sort of silly, but I wanted… I wanted to destroy something.”

“Huh? That doesn't make any sense!”

“I sometimes think about my Lehart and why I can't control it. I don't want to become a monster.”

Gulraj shook his head and stared at Tioja's eyes with seriousness. “Tioja, you have already killed people.”

“No! I would never do that!”

A sigh escaped Gulraj's lips. “Don't you remember when we conquered Senhort? You used your magic to destroy some supporting beams. Well, I just want to tell you that you accidentally killed a few humans. Don't feel bad. They would still be alive today if Didiot hadn't acted like an idiot.”

Horror dawned on Tioja and made his self-loathing even worse. It took every fiber of Tioja's willpower to avoid punching his brother in this instant. “Mom told me everyone was fine! I didn't mean to hurt anyone!”

“Stop hiding from your destiny, Tioja. I saw you fight that day. You enjoyed killing those humans and never even realized it.”

“No!”

As Tioja ran off with tears on his face, Gulraj's beckoning voice was audible from afar. It was laced with arrogance peppered with malice. "Run all you want Tio, you are a murderous harlequin like the rest of us! You will accept killing people someday!"

***

That evening, Hamara seemed impassive as she stared at Tioja and consoled him. Indifferent to his complaints about what truly happened in Senhort, Hamara petted Tioja's messy grey hair and caressed his face. "Ignore those memories, Tioja. Let me enjoy spending these last few moments in your company."

Why was Hamara acting like she was saying goodbye? Was she planning on leaving the city? Tioja shook his head. "You haven't visited Hurrujat."

Hamara averted her gaze. "I had… more important things to discuss with Knight Kashin. Someday, you will understand." Hamara whistled, and the door was opened by a deadpanned Kashin. He gently nudged a startled Gulraj inside.

"Gulraj, please come here." Hamara's arms beckoned, and she hugged both of her children with all her might. "My beautiful sons. Both of you make me feel endless pride. The love you share is a bond that is even stronger than blood. I am about to embark on a journey, and I need your support."

Recalling what happened in the past, Tioja spoke in a whisper. "You are abandoning your husband for a new lover."

A giggle escaped Hamara's lips, and she shook her head. For no reason, a tear escaped her eyelid that she wiped with discretion. "Not at all. Hurrujat will always be my one and true love. I may not have always been the best parent, and I urge you to forgive me. Nobody prepares a woman to become a mother. We all assume it comes naturally. In my opinion, this isn't true. I stumbled and failed in more ways than one, but I will always love you. A mother must do everything she can to keep her children alive."

And then, something pitted into the deepest recess of Tioja's stomach as he recalled a haunting memory from his childhood. "Mom, what happened to grampa Jamen's dog, Jian? You never told me."

Surprised about Tioja's odd inquiry, Hamara drummed her fingers on Tioja's shoulder due to the inopportune timing. "Why do you care about that now?"

"I… I feel it might have something to do with you not visiting your husband yet."

Hamara then stared at Gulraj, who seemed curious to know as well. And so, she conceded defeat. "Jamen killed his beloved dog, and I drank her blood to stay alive. Satisfied?"

From the curtness of Hamara's response, Tioja confirmed his suspicions and nodded.

Hamara stared into Tioja's eyes for a long time, kissed his forehead with sorrow, and stood up. "Gulraj, come with me. I need to speak to you in private."

Befuddled by Hamara's increasingly odd behavior, Hamara and Gulraj reached the hallway while Kashin nodded at them. Kashin knew what was going on and agreed to be Hamara's accomplice. Hopefully, it meant Hamara would embark on a journey after Hurrujat's death to help Gulraj summon his phantom beast.

A few minutes later, Gulraj returned to the room while crying nonstop. Tioja rushed to his side at once. "Oh my! Has Hurrujat passed away?"

Wails and sobs ensued until Gulraj finally calmed down. "Not yet. Hamara… she is going to leave us."

Tioja suspected this and hugged his brother. From the way Gulraj seemed equally sad and horrified, there must have been something else. "Brother, you are acting strange. What did mom tell you?"

"Mom has already found the way to awaken my phantom beast. She has started the preparations alongside Uncle Kashin. I am going to summon my beast tonight."

That evening, Jarahad was seated on a hillside as he thought about his father's words. Jamarnid was cautious, sometimes even borderline paranoid. They were either remnants of his Äimite training or perhaps as a coping mechanism after he saw Chandrice and most of his clan die during the first purge. A part of Jarahad felt guilty for scheming without Sharad's permission. Yet he knew his father was right. Jamarnid could be accused of a plethora of things, but he was very upfront when it came to punishing criminals.

Soon enough, the rising half-moon was momentarily blocked by a black feminine figure with glowing pink eyes that landed in front, packed her wings like a cape, and approached him.

Henrietta's wounds finally healed, and the joy on her face warmed Jarahad's heart. He didn't feel comfortable marrying this woman just to appease her father, but helping a friend was always the right thing to do.

Soon enough, Henrietta's smile vanished upon seeing his worried face. "You don't look happy."

"Have you talked to Talgel?"

Henrietta shook her head. "I think she still feels guilty for injuring me. She has locked the door to her house and doesn't accept any clients. I'm getting worried."

"Don't worry; she can take care of herself." Even though Henrietta sat beside Jarahad, his heart remained steady as concern consumed his thoughts. "The night Anduvio arrived, Talgel fell unconscious for no apparent reason."

"Maybe she suffered from a blood attack. She used her sorcery to spy on me."

"Ignore her threats. You haven't broken your vow of abstinence to your family."

"Uh… let's avoid that topic for now."

"I understand. First, we must settle the issue about Anduvio."

"What about him? I haven't spent any time with him."

"Something is amiss. Have you heard of a kind of harlequin magic that vibrates when it becomes exposed to mana and makes the user absurdly fast?"

A discreet squeak escaped Henrietta's lips which alerted his senses. "A vibration device, you say?"

"Look, don't get any strange ideas he uses it to pleasure himself. I mean…"

A giggle escaped Henrietta's lips. "I am teasing you! I didn't stay long in your palace, so I never got to sense this magic. In case you are wondering, there are legends among my people passed among the noble circles about immortality stones that can bond with a mage."

The pounding in Jarahad's heart throbbed even stronger than before as he began to connect the dots. He needed to know more. "Can someone build one of these things?"

Henrietta crossed her arms and stared at the starry sky. "A third initiate might be capable of such a feat."

"Third initiate? So, the legend is true?"

"Perhaps. My father is just an ordinary first initiate like both of us. Only exceptional warriors from powerful clans can be granted far better training where they unlock greater powers from their swords. Charon might have been a second initiate in his prime, but I am certain Hurrujat wasn't one. This world is vast. Perhaps a third initiate is hiding in the faraway continents. They can perform sorcery beyond the realms of possibility and creating an immortality stone is theoretically possible."

Intrigued by Henrietta's thoughtful answer, Jarahad pondered his scant options. "Have you seen one of these stones before? Do you know anything else?"

"They are more like a legend. I know you won't be able to harm the wielder as long as they remain close to their stone."

"Do you mean that…?"

"If this insane theory is correct and Anduvio holds a stone somewhere in his body, he could remain forever young. You will be unable to cause a single scratch in his body. I pray to the gods that he doesn't have one of those devices because…"

A voiding sensation pitted in Jarahad's stomach when he thought about Tanato. "I have a hunch Talgel predicted this man would arrive, and she is using you as an excuse to continue hiding the truth from all of us."

Before Jarahad could leave, Henrietta grabbed his wrist. "Did your father ask you to get rid of this human?"

"He wants me to perform a test."

"And that is?"

"I need to use harlequin magic without making Anduvio suspicious. My father wants to know if the vibration emanating from his body increases when he becomes exposed to it."

"And if nothing else happens, then what?"

Jarahad stood still as the warm wind blasted against his face. "I can't summon my Rashid in front of Anduvio."

"Why not use it for transport and have him sit on it?"

"Hrm… I guess I could do that. Would you happen to know what happens to a normal phantom beast when it becomes exposed to these legendary stones?"

"The beast will be absorbed. I don't know anything else."

This would prove to be helpful. If Anduvio truly owned a strange stone, testing a phantom beast in front of him might prove worthwhile. But Jarahad had to be cautious. If Anduvio could run several yards in a few milliseconds, even a trained warrior like himself could suffer from an injury if Anduvio felt threatened.

"Thank you for your help, and I feel glad to see you are feeling better."

CHAPTER 12 ♦ TIOJA

As the months passed upon the relentless instruction of his teacher, Tioja could never land a decent hit during their fencing sessions. Whenever he assumed he had a chance, the harlequin would cackle because Tioja fell into a trap and collapsed with horrible pain in his chest. His armor had suffered so many beatings from endless hits he wondered if his teacher might end up killing him by accident.

To further hurt his pride, the harlequin that kept on defeating him so pitifully easily was a teenage woman. Even worse, she was already several months pregnant, which didn't reduce her combat prowess.

After towering over his tiny frame with a menacing glare, she growled with disgust. "You are the worst student I have ever had the shame of teaching. I can't understand why my ruler ordered me to personally teach you."

"I... I am trying my best!"

"No, you are not!" She clenched her practice sword even more firmly. "If I used my harlequin sword, the rage I feel would have easily activated its full power and sliced your body into two." Intrigued, Tioja stared at the faraway table. Whereas Hamara's old sword remained idle, his mentor's sword emitted a blinding green hue. The fact the sword was glowing so much meant her emotions were inciting its nascent bloodlust.

Tioja kowtowed on the ground to save face and offered his cupped hands. Even though harlequins didn't understand the intricacies of elvish bowing customs, offering his undefended neck and hands proved he was serious in asking for her forgiveness. "Sword Master Baa, I am sorry. Your generous clan has offered to initiate me in exchange for desirable engineering knowledge, and I have only proven to be a failure. I swear it isn't because you are a poor teacher or that I am insulting you on purpose because of your age and gender. It's that..." Tears fell from his eyes as he veered away from the table.

Baa sighed as she guarded the blunted sword on a shelf and returned a few moments later. "Look up."

The instant Tioja obeyed, he felt her left fist crashing against his skull, accompanied by dizzying pain. He collapsed on the ground and spent a few moments savoring the experience.

Baa assumed Tioja was stunned by her unexpected act of violence and crossed her arms rather menacingly. "I am not angry at you for assuming women should spend their lives raising children and serving their husbands. If elves believe in those things, I cannot change your pitiable patriarchal society. Gulraj warned me you haven't spent a long time under his care and might unconsciously do or say something offensive." Before Tioja explained that elves were very egalitarian, Baa continued her rant. "You have been the strangest student I ever had the misfortune of instructing. You comply with the inking sessions without displaying any discomfort, recite the spells with a nearly perfect accent, and defeat the clan's warriors in wrestling matches almost every time. Yet you still insist on making rookie mistakes during your fencing lessons. I can't believe even children can trounce you. Over the months you have lived under this roof as our treasured guest, I began formulating a few theories. One, you truly are a genius in combat and wish to humiliate me because you hold a grudge I am a swordmaster at an extremely young age. Two, you never wanted the training, but Gulraj made you oblige. Three, you are absurdly bad at fencing, or… you are afraid of your phantom beast."

Tioja's eyes widened from the final observation. Gulraj knew he was terrified of harming others and could never control his phantom beast despite knowing its full combative potential. "My Lehart wants to destroy me. Right now, I feel the urge to harm everyone. The only reason I have not fallen into madness is because my beast has proven worthless in harlequin cities."

The confession prompted Baa to raise her eyelid with amusement. "Gulraj told me something about you being blessed with strange sorcery. His words were vague, perhaps to avoid veering my attention too much. You must accompany me outside right now."

"What?" Before Tioja could oppose, Baa threw his sword towards him. Fearful of her wrath, Tioja cowered and let the weapon fall onto the stone ground. Baa shook her head in disapproval and marched outside. Obliged to comply with Baa's command or risk getting into even worse problems, Tioja fastened the weapon to his belt. He followed her into the endless hallways of their underground city. Hordes of onlookers hurled insults at him wherever he went. It was a degrading humiliation to be treated with so much disrespect, but there was nothing Tioja could do about it. Baa didn't say a word as she continued marching among the thick crowds. They eventually reached one of the stair tunnels to go outside, prompting Tioja to stop. "Please don't force me to go outside right now. Can't we go in the evening?"

"You will summon your phantom beast and stare at me. If you are half of a harlequin as Gulraj claims, you will find a way to control the urge to kill me. If you do not comply with my command, your clan will be unwelcome in our city. As the niece of Lord Lazarius, I can sever the agreement. Follow me and shut up."

Tioja complied with a discreet sigh. Given that Baa issued him a direct order, he would not suffer a severe punishment if he killed her by accident. Baa didn't even bother to insult him on the ascent, which only increased Tioja's anxiety. Instead, she used a passive-aggressive approach of silence. But Tioja would not fall for the taunt. At first, she was relatively permissive with his failures during the lessons. As each inking session came and went, she became increasingly demanding. It was little surprise why. The one-year mark was about to arrive, and she was obliged to perform the final test. They both knew Tioja was doomed for failure, which would inevitably damage her reputation.

The instant Baa unlocked the steel door, they were bombarded by an explosion of light and went outside to a desolate field. Unlike Murdorhiolan, this harlequin city was located on a flat steppe, and they tried to disguise their secondary entrances within hills. Aside from a few sheep being herded in the distance, he could only see yellowing grass and the sweet aroma from the soft bristling wind. Tioja sighed in tepid relief. At least there weren't that many sources of shadows which might make things a bit easier.

Baa seemed indifferent as she paced a few yards away from the door. She then turned around and crossed her arms. "Well, why haven't you started to attack me, you worthless fool?"

Tioja shook his head and decided he had little choice. Might as well humiliate himself and hope she wouldn't regret challenging him in such a foolish way. Tioja removed his shirt, which only prompted Baa to stare at him with a strange expression. "Don't worry, Master Baa. You will soon understand." As mana invaded his body, her pink eyes glowed ever more fervently in anticipation. "I summon thee, my phantom beast, the Demonic Wing Lehart!" Black wings soon grew from his back, and he once again sensed his surroundings within a fifty-mile radius. Due to the barren terrain, most of the targets Tioja could observe were blades of grass, a few rocks, and meandering ants. The sheep and herders proved to be a far more enticing target. And yet nothing could compare to Baa, whose shadow only accentuated her stern physique and slightly protruding belly. Tioja could even sense the second source of life growing from within. A healthy boy, it seemed. The desire to murder this fine young woman proved to be beyond enticing as he studied her shadow. Oh, how he wanted to rip her into pieces just because he could do it!

"Well? I can sense mana and see your wings, but you have proven to be a disappointment. Where is this mental instability you pride yourself with? I will…" Then, Baa unconsciously grasped her sword hilt and chanted a strange prayer that activated her sword. Little did she know, the soil surrounding her collapsed into a sphere of energy as her wings furiously flapped from behind and were ripped into pieces.

The next thing Tioja knew, a group of herdsmen were fast approaching while hollering something in Harlequin. It no longer mattered. He killed his mentor and didn't even understand why he would do such a thing.

"Well done, Tioja."

"Huh?" Tioja lifted his weary head and gasped at the sight. Baa was in a knelt position while she panted with exhaustion. Aside from a few bruises on her umbre skin and blood trickles falling on her robes, she seemed perfectly fine. "I didn't kill you!"

"Of course, you didn't, you flabbergasted idiot! You'd think a Sword Master would be so weak? Master your weapon, and you too could garner access to many hidden techniques."

A pair of herdsmen approached them with bewildered faces. "Sword Master Baa, are you hurt? Did this pitiful elf harm you?"

Baa shook her head as she attempted to flap her ruined wings. "Tioja passed his test. I will inform Lord Lazarius to prepare the initiation." Despite the offering to stand up, Baa shook her head and stared at Tioja with a sense of pride for the very first time. "You are blessed with a gift I never knew could even exist. Gulraj told me you were shunned by the stupid elves because of a heretic seer. You placed too much blame on yourself by failing to cover their impossible expectations. Fear not, we harlequins value power. You have a gift of the gods that can change the world if you start to embrace it."

"But I injured you!"

Baa spat a bloodied heap of saliva on the ground and rubbed her chin. "Foolish mutt. My sword can activate a powerful shield. The fact you caused me any damage without harming anything else is proof you already know how to control it. Or are you not using mana as we speak?"

This observation left Tioja in a stupefied pit of foolishness. He could still see everyone's shadows, yet he had no genuine desire to harm anyone. Despite the visible damage to Baa's body, he felt a sense of pride to meet someone capable of surviving his magic. He then stopped emitting mana, and the lingering sensation of peace remained. With a sigh of relief, Tioja then observed Baa's ruined wings that strayed in a painfully crooked angle. She would have no choice but to surgically remove them, which filled him with pity.

Anticipating his thoughts, Baa seemed rather indifferent. "I will shed in a year. I can survive without them for a while. What about your wings?"

Tioja's wings flapped for a few moments and again tightened themselves to form a cape. He picked up his discarded shirt and held it tight. "I can't keep them for more than a few hours, or I start to shed.

Gulraj believes it is a weakness of my sorcery."

"Very fine then. Let's visit the medic to have our wings removed. Hopefully, you can perform your initiation tomorrow. Don't be late."

****

The initiation began without a significant variance from the prior sessions. Baa didn't seem even remotely hindered from losing her wings. Despite having her chest wrapped in bloodied bandages, it was as if the kerfuffle from the other day had never happened. Tioja would have almost enjoyed the inking portion of his final test had it not been for the presence of an irritable Lord Lazarius. It was strange how every harlequin leader Tioja ever met was so different. From Hurrujat's overzealous joy to Gulraj's cruelty, Lazarius stood out due to his pervasive dourness. The dolt always had an expression ranging between anger and indifference, making it impossible for Tioja to anticipate his equally unreadable mood swings. To further intimidate him, the harlequin's towering height with broad shoulders only accentuated his fierceness even more. Gulraj was initiated in this city alongside several other nobledemons of Murdorhiolan. At first, Gulraj wanted Baa to train one of his clan's pureblood harlequins to become Charon's replacement swordmaster, but Lazarius had been staunchly unbinding in this respect. If Tioja passed the examination, there was a slim possibility Baa would accept to train someone so that they could become self-reliant.

Knowing perfectly well the importance of passing this test, Tioja tried to feign equal indifference towards the leader and remained still as Baa continued with the grueling task of inking his spinal cord. Unlike Jarahad's experience, Tioja barely noticed the pain at all. Without warning, Tioja felt the same voiding sensation described by Jarahad, but he didn't find it particularly stimulating. Nothing could ever compare to the excitement of harming Baa with his Lehart. In comparison, returning to his body was a mediocre consolation prize. As a further contrast to Jarahad's initiation surrounded by friends, Tioja was alone in a hostile city that only barely started to tolerate his presence.

When Tioja stood up, Baa was already washing her face with warm water. "Well? Are you going to say something, or will I drag you outside again to punch the truth out of you?"

"Huh?"

Baa shook her head in disapproval. "What is wrong with you? Perhaps I have not achieved a Master's status for a very long time, but I had initiated enough students to know they always felt awed when I connected the vantage points. Meanwhile, you are acting as if you forgot how to pee."

"I uh…" Tioja blushed without ever getting used to his mentor's bluntness. "My… brother told me about his initiation with your teacher who is traveling the world. Gulraj enjoyed floating in the air very much. I just… well, it isn't like you failed in your session."

Lazarius's grave voice boomed from afar. "You feel so proud, don't you? You are too blinded because you can summon a powerful phantom beast that could obliterate any human enclave despite being a hostage in my domain. Remember that you have only accomplished the easy part of the test and are pretty much naked."

While Tioja hurriedly dressed in his beige robes, Baa chuckled at the spectacle. "Don't be so hard on him, Uncle. Tioja ruined my wings without even blinking. He could have killed me if I hadn't been such a competent second initiate. Must be real fun feeling your enemy being ripped into pieces." Baa was indeed way too blunt for Tioja's taste.

After Tioja finished dressing without accommodating his unruly hair, Baa shoved a ceramic cup into his hand. "Now for the second test. Drink it and go outside. Don't talk to anyone. I'll fetch you."

Tioja complied with the command, assuming it was just a normal part of the test. Jarahad was not allowed to explain his experience, and neither could Gulraj. Therefore, there was little need to fret about it. Hopefully, the initiation was just as easy as the inking sessions, and Tioja could return home and make Gulraj feel proud. Tioja soon walked outside and observed the passersby in the street, occasionally hollering insults intermixed with skeptical glares. It no longer mattered to him.

"You are a failure, just like your father."

Tioja was well versed in ignoring other people's gaslighting, yet this voice came from a different source. A part of him wondered if a harlequin was using some sort of telepathy. Until he realized this clan's mages were incapable of such a feat.

"Must be painful to be an orphan. And it was your fault. They would still live if you hadn't left your father's side."

Tioja bit his lip and resisted the urge to voice his complaints. Baa was only starting to accept him; he would not fail her now.

"I can't wait to see you fail. A shame. Your mother was a fine master."

Before Tioja had a chance to argue, the taunting voice reverberated once again. *"If you fail your test and attempt to use me, I will devour you and explode into a thousand pieces."*

Baa returned with a grave face. "Wear this hood on your head and come with me." He complied without protest while putting up with the voice's taunts.

"Yes, Tioja. I am the soul of your dead mother's sword. I wanted to communicate with you for so long, but it was only after you finished your initiation that unlocked the spells hindering communication. I must say you have proven to be a complete disappointment. Your father disowned you, your mother is dead, and Gulraj will inevitably murder you to ensure nobody takes his throne away. Not that you ever had a blood claim to it." The sword's voice chuckled nonstop.

None of the insults stirred much of a reaction in the elf. Despite the endless layers of viciousness, Gulraj was still the kind-hearted brother from before that fateful day. Baa eventually yanked the hood off and walked away without saying a word. The instant Tioja opened his eyes, he gasped. Like Jarahad's test, a little child was chained to the floor. Tioja wondered why Baa's studio had a hooked hinge on the floor for a very long time, and a part of him expected it was due to this purpose. Instead of feeling disgusted, the elf sighed. "I have to kill him."

"That is correct, you impertinent fool. Finish the bonding and let us both feast on the blood of an innocent."

"You are no innocent, stupid sword."

The sword cackled even more. *"I like your sense of humor. Don't be a hypocrite. You love murdering just as much as I do."*

"I will not kill a hapless child!"

"Then abandon this city and return to Murdorhiolan in shame!"

The sword began vibrating, jerking itself free from the scabbard. Before Tioja could catch it, the sword collapsed to the ground. "Wait! Let me offer my blood instead!" With a sensation of utter dread, Tioja knelt on the ground, sliced a large wound on his hand, and fed it to the sword in the same fashion Hamara and Gulraj would do on occasion. Unfortunately, the sword remained idle, and he never heard the voice again.

After a few minutes of complete and utter despair, Tioja could only hear the cries of the little child he was unwilling to murder. Before he knew it, someone punched his stomach, rendering him unconscious on the ground. He had failed.

Jarahad's good fortune allowed him to perform his little test during breakfast the following morning. For some odd reason, Anduvio decided to sit next to Sharad, who was hell-bent on trying to reach a basket filled with loaves of bread.

Using air magic to push the food was enticing, but Jarahad opted against it. Taking advantage of the basket's proximity, Jarahad's hands rummaged through the loaves and selected the hardest of them all. "Here, Sharad. Enjoy your meal."

"Geesh, you're the best, Jarahad." If there was one thing that made Sharad stand out, it was the way he could relax his fiercest enemies with a smile.

"My dear, wouldn't you like to apply butter on that? Hrmm?" Before Sharad could protest, Anduvio snatched his loaf. Incapable of finding any knives at hand's reach, the man proceeded to break the loaf in half. Spilled crumbs covered the table.

"We don't make butter over here, old pal. But we have hummus!" Sharad's innocence further kept Anduvio's guard down as he proceeded to dip the loaves in a beige paste.

Taking advantage of this unique opportunity, Jarahad's right hand made minuscule circular movements as he stirred his tea and watched the breadcrumbs slowly drift to the side of the table. While Anduvio's eyes seemed to blink for an instant or two, he continued goading Sharad without noticing anything amiss.

For the briefest of instances, Jarahad felt a slight increase of the soft buzzing. Before he knew it, the vibration surrounding Anduvio's body returned to normal. It might have been just a fluke.

Finding additional excuses to address the man without lifting suspicions would be more challenging. After requesting for permission beforehand, Jarahad accompanied Anduvio into Jamarnid's office the next day.

Anduvio was wearing a brand new green and red costume today, which seemed even more ridiculous than the blue one. Instead of storing the books as he promised, Anduvio spent more than an hour trying to read them in vain. "What kind of language is this anyways? I can't read it, my darling!"

"The book is written in ancient Elvish. Chances are a human merchant sold it for a hefty fee. I don't like to meddle in my father's personal affairs. You have been an immense help. We will also need to replace the damaged window before the rains commence." Jarahad stared outside.

"Ah yes, indeed. We wouldn't like this room to get wet, my sweetest hearts." After growing bored with the illegible text, Anduvio packed some books in the crate. Taking advantage of the distraction, Jarahad held a book covered in sawdust and blew it near the man's shoulder using air magic. Like the other day, the increased humming was barely perceptible and returned to its constant throbbing.

Anduvio was aloof as he continued his tasks. "Yes, these books are covered in dust. I can see why you requested my help."

"Hey, can you use air magic and help me remove the dust? I would hate it if my father saw his belongings looking dirty," Jarahad said.

"For you, I will acquiesce this one time." With a snap of his fingers, trickle amounts of air magic became detectable in Anduvio's body. Dust blew in Jarahad's face. While elation dawned in Jarahad's mind upon realizing his father's suspicions were correct, Anduvio took advantage of his confusion to rush to his side. Terror and incredulity filled Jarahad when he felt Anduvio's lips kissing his mouth while his hands held him in a firm embrace. Disgusted and confused, Jarahad recalled his father's observations regarding Anduvio's prior acts of closeness with him. Feigning stupidity to confirm his suspicions, Jarahad continued kissing Anduvio while his hands prodded the man's neck in search of jewelry… until his tongue felt something round and hard. A pervasive vibration felt cold to the touch. Frozen in fear, Jarahad remained immobile as Anduvio stood away and giggled due to his little prank. "Oops, sorry about that."

"Your tongue, there is…."

"Oh, you're talking about this?" Anduvio opened wide and revealed a strange black stone gem adorning his tongue. Horror dawned on Jarahad.

If Henrietta's story was true, then Anduvio possessed a legendary immortality stone that had bonded to him as a human air mage and made him unbeatable in combat. Worse, the man was madly attracted to him. Jarahad had no idea how to approach this touchy subject without risking the clan.

***

With deft theatrics, Jarahad excused himself after showering Anduvio with appreciation for his assistance. Taking advantage Anduvio was busy, Jarahad spent the better portion of the day pacing across the city's wide streets as he garnered his thoughts. From the interactions of the past two days, Anduvio was indeed a pureblood human. He was also capable of summoning some kind of invisible phantom beast that didn't increase the constant throbbing of his stone. Jarahad shook his head after recalling the man's advances. It was more than obvious Anduvio's unrequested love would become a huge problem. Before Jarahad realized what he had been doing, he was standing right in front of Talgel's fanciful two-story home with a flat roof covered in colorful wooden motifs. "I guess old habits die hard." With a shake of his head, Jarahad knocked on the door. "Talgel, are you home? I would like to speak to you."

No answer, which made him wonder whether she was even home. Suspicious, Jarahad eased to the kitchen window and wafted the discernible scent of boiling vegetables. Certain Talgel was home, he spoke through the window in a commandeering voice. "Talgel, I know you're home. I don't want to talk to you about Henrietta. Please let me inside."

"Go away! Leave me! Please!"

Fed up with Talgel's latest mind game, Jarahad rushed to the entrance and used air magic to unlock the door. He didn't even bother to remove his muddy boots as he marched inside, cruised through the colorful drapes, and saw the most pitiful sight. Talgel was huddled in a dark corner of her bedroom, crying her heart away as a bottle of liquor was vacating its content on her brand-new rug. If her odd behavior wasn't disturbing enough, this was the first time Jarahad had seen the disheveled halfling dressed in her underwear. Ashamed of the sight, Jarahad didn't even think twice before covering Talgel with a blanket and sitting nearby. "Talgel, I know that things have been very rocky between us. I forgive you for your outburst the other day. If you don't wish to see Henrietta again, I will respect your wishes."

"This has nothing to do with that sniveling worthless bitch! Get out!"

In a pitiable fashion, Talgel's hands clasped on the closest bottle she could find and tossed it near Jarahad. Her aim was so poor that he didn't need to worry about dodging it. Knowing she would hate him for this, Jarahad sat beside her, grasped her shoulders, and wiped the tears from her empty eye sockets. "I have known you my whole life, Talgel. If you choose to return my feelings, I will always accept you in my heart. I urge you to calm down and let me ask you something. It is very urgent."

"Have you entered contact with the calamity stone?"

This comment that came out of the blue warranted a wave of fear to envelop Jarahad. "I believe the human that injured my father is wearing something on his tongue. The gem is round and feels unusually cold to the touch. I dread going back to the palace because I have no idea how to evict him without facing retaliation."

"Hahaha, the little bastard kissed you. Is that so?" This was perhaps the first and only time Jarahad would ever feel glee to see Talgel's usual cruelty resurface. The fact that she seemed to already know everything that happened from the past few days was proof she was withholding a vision. For what reason, he couldn't quite understand. "I beg you to please tell me why you didn't warn us. Who is Anduvio, and what does he want?"

"My future has been sealed in stone. If you walk outside and make the right choice, you still have a chance to save Almjarhad. Go outside right now! Please!"

"What about you?"

Taken agape by Jarahad's pestering, Talgel covered herself in the blanket, stood up, and shoved him toward the hallway. "Let me dress first! Go to the street right now!"

Assuming Talgel's abrasiveness was due to the need to dress in privacy, Jarahad stumbled outside and bumped into Anduvio's firm embrace. How could it be possible this human moved so fast?

"You are a flirt, elf Jarahad. What are you doing in this obscene-looking building, hrm? Are you cheating on me?" Vibrations hummed with increased intensity as Anduvio's brown eyes gazed with such fierceness, Jarahad pondered whether the man was teetering on the verge of madness.

Annoyed, Jarahad tried to shove him away. "What are you doing? Why do you act in such a way with me?"

Before Anduvio could explain, they were approached by an inebriated Jamad who stood across the street with a wobbly gait. "Hey! Why do you disrespect my Lord? Ja- hic! Is zer Lord of zis city, and we must gup him respect."

"Pensennovante embriagado! Get away from me, you piece of filth!" Anduvio hollered.

Jarahad's worst fears played before his very eyes. His hopes of avoiding Tioja's alcoholic father from antagonizing Anduvio had vanished in an instant. In Jamad's current state, he would neither heed orders to back off nor abscond from the inherent risks of angering the mage. Just like his prior outbursts of anger, Jamad summoned his phantom beast. Jarahad's heart pounded as he saw the bluish gelatinous quadruped beast charge in Anduvio's direction and collided against his body. Much to everyone's shock, it vanished in the blink of an eye.

While the drunk elf tried rubbing his eyes from disbelief, Anduvio laughed hysterically without showing a single scratch on his body. "Insolente! Do you think a disgusting drunkard can harm the wonderful magician Anduvio? I have lived for over 600 years, and I have never been defeated. Take this!"

What happened next would haunt Jarahad for the rest of his life.

The shockwave from Anduvio's sorcery also ricocheted him backward. Overwhelmed by the magnitude of Anduvio's power, a desire to survive ignited Jarahad's most primal instincts. Before he knew it, his body became enveloped in the safety of his magical armor as he crashed against the closest building.

Dazed from what happened, Jarahad's hands prowled the bricks aside. With all his might, he coughed dust from his lungs and pushed, shoved, and dug back to freedom. The instant Jarahad could feel the caress of wind wafting against his face, Jarahad's heart sunk at the sight. Anduvio stood completely unscathed as he kicked and stomped on the prone Jamad.

Was Jamad still alive? Due to the angle, Jarahad was unable to know at this point. With great effort, he crawled on top of the broken rubble and thanked the elf gods for gifting him armor that had just saved his life. Jarahad mentally retracted the helmet that flattened on his back and was granted a clearer view of the destruction. Ruined houses within a 30 feet radius were intertwined with screams of pain, calls for help, and uttermost chaos. After seeing Anduvio's work of destruction firsthand, Jarahad cowered in both fear and respect for Tanato, whose quick thinking saved both his father and everyone inside the castle when they were attacked.

Anduvio heeded no worries as he continued kicking Jamad with an enthusiasm that made Jarahad's blood boil in rage. For the briefest moments, he formulated a silly plan to charge toward the mage and rescue Jamad. A sense of horror dawned on him when he saw Jamad's head tilt backward from a broken neck while his body was resting on top of a pool of blood. "I… I failed him. He's… Tioja's father is dead."

By this time, Anduvio knew something felt amiss. Jarahad sensed the vibration that accompanied Anduvio everywhere had increased an imperceptible notch and was clinging ever slightly stronger to its master than before.

Anduvio screeched upon spotting Jarahad with an unmistakable sense of terror and stomped towards him. "You can use magic, and you never told me!"

Fearful for his life, Jarahad was close to drawing his weapon and attempting a fool's errand of attacking Anduvio heads on with his sword. Until something grasped his ankle.

Coughing and moans were audible from below. If seeing Jamad's horrifying demise wasn't agonizing enough, Jarahad's heart sunk in terror upon seeing a thin arm trying to claw his ankle. Jarahad was so preoccupied staying alive that he never realized Anduvio destroyed Talgel's home. The blind seer heaved with coughing fits as she dragged her uncompliant body from the rubble. With some effort, Talgel crawled to freedom without releasing Jarahad's ankle. For unexplained reasons, Talgel never lifted her head, so Jarahad could only see her matted grey hair.

Talgel continued staring at the rubble as she spoke. "Don't fight against the mage with your sword, Jarahad. He will take this action as a declaration of war and murder everyone in the city."

"Talgel, my love! Good lord, you're wounded! I…"

Howled screeches erupted from Anduvio's lips as he saw Talgel's odd behavior. The increase of mana permeating from the human echoed in every direction, worrying Jarahad even more. "You bitch! You are Jarahad's lover!"

It was Talgel who spoke first as she heaved for air. "Anduvio, you don't love Jarahad. You only idolize him like a statue without seeing his many defects. I saw your fortune a long time ago and was well aware you would visit us. After reaching a new city, you would always fall in love with an unsuspecting victim and throw childish temper tantrums whenever they don't cower into your web of abuse. When you outlive your victim, you destroy the city and hunker off in your birth island for several decades in the hopes everyone forgot about you."

A tremble escaped Jarahad's lips. "Anduvio… he's visited other cities and destroyed them?"

Talgel's hand clasped Jarahad's ankle even more firmly. "Yes. Anduvio hides in his palace once he does his misdeed so that unsuspecting humans never discover he has attained immortality. He is either very cunning or just plain lucky that the Elf Kingdom never knew about his existence. The guard would have tried to assassinate him long ago." Ignoring Jarahad, Talgel tried to lift her head, and her hollow eyes stared in Anduvio's direction. "Of course, both of us know your stone can survive even the most powerful phantom beasts. If you had the guts, you could walk straight into the Elf King's palace and murder Master Salman anytime."

Both Jarahad and Anduvio blinked from the absurdity of Talgel's threats. Jarahad observed the man and tried to recall something. A sense of dread dawned on his face. "I remember reading a book in Orsenmuray just a few days after Talgel first awakened her phantom beast. It was a book about extinct human languages. Anduvio, you're an Itorani? I thought those people vanished from the face of the earth centuries ago due to some mythical cataclysm!"

This brought a cruel smile on Anduvio's face as he twiddled with his mustache. "Why, I never knew there were still books about my kin. I killed them all when I first became immortal. My sorcery was far too powerful to control at the time. I have wandered around like a nomad ever since. How could any of you know all of this?"

Crowds began gathering in a circle to see the commotion. Jarahad felt increased fear Anduvio would kill everyone with each passing minute. Worse, Sharad knelt beside Jamad while carrying a pair of boots that needed to be polished and screeched. Knowing his options were limited, Jarahad spoke to Talgel while he kept a close watch on Anduvio's movements. "What can we do, Talgel? You have seen this man's future. Tell me! Help me save my people!"

Talgel's voice faltered as she responded with subdued resignation. "Give Anduvio full reign of this city in exchange for the lives of its inhabitants."

"What?! I can't follow such a ridiculous command!"

"Give Anduvio the city immediately before Sharad does something stupid and has everyone murdered. I command you to abide at once and evacuate to Soremin's temple!"

Left without better options, Jarahad sucked his last figment of pride, and made his armor vanish. Jarahad approached Anduvio, who seemed amused more than anything. Going against his infantile sense of justice, Jarahad kowtowed in front of Anduvio and spoke in a firm yet apologetic tone. "Magician Anduvio, I have never caused you any harm. As the ruler of Almjarhad, I will barter a deal you will be hard-pressed to refuse."

"Oh, and what would that be?" Anduvio's foot slithered on Jarahad's head and pressed hard.

"Jarahad, what are you doing?" Sharad screeched from afar.

Knowing Sharad would ruin Talgel's plan, Jarahad spoke in a commandeering voice. "Sharad, don't you dare move an inch! As your cousin and current ruler of the city, I beg of you to obey for once in your life!"

Anduvio knelt low and a slithering voice reverberated within Jarahad's ear. "What a pesky little bugger, aren't we? Coming to think of it, you're not as attractive as I initially thought. Maybe I will accept your offer, and we shall be at peace?"

Without daring to lift his head, Jarahad spoke loud and clear. "I, Lord Jarahad, ruler of Almjarhad, hereby grant Magician Anduvio full ownership of every possession in this city effective immediately. This must be under the condition that he allows me to rescue any survivors and move into the nearby temple. You can take or destroy everything inside the city. In exchange, you must grant us safe passage to the temple, or else the deal is off."

Silence was imbued everywhere as the howling wind intertwined with the crashing waves. After pondering for a moment and pressing his foot on Jarahad's head with increased firmness, Anduvio nodded in agreement. "You have a deal, my dearest hearts. I give you one hour to take every inhabitant of the city to the priest's temple with just the clothes on their backs. Anyone who disobeys by smuggling my possessions or stays behind will be murdered. Leave at once!"

Jarahad bowed at Anduvio and stared at Sharad's horrified face. Knowing Jamad was dead, Jarahad still had a responsibility toward his deceased friend. "Let me take the dead bodies as well. Their blood will stain your new robes."

"Oh yes, yes, take them. I don't like seeing corpses. Leave!"

The trail of Anduvio's laughter echoed as Jarahad lifted Jamad's ruined body and stared at the infuriated blond elf standing by his side. Sharad raised his fist with the full intention of slapping Jarahad, but his blue eyes faltered from the tears he could not contain any longer. "Cousin, what... You're going to condemn us to death if we leave Almjarhad like this."

"Sharad, I know I don't have the right to boss you around. I only beg you to follow Talgel's plan. If you issue the order, we won't waste time arguing. Help me!"

As everyone scampered off and Jamad's corpse was hauled on someone's back, Jarahad rushed towards Talgel. His heart fell with dread because she was no longer moving.

CHAPTER 14 ♦ JAMARNID

For the rest of Jamarnid's life, he would never understand why Talgel plotted and schemed with so much fervor to avoid the downfall of Almjarhad. And after so much effort, she ordered Jarahad to offer the entire city on a silver platter to some loathsome human. The evacuation happened quickly enough.

During their frantic escape, there was one event that was particularly aggravating. Jamarnid's wheelchair was being pushed on the cobbled road while he barked nonstop orders at his populace to evaluate in an orderly fashion. In retrospect, Jamarnid's behavior made sense. Jamarnid distrusted Anduvio from the very beginning and agreed to evacuate the city after what happened to Tanato.

Anduvio was standing right in front of the wheelchair while he patted a hammer in his arms. "No, no, no. My orders were clear. Jarahad begged me to let your people leave the city with nothing but the clothes on their backs. Right, guys?"

A group of human thugs jeered as they yanked scarves and hidden bags of money from wailing evacuees. As annoying as it was, Jamarnid remained undeterred. "My wheelchair is a part of my body. I need it."

Anduvio cackled even further as he twirled around while caressing the cheeks of an errant male refugee that shimmied away from him in terror. "A chair is not a piece of clothing. Or am I wrong?"

The band of thugs agreed while one of them wrestled against the poor servant and grasped the chair handles. Even though the man shook the chair several times, Jamarnid tried to hold on by hugging the armrest with his forearms. "Stop it! Why are you abusing a disabled man? Don't you have any decency?"

A frantic Jarahad came running and gasped at once. "Please! Grant my father an exception to this rule! I beg of you!"

Anduvio caressed Jamarnid's jaw and pressed it hard. Despite the pain, Jamarnid showed great restraint while clinging on to his chair.

Anduvio shook his head and stared at Jarahad with a maddened grin. "I only offered you one exception: to bring the corpses. You have two choices: your father, or his chair. In exchange, I get to either keep his chair or his corpse."

Recalling Talgel's warning, Jarahad slumped his shoulders and Jamarnid accepted staying alive was more important. The human raised the chair, and he slipped off and fell against the ground unceremoniously.

Anduvio then dragged the chair to the side. With malefic disdain, Anduvio smiled at Jarahad as he lifted his hammer and smashed the beautiful chair that had become a part of Jamarnid for the past few decades. Crunch, pound, and toss. Jarahad closed his eyes as tears fell while hearing wood being crushed into pieces, whereas Jamarnid watched with hopelessness. With his misdeed done, Anduvio dropped the hammer on the ground and caressed one of his goons. His sneaky hand lowered until it grasped the man's buttocks. "Let's go to my new home, guys. I am hungry for some steamy action."

As the cackles lessened from their departure, Jarahad approached Jamarnid while he stared at his ruined chair with sorrow. "Pick me up, son and take me to Soremin's temple. Before that lunatic changes his mind."

Jamarnid was incredulous that the rumors of Talgel's demise were true. Did she move the chess pieces and toy with everyone's actions so that she could die alongside Almjarhad? No, as twisted as she was, Talgel had plenty of chances to lure everyone into a trap. Yet it was thanks to her predictions they ended up founding their new city in the first place.

Talgel could have accompanied Hurrujat to his uncertain fate. Instead, she chose to stay behind. Jamarnid's mind revolved in mixed emotions as Jamad's body was settled down on the altar. With great effort, Jamarnid crawled toward it. At first, Jamarnid hoped that Jamad was still alive, but there was no point in fooling himself. Jamad's neck was broken, and his innards were covered with shrapnel wounds. Recalling Tanato's injuries, it was apparent this misdeed was Anduvio's doing. While Jamad was an elf with plenty of defects, he was still a loyal friend whose unceremonious death at the hands of a madman would not go unpaid.

Footsteps were audible, and Jamarnid spotted a weary Soremin approach him. "How terrible. Jamad… he's gone."

With enormous effort, Jamarnid withheld the tears as the dorso of his hand caressed Jamad's inert face. "Did we do the right thing, Soremin? Fight against the Äimite Guard in exchange for this life sentence in exile? What was the point of condemning Hurrujat's clan when my friends would perish anyways?"

Daunted by a question with no clear answer, Soremin paced toward the main effigy in the room and retrieved a large wooden object from the ground. Much to Jamarnid's surprise, Soremin opened the box. A smile covered Soremin's face after revealing a chest filled with dozens of coins. "My students organized cooking festivals with neighboring human enclaves. It isn't much, but we have enough money to survive for a few months."

While Soremin's actions would keep his people alive for a while longer, that didn't solve their most pressing problem. "We can't leave Jamad to rot away like this."

Soremin locked the chest and paced toward Jamad. With deftness, he sliced a strand of Jamad's brown hair with a dagger.

"What are you doing, Soremin?"

"I respect your feelings, Lord Jamarnid. If we survive our ordeal, I plan to deliver this to Tioja. He deserves to know his father was murdered."

"Tioja has left us, you hear me? I need to save our people!"

Ignoring his friend's latest tirade, Soremin approached Jamarnid and knelt before him. His sea green eyes burned with incandescence as he gazed at his eyes with a fierceness Jamarnid had seldom seen before. Soremin's soft hands wiped several errant tears that spilled from Jamarnid's eyes that left him speechless. "Talgel is still alive, in case you wanted to know."

"She is? I thought…"

"Her body has been pierced by wooden supporting beams. She will only live for another few days at the most."

"No, no, no, no! My son is going to throw a fit if she dies! Soremin, dear friend, can't we do something?"

"Such as what? I never learned medicine and none of the water mages know how to heal wounds."

"What if Jarahad brings her to the Elf Kingdom?"

"Are you insane? Both of them will get executed the second they cross the border!"

"Maybe Jarahad risks death, but Talgel wasn't even born when we got exiled! Your phantom beast could carry her! Please!" With a shake of his head, Soremin walked outside and assisted the weary horde of refugees. Despite the issues Jamarnid had with Talgel, he hated finding out her life would soon end.

***

Sucking his pride, Jamarnid crawled through the hallways of the crowded temple and entered Talgel's room where Henrietta and Jarahad were weeping. Accustomed to Talgel's vivacity, Jamarnid felt surprised to see her sweaty skin turned into a vile shade of dark grey. Given her mask was destroyed, her eyes were covered by a scarf.

With hurried gasps of pain every time his hands shoved his body one inch closer to the flatbed, Jamarnid sat beside his son. "Jarahad…"

This was no time to offer a pitiful pep talk, and so Jamarnid hugged Jarahad as well as he could and stared at Henrietta. The mysterious woman was hell-bent on remaining by Talgel's side despite what happened a few days ago. "Why are you still here? This isn't your home. Go back to your father's city and leave us to our suffering."

Henrietta shook her head between attempts to control her sobs. "There must be a reason why my ladyship has sacrificed herself to keep all of you alive. I know she may say horrible things every now and then, but her actions are always for an ulterior purpose. She wanted to keep this city safe."

"Safe, you say? Almjarhad is ruined! My son has confirmed my suspicions the mage possesses some kind of magical artifact that makes him indestructible. Forced to barter our lives in exchange for the city. And now the seer is going to die!"

Talgel regained sufficient composure to pinch Jamarnid's hand and heckled a laugh from his squeals of pain. "Dammit with you, Talgel!"

Talgel smiled in between gasps of pain. "I don't care what you think about me. And no, Almjarhad still has a sliver of hope. I believe the time has come to tell you why I have lost my eyes."

Jarahad's ears perked, and he stared at Talgel's face. "My love? You're just delirious from fever!"

"No, I am not! Let me tell you this confession before I die, will you?" Talgel's trembling hands prodded the coarse bedding and pressed Jarahad's hand. "When I summoned my beast and became cursed, the very first vision, the cause of my blindness was seeing my death. This was not just some random vision. It was the most agonizing torture I ever had the misfortune of experiencing. I not only died once, but thousands and thousands of times in all sorts of horrible ways in the flash of a second. This experience writhed my body in so much pain that my eyes died to save my mind from going insane. My beast, the demonic beast that has imbued itself to my soul and will haunt me forever did it on purpose. I truly wanted to marry you from the beginning, Jarahad. But the demon ensured he would sabotage every future we would be together and fill it with complete misery. No matter what happens, I will always love you and chose the actions that led us to our current situation to give you the best chances of living a long and lasting life."

"My love, stop talking, you... you're going to make it!"

"No, I will die! Dammit, Jarahad! Get over me and find true everlasting love. I don't care at this point if you marry Henrietta or some other person. Order everyone to stay inside of this temple, do not antagonize the mage in any way and wait for our savior."

"Savior?"

Everyone lifted their heads and pondered at the same time.

The smile of Talgel's face increased just a few notches. "Tioja is heading right this way. He is the only person in the entire world who can defeat the mage."

"What?" Jamarnid was tempted to begin one of his endless tirades, but his son Jarahad grasped his shoulder and shook his head.

Determination covered Jarahad's teary face. "Talgel has taken us as a fool the whole time. I told you many times Tioja was not the cursed demon of your sick fantasies."

"Good to see you have come to your senses, Jarahad." Talgel squeezed his hand even more than before in between labored breaths. "Anduvio cannot suspect anything. If anyone leaves this temple to greet Tioja, Anduvio will take this as an act of war and kill us all. I am certain Tioja will come here very soon. When he does, I want him to talk to me immediately." And with that said, Talgel released her grasp and fell asleep.

***

The following day, it had been decided to bury Jamad in a garden next to the temple. Even though the cemetery was away from the city limits, Jamarnid didn't want to risk Anduvio's wrath and ensured it would be a simple and private affair.

With Jarahad and Henrietta too preoccupied with Talgel's dire situation, only the surviving pureblood elves, Jamad's mother-in-law Svetlana and the rest of Hamara's immediate family were present. Unable to construct a spare wheelchair with the scant materials available in the temple, Jamarnid was placed on a chair while Sharad held a palm tree sapling in his arms.

Disconcertion imbued Sharad's freckled face as he stared at the plant. "Uncle Jamarnid, can't we bury him with everyone else and plant an olive tree?"

A sigh escaped Jamarnid's lips. "Everything within the city's limits is now Anduvio's property, and he ordered us to take Jamad's corpse with us. I wished I could have done more for him. There was no other way."

Svetlana wiped some tears from her face. "My Lord, if what the seer says is true, can't we wait until Tioja returns so that he says goodbye to his father?"

It was a thoughtful comment, but unideal. Jamarnid shook his head. "Our water mages are overworked trying to desalinate water for everyone. We can't waste their mana keeping his body cold. Maybe if we knew the exact date Tioja will return, I would consider it. This is for the best."

With a nod of resignation, Svetlana caressed the cotton shroud covering Jamad's body and ushered a prayer in Harlequin. The rest of the guests offered brief goodbyes; their faces stained by the increased indifference only shown by those who had seen endless death. The funeral performed by Soremin was simple and brief, which is what Jamad would have wanted. Everyone took turns dropping soil into the ground, including Jamarnid who had someone place soil on the dorso of his hands that he dropped into the pit. Using magic, Jamarnid summoned his earthly phantom beast that hardened the ground, leaving a small part in the middle. Sharad placed the sapling in the ground, patted it twice, and marched away without ushering a word.

Three days passed with no sign of Tioja. Jarahad had spent his days by Talgel's bedside as she clung to life. Much to everyone's chagrin, Talgel no longer wanted to speak to anyone.

With each passing day, Talgel's fever worsened, and her body became imbued with a vile stench that was an announcement of certain death. Jamarnid never had any intentions of loving the miserable creature that caused so much pain to his dear son, but he still believed Talgel deserved to live. He pleaded Soremin an additional time to take Talgel to the kingdom to no avail. "Dammit, Soremin! Save the brute! Do it as a personal favor!"

"No, I will abide with her wishes. The day I cut my hair, I made an unrelinquishable oath to the seer I would give her the death she sought for so long and I will not yield to you. Wait for Tioja's return and pray he agrees to help us defeat the mage."

Jamarnid had never felt more powerless in his entire life. Even when he saw Hormandra, Chandrice and the rest of his family die in the first purge, none of those memories could ever compare to seeing the despair on his son's face that increased as Talgel's life slipped away. If the first worst fear was for a parent to outlive their child, the second one was to disappoint them. And so, Jamarnid started to question the seer's true intentions. Maybe Talgel's fortune will come true after all.

On the 7th day of Almjarhad's downfall, Talgel had grown weak from sepsis. Wondering whether Tioja's arrival was just Talgel's final prank before her untimely death, everyone gawked when they heard someone standing guard on the rooftop. "I see him! It's Tioja! He's back!"

When Tioja left Almjarhad 30 years ago, he had run away as a discarded piece of trash that deserved to die. Much to Jamarnid's shock, he was now a grown adult with his head lifted high as he walked straight towards the temple among a standing ovation.

Relieved to see the halfling that didn't harbor resentment for his prior ill deeds, Jamarnid bowed his head very low in sincere apology from his chair. "Tioja, I… You've come back."

As much as Jamarnid wanted to apologize, Tioja shook his head with a strange expression of solace and walked straight into Talgel's room. Nobody told him to go there. It was like a greater force of nature pulled him into the line of fire. To save the clan.

CHAPTER 15 ◆ TIOJA

An expression filled with hurt was the only emotion on Gulraj's face after Tioja suffered yet another brutal beating. This was nothing new. Ever since Tioja returned to Murdorhiolan alongside the infant he was incapable of murdering, Gulraj made his life miserable in every way.

Tioja had grown numb long ago to Gulraj's relentless tirades that were thankfully only done in private. This was done on purpose to avoid tempting the city's inhabitants from overcoming Gulraj's authority. Nonetheless, Tioja always felt confusing feelings whenever he was brutalized behind closed doors.

It had become a sort of daily ritual at this point. Wake up by being met with a broken nose, tossed on the ground, stomped, insulted, and then perform the city's daily activities as if nothing ever happened. Rinse and repeat every day. Whenever Gulraj was in an even worse mood, he would do these honor repayment sessions as he liked to call it at random intervals. Usually, these additional beatings were severe enough to break a rib or two. On a few occasions, Tioja would lose consciousness after being bludgeoned in the head with a mace or any nearby blunt object. Having a greater inclination for water magic, Gulraj's air magic wasn't good enough to lift heavy objects with precision. That still didn't stop him from tossing a drawer or two every now and then.

Every time Gulraj's anger abated, the delightful abyss of pain was replaced by Gulraj's impervious water magic. It could heal the worst injuries imaginable within seconds. The downside from such gifted healing magic was that Gulraj could punish his brother in any way conceivable whenever he wanted with zero consequence.

It was a position nobody would ever envy. As Hurrujat's adoptive son, Tioja didn't have the blood claim to inherit the city. If Tioja attempted to run away, it would be very easy for Gulraj to order his knights to track him down and suffer an even worse punishment. Before Tioja had gone to Lazarius's city to train, Gulraj was already bartering deals to marry him off to the highest bidder. This highly anticipated event had to be cancelled at the last minute when the bride found out that Tioja returned as a failure instead of an initiated swordsman. Such a loss of face ensued it was doubtful Tioja would ever marry anyone. Something Gulraj felt to be unacceptable.

And so, the next few years were nothing but utter hell. The only thing that triggered Gulraj even more was the fact Tioja never begged him for mercy. He had become so numb to this new family dynamic that he even enjoyed being on the receiving end of his brother's wrath. It was the only time in the day where he could still feel the closeness they once shared as children.

Today's midday beating was worse than the other times. A familiar and inexplicably delightful throb pounded in Tioja's skull as blood oozed from his scalp. Tioja was certain his skull, left shoulder and ankle had fractures. As the veil of unconsciousness tempted him, the waning pain was met instead with a soothing cool energy Tioja had grown far too accustomed by now. Soon enough, the pain had gone away, and he spent the following few minutes using his own water magic to clean the remaining vestiges of blood from his body.

Safe within the confines of Gulraj's office, Tioja felt befuddled to see an impassive Gulraj retrieve a mysterious wooden box from his desk. Ever since Tioja moved into the city, he had been staunchly forbidden first by his mother and later by Gulraj to even touch the box. Up until now, he had no idea what was inside of it.

"Are you presentable?"

Tioja bowed without showing any hint of anger. "I am, dear brother."

"Sit down."

After obeying the command and sitting upright, Tioja couldn't help but stare at the rather large wooden box covered by a layer of black lacquer paint emblazoned with colorful shellfish motifs. His brother's behavior intrigued him even more.

Much to Tioja's surprise, the box contained several dozen letters written in Harlequin script. Upon closer inspection, there was something about the shape of the vowels attached to each name that flashed memories of Almjarhad into Tioja's mind for reasons he couldn't quite understand.

Gulraj seemed unfazed as he fetched a letter with Tioja's name. He placed the missive on the desk, locked the box and returned it to its place with frightening coolness. "When Hamara first departed Almjarhad, the seer commanded her to safeguard this box. It contains the fortunes of present and future inhabitants of my city which I have been honor-bound to deliver when the time came."

"This… this is my fortune?" Tioja's trembling hands touched the yellowed paper.

Gulraj's face remained emotionless. "There was a letter directed to our mother. She had to locate a certain harlequin mage that helped her give me the magic I now possess."

"Why didn't you give this letter to me sooner?" Tioja furrowed his brow.

"The day Lazarius brought you back home alongside your burden 8 years ago, I returned to my office and opened the drawer. I never cared to study this box until that fateful day. Sitting right in front was a letter with my name inscribed on it. My letter had a specific date to open it, which just happened to be today. I felt quite fascinated by the truthfulness of its prediction. The seer you hate so much predicted your failed initiation years before your arrival. It also stated I was obliged to let you return to Almjarhad precisely today and to give you ample freedom to return to my side whenever you required my help."

Incredulous, Tioja stared at his brother's face and realized there was zero malice in it. It was obvious Gulraj was retaining some tidbits of knowledge from him. Chances are Gulraj was only being truthful due to an unpaid debt to his deceased parents. Tioja's fingers caressed the sealed envelope and noticed his letter had today's date etched on top. "Can I open it?"

"I am obliged to let you read it without pressure or hindrance of any kind. Feel free to keep the knowledge to yourself if you so wish." With his statement said, Gulraj stood up and left the room.

Uncertain of his brother's ulterior motives but emboldened to read the letter, Tioja ripped it open and read its contents in silence.

"Dear Tioja, I have manipulated your life in so many ways to reach the crossbends you have right now. Your brother will give you a bottle of söma. Take it with you to Almjarhad Temple and deliver it to a halfling named Tanato. There will still be enough left for another two halflings. Soremin possesses his own box of instructions, and he will give the rest to two candidates that need it to awaken their phantom beasts sometime in the future. Your fate continues to unweave in uncertainty, and you still have the chance to choose.

If you opt to spend the rest of your life in Almjarhad, you must leave Murdorhiolan before sunrise. Gulraj will not hinder your trip in any way because he still harbors hopes you will regret it and return to his side for good. I want you to come straight to Soremin's temple to discuss your future. If you choose to stay in Murdorhiolan, this will mean you have given up on the elves and they will be exterminated. Choose wisely and destroy this letter. If your brother reads it, he will betray you. Good luck."

Talgel

After reading the letter a second time, Tioja heeded the warning and burned it in the fireplace at once. Within a few minutes, Gulraj returned without showing any hints he would prod Tioja for the truth. Just as the letter said, Gulraj was holding a travel sack and a bottle of söma in his hands. "So, brother? What do you plan to do?"

The decision was obvious and Tioja was surprised by the speed he snatched both items and stored the bottle inside the backpack. "Brother, I must leave for Almjarhad immediately. Whatever happens between us, I love you very much."

True to his word, Gulraj didn't stall Tioja's departure. This new sense of freedom made Tioja queasy instead of glad. Uncertain of Talgel's urgency, Tioja summoned his phantom beast to grow his wings and soared in the air towards Almjarhad. When his bloodthirst became too intolerable, Tioja landed, ripped off his wings and gawked at a bottle of blood wine in the sack, courtesy of his brother. With his thirst quelled, Tioja traveled the rest of the voyage on foot and soon spotted a pitiable group of hundreds of refugees inhabiting tents within the perimeters of Soremin's temple. Incapable of understanding why everyone huddled together, Tioja was even more obfuscated by the warm reception of his unannounced arrival. Even Jamarnid seemed gleeful by his return. Hard-pressed to know the truth, Tioja stepped inside Talgel's room out of instinct.

Henrietta and Jarahad where nowhere to be seen. Upon going inside, the stench of death invaded Tioja's nostrils and he hurried to Talgel's side. Talgel was at the gates of death, and yet the instant he sat down, the dying woman spoke in a soft voice. "Hello, Tioja. You have come right on time."

"Oh my, you're injured. Maybe if I take you to Gulraj…"

"No, Tioja. Don't condemn me to a blood debt with him. This is how I want to die."

"No! Your ladyship, I thought the letter stated you were fine and only wanted to see me."

"You're the reason why I have fought to continue living for a bit longer, Tioja. You have chosen to serve Almjarhad, and so it shall be done."

"I have a mission?"

"Tioja, a human mage has seized Almjarhad. He possesses a magical stone that grants him imperviousness to any weapon or magic in existence… except for your Lehart."

And then Tioja's initial glee turned into despair, and he tried to stand up and run away. Talgel grasped his hand with the last remaining figments of strength. "No! I can't control it! I tried everything and it is useless!"

"There is no other choice. By visiting me, your future is forever tied to this city. I am sorry for the hardships you will endure from now on. You must return to Gulraj's city alongside any volunteers and beg for him to summon his demonic beast into your body."

"No! I don't want to return to that city for as long as I live!"

Fury emblazoned Tioja's face as he saw Talgel's pitiful state. She knew just as well as he did asking Gulraj to save her life would entail the steepest price. Knowing him, Gulraj would force her to become his wife and live in a cage. A life that would only serve to give Gulraj additional children and unlimited access to her predictions. Despite the hatred he felt, Tioja still felt a modicum of respect for the seer. Death would always be preferrable to being imprisoned in Gulraj's palace. Tioja had an idea, and he lifted his hand. Without uttering any words, Tioja tried sending water magic into Talgel's body… until something happened.

With a wicked grin, Talgel heaved in bouts of laughter alternated with grunts of pain. The dratted woman was blocking his magic!

Talgel relished hearing his mumbled complaints. "Gulraj's Giltemarraj is the exact same beast that ruined me, and you know the risks entailed with using its power. However, it can help you defeat the mage and save the city. My fortune foretold I was destined to die upon your return."

This confession angered Tioja even more, and he sent curative water magic with increased fervor. "Don't you dare die on me, seer! Jarahad needs you!"

Talgel lifted her feeble arms and tried shoving him away in between bouts of clattering teeth. The woman was adamant in dying, but Tioja would not let her die so easily. Talgel deserved to pay for the hardships he endured.

Aware of Tioja's plan, Talgel opted to change tactic. "Goodbye, Tioja."

Flustered about these strange last words, Tioja sensed demonic air magic that made air escape from Talgel's mouth. What in the hell was the woman doing? Unaware of the fact Talgel's second tuning element was air, the woman took advantage of Tioja's surprise by vacating her lungs. A burning and cruel suffocation enveloped her body as she opted to die under her own terms in front of the poor halfling that was trying everything to save her. Within seconds, Talgel's lips shifted into a deep violet, and her pulse slowed. Before Tioja could stop her from committing suicide, Talgel heaved her last breath in front of Tioja's eyes. Right in front of a terrified Jarahad.

CHAPTER 16 ◆ JARAHAD

After seeing Talgel exhale her final breath, a crumbling sensation never felt before withered into the deepest recesses of Jarahad's soul. Talgel, his childhood playing companion, confidant, love interest and perpetual motivator had just been welcomed into the cold clutches of death, never to return.

Ignoring the trail of events that reached this very moment, weakness invaded his legs and he collapsed to her side. Could it be true that Talgel was dead? Incredulous at first, Jarahad's trembling hand touched the stickiness of Talgel's sweaty skin, only to feel disdain because the warmth was vanishing from her body. Still unconvinced, the taciturn halfling touched her neck. No pulse. By the time Jarahad lowered his head to hear the heartbeat that would remain silent, someone tried to pat his shoulder.

Much to Jarahad's chagrin, it was his father Jamarnid, who tried his earnest to crawl to his side despite the pain from his maimed hands. "My son, I… I know these are not the words you wish to hear. You know better than anyone I disliked this woman because I knew she was deceitful."

"Shut up! How dare you criticize my life decisions and continue to manipulate me! Talgel never wanted to lose her eyesight. Instead of being supportive, you did everything possible to ensure my Talgel died!"

"Son! I swear I wanted to save her! For you!"

"Everyone! Get out of here! Stop torturing me with your sick lies and let me mourn my loss!"

Jamarnid's eyes squinted for a moment. For the briefest moment, he lifted his forearm to slap Jarahad's face into submission. Knowing he risked losing his son's respect forever, Jamarnid nodded in defeat, and crawled outside alongside a belligerent Soremin.

Standing in the room was a tearful Henrietta who had just arrived and an unwitting Tioja. Heaves escaped Jarahad's lips as he stared at both people who he didn't have the heart to insult. As he fought the tears, Jarahad averted his gaze. "Henrietta, follow my father's suggestion and go home."

"Jarahad! Why would you do this to me? Talgel is my friend and I have the right to choose what to do."

"Please don't make me kick you out. Anduvio has killed two of my closest friends. I can't lose anyone else."

Frozen, beguiled and insulted in equal measure, Henrietta's pink eyes glowed with increased fervor and her hands trembled. Instead of expressing rage, Henrietta shook her head and her bare feet stomped outside. Jarahad and Tioja were alone alongside Talgel's earthly remains.

Unlike Jarahad, whose heart had been shattered into pieces the instant he knew Talgel had been wounded, Tioja stared at her body with deferential terror. Unaware about the brief conversation they had before Talgel's demise, Jarahad tried to ignore the remains of his former lover and speak before he crumbled into despair. "Why did you return, Tioja?"

"I…" Tioja's shoulders slumped from defeat. "I don't belong in Murdorhiolan."

"Are you willing to forgive my father and everyone else after they evicted you? Why would you do such a thing?"

Disconcerted, Tioja averted his gaze. "I think I know why I am here. But what Talgel asks of me is impossible."

Before Jarahad could continue prodding, Tioja shook his head. He then bowed at Talgel with utter respect and marched away, leaving Jarahad alone to give in to his latent sorrow. It didn't take long before the tears started pouring and he collapsed on Talgel's inert body and cried his heart out.

***

Before Jarahad knew it, it was already morning. Standing by the doorway was a timid Sharad, who was dressed in white priest robes. "Jarahad, it is time."

Forced to comply, Jarahad raised his head and whimpered. "Do we have to bury her so soon? I…"

"I don't wish to be insensitive. The corpse is already rotting. If we don't bury her soon, our people will start getting ill from disease. The stench has permeated the entire temple."

This was a painful truth, but Jarahad couldn't disagree. Talgel had been rotting away for half a month, so his nose had acclimated long ago. Even though Jarahad would have wanted to mourn over Talgel's body for a thousand years, the last flicker of hope soon evaporated from the back of his mind. If there was any solace Jarahad could attain from this inevitable nightmare, it was the possibility Tioja's return was predated from the very beginning. He might be the city's last hope after all.

***

A mixture between sorrow and glee invaded Jarahad upon seeing the coffin Sharad made from spare wood. There were no hints Soremin expected Talgel's demise prior to Anduvio's arrival to have hidden building materials until the right moment. Even so, it was a small solace to know Talgel would be buried under more redeeming circumstances over Jamad's thankless funeral from just a few days prior.

Adamant he participated in every step of the way, Jarahad helped Soremin and the other priests in undressing Talgel's body, washed it clean with purified water and helped them dress her in fine silk robes. Henrietta decided to remain and placed stone jewelry on Talgel's neck and wrists. Puffiness in Henrietta's cheeks hinted she had spent the better half of last night crying nonstop over her friend's demise.

Even though Daedoman didn't have access to his prized workshop, he still managed to construct a decent mask with gold leaf decorations from the temple's altar. For the briefest of moments, Talgel seemed to be once again alive in her new wooden prison. Jarahad then shook his head. No matter how much makeup was applied, the stench of death was proof of Talgel's demise. Jarahad knew the woman he once cherished was gone forever.

Jarahad felt his mind split as he watched Soremin perform her funeral. As the closest of kin, it was his duty to plant the fruit tree that would grow from her remains. He made a promise to care for this tree if they became successful in evicting the mage.

While everyone paid their respects, there was one person that was purposely giving his back to the crowd. Rage imbued in Jarahad's heart seeing Tioja ignoring the funeral. Why would he do such a thoughtless thing? Anger soon ebbed into acceptance upon realizing Tioja was staring at Jamad's tomb. A strand of brown hair was held by Tioja's clenched hand. Soremin must have told him the truth about his father's recent demise.

Jarahad spent the better portion of the next day seated in front of the sapling with a sense of disconcertion. While it made perfect sense to plant a date tree on Jamad's tomb, Talgel's sapling was an almond tree of all things. Why would Soremin's nursery have a plant that required ample amounts of water? Talgel never mentioned she liked eating almonds when she was still alive. Was this just another mind game to confuse Jarahad long after her death?

Whatever the purpose, processing these thoughts proved to be helpful in keeping the sadness at bay. If Talgel planned to be buried under a tree whose proper care would prove to be time consuming, it meant she was certain Tioja would defeat the mage and save the city. Knowing Talgel would forgive him for this, Jarahad caressed the leaves and muttered a silent whisper. "Wait for me, my beloved Talgel. I promise to return to your side when the mage is defeated. I swear upon my honor."

Knowing the full implications of such an impossible feat, Jarahad stood up, and marched off. Instead of standing by Jamad's tomb like the other day, Tioja was staring at a campfire while he was busy braiding the errant strand of Jamad's hair. Dozens of elves sat by his side encouraging him to drink some alcohol to alleviate his woes. Tioja ignored them.

Intrigued, Jarahad approached the group and wiped the tears from his eyes. "Have they told you the truth yet?"

Tioja smirked as he continued fumbling with the braid. "Lord Jamarnid apologized earlier today about burying my father before I could return. Given I insulted you yesterday by not paying any attention to the seer's funeral, I concluded we are now even."

Jarahad sat down and observed Tioja. "Were you evicted from the harlequin city? Is this the reason why you returned?"

Sharad who was sitting by Tioja had a sip of hard liquor. "Sorry about stealing the priest's ceremonial liquor, cousin Jarahad. Things have been well, shaky lately. Hic!"

For the first time in ages, a tiny smile appeared on Tioja's face. "I missed hearing your uplifting comments, Lord Sharad. I just wished I had returned to this city sooner. Maybe…" Tioja shook his head and finished fastening a ribbon on the braided hair. His odd behavior only intrigued Jarahad even more. "Did you know I have a younger brother and he is the ruler of the harlequin city?"

"Really? What happened to Hurrujat?"

A rapid blink and a stutter escaped Tioja's lips due to an unexplained reason. "My adoptive fath… your great-grandfather passed away 15 years ago. I feel regret that you couldn't say goodbye."

"Don't apologize for that. I was aware about his disease when he left Almjarhad."

The crackling of wood was the only sound in the vicinity for the next few minutes. After struggling to garner the words for a long time, Tioja spoke. "Before I tell you what the seer wanted from me, why are all of you huddled in the temple? Why did my father die?"

And so Jarahad spent the better portion of the evening talking about the events of the city after Tioja's departure. The story was told alongside the company of Hamara's surviving family members, Henrietta's uplifting chattiness, Sharad's jokes and Soremin's occasional intromissions. Jamarnid still felt callous disregard about being near Tioja and sat far away while overhearing the conversation. For brief moments, Jarahad forgot about Talgel's sacrifice. Knowing Tioja was receptive to hearing what everyone was up to had given him a new sense of purpose. The fact Tioja didn't harbor hatred after being evicted from the city meant he might be willing to fight the mage.

Tioja listened to Jarahad's story about Anduvio's arrival, Tanato's injury and the series of events that culminated in their current situation.

By the time the pinnacle of their conversation arrived, Tioja stood up and stared at the sky. It was almost dawn. "I forgot how long the days are in the summer. I spent so many years underground that I forgot what it felt like to see the stars."

This odd comment intrigued Jarahad the most. "Were you hiding from the sun by any chance?"

"At first, I lived within the safety of the underground caves. It's that… well… my brother ordered me to always remain by his side and keep his city in order. I could always leave the city's limits for brief business trips, but only after seeking Gulraj's permission. Oh! Before I forget, here is a bottle of söma, priest Soremin."

Gawking and awe echoed in the campsite as Tioja gave a bottle of the priceless magic endowing potion to Soremin, who cradled it in his arms with care. After uncorking the bottle and savoring a drop of the oily transparent liquid, Soremin soon felt convinced. "This is without any reasonable doubt to be söma. How did you get it?"

Tioja's eyes fluttered towards his grandparents Jamen and Svetlana. Being extra careful not to reveal the whole truth, Tioja remained vague out of convenience. "My brother does a lot of trading with neighboring human and harlequin enclaves. A few human mages know how to make the potion, and he always finds the way to get it. Please tell someone named Tanato to start the fast. He must drink it at once so that he can awaken his beast."

With a nod, Soremin carried the bottle inside. Feeling more relaxed, Tioja stared at Jarahad's face with determination. "I am well aware the human mage is a threat to us all. I can feel his magical artifact all the way here."

"You can? I can barely feel it and the pureblood elves don't sense anything at all!" Jarahad gasped.

Tioja seemed amused more than anything. "You forget that I spent a good portion of my exile mastering my harlequin magic. Just like Henrietta who knew about the stone, some of the pureblood harlequins that moved in Murdorhiolan have spoken about these legendary devices. I always assumed they were complete bollocks."

This only infuriated Jarahad even more. "Well, the stone is the reason why your father and my… the seer have passed away. I couldn't do anything to stop him. Tanato ended up badly injured trying to protect my father from his attack. Do you have any useful clues on defeating him?"

"I…" With a shake of his head, Tioja confirmed Jarahad's worst fears. "Let's rest for a while. When it is midday tomorrow, I wish to visit the mage and talk to him."

"No! He is a madman! If you enter the city, he will believe it is an act of war!"

This didn't seem to bother Tioja for odd reasons. "From what Soremin claims, the agreement you made with him doesn't apply to me because I was not considered to be an inhabitant of Almjarhad when he took over the city. So, I will speak to him in private. With a little luck, he will take the city's gold and leave us alone."

It was pointless convincing Tioja otherwise after he made his decision. No matter the inherent dangers, Tioja didn't seem even in the least concerned. Up until this point, Jarahad wasn't aware about Tioja's private conversation with Talgel. Knowing the elf, Jarahad was certain Talgel wanted Tioja to return to Murdorhiolan, which seemed to be the last place he wanted to go. Whatever the reason, returning to that city was a far worse fate than facing certain death confronting the mage.

And so, with great difficulty, Jarahad was left with no other choice than to accompany Tioja to the city.

CHAPTER 17 ◆ TIOJA

Despite everyone's constant begging and Jamarnid's thinly veiled threats, Tioja left the campsite by midday alongside a reluctant Jarahad. The city had changed very little from the last time Tioja had seen it. Some residential estates had been divided to house grown children, others had a second level. His home in comparison was left unattended for so long due to his deceased father's alcoholism that ravines covered the garden.

Whatever Jarahad was saying as he wandered around the desolate city went ignored. Most likely he wanted to beg him to head for Murdorhiolan immediately. No, pleading Gulraj for help was too risky. It would be preferrable to barter an amicable agreement with the mage and forget he ever had a brother.

Tioja wiped away some sweat from his brow. He hurried away from Murdorhiolan at such a pace before Gulraj changed his mind, he never anticipated returning to Almjarhad in the middle of the summer. Given the dire situation, the refugees didn't have spare clothes, so Tioja was forced to visit the mage wearing black harlequin robes that were totally unsuitable for the local climate. The only comfort was that his present robes were designed to accommodate his demonic wings. Chances are he could convince Anduvio without summoning his Lehart.

Soon enough, they reached the bay and were spotted by groups of humans that spoke a myriad of strange languages. A man that made Jarahad jolt a step backward and grasp his sword stood in front. Unlike the others, this one spoke in the common tongue. "Lord Jarahad! Why have you set foot in these lands? I heard you have been exiled!"

Seeing the mighty Jarahad cower to this man was maddening. Even worse, his apologetic tone of voice made Tioja's blood boil. He always had this false image growing up that Jarahad was fearless, and now he had been shriveled into a pitiable husk. If Jarahad's will had been beaten so easily, he stood no chance against Gulraj's wrath. This only further emboldened Tioja's resolve.

Both halflings were surrounded by humans who pointed weapon

in their direction. Adamant in not surrendering his sword, Jarahad sighed in relief the humans they encountered seemed decent enough and escorted them to Almjarhad Castle. Unlike the rest of the city, the palace was quite alive with the relentless stomping of humans dismantling Sharad's beautiful wooden doors and whisking away furniture. Sadness invaded Tioja's heart to return to his home city and see people pillaging everyone's belongings.

Within a few minutes, they reached the throne room which looked the same as always. The room was empty. Unlike Jarahad who knelt at once, Tioja stood tall to prove to everyone he didn't fear Anduvio. Uneven footsteps were audible, and the man finally appeared… butt naked except for a chemise while licking something from his fingers.

While Jarahad rattled from nervousness at the disconcerting sight, Anduvio's careless attitude amused Tioja. If this is the best Anduvio could do to intimidate his enemies, he will be easy to defeat.

A sing-song voice escaped the man's lips while hints of wine emblazoned the air. "What is this? Forfeiting your agreement, Jarahad? Do you believe I would let you return so easily? Or perhaps you wish to become my sex slave?" Jarahad's back cowered further low.

Ignoring the imminent threat, Tioja studied the man's tongue. The vibration he felt from afar increased a discernible notch from the man's display of emotions. He was indeed bound to its magic. "My name is Tioja. Jarahad only accompanied me as a trustworthy guide and has no plans on staying here longer than necessary."

The man lifted his eyebrow as he studied Tioja for a few moments. "Nobody in their sane mind would wear winter attire in the summer."

"As you can see from my robes, I am not an inhabitant of this city, which makes me exempt from your little agreement."

"Little, you say? Hrmm? You don't look too impressive. Messy hair, beady eyes, you really believed I would return the city… for you?"

"Tioja! Please, let's go! Don't anger him." Jarahad's firm hand pulled Tioja's pants to coax him into leaving.

This only enticed Tioja's boldness even more. "I am quite intrigued by your calamity stone. Did you murder a third initiate to obtain it?"

As expected, the vibration in the stone increased in equal measure to Jarahad's begging. Before Tioja knew it, he sensed a blast coming his way. Thrown into the air from the shockwave, the dizzying and delightful sensation made him feel even more alive. Just as they previously agreed before their departure, Jarahad was instructed to summon his armor to protect himself and to not interfere. Tioja used his air magic to ricochet forwards and land on the exact same spot where he first stood. Unbeknownst to anyone else, Tioja had learned how to emulate Gulraj's curative water magic. With seamless effort, the painful throbbing in his neck from the whiplash and bruises on his arms vanished within an instant.

It only delighted him to see the awed expression on Anduvio's face. What was even better, a thankfully unhurt Jarahad stared at him as he tried to reincorporate with such an expression of astonishment that it made him feel immense pride. Taking advantage of the brief distraction, Tioja said something incredibly stupid. "Nah, this can't be the terrifying mage that almost killed Tanato. Your hits are so slow that even the worst first initiate harlequins could defeat you with their eyes closed."

"Why you little…"

Ah, the mage was so pathetically predictable, it was joyous! Just as Tioja expected, Anduvio thrashed a barrel of hits using his insane speed. While Jarahad remained at a safe distance, Tioja did the complete opposite: with the aid of air magic to move his body beyond the speed of sound, Tioja marched forward. A deft grin imbued his face as he dodged blasts left and right and began absorbing Anduvio's mana.

Whenever Anduvio thought he had won, Tioja taunted him again with a never-ending barrage of childish insults. Saying such inappropriate things were predictably followed by more melee attacks that Tioja dodged with ridiculous ease. This went on for the better part of the afternoon, and yet Anduvio's mana never ran out.

Jarahad ran out of mana and was forced to hide behind several walls of stone. From his labored breathing, it was obvious Jarahad would soon suffer from a blood attack. Despite his excessive arrogance, Tioja was also starting to feel the effects of the extended battle. Instead of feeling exhaustion or bloodthirst, heated pain pulsated through his hands due to absorbing too much mana. This was a new sensation that Tioja couldn't quite process. Was the pain enjoyable like usual or something else?

Glass shards crashed against the ground from the domed ceiling, which prompted Tioja to look up. The sky was already starting to change into a reddish hue, a bad omen. Knowing his current plan of stealing Anduvio's endless mana would take too long, Tioja was left with no other choice. "I summon thee my phantom beast, the Demonic Wing Lehart!"

Tioja gloated at Anduvio's confusion upon seeing the black wings grow on his back. The instant Tioja summoned his beast, the pain in his hands subsided to a tolerable level. Much to Tioja's dismay, the throne room didn't have enough sunlight to see Anduvio's shadow. His wings flapped and he elevated a bit into the sky with the aid of his air magic. "Come fight me outside. If you dare. Or are you a coward?"

Enticing Anduvio to abide with his commands was easier than stealing candy from a child. Knowing Jarahad was perfectly capable of taking care of himself, Tioja used his augmented air magic to blast through the hallways and was soon outside. Tioja then focused his beast and studied the shadow of the castle. Anduvio could be considered many things, but the man had enough decency to avoid causing major structural damage to the castle. It was obvious he had no plans to flatten the city for the time being.

With a few flaps of his wings, Tioja reached a desolate area and stood on the ground while he patiently waited for Anduvio to arrive. Giggles escaped his lips at the humorous sight of the naked man huffing from exhaustion.

Anduvio's voice faltered into atonal sounds from the perceived blight. "Why are you laughing, you inbred mutt?"

"Your dick is smaller than my thumb."

Once again, Tioja took advantage of the man's excessive insecurity. A pummeling of punches soon ensued that Tioja eagerly accepted, tainting the ground with blood splatters. Despite relishing the onslaught of pain, Tioja was starting to become bored by Anduvio's predictability. Tioja only tolerated the abuse because it offered him the unique chance to study Anduvio's shadow and learn more about his strange stone. It didn't take long for him to become familiarized with the unique throbbing of the artifact, which became even more energized from stealing his mana. Aware of the mana stealing ability of the stone, Tioja continued letting Anduvio pummel his battered face while he stole the mage's mana in a fruitless attempt to subdue him before nightfall. Much to his chagrin, the man's mana seemed to be endless, and so he had to change his plan. Taking advantage of his immense skill with hand combat, Tioja pinned the man down on the dusty ground.

As Tioja stared at the man's astonished glare, he twisted Anduvio's shoulder backwards in an absurdly painful angle. With increased focus at the man's horrified face, the Lehart took aim and fired a blast. Pulsating superpowered water and air magic combined into one, channeled through both of their shadows and crashed against the man and any object in the vicinity. Soon enough, dust and debris filled their surroundings and a crater formed around both mages.

Initially satisfied his attack hit its mark, something felt wrong. As the hues of the sky shifted colors into the imminent sunset, the man's light brown eyes were staring in his direction. Anduvio was still alive! Horror dawned on Tioja as haunting memories of his failed initiation resurfaced, and the man took advantage by tossing Tioja into the air with a huge punch.

"You bastardo!"

Conflicting thoughts invaded Tioja's mind as his water magic healed some of his wounds. In his distraction, Anduvio charged forward and Tioja felt a crunch in his ribs. He stumbled backward as blood oozed from his nostrils. Knowing these injuries were crippling but non-life threating, Tioja felt gratitude for his brother's punishment sessions because they hardened his inner focus. There was something else that left Tioja speechless. For the very first time in his life, Tioja no longer felt any fear of using his Lehart. Knowing Anduvio's calamity stone could protect him from the Lehart's immense power, Tioja sent several blows in his direction in successive waves. While the effect was minuscule, each blast caused trickle amount of damage to Anduvio's stone. If Tioja had used the Lehart from the very beginning, he might have been able to defeat him. Tioja's hopes of defeating the mage vanished when the last rays of sunlight escaped from the horizon. With the vanishing light, Tioja's beast became unable to read Anduvio's shadow. All hopes were lost.

Exhausted and blood thirsty, Tioja collapsed on the ground, heaved with exasperation, and stared at his opponent. Anduvio was nursing the sprained ligaments of his left shoulder while remaining otherwise unscathed. They both ceased using mana and stared at each other's faces for a moment.

"Tioja! Tioja!" Jarahad ran in their direction while he held onto his magical sword and aimed it at Anduvio's flustered head. After realizing Anduvio was in too much pain to stand up, Jarahad felt temped to decapitate him.

Knowing this would be futile, Tioja grabbed his wrist and clenched hard. "Don't dishonor the agreement, Jarahad."

"Huh? But Tioja! I saw your battle from far away and you injured him."

"Yes, that is true. But I am injured as well and ran out of mana. Neither one of us will be able to continue fighting… for now."

For the first time ever since he met him, Anduvio stood up with a stumble and stared straight in Tioja's eyes. There was a sense of self-awareness the human had seldom ever shown before. Anduvio's voice sounded stronger, more decisive than the usual mocking jingle. "I am impressed with your abilities, mutt. For 600 years, I have never been injured before. You have earned my respect. But you have reached your limit while I can keep on fighting. As a token of my goodwill, I will not harm the refugees. In exchange, you must leave my city by tomorrow morning."

A sense of dread invaded Tioja as he watched the man stumble back to Almjarhad without showing any regard for Jarahad.

***

153

The journey back to the campsite was an agonizing affair. While Tioja initially had high hopes that only Jarahad saw his battle, the anticipation on everyone's faces made his stomach churn.

Henrietta was the first person to rush to greet them. "Lord Jarahad, Tioja! Did you defeat the mage?"

A sigh escaped Tioja's lips as he focused on the burning thirst from an imminent blood attack. Yes, Tioja displayed an illustrious combative ability that wasn't deemed to be possible. In fact, he should have felt proud for his feat. Any remaining vestiges of hesitation and fear mongering from summoning his demonic beast vanished forever upon seeing Talgel's death. She knew just as much as he did that being indebted to Gulraj would backfire. And she preferred to die in the hopes he could save the clan that once again accepted him with open arms. Knowing he had failed to defeat the mage only worsened the relentless guilt. And so, he averted his gaze because it was too painful to acknowledge the truth to Henrietta.

Knowing there was no other choice, Jarahad shook his head. "Tioja taunted Anduvio and tried stealing his mana. Henrietta, his mana is seemingly endless. Tioja attacked him with his phantom beast and didn't even cause a scratch!"

Henrietta's eyes glowed ever more fervently from the dire news, and she stared at Tioja with weariness. "I truly felt happy when you told me that one time you were excited to become a mage, Tioja. Thank you for trying to help… My ladyship…" A whimper escaped her lips as she ran off.

Haunting memories churned Tioja's stomach and made him want to dig himself into a hole and die after failing Talgel. It only made him wallow in self-doubt when he recalled Talgel's final words. A whimper escaped his lips. "Jarahad, call everyone. There is something important I must discuss with you guys."

With Jarahad's help, Tioja reached the campsite and sat on a stone bench. Seemingly aware of his impending attack, Soremin was already standing there with a cup of blood wine. "You will need this."

Bashful because he didn't expect to see Soremin with a new haircut, Tioja grasped the cup with a tentative nod and sipped its contents. Within a few minutes, the pain receded to a tolerable level.

"Tioja, can I apply this medication on your body? It looks bruised." Soremin had returned with a canister in his hands and nodded. With some difficulty, Tioja removed his shirt. It filled him with sadness that there were a few holes in it. His mother always told him he looked nice in this shirt, and now it was one more pleasant memory, a distant past that was forever gone, never to return. As the priest applied some ointment on his chest, the pain was soon replaced with a soothing sensation that made him relax his shoulders. Under normal circumstances, Tioja would have been able to heal these bruises with his own magic. Given he ran out of mana, he would have to put up with the pain for the next few days. Soremin was meanwhile flummoxed about something on his chest and pressed a rib.

Tioja clenched his teeth from the pain. "Ow!"

A frown etched on Soremin's face. I think your rib is broken."

"Leave it, I can breathe fine with it there."

"But you must be in terrible pain!"

Before Tioja had the chance to talk about his brother, an invisible but overreaching desire to respect Gulraj's authority forced Tioja into silence. His lips trembled and he soon slumped in defeat. "Just place a bandage. I'll be fine."

Jarahad soon returned alongside Henrietta, Sharad and Tioja's immediate family. From the despair on their gaunt faces, there was no need to explain anything. Jarahad must have told everyone while he recovered from his blood attack and spoke to Soremin.

Hundreds of refugees stood in a circle around him, their faces unanimously covered in sorrow and disappointment. Seeing their hopes and dreams become abated from his failure only made the pain even worse. Even Jamarnid, who mistreated him before his self-exile was present, albeit the whereabouts of his wheelchair were unknown. Chances are it ended up broken during the clan's frantic escape. Out of everyone present, Jamarnid was oddly the person that seemed the most downcast about his failure. It sent chills to his spine seeing the elf staring at him with a penetrating glare.

Jarahad finished drinking a cup of blood wine and relaxed his shoulders. "Do you have a plan, Tioja?"

A sigh escaped Tioja's lips as his fingers continued rubbing his shirt. "I was trained by some of the continent's finest harlequin mages, and I am convinced Anduvio's stone has immense mana reserves. It is inconceivable someone could fight against me for half a day and still have mana to spare."

"Do you think the plan would have worked if I had helped you steal his mana?" Jarahad asked.

Tioja shook his head. "Even if every halfling in this city tried to steal his mana, it wouldn't be enough. I learned a great deal about this stone with the aid of my phantom beast. Nobody can defeat him."

Murmurings and moans echoed in every direction as everyone lamented hearing the bad news. Jamarnid began arguing with Sharad in the distance. Whatever was being said, Tioja was unsure due to the excessive noise.

Sharad's face was on the verge of punching Jamarnid, until he showed self-restraint and stomped in Tioja's direction. "Tio, my uncle.. no… I apologize for causing you so much hardship. Talgel should have never accused you of being cursed. You're the most awesome and gifted mage I have ever seen." Sharad's blue eyes twinkled in sheer admiration, prompting Tioja to blush for a moment. His life had been marked by so much pain that he had forgotten what it felt like to be praised by someone.

"Umm… that is all right, Lord Sharad. I came back here because I genuinely want to help you. I never expected receiving any prize. Or your kind words," Tioja replied.

Sharad bit his thumb for a moment. "Even though my uncle is against it, I believe we should cut our losses and abandon Almjarhad."

"What?!" Tioja and Jarahad screeched at the same time.

Sharad shrugged his shoulders. "Soremin hid some money in this temple, so we could survive for a few months. But if we stay any longer, we will die of starvation. I doubt the mage will let us tend to the fields or build houses here. He will just barge right through and continue making our lives miserable until we all die."

Tioja set his shirt on his lap while he winced. Soremin began strapping bandages on his chest to secure his wounded rib. Ignoring the pain, Tioja's mind was busy anticipating Sharad's plan. "You believe I should bring all of you to Gulraj's city and let you all live there. While I cannot stop you, I believe you should not ask him for his help. You will regret it."

Jarahad chimed in. "Is it because of what happened to Hurrujat's city? This won't happen again. There are far more mages than before, and I now have my sword. As Gulraj's nephew, I would be glad to barter some kind of agreement!"

"Don't do it! You may never be allowed to leave his city ever again!" Tioja froze upon realizing he was screaming, and tears fell from his eyes. His fingers touched his cheek and felt the droplet of salty liquid. This wasn't from the pain inflicted by Anduvio. It was far more visceral and terrible.

Before Tioja marched off in a flurry of emotions, a soft hand touched him and allayed his concerns. It was his grandmother Svetlana. She had aged quite a lot from the last time he had seen her, with strands of grey replacing her previously black curly hair. Now that Tioja had experienced living with harlequins, he felt a pang of increased respect for his grandmother. She had shunned her own people for love. His grandfather Jamen stood by her side and held onto his wife's shoulders.

Knowing everyone deserved an explanation, Tioja breathed until his anger melted away. "My brother Gulraj will never let you seek refuge in his city. I wanted to escape from that horrible place ages ago. He only let me leave because he thinks you will betray me. Which would entice me to return to his side for good."

Jamen raised his eyebrows from the odd comment. "Grandson, can we ask my daughter Hamara for help? Ever since you arrived, you have never told me how she is doing."

Everyone stared at Tioja in the hopes for an answer. Knowing it was best for everyone, Tioja shook his head. "My mother has been deceased for over 15 years. Gulraj rules the city with my help. I'm sorry, grandpa."

Wails erupted within the campsite as Svetlana and Jamen scampered off. Any attempts to probe Tioja for answers came unheeded as he focused on greater matters. After Jamen and his wife marched away to mourn the loss of their daughter, the campsite became silent.

An intrigued Sharad sat on a stone slab and stared at the campfire. "I am sorry about what happened to your mother, sweet Tio. Is there anything else we could do? Maybe stop by for a visit and ask if Gulraj can lend some of his mages?" Sharad then remembered something, and a smile filled his face. "Wait a second, everyone!" Curious about what he planned to do, Sharad rushed off and soon returned.

A gasp escaped Tioja's lips when he recognized what the blond elf held in his hands. "I remember that sword. Hurrujat gifted it to you before he left. Wasn't it in the city when Anduvio conquered it?"

Jamarnid grinned from afar. "I might have allowed that prick to conquer my city and destroy my wheelchair, but there was no way in hell I'd let his grubby fingers steal Lord Sharad's sword. I ordered a servant to hide it beneath their robes when he evicted us from the city and Soremin has been safeguarding it in his temple ever since."

Feeling convinced with Jamarnid's cleverness, Tioja admired Sharad's sword. Despite being made of ordinary steel, it was still a gorgeous weapon that would be worth a fortune. Tioja soon understood what Sharad had something in mind. "You owe Lord Hurrujat an unpaid debt. Am I correct?"

Sharad nodded in agreement. "Lord Hurrujat gave it to me for no apparent reason. I will never understand every rule about harlequin society, but they take verbal agreements very seriously. From what I remember growing up, a verbal agreement can become passed to the next generation. I owe the harlequins a favor and would wish an audience with Lord Gulraj, effective immediately."

Jarahad then stared at his own sword and his eyes fluttered with disbelief. "My sword was loaned to me. Before Hurrujat left, I agreed to help his clan at a time of need, and they would do likewise for us. Would you happen to know if Gulraj has a magic ability that could come in handy?"

Tioja swallowed some saliva just thinking of it. He observed the hordes of refugees that were hoping for an answer. Talgel's haunting final words echoed in the back of his head. "My brother has a demonic beast like nothing you have ever seen. There are no guarantees he will fight Anduvio."

More heated gossip was exchanged among the crowds of refugees. Knowing he would regret it for the rest of his life, Tioja still believed he should be honest to his peers. "If you remind him about your debt, he will be forced to at least consider summoning it."

The ambience eased a bit from this statement, which prompted Jarahad to sit down. By this time Soremin had finished tying the bandage. "Tioja, I wished I could loan you some priest robes, but…"

"Nevermind. I don't want the mage to think I am planning on staying here," Tioja mumbled.

Jarahad's eyes glistened at once. "So, will you do it? Will you let us visit your brother?"

Tioja sighed. "I risk Gulraj's wrath if I don't straighten the issue about Lord Sharad's honor debt. When it comes to my brother, you have to always be very upfront with him. Even though I would rather avoid asking for his assistance, the sooner his lordship's debt is paid, the better."

After hearing the good news, Sharad beamed with joy. "Then it is settled. We depart tomorrow!"

Cheers and some improvement in the darkened ambience allayed some of Tioja's fears. For a brief instant, the refugees were tempted to celebrate with song. That was… until Tioja spoke. "How will you pay him? Jarahad? Sharad?"

This was a question with no right answer, and so both elves stared at each other and shrugged their shoulders.

Tioja's concerns increased a notch. "That is what I feared. Neither one of you have any gold or anything else my brother would want. Except…"

"I don't understand riddles, Tio. I'm just a not-very-bright elf!" Sharad giggled.

The far more level minded Jarahad surmised a possibility. "Gulraj will want someone to donate him mana. Is that his price? To have some mages live in his city and offer him mana?"

Such a thought disgusted Tioja. Mindful he had to remain neutral, Tioja opted for a half-truth instead. "It is a possibility, and Lord Sharad will have to be aware my brother is capable of forcing him to marry a harlequin and remain under his service indefinitely."

"No! I will not allow it! Over my dead body!" As expected, Jamarnid was shoving his arms and attempting to pounce off his chair. Soremin was forced to stomp in his direction and say something in his ear that made him calm down. A stern expression from the priest was all that was needed to allay Tioja's concerns of Jamarnid attacking him.

Sharad crossed his arms. "An arranged marriage and living in that city seems like a huge price for a sword."

It was obvious Sharad was completely oblivious to how devious Gulraj truly was. Knowing he wished to offer better answers, Tioja drummed his fingers on his lap for a few moments. "Perhaps if I accompany you and explain it further, Gulraj will be lenient and demand something else. If you promise to trust me, I will convince him to be reasonable so that your debt is pardoned."

Jarahad decided to intervene. "Couldn't he return the sword?"

"No, that won't work. A payment for a debt is one of the most important rules of harlequin society. You also must understand the sword will only allow him to enter his city. Gulraj will not summon his phantom beast under any circumstance."

"Not even for you? His brother?" Jarahad scowled.

Tioja sighed. "There is something you need to know about Gulraj's phantom beast. It gives him the power to grant one wish to the recipient."

Sharad lifted an eyebrow. "A wish? Could anyone use this thing to make the mage drop dead and, poof! Our problems are solved?" After Tioja remained steadfast for a few moments, Sharad became impatient like usual. "Well? Isn't that how it works? I mean. If I had a power to grant me wishes, I'd be using it every day. Have some wood to build a chair, kiss a girl, see…" Tears began welling from Sharad's eyes recalling his greatest hidden desire. "See my mom, dad, and brother Hormandra and sister Carpathia… just one last time. And be tucked in bed and have mom kiss me goodnight."

Tioja knew Sharad wanted something impossible, and not even Gulraj's magic could do that. "Forgive me for hurting your feelings, Sharad. I never intended to make you feel sad. You are also mistaken. My brother's gift will not bring your family back to life, or anything of the sort."

"Then what can he do?" Jarahad asked.

"I think I am starting to understand why Talgel stayed alive. And it was because she knew I would be unable to defeat the mage without his help. Gulraj's magic will let me know how I can defeat the mage."

Everyone except for Jamen and Svetlana smiled, cheered, and clapped. Under normal circumstances, Tioja would have felt glad Sharad had an excuse to visit Gulraj. Knowing him, Sharad would pay whatever Gulraj wanted without complaint as long as it didn't entail living in Murdorhiolan indefinitely. There was only one problem about this plan. It wasn't the fear of being beaten by Gulraj when they were alone or potentially being forced to remain in his city. In Tioja's point of view, he was hoping remaining with his brother would be the price to pay for saving Almjarhad. If he had to live the rest of his life under Gulraj's yoke to save the city, he would agree without complaint.

Sharad had already forgotten about his past childhood trauma and was already drinking wine to celebrate. How foolish he was! Silly, clueless, dopey Sharad. Maybe Tioja should enjoy these last few minutes of happiness before he was forced to confront his brother. Not that he minded the celebration. These people, who had once shunned him out of fear were now heralding him as a hero even though he didn't deserve it. Doubt, fear, these were feelings Tioja should try to embrace and accept as something natural. And so, soon he was starting to forget his concerns and was already singing songs and became inebriated with some of Soremin's last bottles of liquor.

By the time dawn was approaching, Tioja rubbed his eyes and saw Jarahad seated on a stone. He was dressed in travel attire and beaming with joy about his impending adventure. Foolish elf indeed!

Tioja shook his head and felt glad he was not suffering from a hangover. His body had been unable to recover enough mana to heal his wounds, but the pain in his rib helped the fogginess of somnolence vanish sooner.

From the pained expression on Tioja's face, Jarahad knew there was something Tioja wanted to say, but it had been lost in the frenzy of the celebration last night. "One of my men paid a human merchant some money to lend us some horses. My father has decided to stay here alongside most of the refugees."

"I feel troubled you will end up spending so much money. It will take us almost a month to reach Murdorhiolan. I suggest we should travel by phantom beast part of the way to save time."

"Very well, we'll travel to a village that is sufficiently far from Anduvio and summon our phantom beasts." Jarahad's face became sterner. "Tell me, Tio. There is something you haven't said about your brother's magic. It has been troubling me this whole time, but I didn't know how to say it."

Tioja frowned because he had forgotten how clever Jarahad was growing up. "You are probably wondering why Gulraj doesn't use his magic even though it can grant you unlimited knowledge."

"Yes. Talgel always mentioned there was something about her magic. And thinking about it, I have concluded your brother has to pay a high price for this gift."

If only Jarahad knew! The truth was so absurd that Tioja shook his head and resisted the urge to laugh at the degree of Jarahad's correct assumption. "Gulraj already paid for his gift. Now it will become the recipient's turn."

"What will happen if he uses his beast on your body?"

A shiver escaped Tioja's lips, and he felt the urge to spill the truth immediately before they departed on their suicide mission. Knowing he didn't want to disappoint everyone, Tioja spoke in a subdued whisper. "I'll either end up insane… or die."

Upon seeing Gulraj's face for the first time, Jarahad soon regretted visiting the harlequin. Fitted with an imposing sense of authority that made Hurrujat seem like a pilfering buffoon, Gulraj imbued immense fear on everyone. There was something about the way Gulraj's eyes darted left and right to observe their small entourage. Worse, Gulraj focused most of his attention on the handful of pureblood elves. Would he take them hostage to become mana donors?

If there was one thing that kept Jarahad's emotions in check, it was the neutral expression on Tioja's face. Any tints of fear regarding Gulraj's magic were well hidden. If Tioja felt any concern about his impending doom, he kept those feelings to himself. Tioja's display of subdued bravery prompted Jarahad to keep a level head. True to his oath, Jarahad respected Tioja's desire for discretion regarding Gulraj's magic.

Gulraj was seated on his throne, and soon grunted at Tioja with seething rage. "What is this?! I only permitted you to leave my city to realize the elves had exiled you, and you brought them here to beg for my help. Is this a joke?!"

An unusually grave Jarahad approached the throne and knelt in front of Gulraj with utter obedience. "It is a pleasure to finally meet you, Lord Gulraj. We have never met before, but I was a close friend of your deceased father. My name is Lord Jarahad, and I am the ruler of Almjarhad."

The throne room was invaded by disturbing laughter that caused the pureblood elves to shiver with fear. However, Jarahad remained tranquil as he observed the frown on Gulraj's face.

"The pleasure is mine. From what I understand, you are currently not the ruler of Almjarhad."

Jarahad clawed his knee with his left hand, but he remained tranquil. "That is unfortunately correct. A powerful human mage conquered my city and murdered several of my men."

Gulraj skimmed through the room and observed the handful of pureblood elves. A wicked grin appeared on his face. "Is any of these exiled immortals Tioja's father?"

"Jamad was murdered a few weeks ago, my Lord. However, his grandfather Jamen is here."

Gulraj's eyes widened when the brunette elf bowed at him with politeness.

Jamen's voice tittered as he spoke. "It is a pleasure to meet you, Lord Gulraj. I am your grandfather, Jamen."

"I imagined you to be different. Even though my mother had her differences with your people, I am grateful for your blood."

Jamen was uncertain if Gulraj's comment was a compliment, but he bowed once again and remained standing at a safe distance.

Tioja, however, remained frozen as he stared at the stone floor of the throne room. "Brother, I know we have our differences, but your amazing sorcery is my only hope!"

A frown soon appeared on Gulraj's face, and he crossed his arms with disbelief. "Why is your clan so obsessed with recovering that worthless piece of wasteland? Go settle yourselves somewhere else and leave me alone."

Jarahad sighed and stared at Gulraj's face with increased empowerment. "Lord Gulraj, I am conscious you were born in this newly established city, so you don't understand our plight. My father committed a capital sin by giving me life, and the Grey Clan Leader was unwilling to allow Master Lord Salman to murder him. He truly believed Jamarnid didn't deserve to die after he committed the crime of falling in love and wanted to save his life at all costs. The elves accompanying me today had no desire to topple the kingdom. They only wanted to save Jamarnid's life, which they did."

"And it's amusing because I heard he was left as a cripple! A pathetic shell of his former glory that can no longer even feed himself or clean his body. I'm certain he isn't present today."

Jarahad didn't fall for the taunt and remained tranquil. "My father was against visiting your city. He has lost all hopes of setting foot in the kingdom again and is waiting for the Eirmite guard to finish the execution in the hopes my kin can return. However, I beg of you to understand! I don't believe Master Salman will ever forgive our clan after what happened. But I know what is best for my people. I am certain you feel a tint of anger deep down inside that your clan lost their home as well."

"This city is all I have ever known, and my people aren't leaving this place if that is what you are thinking."

"I understand your position that we cannot remain here, but I beg of you! If the Elf King brings his army to Almjarhad to wipe out the remainder of the clan, I will accept the punishment. But I cannot fathom being killed in the wilderness like savage animals. Please help us recover our new home! Your father would have agreed to help us!"

Despite remaining unconvinced, Gulraj calmed down. He observed Tioja's eager face and realized that recovering the city seemed like a fair truce if he ever wanted to gain his loyalty. "There might be a way to convince me to assist your clan. As you can see, I am not as foolishly generous as my deceased father was."

The elves stood up to protest, but Jarahad lifted his arm to tranquilize them before a bloodbath ensued. "What is the price? I will be more than glad to pay it if it is a reasonable condition."

For unexplained reasons, Gulraj shook his head, making Jarahad frown.

"I don't understand."

"You're intelligent, Jarahad. I can see why my father maintained his alliance by housing your kind in his birth city that was cruelly taken away from him nearly 200 years ago. While I respect you, you have nothing I want... except perhaps your sword."

Jarahad swallowed some saliva as the horde of harlequins gossiped with each other. He unconsciously removed the sword from his belt and offered it to Gulraj with overt obedience. "If you want my sword, I will grant it to you as a token of my goodwill."

Even though Gulraj enjoyed Jarahad's offer, he shook his head.

Tioja was the first to protest. "Brother, why don't you accept that sword? It's a priceless treasure of my clan!"

"There is an important motive, Tioja. I must honor my father's agreement that the sword cannot be returned to my clan until Jarahad dies. I am an honorable nobledemon, and you can safeguard that sword for as long as you remain alive."

Jarahad sighed in relief and returned the sword to his belt. However, he remained cautious. "Then what is wrong? Is it because my father is an Eirmite guard like the soldiers that killed your people?"

Gulraj once again shook his head, confusing everyone even more. "Despite his cowardice, Jamarnid is probably your better half. Thanks to him, you can summon an impressive demonic beast and will easily outlive most of the harlequins in this throne room."

"So, you have an obvious problem with my mortal blood."

"I am a harlequin, and we respect our race. Sadly, you have been tainted with the filth of human blood. Therefore, while I abide by your request, there is nothing you have that I want."

While Jarahad was uncertain about Gulraj's comment, a smile appeared because he was willing to help him.

One of the pureblood elves stood up and bowed at Gulraj. "Thank you, my Lord, for your mercy! Tioja already explained your sorcery to me, and I am willing to offer myself! I am certain I will be of some use!"

Oddly enough, Gulraj shook his head with a furious growl. "No immortals. I will not risk my Giltemarraj on one of your kind."

At first, Jarahad didn't heed much warning regarding the odd comment from the pureblood elf that was standing among his small entourage. When Tioja confessed to him the price of Gulraj's magic, it would make sense for Gulraj to issue an endless list of demands in exchange for his help. From Tioja's skittishness that warranted him to risk his life taunting Anduvio instead of visiting Gulraj, Jarahad knew Tioja didn't want to become the sacrifice. Why would anyone want to endure undue suffering just because Talgel said so?

A revolving flurry of thoughts raced in Jarahad's head as he pondered why Tioja felt comfortable enough revealing this secret to someone else. Who could have offered himself at a time like this? Was it Jamen? Jarahad stared at his friends and Jamen lurched far away from view with a concerned expression. No, Tioja would have never risked Jamen's life after losing his father.

The answer came soon enough. Much to his chagrin, Tioja was peering at the suicidal volunteer with a keen disdain on his face. It was Sharad. Bloody fool! Before Jarahad realized it, he marched towards his foolish cousin and grabbed his shirt. "What are you doing?"

Sharad shrugged his shoulders as the room fell silent. "What choice do we have, Jarahad? Lord Gulraj doesn't want your sword."

"This is out of the question! Tioja must be the sacrifice!"

Gasps and murmurings surrounded Jarahad in every corner because he mentioned Talgel's final vision out loud. Everyone was aware their position was precarious. The fact Gulraj wasn't going to accept his sword as payment meant they had few other things to barter. Dratted selfishness! Whether Sharad was aware about the risk of death from Gulraj's magic, how dare Jarahad prioritize the life of his cousin over the feelings Gulraj harbored for his older brother! And now, the fact Gulraj knew his own family could die for nothing might entice him to evict everyone immediately.

Several of Gulraj's foot soldiers were already lifting their spears. If Sharad continued screwing things up, Gulraj could kill everyone. Gulraj cleared his throat. "Let's assume I grant my own flesh and blood his death wish to save your city. What could you possibly give me in return? From your tattered appearance, I doubt you have anything valuable."

Jarahad swallowed saliva and felt a gurgling heave of bile raising from his stomach. Was it possible Gulraj was already aware about their visit? Could it be possible Talgel relayed this knowledge ahead of time?

Without showing concern for the guards that could kill everyone, Sharad unfastened the sword on his belt and drew the weapon.

"Don't threaten him, you idiot!" Jarahad screeched as he felt tempted to punch his cousin's face.

Sharad seemingly ignored him as he stepped forward and showed Gulraj the sword. From the blatant clumsiness in his movements, it was obvious Gulraj didn't feel threatened by him and only crossed his legs. "If you are unwilling to let me become the sacrifice, then I must offer something else that you want. Don't show anger at Jarahad for his behavior nor lash out at Tioja. It took a lot of pushing Tioja's buttons during our voyage to learn the truth of your magic, and I accepted the risks. Perhaps you have not noticed it earlier, but this sword is special."

This last comment only emboldened Gulraj even more and his serpentine tongue caressed the points of his sharp teeth. An increasingly fierce glow from his iridescent reddish-pink eyes made him even more dangerous. "Special? Nonsense! This is just a worthless toy in comparison to harlequin steel. Not even the peasants would want this piece of trash."

Once again, the ambience of the throne room eased as the harlequins cackled from Gulraj's comment. Whether Sharad's nonsensical behavior was done on purpose or sheer accident, Jarahad felt glad everyone guarded their weapon.

Sweat droplets fell from Sharad's temples because Gulraj didn't feel impressed with his speech. With a stutter, Sharad had no other choice but to sheath his sword. "That is a bummer. Your father Hurrujat begged Charon to make it for me right before they left Almjarhad."

Gulraj lifted his eyebrow upon hearing that. "My father gave that trinket to you? What for?"

"I don't know. We were never very close, and everyone knows I am terrible using it. When we lost our city, I presumed Hurrujat gave it to me for an important reason. Perhaps you are familiar with the concept of an honor debt?"

Before Jarahad could speak, Gulraj stood from the throne with abruptness and spent the better portion of an hour examining the faces of his small entourage. For unexplained reasons, he seemed rather indifferent regarding Sharad's question. It was most disconcerting.

Sweat beaded from Tioja's face as he diligently knelt in front of the throne, anguish teetering on the verge of crying because he was incapable of doing anything else. How was it possible that someone could exert so much authority on the normally dauntless elf?

On all accounts, there really wasn't much Jarahad could do. So, he remained still while Gulraj began asking somewhat troubling personal questions to his entourage. What disturbed him the most was Gulraj's utter disinterest in Sharad's unpaid debt. There was no doubt Gulraj didn't want Sharad's sword, yet the fact he hadn't even demanded a ridiculous payment for his help was troubling. Still, the fact Gulraj ceased to be angry gave him a small hope he would change his mind.

At first, Gulraj asked the usual pleasantries, such as everyone's names and magic skills. Gulraj didn't hesitate to nod in agreement whenever a halfling confessed they could summon a demonic beast. A shimmer appeared on Gulraj's eyes whenever the truth was prodded by his adept questioning skills. It was obvious Gulraj was going to offer safe passage for these people. The adult halflings didn't seem impressed with Gulraj's boastings. At least one of the youngest halflings who lacked exposure to harlequin culture had an excited expression on their face. There wasn't much Jarahad could do in this regard. If they successfully defeated the mage, Jarahad would have to get used to greeting delegates that invited his city's inhabitants to Murdorhiolan. As annoying as it may be, this would be a small price in exchange for Gulraj's invaluable help.

When it was Nurran's turn to speak to Gulraj, the defiant halfling crossed his burly arms and shook his head. "Nope, I am a terrible mage. I only have one element and doubt I'll ever be of much use!"

A twitch emanated from Jarahad's eyebrow, and he hoped none of the harlequins saw his reaction. Despite his brashness, Nurran suspected something was amiss. It was obvious Gulraj was asking these questions for an ulterior motive and didn't fall for his trap.

Much to his chagrin, Jamen screwed things up. The foolish elf bowed at Gulraj somewhat apologetically. "Nonsense! My beautiful son Nurran fills me with immense joy! His phantom beast can change the properties of any metal, which has been quite useful. He plans on being a blacksmith someday!"

Jarahad cursed under his tongue and wasn't surprised both Nurran and Tioja shared a horrified facial expression. While Nurran continued trying to downplay the usefulness of his sorcery and shove his father away, Tioja's relentless shivering indicated that Gulraj disliked being duped.

Tensions soon eased when Gulraj lost interest in Nurran and began a lively conversation with Jamen. He tried to convince the elf to accept his invitation to live in the city alongside Svetlana as a true token of his generosity, but Jamen did not relent.

"You give me so much pride, my dearest grandson Gulraj! My humble upbringing happened in a remote village far away from Teryoura, and I barely escaped the kingdom alive. After seeing my entire family being murdered, I firmly believe that blood ties are important. Your offer is tempting because families should live together. However, Almjarhad is a sort of pet project of mine. It fills my heart with joy to know my earth sorcery has made the lands very fertile, so I must decline your kind offer. A simple little peasant like me would never feel comfortable living in this palace. I would, however, like to know if I could spend some time with my son Kashin. Is he here?"

It was as if a small fire ignited in Gulraj's glowing eyes. Gulraj skittered through the room and spotted Kashin cowering in the corner. A cruel grin invaded his face, and he soon returned to Jamen's side with a glass of wine. "I understand, my beloved grandfather. Perhaps you could… stay with your son Lord Kashin. I agree that families must stick together." As if on cue, the second Jamen's hand clasped the glass, Jarahad sensed a small amount of water magic that made the glass break and blood spilled on the ground.

"Jamen!"

Jarahad felt someone grasping his shoulder. It was Sharad, whose face seemed unusually defiant. "Try to stay put, Jarahad. I think it was just an accident."

Taking Sharad's cue, Jarahad tried to feign concern for Jamen without antagonizing Gulraj. As expected, Jamen chuckled with forced restraint while he let Gulraj clean the wound with a handkerchief and bandage it. "I am so sorry for that, Gulraj. The glass must have been fragile."

"No insults taken. I believe you will have a lot of fun spending time with… your son." Instead of throwing the bloodied handkerchief away, Gulraj pocketed it in his coat. Suspecting Gulraj had ulterior plans, Jarahad felt further convinced the cowering Kashin had offended his master and would be punished. Whatever blight Kashin committed, Jarahad had to respect Gulraj's authority because Kashin was no longer a citizen of his city.

After Gulraj felt convinced with the entourage, Jarahad drew a sigh of relief alongside Tioja because it seemed he wouldn't evict them.

For the first time, Gulraj's face became imbued with a smile, and he opened his arms. "Let us return to business some other time. You seem most weary and deserve to enjoy the hospitality of my city. Please join me to the dining room and enjoy a feast."

The guests were ushered into a large dining room which already had empty plates prepared for the guests. Assuming the obvious due to his social position, Jarahad approached a chair beside the most oversized and elegant chair in a far corner of the table.

A servant shook his head and curtly dragged the chair back in its place. "This isn't your assigned chair. Please sit alongside Knight Kashin."

With a lifted eyebrow and his feelings hurt due to the blight, Jarahad hid his genuine emotions. He ambled to a chair several seats away and sat down. Kashin's chair was currently empty. In fact, Gulraj and Tioja were nowhere to be seen. Had Gulraj arrested his brother? Nonsense! From the smiles on everyone's faces, chances are Gulraj was arranging appropriate housing for his entourage and ordering servants to prepare a feast. Considering they were around 20 people; the palace cooks would be in a rush to prepare a decent meal in a short amount of time.

The same servant that ushered him to his chair soon returned with some loaves of bread. Mindful of the vegetarianism of elves, Jarahad felt glad for being treated like any guest. After being served some wine, Jarahad had a sip and studied his surroundings. The dining room was rather reminiscent of Hurrujat's old palace in Orsenmuray. With black stone pillars imbued with Corinthian engravings, the room like most of this palace had an unusual octagonal shape, with endless lichen that filled their surroundings with an eerie fluorescent green hue. The stone table was made of a black marble stone with colorful pink veins. Chances are earth mage artisans placed the same lichen that artificially brightened the city into the table. Even the walls possessed this quality, albeit to a lesser degree.

Contrary to Tioja's harsh opinions of Gulraj, it was delightful to know the dining room had a myriad of family portraits on the walls. One painting had Gulraj standing alongside various pureblood harlequins and there were several paintings of his parents posing next to purebred steeds. Facing right behind the currently vacant chairs for Gulraj and Tioja stood a gigantic painting of both siblings when they were younger. If Jarahad had the chance, he hoped he could stand closer to the portrait without offending anyone. There was something different about the way Gulraj looked in that painting. His features remained just as striking and beautiful as today, but the countenance seemed softer, kinder perhaps. Tioja stood by his side with a relaxed expression that hinted a sense of true brotherly love. Given Jarahad was an only child, he was unfamiliar with the concept of having a sibling. Could it be the true reason Gulraj and Tioja were not present was because of Sharad's offering? Whether Tioja's concerns about Gulraj were true or not, it was obvious from the portrait that Gulraj didn't want to lose Tioja. In a worst-case scenario, Jarahad was willing to convince his father to live in this city under the condition Gulraj didn't treat the refugees like a tyrant.

Soon enough, a few nobledemons dressed in elegant attire returned to the dining room. Gulraj's face was pensive, whereas Tioja's deadpanned grimace didn't offer any hints over what they talked about in private. The nearby chair screeched, and Kashin finally sat down.

Jarahad then realized he was sitting next to Hamara's older brother, who he hadn't seen in at least 30 years. Kashin was a changed man. From an ordinary farmer, Kashin was transformed into a nobleman who wore elegant attire and four gold bracelets on his arms. In a way, Jarahad quickly felt satisfied to be placed in this part of the table. "Kashin, look at you now! Dressed like a true nobleelf! Your mother would feel so impressed."

Red eyes dilated, and the halfling turned around. Softness imbued Kashin's face, albeit no hints of a smile were visible. "I am glad to hear that my mother still lives. Thank you for telling me."

"What is wrong? I thought you would have run to your father's side to greet him the second we arrived." They both turned their attention to the assembly. Jamen and Nurran were seated very far away alongside the other peasants. Kashin might have felt tempted to stand up and talk to his family for a few moments had it not been the other nobledemons were staring in Kashin's direction.

Without engaging in pleasantries, Kashin ate his meal with a downcast head. When Tioja first heard Talgel's final prediction, Jarahad couldn't understand why he was so adamant in trying to defeat Anduvio without his brother's help. The way he didn't seem even remotely frazzled from his injuries or intimidated by Anduvio's magic made Jarahad more curious about his years in this city. At first sight, Murdorhiolan seemed far more prosperous than Almjarhad. However, Gulraj's insistence on interrogating the halflings and only showing interest in the ones with demonic beasts hinted at a more sinister agenda. Suspecting Gulraj didn't trust him due to being Hurrujat's only remaining blood heir and thus a genuine threat to his authority, Jarahad studied everyone else at the table. Sharad was seated on the chair he tried to occupy. It made perfect sense Gulraj would place the true heir to the clan in the most respected chair on the table! Shaking his head as he slurped spoonfuls of spicy mushroom soup, a smile imbued Jarahad's face. It had been so many years since Orsenmuray fell that he had forgotten the pleasant memories of his childhood. Most harlequin dishes can be replicated anywhere, but you need specific weather conditions to grow some of the more exotic fungi in their cuisine. Tears fell from Jarahad's eyes because the agglomeration of forgotten smells and tastes brought him back to those wonderful memories. Such as the occasions he visited uninhabited caves to hunt for mushrooms with a beautiful halfling that always made his life more worthwhile. "Talgel…"

Kashin showed a modicum of interest in his company for the first time since they began eating. "Something happened to the seer. Am I correct?" From the welling of tears falling from Jarahad's eyes that he dried with his handkerchief to avoid suspicion, Kashin surmised the obvious. "I presume she died recently. The seer knew how to evade death, so I will presume the mage caused her demise, and she could not change that future. I am sorry for your loss."

A sigh of relief escaped Jarahad's lips, and he resumed his meal. "Thank you for your kind words. The mage also killed Jamad."

Unlike the first revelation, hearing Jamad's demise made Kashin promptly return to his façade of indifference. Perhaps it was because neither elf shared a close bond, so Jarahad didn't continue approaching the topic.

Kashin's mouth furrowed for a moment as he thought about something potentially dangerous or self-incriminating. Fighting against common sense, he whispered while a handkerchief covered his mouth. "Gulraj's magic could have saved the seer, and Tioja did nothing about it. He wanted her to die. Don't tell anyone else. Just keep it to yourself."

Emotions began to reignite deep within Jarahad. Tioja had the key to saving the seer and didn't share? Why? Jarahad had to calm down to avoid a bloodbath. There was no proof Gulraj possessed this ability or Tioja had nefarious plans. While his behavior during Talgel's funeral was insulting, chances are Tioja was too preoccupied with his father's demise to be in the right state of mind at the time. Judging from the gallant way Tioja fought against the mage without showing fear of death, asking for Gulraj's help was too much of a risk to be worth it. Jarahad lifted his head when the servants replaced the bowl of soup with the main dish: a potato and mushroom salad alongside an assortment of grilled vegetables. Curious, Jarahad turned toward Gulraj's chair, and he felt shocked. Gulraj and Tioja's assigned chairs remained empty. "Where could they be?"

This utterance ignited Kashin's attention, and a discreet squeak escaped his lips. A clang of metal echoed as Kashin released his fork and slumped on his chair.

Soon enough, Gulraj and an impassive Tioja sat on their chairs and began eating as if nothing had ever happened. Sharad spent his dinner telling Gulraj funny jokes to alleviate the mood, which felt like a good sign. For brief moments, even Tioja laughed. It was then Jarahad realized Tioja's bruised face had become healed and he ceased cowering in pain from his broken ribs. Chances are Kashin's claim that Gulraj could use curative magic was true. Despite the discovery, Jarahad didn't want to buy Kashin's accusation that Tioja let Talgel die on purpose. There was plenty of time to ask him the truth in private. Snickering was audible nearby, so Jarahad focused his attention on the four nobledemons that sat down at the same time as Kashin: three male, one female. He recognized one of the males who was named Teris. A halfling that was only a child when Orsenmuray fell who developed prominent combative abilities at a young age. Rumors are that he killed an opponent for the very first time at the tender young age of twelve.

Before dinner ended, Gulraj paced toward Kashin and stood behind him. The poor halfling froze at once. "Stay there, Kashin. I have a little gift for you."

Gulraj retrieved something from his pocket: A strange gold bell with a chain. Kashin's entire body trembled from fear as Gulraj bent very close and whispered something to his ear in Harlequin. "You know what the punishment is for lying to me. I forbid you to leave my city until the conditions are met. Bell of restraint, bind to thee."

The tips of the necklace flittered and snapped together like a magnet on Kashin's neck for a brief instant until it settled down. Kashin tried earnestly to remove a small tear from his eye with his napkin while Gulraj patted his shoulder.

Gulraj then focused his attention on Jarahad. "Your kin are welcome to stay in my city to rest. It has been a long voyage, and I must continue to think about your petition to use my demonic beast."

"I am appreciative of your hospitality, my Lord. Has my room been prepared?" Jarahad asked.

Gulraj shook his head and gave his back to him. As he began walking away, Gulraj's voice echoed loud and clear for everyone to hear. "The only person welcome to sleep in my palace is my brother Tioja. Neither you nor Sharad can stay here. My men will guide you to the exit."

As Gulraj marched away, Jarahad's heart sank from the announcement. His uncle was indeed as Tioja claimed: a wicked and cruel man with no loyalty to his family.

***

After the meeting, Jarahad accompanied Kashin through the streets of Murdorhiolan. Unlike Orsenmuray, this city was in a cavern with an elevated roof. It was immaculately clean, with a drainage system that surpassed even Almjarhad. "Lord Kashin, I am impressed with your new home. Jamen, don't you feel proud of your son?"

Jamen offered a kind pat on Kashin's shoulder, prompting him to cower in an automatic reflex. "Son?"

Kashin remained silent as he stared at the ground and paced through the throngs of inhabitants that gawked in awe at their visitors. Chances are, most of them had never seen a pureblood elf before. "Yes. Murdorhiolan is a grandiose city. It was designed by the halflings that you mentored over the years. If there was one thing that made our suffering in Almjarhad worthwhile, it was how you and your kin helped us learn the foundation of innovative masonry."

An equally vague and relatively self-explanatory response. This prompted Jarahad to shrug his shoulders as he watched Jamen make several stops to salute and speak to the handful of halflings and harlequins that abandoned Almjarhad several decades ago. At first sight, they seemed affable and most welcoming. There were no signs of disease or malnutrition among the city inhabitants. The pureblood harlequins were in equally good health, with no signs of anyone suffering from the rotting ailment that afflicted poor Hurrujat.

Even Jarahad spent a minute or two engaging in menial conversation with the citizens, but this only filled his heart with despair. Could he have done more? Perhaps tried being more convincing?

Jarahad cursed himself for his weakness. He should have begged Charon to initiate him when they lived in Orsenmuray. And now the clan will be split apart where Hurrujat's true heir gets to live in prosperity while the elves must grovel for Gulraj's help to defeat that monster.

Jamen smirked from the tension spewing on Jarahad's face and stopped talking to the citizens. "Lord Jarahad. You must trust Lord Gulraj. Maybe you never met him before, but he is your uncle. You are family."

"I…" Jarahad shook his head and sighed in defeat. Why did Gulraj behave in such a strange manner? Hurrujat never showed any degree of hostility towards him. And then there was Kashin, a halfling that became lured by Hamara's empty promises and got what he wanted: money, power, and his own sword. In all respects, Kashin should have been overjoyed to see his father alive and well despite everything, but he spent his time trying to coax him to continue walking. Something was wrong. "Lord Kashin."

"Uh… yes?"

"When we reach your home, I would like to have a private word with you," Jarahad said.

Kashin's red eyes shimmered from the request. Undoubtedly, he wanted to reveal Gulraj's ulterior motives in a more private setting. After a lot of insistence, Kashin convinced his father to accompany him to his gigantic monstrosity of a palace.

At first, Jarahad found it quite odd that Murdorhiolan was so surprisingly devoid of dwellings. From the size of Kashin's palace, Jarahad felt marveled at the star-shaped cylindrical stone buildings with glowing lichen balconies and pools with fish whose exoskeletons glowed various hues.

Even with the darkness, Kashin's home was magnificent, which made Jarahad feel an increased desire to learn more about Murdorhiolan's new noble families.

Arriving at the front door, Kashin stepped backward and squeaked at the strangest sight: a young human woman with long brown hair in a braid, medium-dark skin, and elliptical eyes. The woman was dressed in a modest brown uniform and puckered a kiss on Kashin's cheek.

"Welcome home, my love."

Jamen gasped at once. "Kashin! You're married! And… she is…"

With a pleased demeanor, the woman hugged Kashin while he averted his gaze. "Who are these guests?"

Before Jarahad could ask the obvious, Kashin laughed intermittently in the hopes of not causing too much of a scene. "Linda, I want to present to you two very important inhabitants of Almjarhad: Lord Jarahad, who is the second interim ruler of the city, and my father, Jamen. This is Linda. She's…"

"Papa!"

To make things even stranger, a horde of several small halflings rushed towards Kashin and soon began a rather comical scene where they were all cajoling for his time and attention.

A small giggle escaped Jarahad's lips when he realized Kashin had indeed spent his years being very busy.

While Kashin seemed amused as he tried to beckon his half-dozen children to stand still, Jamen froze at the odd sight. "I… Kashin, why didn't you tell me you had children? Oh my, I'm now a grandfather once again! Amazing!"

"Please come inside." As Kashin offered a small tour of his magnificent palace, Linda was pacing a fair distance behind. Jarahad's eyes screened her even further, and realized she wasn't wearing a ring on her hand. He kept these suspicions to himself so that Jamen's wondrous reunion wasn't ruined.

Kashin's estate was an agglomeration of 5 semi-independent houses interconnected by long tunnels. At first, when they first arrived,

Jarahad only spotted a servant or two keeping things tidy and saluting the master. Eventually, as they crossed another corner, Jarahad saw from the window armed guards patrolling outside.

Kashin would sometimes offer brief glances in his direction as he pulled on the strange necklace that carried the gold bell.

Soon enough, servants opened several doors, and they reached a luxurious circular bedroom with violet-draped curtains and soft silk linen. The room even had a bookshelf, a small fountain, and a bathroom. The only thing missing were windows.

Jamen didn't seem to notice anything amiss as he plunged onto a lounge chair and soon had Kashin's children on his lap, asking him all sorts of inane questions about his life.

Linda was standing right next to the room's only exit. Intrigued and concerned, Jarahad approached Kashin, who stood far away. "Lord Kashin, is this going to be our room? It's rather odd that Lord Gulraj has not allowed me to reside in his venerable palace."

Kashin smirked from that comment.

Realizing he might have offended Gulraj, Jarahad bit his tongue. "I don't wish to sound unappreciative of his hospitality. I would like to know if I will share the same bed as Jamen. You do realize we are not related."

Linda giggled from afar.

Kashin spent most of his time staring at the four gold bracelets on his wrists. "Do you know what these are?"

Jarahad had his suspicions and knew part of the answer already. "Linda is neither your wife nor the mother of those children. Am I right?"

Kashin sighed. "Hamara knew my weakness. You must understand, my Lord. Walking in that miserable voyage, trying to build a new city only to be evicted repeatedly. I know what it felt like to live in the comforts of Orsenmuray and miss it. Yes, I was young and stupid. Beguiled about positive memories of my childhood and ignored the more… difficult aspects of harlequin society. As a fellow survivor of the second purge, I believe you will understand better than most why I abandoned Almjarhad."

Even though these excuses didn't convince Jarahad, he let Kashin continue his rant. "I made an oath to Hurrujat. Helped him build this place, and I was sent to train in another harlequin city when things became more stable. Tioja was brought here by Hamara when I was training elsewhere."

Jarahad noticed Linda was staring at him with a degree of sorrow on her face. There was something increasingly intriguing about her. "I see. Your successful initiation is proof of the devotion you now harbor toward this city. I... I know what it means to sacrifice everything. Trust me." Jarahad's hand grasped Kashin's shoulder, and the halfling controlled the urge to hold back his tears without saying a word. Jarahad then continued to voice his thoughts out loud. "When did you meet Linda?"

A timid smile etched on Kashin's lips for a brief instant. "Hurrujat selected 5 of us to train in three different cities, and we all inhabit our own palaces. I met Linda during my training, and our forbidden love increased over time. I told her the likelihood I would be allowed to wed her was low, but she remained optimistic."

"You have four bracelets. Did you seriously wed four women?"

"I promised Linda I would speak to Hurrujat. She is the true reason why I passed the final initiation. I was desperate to prove to Hurrujat I was loyal enough so that he could consider letting her become one of my wives." Without realizing it, Kashin's hands began rubbing the gold bracelets and grasped them tightly. "Did you know these things can't be removed? They are different from normal restriction collars. If two initiated clan leaders place them on the wrist of two initiated people, they become locked for life. I can't even touch Linda without their permission. Believe me; my wives know my weakness and like to exploit it."

Jarahad began to feel a pang of regret for the poor elf. Kashin would constantly smile at Linda, but it was useless. Despite the contentment from Kashin's new home, the throng of servants, and the respect he garnered in the city, not even his children gave him the solace he desired. "Can't you marry Linda? Boshi has a lot of wives."

"Haha, poor Boshi. I now understand how it feels to have so many wives demanding all your time and devotion. Believe me, harlequins are the most relentless of women. I suggest you should never marry one if you have the chance."

"Come on! Svetlana is a delight!"

"I…" Upon hearing that name, Kashin shook his head with defeat, and his hand touched the bell on his neck. "Yes, my mother is different. How is she?"

"Her age is catching up to her. She will remain safe in Soremin's temple. I promise."

"I see. Lord Jarahad, I believe you were mightily foolish to have come here to request Lord Gulraj's help."

"I know he doesn't want this city to be destroyed in a third purge from Master Salman. If Tioja cannot make him change his mind, I will pack our belongings and tell my father that we must abandon Almjarhad. There is no possible way we can defeat the mage with our current power."

"You are a fool."

"Huh?"

Before Jarahad knew it, the door was opened and Linda stood to the sidelines. Kashin's face blanched when he spotted four pureblood harlequin women wearing identical gold bracelets on their wrists. Jarahad knew who they were at once.

The children soon rushed towards their mothers and relayed Jamen's stories in Harlequin. Unsure of Kashin's strange behavior, Jarahad offered the elf a kind smile. This visit gave Jamen a certain degree of joy he had seldom experienced during his long life.

Kashin's four wives were young, with average beauty and varying heights and body complexions. They all wore beautiful dresses and dragged their black wings like capes. One of them was currently bald due to a recent shedding. They all snickered amongst each other and whispered menacing taunts to Kashin, who nodded with nervousness. From the looks of it, none of the wives realized Jarahad could understand their language. Whatever seemed to be troubling Kashin meant Jarahad had to be extra careful. There was a possibility Gulraj was planning on deceiving them.

Deciding to test the waters, Jarahad spoke aloud in the common human tongue. "Lord Kashin, as I said a few moments ago, where am I going to rest?"

One of the wives stood forward and crossed her arms. "Welcome Lord Jarahad to Murdorhiolan. My name is Golana, second wife of Lord Kashin. As you can see, you will not stay here."

Jamen soon showed overt disappointment. "Oh my! But Lord Gulraj told him he couldn't stay in his palace either!"

Another wife snickered. "I am Yurivia, third wife. Jarahad can stay in any part of the city under the condition it isn't inside Gulraj's palace or in your room. He could even leave the city if that is his desire."

"Huh?" Jarahad was soon getting nervous and looked at the hallway outside. Two armed guards were standing by the front entrance while Linda went to fetch something. "Can Jamen leave this building?"

Kashin interjected at once. "I am afraid he is my prisoner."

Jamen rushed towards his son with a shriek, but Golana was faster and aimed her harlequin sword at his neck. "Stand back, pureblood elf. I cannot hurt you. Lord Gulraj will have me decapitated and grant my husband the wife he has been dreaming of for ages."

"But what is wrong? I have never harmed Lord Gulraj or his father. Why are you locking me up in here?" Jamen bellowed.

Another wife snickered as she saw Linda pushing a wheeled service tray with small glass vials. Following behind were dozens of young women, both pureblood harlequins and halflings. They all wore absurdly skimpy robes of varying colors, faces imbued with makeup and intricate hairstyles. Some of them encircled the bed and giggled.

Soon enough, Linda closed the door to the room and offered Jamen one of the vials. The poor elf sniffed it and gagged. "Is this poison? Please, Kashin, I don't understand."

Jarahad soon tried to recall his conversation with Gulraj a while ago. "Gulraj knew about my human blood and didn't want anything from me." And then, his heart sunk in overt fear when he saw the horde of scantily clad women offering Jamen to lie on the soft bed. Horror dawned on his face. "Jamen, I am so, so, so sorry. Lord Gulraj has duped all of us."

"Huh? Lord Jarahad, what do you mean? I don't understand. Does he need something from me?"

Before a teary Kashin could speak, it was Linda who murmured. "Lord Gulraj wants Jamen to give him 100 children. Give him what he wants, and he will help you save Almjarhad."

CHAPTER 19 ♦ JARAHAD

As a token of respect to his father, Kashin did not allow the women to force themselves on Jamen until he was ready. Jarahad dragged the halfling into an adjacent room and shoved him against the wall. "Do you know the amount of suffering you are inflicting on your father? Jamen doesn't deserve this!"

Kashin knew it better than anyone and spent his time either clawing the bracelets on his wrists or the bell that dangled on his neck.

Feeling fed up with Kashin's evasiveness, Jarahad tried to yank the necklace. It was useless. "What in the hell is this?"

In that instant, a soft chime was audible from the device, and Kashin hollered once again in agonizing pain. "No! Please make it stop!"

"Tell me the truth, Kashin! It's the least you can do for your poor father, who is crying his heart out in that room!"

For the better portion of an hour, Kashin cried like a baby. From the shadows under the doorway, it was obvious his wives were overhearing everything in a conniving fashion. Jarahad formulated a plausible explanation. "That collar is like the bracelets, right? Gulraj put that stupid thing on your neck after we arrived and told you something."

"I can't say! It's too painful!"

"I order you to tell me everything, or I swear I will hurt Linda!"

"No! Don't you dare touch her!"

"Then tell me, dammit!"

Kashin collapsed on the ground and tried pulling the necklace off, but the chain was too small to fit through his neck. In a final act of desperation, Kashin drew his sword and tried sawing the necklace off in vain until he gave up. "The necklace has a powerful curse that is similar to the bracelets. Gulraj knows I am not fully loyal to him. Tioja accidentally enticed Hurrujat to wed his knights to the highest bidders in exchange for söma, but Gulraj could not awaken his mana. I always felt resentment towards Hurrujat for not letting me marry Linda when I had the chance, and now I must wait until one of my wives die."

"I know the bracelets keep you loyal to your wives. You still haven't answered my question. Tell me!"

Kashin sighed once again. "I am a prisoner of this city."

"Huh?"

"I swear I am telling you the truth. Gulraj knows I want to bolt out the door and return to Almjarhad. I would still be unable to sleep with Linda, and my children would have to stay here as Gulraj's hostages. For my dearest mother, I would consider the hefty price. I detest even thinking of the painful thing my father must do. If he complies without too much of a qualm, I promise never to say anything to Svetlana in case I see her again." To further prove his point, Kashin jingled the bell, but it remained silent. "The necklace I'm wearing is a bit like Boshi's curse. The bell rings at variable intervals as long as Jamen remains in this city. The closer I am to my father, the more frequently it chimes."

Incredulous, Jarahad touched the bell and felt magic that briefly made his harlequin tattoos glow. Kashin was telling the truth. "What happens when the bell rings?"

"My prison sentence is extended."

"What?" This time, Jarahad focused more on the bell and saw an inscription etched with harlequin magic. "I see a number two. Two days?"

"Dammit, I have barely seen my father, and my sentence is already two years?!"

Jarahad soon understood Kashin's punishment and began feeling decreased animosity towards him. While he disagreed with the halfling's selfishness, he could understand why he felt bitterness towards Hurrujat for forcing him to marry four demeaning women that exploited him for their amusement. If it wasn't because Jamen would suffer so much, Jarahad would feel sorry for the halfling. "I could try to reason with Gulraj and..." Kashin grasped Jarahad's arm firmly enough to twinge in pain. However, Jarahad remained adamant. "I know Gulraj is your master and you are honor bound to obey him. But he is my uncle. As Hurrujat's second heir, I also have the right to make decisions about this clan."

"Jarahad, no matter what you do, I urge you to never anger Master Gulraj. I beg of you to obey me for the sake of our friendship or whatever. If I am lucky, the pureblood elves will get their misdeed done soon, and maybe I'll be able to visit Almjarhad to see my mother one last time. Please!"

And then it was Kashin who gasped when he realized he said a tad bit too much and covered his mouth. Realizing he was being cornered, Jarahad lifted his trembling arm to punch Kashin in the face, only to avoid aggravating the situation even further at the last minute. "Does Gulraj plan to do this to Lord Sharad as well? The true Grey Clan Leader deserves respect!"

"Ha! Gulraj couldn't care less. All he sees are devices that will give him the halflings he wants. As a fellow halfling that can summon a demonic beast, you must understand Lord Gulraj's position. We don't have any pureblood elves to serve as mana donors!"

For once, Jarahad began understanding Gulraj's twisted point of view and sat alongside Kashin. It all made perfect sense. "Why doesn't Gulraj let me take the brunt of the punishment? If he wants mages, let me do it. I am unmarried and would not complain. Having human blood doesn't impede me from summoning a demonic beast!"

"I know how helpless you feel better than anyone. But you didn't see the despair on Gulraj's face when he watched his mother and Tioja summon their beasts. He only wants the same thing you do which is to protect our clans from harm. If Gulraj believes your human blood makes you unsuitable for the grim task, he will stop at nothing to get what he wants. I swear I will try to make my father's stay less miserable. Once Gulraj feels satisfied, you will all be able to return to Almjarhad and meddle with that mage for all I care. Whatever happens in this house will not be shared with anyone else. My mother doesn't have to know anything."

It was a painful realization. While Jarahad understood there wasn't much he could do, he still felt disgusted. Jarahad stood up and dusted his pants. "Fine. Don't let your wives get near Jamen. Try to explain Gulraj's reasons. If Jamen insists on staying true to his wife, I will barter a deal with Gulraj that will at least spare Jamen from any further humiliation. If you may excuse me, I wish to visit Sharad."

***

Kashin's comments regarding Jarahad's freedom of movement were true. The guards didn't even bat an eye when Jarahad stepped outside alongside Linda. As they walked across the city's wide streets in unbearable silence, Jarahad decided to allay his suspicions. "Can you speak the sacred elvish tongue?"

Linda smiled at him. "So, you discovered I am not a pureblood human. You are quite insightful."

Just as Jarahad suspected, Linda spoke Elvish with a heavy accent he couldn't pinpoint. Taking advantage that the streets were devoid of people so late at night, Linda felt it was safe to move her hair a bit and expose her pointed ears.

Linda covered her ears once again. "I try to keep a low profile so that other harlequins don't get any ideas. It would be preferable that you never speak to me in Elvish in front of the city's inhabitants. Most of the adults speak it fluently."

"Will you get harmed if anyone finds out?"

"I am not sure. I always suspected Kashin didn't want Master Gulraj to know because he might be tempted to marry me off even though I am not a member of his clan. If Jamen and the others cooperate and the clan births enough mages, Gulraj won't harm me."

The two stood still in front of a major avenue. Linda turned both directions beneath a lamp post that emitted a dim green light. It was hard to discern her eye color in the dark, albeit Jarahad suspected something else. "You're not a halfling either."

Linda turned around and smiled. "You're right. My mother is a pureblood elf merchant that became pregnant by fooling around, so to speak. She lived with one of the nomadic human tribes further south but soon grew homesick and brought me to the kingdom."

This tidbit of knowledge prompted Jarahad's legs to tremble from shock, and his hand unconsciously fumbled for his sword. His concerns were soon thwarted when Linda's hands pressed his wrist until he guarded his weapon.

"Kashin told me about his father's exile and reacted like you did when we first met. He even accused me of being a spy from the Elf Kingdom."

Jarahad sighed in relief. "Kashin was lucky he accompanied Jamen during one of his frequent business trips in the human villages and was spared the worst of the second purge. I apologize for his behavior and hope it didn't cause too many problems with the harlequins in the city where you first met."

Linda shook her head. "A member of my human tribe was a close friend of the clan leader. Kashin's teacher told him to stop saying nonsense, or else he would fail his initiation and risk Gulraj's wrath. He tried to ignore me for the better part of his training. That didn't stop him from finding excuses to bump into me when I visited the city to bring merchandise. He's quite endearing once you get past his rough exterior."

"I am quite surprised. I thought hybrid elves never wanted to leave the kingdom."

Linda shrugged her shoulders. "Even though I am a citizen and grew up bilingual, well… I didn't quite blend in." A frown soon etched on her face. "I think this is one of the things that made me feel attracted to Kashin. Pureblood elves all look the same, with pale skin and slender bodies. I also had a hard time growing up because there weren't any children to play with."

"No children? Really?" If Jarahad ever had the chance to return to Almjarhad, he would prod his father for more stories about the kingdom from now on.

Linda gawked at his reaction. "You didn't know children are a rarity in the kingdom?"

"I thought having children would make a lot of sense. It seems so unfathomable to me."

"My mother explained it has to do with their immortality. If you live long enough and never grow old, what's the rush to get married and have children? Elf society is rigid in many ways, but they don't have major qualms if you become a single parent."

"You don't sound like you missed the place."

"Well, I was arrested."

"What?"

"It was terrible. An Äimite guard showed up one day and accused me of being a member of your clan. I found the accusation to be complete rubbish. After they arrested my mum under false charges, it was the final straw from a long series of events."

"Oh, please don't tell me your mother was killed!"

With a sigh, Linda recovered her joyfulness. "She is still busy paying the lawyer's fees. They had to release us after she provided a legitimate birth certificate that absolved her, but I kept getting pestered for several months after being liberated. I applied for jobs, and nobody would hire me because they were worried about getting in trouble with the law. So, I ended up as a burden to my poor mother."

"Oh my! But you don't have ancestors from my clan!"

"The problem is that my mother doesn't even remember who my biological father is. She is a very liberal-thinking elf, and most nomadic human tribes don't have birth records. Half of them are illiterate. The harassment was the reason why I grew fed up living in the kingdom and left."

"What a terrible story. Have you ever returned?"

"The kingdom can't exactly arrest me for stopping by for a visit. I must put up with excessively long interviews with guards at the border to prove my innocence. My mother learned the hard way it was easier for her to camp near the border and convince the guards to let me in. For those reasons, I can't get a job in the kingdom. I only stay during the winter." After pilling her life story, Linda nearly collapsed on her knees in relief.

"Linda! Are you all right?"

"I'm fine. Feels great to lift this burden from my chest, and the excuse to speak to you in private couldn't have been better. But we must reach Sharad before the city's inhabitants suspect anything. Everyone knows I am somewhat engaged with Kashin, and it will cause him problems if people start having some ideas."

"I agree. Let's get there quickly. If we manage to liberate Almjarhad from that mage, you are welcome to visit us."

"I appreciate it."

The two hybrid elves crisscrossed the streets until they reached a similarly elegant palace on the other side of the city. Guards were standing at variable intervals and observed Jarahad with a mixture between boredom and bemusement. Nobody seemed hostile from his presence, which was a good sign. Linda stood in front of the front gate as the guards unlocked it.

Before Jarahad stepped inside, he turned around and realized Linda remained standing far away. "Aren't you coming with me?" Jarahad asked in the common human tongue to avoid unwanted attention.

Linda shook her head. "This is the palace of Lord Deshueila. He was still underage when he abandoned Almjarhad and became knighted somewhat recently. It was a pleasure to be your guide, and I bid you a good evening."

Knowing Jarahad had to continue the same ruse, he bowed at the woman with the same degree of indifference and marched inside. He couldn't pinpoint Deshueila's face. Chances are he was just another ordinary child that scrambled around the city, so they barely got to know each other. Deep inside, Jarahad couldn't harbor disdain for the underage halflings that moved to this city with their families. If any of them decided to return to Almjarhad as legal adults, he would always welcome them.

Waiting at the doorway was Deshueila himself. He was reasonably short with a thin face, sad-looking reddish glowing eyes, and dark grey hair in a mullet. His face had a burn scar on his upper right lip and some dark cracks on his skin. From the looks of it, the halfling would shed in a few weeks.

Deshueila saluted Jarahad without showing any emotions on his face. Just like Kashin, he had two gold bracelets on his arms. It was obvious either Gulraj or Hurrujat married off all the clan's highest-tiered nobledemons to ensure their loyalty.

"You probably don't remember me, Lord Jarahad. My name is Lord Deshueila, and I am the custodian of this castle. I will suppose you wish to spend the night here."

Jarahad scratched the back of his neck and shrugged. "I wanted to speak to Lord Sharad immediately."

"That can be arranged. I'll prepare your room so you may stay here for as long as you wish."

"I appreciate your hospitality."

"It is my deepest pleasure." Deshueila seemed rather polite, albeit characterized by a dryness to his mannerisms which was typical of pureblood harlequins. Jarahad supposed it reflected their harsh society.

"Is the elf visiting us so soon? Why did he come so late?" Standing in front of the circular staircase was a short harlequin woman wearing a bathrobe and fluffy slippers. She was wearing a gold bracelet on her left wrist.

Deshueila spoke in a soft voice. "Please be kind, Usana. Lord Jarahad is the clan's leader in his lordship's absence."

"Hush! The two of them should be residing in Gulraj's palace! Why would he insult us with such vile treatment?" Usana stammered.

Even though the woman was a tad bit too brash, Jarahad had to agree with her. "I found Lord Gulraj's behavior to be rather concerning."

Deshueila sighed. "Lord Jarahad, I apologize for my wife's rudeness. I also believe it was unfair to be housing you in my simple abode instead of Lord Gulraj's palace, where you belong."

"Do you know why he rejected us? Did I say something that insulted him?"

Deshueila shook his head and began his ascent. "It was an order by Tioja."

"What?!" Jarahad strode several stairs to catch up while Usana observed them from the first stair with a pursed lip. "Why would Tioja do that? What is going on?"

"I am honor bound to remain silent about Tioja's wishes and can't divulge everything. He has personal reasons for keeping you at arm's length, so you must accept it. I am glad to let you stay here for as long as you want, but Lord Sharad must remain imprisoned."

"Oh no! Is he…"

Before Jarahad could protest any further, they reached a bedroom door, and the guards stood far away to let him inside while Deshueila wandered elsewhere. Like Jamen's arrangement, the luxurious room had a large bed, trays of food, vials of liquid, and hordes of scantily clad women. The guests were giggling and conniving as the heated throbs of passion intertwined with the stench of sweat and metallic springs reached further highs until a shrill voice hollered: "Booyah!"

"Sharad?" Terrified of what was going on, Jarahad's trembling feet stumbled with each step, and the noise stopped.

"Would you like to wear a bathrobe, my Lord?"

Laughter echoed within the room as some women seated against the bed offered the blond elf ample space to stand up, fasten a silk robe and stretch his muscles. Unlike Jamen, Sharad was lifting his fists in the air and cheering. "Score!"

"Sharad?"

Sharad didn't seem bothered about Jarahad's presence and grabbed some grapes from a tray. His mouth made his unfathomable circular crunching noise as his way of eating food. Jarahad had never realized how obnoxious and unpredictable his cousin truly was.

"I know why you are bothered by all of this, Jarahad. Lord Deshueila and his two wives explained everything. They really are quite awesome people, you know. Great hosts, straightforward that I am supposed to be 'their prisoner'." Just as he said this, Sharad bent his index and middle fingers from both hands to prove his point.

"But you're a prisoner, my Lord! I was told you can't…." Jarahad's mouth opened agape as Sharad bridled past him, exited the room without stirring any attention, and soon returned with a bottle of champagne and two glass cups.

"My Lord, I would have been more than happy to have brought these for you. It is rude for you to be serving yourself, I…" A harlequin man chased after him.

"Sorry, Gus, you're a great butler. Here, have some fruit, and just let me do everything."

After evicting the confused butler, Sharad plopped on the nearest sofa, and a few women huddled on both sides. Sharad couldn't stop smiling as he served two glasses and offered one to Jarahad. "Take it. Don't worry. Deshueila would never poison any of us. If we suffer from any harm, he will be beheaded, and I believe he treasures the good life he has right now."

"Oh, Sharad, you're such a flirt!"

"Sharad, I feel so lucky to have been assigned to you!"

"Can we go again, sir?"

The sense of perplexion forced Jarahad to swallow his beverage in one gulp and leave the empty glass on the nearest table. "Just what is going on, Sharad?"

"I told you! Ugh, you always tell me I am the ninny with an attention deficit problem! Lord Deshueila and his wives told me I must give this clan 100 children to protect them from possible invaders."

"Well, yes. It's just that…." Turning around, Jarahad realized the women seemed rather at home with Sharad. "I thought you were… well… new to all of this."

Sharad served himself a second cup of champagne and swirled the liquid in circles to smell it with glee. "Why else would I become best buddies with those pirates and get my rad tattoo?"

"That is not a tattoo. It's a blue blob on your arm, and you squealed like a pig when you felt the first prick and chickened out."

"Small details, more like single dot tattoos are in, and women find me irresistible. I dunno. They think I am a good listener; you know. I joined the pirate gang to impress a girl, but things didn't quite work out. It was still a lot of fun riding the seas with those pals."

"What?" Jarahad wanted to scream at the top of his lungs from the fear Sharad had possibly broken laws in human nations, which could imperil Almjarhad even further. And yet here he was telling his fantastical life story to all these women without a care in the world. Jarahad had difficulty deciding whether his cousin was a master of manipulation or a lunatic.

Sharad soon realized Jarahad was still standing there. "Well, you sure are quite the party pooper. Maybe you'd like to get in on the fun as well? It will help you to relax!"

"No! I…" Jarahad shook his head and clenched his fists. "Are you enjoying this? Sleeping with these women knowing you won't be able to claim any of their children as your legitimate heir?"

One of the women began twirling Sharad's hair and nibbled on the jeweled earring on his right ear. "Yes, Sharad, what do you plan to do now? Will you stay here with me?"

"Sorry, gals. Um… look. All of you. I know it is weird and gross. None of you ladies are married, and neither am I. We are all in a sort of free arrangement. I need Lord Gulraj's magic to defeat the mage that is terrorizing Almjarhad because I sure can't defeat the bugger. He's scary, like, um… real bad. Jarahad hates him to pieces, and I agree that forcing yourself on someone is just not cool."

"The mage is attracted to you, Sharad?" Another woman asked.

"Nah, the guy has the hots for poor Jarahad here and well… My cousin said no thank you, and the guy took the rejection in the wrong way. Now we are enemies or something. Right, Jarahad?"

Ashamed because he wished the mage had not reacted the way he did, Jarahad was forced to agree. "I don't harbor negative opinions towards people that want to be with someone of their same gender. He could have just accepted my rejection with good stride and left us alone. And no, we…." Jarahad tried to hide those daunting feelings that burned inside his broken heart. Whether it was the strong emotions from the day or the alcohol, every negative thought about his current situation returned to the memories of her demise. "Talgel… My love is dead! He killed her! Why did he have to do that? Why didn't she predict his imminent arrival and warn us? Why????"

Feeling unsure of how to respond, the women stared at Sharad, who remained as aloof as always. Sharad finally spoke. "I'm glad that you are staying here with me, Jarahad. Gulraj could do something terrible if he saw you whimpering like that."

"Stop saying those things, dammit! The mage killed Talgel! And he murdered Tioja's father! The bastard! I… why doesn't anyone care about the lives he cruelly took away from all of us!? Dammit, I need an answer!"

With a sigh, Sharad savored his drink long enough for Jarahad to calm down. "The first step of grief is anger. You are on your way to making amends."

"Dammit with you, Sharad!"

"I reached acceptance a long time ago. But I read in the books that grief can bounce back and forth, and you might endure periods of sadness and denial. In your case, I think the riskiest one is to barter a deal with Gulraj in your present state. Tioja must have sent us here so that you don't screw it up."

"Huh?" And then, as Jarahad tried to control the urges of his repressed emotions that were finally spewing into the open, he dragged a chair, sat down, and stared at Sharad's blue eyes. "You are up to something."

"Me? Nah, I'm not that bright. We are facing a psychopathic mage with rejection issues who possesses an invincible magical device that nobody can beat. Tio grudgingly lets us accompany him here to ask for help. His crazy brother Lord Gulraj acts like a turd with us for unclear reasons, but he doesn't chop off our heads or kick us out. Next, Gulraj lets us stay in the best palaces in town with Tioja's help, so that you can get your act together."

"And you have to impregnate 100 women."

"Yeah, it's a tough job. But someone's got to do it so we can defeat the mage."

"What about Jamen? He's a hysterical mess because he doesn't want to cheat on his wife!"

Sharad's eyes sharpened, and his fingers swirled against the glass, imbuing the room with a soft musical tone that delighted the women. "I thought Gulraj only wanted bachelors to do this."

"Well, he has not only forced Jamen to cheat on his wife, but he also placed a leash on Kashin's neck to punish him for some misdeed!"

Intrigued, Sharad stared at the woman seated to his left. "Mako, does Gulraj want the kids like... right now?"

Mako was a halfling that Jarahad scantly remembered seeing in Almjarhad during one of Soremin's many marriage dissolution ceremonies. She had a cute button nose, freckles on her flat face, and spoke with a squeaky voice. "Lord Gulraj only said he wants 100 women to get pregnant.

The command sounded vague. I believe he is demanding so many pregnancies by anticipating any miscarriages or preterm births."

Soon enough, Jarahad screeched upon being surrounded by the rest of Sharad's concubines as they spoke amongst each other in a blend of Elvish and Harlequin. Contrary to his initial concerns, they all seemed concerned about Jamen's situation.

"Yeah, forcing a dutifully married man to do this isn't nice."

"But they need Master Gulraj's sorcery to save their city!"

"Master Gulraj doesn't use his beast to help others."

"Maybe he has something in mind?"

"But our clan needs mana donors! We don't have any pureblood elves!"

Jarahad's head was about to spin after listening to so many opposing voices.

Fed up, Sharad tapped the glass bottle against the table with a spoon, and the room fell silent. "Ladies, I think we have heard more than enough gossip. Maybe you want to go to bed, and we'll continue the fun early tomorrow."

"Okay, my Lord!"

"Don't forget, you have a date with me!"

Sharad kissed each woman on the cheek as they giggled and waved goodbye.

Jarahad would never comprehend how the elf could understand the opposite sex so well. It was mind-boggling. "Well, now we're alone."

"I have a plan, Lord Jarahad. You must come with me to the palace and ask for Gulraj's permission."

"Kashin already told me Jamen will not be liberated until he complies. I am certain the other three hostages must do the same. It is doubtful they are being as cooperative as you are."

"Maybe yes, maybe no. They are bachelors, so it isn't too much of an issue. Jamen is the problem here. As his friends, we must set things right before it is too late." For the rest of the evening, Sharad whispered a clever plan to Jarahad's ear, and he soon felt emboldened by it. There were no guarantees it would ever work. But if they offered Gulraj a deal he couldn't reject, they might be able to leave the city even sooner than expected.

CHAPTER 20 ♦ TIOJA

The instant Tioja closed the door and ushered the visitors away, a tear fell from his eye that he wiped with his sleeve. He couldn't show weakness in front of his younger brother.

A cruel chuckle from the other side of the room meant it was too late. Gulraj stood at a fair distance as he admired a familiar sword. "The harlequin clan that initiated me thought I was a heretic when they found out I bonded with Hamara's sword. Do you feel jealous that I got away with it?"

Knowing this was just another one of Gulraj's plentiful mind games; Tioja remained ambivalent and shook his head. "You are the most adequate person to inherit your mother's possession. Take good care of it, brother."

From the smirk on Gulraj's face, it meant Tioja had won this battle. Gulraj guarded the weapon and stared at the departing refugees from a window. "You know what I will do to these elves now that they are my hostages."

"You are only doing this to punish me."

"Why did you tell me to kick out Sharad and Jarahad?"

Tioja's hand trembled for a moment. "I don't want them to discover what you did to Toby."

A cruel grin invaded Gulraj's face. "I always found it endearing you gave that sniveling slave a name. A part of me wanted to kill him the instant you returned home after failing your initiation. Lazarius was adamant Toby had to become your burden as proof of your failure. Aren't you glad he is no longer wandering around?"

The voiding sensation in the pit of Tioja's stomach had returned. Jarahad might feel anger for being kicked out of Gulraj's palace, but it was for the best. "Yes, brother. I am very happy Toby is no longer walking around in your grandiose city that we once ruled together."

Feeling pleased, Gulraj walked away. "What do you plan to do once I get what I want?"

"I have not yet made my decision."

"Very well. I order you to remain within the premises of my palace. I don't want you lingering around."

"I shall obey my master's desires and wish you a good night."

Sleep became elusive as Tioja twisted and turned in his bed. The anguish, the screams, this was the reason why he feared returning to Murdorhiolan. The memories continued to haunt him, but he had no other choice. Gulraj's demonic beast was his only hope to save Almjarhad from the mage.

The next morning, Tioja woke up in the bedroom he used to share with Gulraj and his heart sunk after seeing the glowing jewels adorning the walls. Out of habit, he began to count them in silence and a tear fell from his eye when he reached 7465. "They are all accounted for."

Such a sense of familiarity was distressing. Even though Gulraj already had several children with his myriad of concubines, he never allowed anyone to reside in this specific bedroom. It was an obvious sign Gulraj would do everything in his power to convince him to stay.

Due to his oath of honor, Tioja was forced to spend most of his day alongside Gulraj. Whether it was sharing food on the table or his lengthily throne room meetings, there was no need to wear a necklace like Kashin because Tioja's will was already crushed long ago. The one thing Gulraj didn't realize was that a lot of Tioja's submissiveness was a ruse to protect Jarahad and the others. If Gulraj wanted to hit someone, he would take the blow with a meek smile so that his friends remained unharmed. As long as they gave Gulraj the children he wants, they would be free to leave his city.

Gulraj was looking at paperwork in his office the following afternoon while Tioja helped him organize logbooks on the shelves. All five knights entered the room together. Lord Kashin's ashen expression and hunched shoulders were the greatest proof he had the worst news to deliver, whereas Deshueila, Kibito, Oshana and Teris stood with lifted faces and a firmer stride.

Gulraj stopped whatever he was doing and studied his knights with cruel intent. "Have the pureblood elves begun their deed?"

Deshueila stood first and nodded with his usual inexpressive face. "Lord Sharad began his duty the instant I informed him about the situation. He works very hard keeping the candidates satisfied and I am certain our first successful pregnancies will happen soon."

Gulraj's eyes softened at once. "I am very pleased. I expected Lord Sharad to give us trouble because I will now have a strong blood claim to the Grey Clan. Any false move from now on and I will be able to crush Almjarhad and rule their city as a proxy state. There is nothing Lord Jamarnid could do to stop me."

Tioja swallowed some saliva. Knowing his brother, he had taken great care in keeping a strict control of the bloodline registry of the city and selected the perfect candidates for Sharad's seed. Jarahad would have to tread very carefully from now on and never incite Gulraj's wrath.

Feeling pleased with Gulraj's approval, Deshueila stood back. The burly Kibito stood forward. Even though Hurrujat allowed any candidates with the capacity to summon a demonic beast to become his knights, Kibito's lower elf ancestry made him the weakest of the five. Aware of this defect, he tried extra hard to grovel on Gulraj's feet. "The elf I am watching over named Kukuro was hesitant at first. Lord Jarahad visited him the following day with a letter from Lord Sharad to only follow suit when he felt ready. I continued to plead with him to comply and right now he has begun to work."

While a bit concerning, Gulraj knew not everyone would be quite as cooperative as Sharad. "I hope your daughters become impregnated soon. They have so far proven to be useless. If they continue to be incapable of summoning a demonic beast, I will lower their nobility status."

Kibito swallowed some saliva. "My Master, I am aware of this problem. I wished I could have married a halfling, but my hands are tied due to your father's poor planning." Kibito's four bracelets glistened in the enclosure, and he stared at them with disgust.

The other knights whispered amongst each other for a moment, much to Gulraj's delight. He enjoyed seeing division and treachery among his nobledemons because it opened further weaknesses he could exploit. "Neither one of us can murder your wives, Kibito. It is part of the magic of the bracelets. I can only execute your wives if they commit treason. If you are lucky, you will someday become a widow and I'll arrange a marriage with one of Sharad's daughters so that your heirs get a blood claim to the Grey Clan as an apology for your troubles. Keep on offering Kukuro those potions to increase his endurance and fertility. I want all of them drinking the potion nonstop until they give me the children I want."

"Yes, my Lord!" Kibito then stood back.

As the only female of Hurrujat's knights, Oshana stood forward. Her face was devoid of beauty, with a rather asymmetrical bone structure and pocketed eyes that were too close together. Her curly hair was adorned with flower shaped jewels that granted her an unusual blend between warrior and femininity. "My hostage is the same. Imano had a hard time copulating with one of my candidates. Claimed he last saw her when she was growing up in Almjarhad and felt disgusted he was touching a child. I was forced to slap him for disrespecting our city's adult citizens."

Tioja gasped at once and stood forward to protest. "You were ordered to treat the prisoners well! Touch Imano again and I will cut off your fingers!" Tioja soon cowered after finishing his little outburst. Oshana stood back and averted her gaze so that she didn't get punished.

Gulraj felt impressed. "I told you many times you have a great future waiting for you in my city. You understand the needs of our citizenry and are capable of following suit with your threats. I can't wait for you to embrace your harlequin blood."

Ashamed of enticing his brother's false hopes even further, Tioja returned to his duty accommodating the shelves. He even used air magic to remove dust so that his brother could ignore him, which seemed to work.

Teris stood forward. He was born in Orsenmuray and his battle-hardened face was proof he had ample experience fighting opponents. The proud halfling batted his wings for a moment and spoke in a commanding voice. "Guma has done his job pretty well. He asked me if we had rice wine to soften him up and I complied. I suggest we should try to barter shipments of this drink with our human contacts. If the elves get a taste of their home nation, the pleasant memories will make it easier for them to relax and finish their duty. The longer we keep them here, the higher the likelihood the mage will continue killing the survivors in Almjarhad. We can't risk losing more members of the sister clan."

Teris was always a good strategist and it was no wonder why Hurrujat was so eager to send him to train. He was capable of tempering Gulraj's whims thanks to his extensive life experiences after surviving the second purge. Chances are the rumor of his first kill at a young age was true.

Gulraj remained pensive for a while as he thought about Teris's concerns. "Yes, the citizens of Almjarhad are not safe. Tioja, I might be able to change my mind."

"Do you mean the part about forbidding the pureblood elves to live here?" Tioja asked.

"I am aware they made their choice when the clan split in half. But my father worked very hard to keep them alive and lost Orsenmuray because of it. If our clan breeds enough mages with the assistance of our hostages, I will offer them the chance to live here."

While the proposal seemed innocent at first and the 5 knights nodded in effusive agreement, Tioja had to avoid displaying concern. He kept his back against Gulraj and pretended to continue dusting the bookshelf. "With your magic, I am certain we will be able to defeat the mage. If you want, I will be more than happy to relay the good news to Jarahad. When we return to Almjarhad, he can invite everyone. I am certain Lord Jamarnid will say no."

"I don't care about that sniveling coward. If he had come with you to visit me, I would have been more than happy to cure his wounded body."

Tioja froze when he heard that. "You would do that for him?!"

The knights began laughing rather hysterically. Deshueila stood forward and knelt before Gulraj. "My Master, the scar on my face was done by a human's fire beast and it can't be healed with regular sorcery. I was waiting until I shed to get rid of it, but you have my blessing to show off in front of your brother."

Gulraj always loved to display his superior magic in front of an audience and who could be better than Tioja of all people! He strode forward with a cunning grin and imbued Deshueila with harlequin water sorcery. Even though the cracked wounds on Deshueila's skin didn't fully disappear, they were reduced in size. The nasty scar on his lip had vanished.

"Amazing! You… I believe you are the most gifted water mage to have ever been born, dear brother!"

Gulraj knelt in front of Tioja and caressed his face. "I know why you still feel angry at me after all these years. My magic has made me increasingly powerful. The more I use it, the more unstoppable I shall become. My city will not suffer the same fate as Orsenmuray. And it is all thanks to Kashin."

Tioja's face soon lost its luster, and he averted his gaze. He should have known better than to fall for Gulraj's taunts.

***

As the days passed, candidates started to miss their menses and would arrive single file into Gulraj's palace. It was Tioja's duty to scribble their medical findings in a logbook for safekeeping.

Not only was Gulraj capable of curing all sorts of physical wounds, but his miraculous hands could also sense a pregnancy even in its earliest stages. All he had to do was touch a woman's belly and maintain his focus for a few moments.

Mako was already having a difficult time with her constant belching and was only able to get examined after she finished drinking a malodorous green tonic. It only took a few moments before Gulraj's eyes glowed ever more intensely. "Congratulations, Mako. You are pregnant, with twins!"

The typically constrained Deshueila escaped a small cheer. "I dare say Lord Sharad is beyond impressive. How many children has he sired already?"

Tioja rested his quiver on the table. "I have registered 46 pregnancies in just 3 weeks. This is his third twin pregnancy."

Tears welled from Mako's eyes as she caressed her belly. "Can't we tell him a little white lie, my Lord? I would love to continue sleeping with him!"

Even though Gulraj's plan was cruel, he remained impassive from the request. "The answer is no. I cannot allow him to become your toy. I only want my 500 demonic beasts. Now that he has reached his part of the bargain, you will return home, visit me for frequent examinations and pray those two infants aren't born premature. If Lord Deshueila sees you sneaking into his estate, you will be arrested. Get out of here."

With a sigh, Mako rushed off while trying to contain her tears. Unlike Gulraj and Deshueila who were laughing at the sight, Tioja felt a mixture between relief and contained amusement.

"Tioja, continue writing on the logbook! We have yet another pregnancy from Lord Sharad!" Gulraj seethed.

"Yes, I will!" Due to clumsiness, an ink blot dyed the paper. Hopefully the mishap wouldn't irritate his brother too much.

Deshueila was most impressed as he saw another excited candidate run outside. He then brushed away a blood smear from the cracks in his forearm due to his impending shedding. "At the rate we are having success, Sharad will be reaching his 100 pregnancies in only another 3 weeks."

Gulraj didn't lift his head as he continued examining each woman. "Teris's prisoner has also done a marvelous job. Guma drinks those potions like water, and he might reach his 100 pregnancies sooner than Lord Sharad."

Deshueila nodded with regained indifference. "Ever since Lord Jarahad talked to those peasants, they started their duty. We might have 400 pregnancies in 2 months at the most."

Tioja's heart sunk. "Jamen hasn't started working. Brother please, I urge you to find a solution!"

"His vows are not my problem. Jamen must give me 100 children or else I won't help you. My decision is final."

***

It only took two weeks before Sharad and Guma reached their required 100 pregnancies at the very same time. After being liberated, Tioja welcomed both elves into the privacy of his bedroom alongside a determined Jarahad. For some strange reason, the three visitors were carrying several boxes and set them on his bed.

Intrigued, Tioja lifted his eyebrow and locked his bedroom door. "I apologize for everything, my dear friends. I didn't expect my brother to issue such a cruel command."

Sharad was too busy touching the jewels on the walls to really care. "I knew your brother was going to demand something in return. I believe we bartered a sweet deal."

"Huh?"

Guma stood before a perplexed Tioja. Unusually short for an elf, Guma had stubby platinum blond hair and crystalline blue eyes which offered a stark contrast between old age and youth. "At least Teris got me some rice wine. I discovered if you mix the wine with that virility potion, the flavor becomes rather good and that is how I finished my duty so quickly," Guma gloated.

Jarahad shuddered even thinking of it. "Let's get to business before someone alerts Gulraj we are trying to outsmart him. Tioja, I am aware your brother won't release Jamen."

Tioja's shoulders slouched at once. "I presumed my brother would demand a lot of gold and have constantly begged him to exempt Jamen from the punishment. It has been useless. If Jamen doesn't abide with the command, we will never defeat that dratted mage."

"I expected he would say that," Jarahad mumbled.

Before anyone could protest even further, Tioja spoke with a softer voice. "Gulraj changed his mind about offering asylum thanks to Teris's unwitting help. Jarahad can go to Almjarhad to fetch for the refugees anytime."

"Sharad and Guma are still imprisoned in this city?" Jarahad asked.

Tioja sighed. "Gulraj will rather say: they are being protected. Once he gets his 500 children, he will accomplish his side of the deal and we can all forget visiting this city for as long as we live."

Sharad approached the bed and opened the closest box. "Look, we all know Jamen will not break his vows. Gulraj won't let us leave and we can't wait another 50 years for Svetlana to perish from old age to convince Jamen to help us."

"I know! But..." Tioja squealed.

Before Tioja could complain any further, Sharad snatched a small glass vial from the box and offered it to him.

His reddish-green eyes glistened with wonder as he touched the ice-cold vial imbued with a whitish goop and someone's name scribbled on a tag. "What is this?"

Jarahad beamed at once. "We are giving your brother a valuable offer he can't refuse. This is the first shipment. Everyone knows a lot of those pregnancies will end up as miscarriages. Gulraj already gave us his word that we didn't have to wait until the 500 children were born. So, Sharad offered to give you 100 vials with his seed that Gulraj can use anytime."

Reality struck Tioja's battered soul and a sense of hope returned. "Amazing! You... how did you find the free time to do all of this?"

Sharad shrugged his shoulders. "Those virility potions taste like muck. But if you mix it with some rice wine, it works like a charm. The other box is compliments of Guma and the third box comes from Kukuro. Our little buddy Imano is still a bit busy with his task. If Gulraj accepts our counteroffer, I think we can convince Jamen to help us in exchange for staying true to his wife."

***

Tioja spent all night thinking about Jarahad's idea. Concerned about inciting Gulraj's paranoia, Tioja urged them to leave the boxes with the halflings. Even though he doubted Gulraj would rummage through Tioja's belongings, a scant trace of mana was emanating from each box due to a cooling incantation spell. This could warrant unwanted attention from his servants. Tioja rested on his bed and stared at the ceiling. It was clear Jamen would rather risk having the mage murder the remaining refugees instead of cheating on his wife. Sorrow filled Tioja's heart as he stood up, reached the jeweled wall, and used a memorized sequence of air magic that opened a secret lock to his safe. This crevice was the one and only part of the entire city that was off-limits to his brother. His trembling hand extracted a strand of grey hair and then a brown one.

When his mother died in flames that fateful day, the only thing that made the pain tolerable was finding a few strands of Hamara's hair in her hairbrush. Whenever Tioja felt heartsick, he would reassemble the clump of hair, separate it and he now had a small piece of his mother that he would treasure forever. His eyes then set upon Jamad's strand of hair. When Tioja first returned to Almjarhad and heard about Jamad's death, he was too stunned from Talgel's final fortune to process his father's demise. Now that Tioja had gained sufficient life experience, he now understood why Hamara abandoned him.

Concern over the wellbeing of the refugees irremediably made him think about being the sacrifice. Whenever they were alone, Gulraj would continue pestering him to select a different mortal candidate for his sorcery. When Tioja first confessed to Sharad about Gulraj's ability, he never expected Sharad was willing to sacrifice himself. Growing up, they were never close friends. In fact, Tioja barely even knew the kooky elf that was supposed to be his leader.

Was Sharad brave or foolish? Either possibility could be correct. It was unlikely Sharad was being suicidal on purpose. And then, another feeling crept deep inside. Sharad had never liberated Jamad from his community service sentence even after he abandoned the city. Could his offering have been a way to expiate his sins for indirectly causing Jamad's death?

No, out of the question! Jamad was a spiteful alcoholic that frequently bickered with his peers. As painful as it was to admit it, Jamad would have ended up antagonizing the mage over a petty squabble. Whether this was the reason why Sharad was willing to die for the city, his prior concerns about Talgel's premonition were allaying with each passing day.

However, this didn't mean Tioja was excited about being the sacrifice. Deep down, he felt morbidly terrified. Could he even do it? Sacrifice most of his lifespan or his mind? Once he obtained the secret towards destroying the calamity stone, would his mind even cooperate?

Tioja's failed initiation always dwelled on him. The one thing that brought him back to reality was recalling the smell. Talgel's body rotted for days while she fought to stay alive and give him his final fortune. The very same woman that ripped his family apart and had him expelled from Almjarhad. She was a heinous and spiteful person who preferred to suffer in agonizing pain over a swift death… just for him. Upon processing this thought, a small spark ignited deep inside of Tioja. Imano and Kukuro will soon fulfill their payment, but his grandfather Jamen would not.

With a final caress of the locks of hair from his dead parents, Tioja shut the safe and pulled a chair aside. He then placed an empty canvas, dabbled paint, and started painting. As the paint morphed itself on the canvas, Tioja wondered about Svetlana. Nurran once mentioned Talgel sometimes told Svetlana her fortune in utter secrecy. There must have been an ulterior motive for retaining the knowledge to herself. Talgel might have warned her Jamen was being forced to choose between sacrificing Almjarhad or his vows.

Stroke, shape, dry. Little by little, the once blank canvas transformed into the shape of Svetlana when she still had few grey hairs on her naturally black hair, a soft face, pointed ears that were so reminiscent of an elf, and her omnipresent smile. Yes, Tioja would offer his grandfather a symbol of what he was fighting for. Knowing Svetlana, she would forgive him if it meant the city could be saved.

By the time someone knocked on the door, Tioja was putting the finishing touches of his grandmother's glowing eyes. A frown imbued on his face due to frustration.

His conundrum was interrupted by a surprised Gulraj. "Who is she? A lover, perhaps?"

It took a ton of willpower to keep Tioja from giggling because Gulraj could take his reaction the wrong way. With a perfectly rehearsed act of self-restraint, Tioja remained outwardly emotionless as he continued painting. "This woman is my grandmother, Svetlana."

"Don't you think it is rather tasteless to display an image of the woman Jamen has to cheat on to regain his freedom? I am quite impressed by your cruelty."

Ignoring the thinly veiled taunt, Tioja sighed. "I want to improve her eyes. They don't glow… like our painting."

Knowing this would improve Gulraj's mood, the ruse worked like a charm. Gulraj strode outside and returned a few moments later with a small leather pouch. "This is made from our city's lichen. Mix it with your paint and make her eyes glow. I will even accompany you to Kashin's residence and gloat at Jamen's face."

Just as he promised, Tioja walked alongside Gulraj while servants carried the magically dried painting across the city. Upon their arrival, Tioja felt surprised to see the hordes of women that had to loiter in every available part of the building. Even odder was the sight of a frustrated Nurran wandering in the hallway.

The instant Nurran saw Gulraj, he bowed with politeness. Chances are Jarahad instructed him to keep his mouth shut whenever Gulraj was around. "My Lord, I am humbled by your visit."

Recalling the cause of Kashin's punishment, Gulraj couldn't avoid gloating like usual. "It is a pleasure to see you again, dear uncle. You look rather strong. I can't wait to see your demonic beast." A gulp escaped Nurran's throat, which amused Gulraj even more. "If the mage remains undefeated, I would be more than glad to accept you as a nobledemon of my city. I could offer you wealth and your very own harlequin sword. I will even sweeten the offer and let you choose your wives. So, how about it?"

Instead of blurting his answer immediately, Nurran's anguish was palpable as he stared at Tioja's stunned face. His bright red eyes preferred to focus on the painting. "Hey, is that my mum?"

Gulraj frowned from the blight, but chances are he already knew Nurran would say no from the start. If Gulraj felt offended by Nurran's carelessness, he kept these thoughts to himself.

The instant Tioja displayed the painting, excitement filled his uncle's face. "Wow! I never knew you could paint, Tio! You continue to impress me! She looks just like when I was a child."

Warmth embellished Tioja's cheeks. "Yes, grandma was always very good to me. I want to show it to Jamen immediately!"

Upon reaching the heavily guarded room, Tioja's heart sunk because Jamen was arguing with Kashin while his four obnoxious wives laughed.

Irate, Gulraj strode towards Kashin for not saluting him and slapped his face. The room fell into deathly silence.

Scared out of his wits, Jamen kowtowed before Gulraj at once. "I am so deeply apologetic for offending you!"

Instead of feeling pleased, Gulraj's boot pressed against Jamen's shoulder. "You are a disgrace to my blood, grandfather. My brother warned you I would not summon my demonic beast without getting something in exchange. Yet, you foolishly volunteered to come here anyways. Why haven't you started to work like the rest of them? Even Lord Sharad has fulfilled his duty, and I am pleased with his efforts."

"Brother! Leave him alone!"

Everyone gasped from Tioja's act of defiance. Even the belittled Kashin dared to lift his head.

Instead of feeling insulted, Gulraj approached him with an expression of awe in his face. "Why do you defy me? What are you hiding?"

Knowing this was the perfect chance to espouse Jarahad's clever plan, Tioja stood straight and stared at Gulraj's eyes. "Brother, how would you feel if your beloved father Hurrujat had been bullied to break his vows to our mother Hamara?" From the silence, it seemed like Tioja found a weakness in Gulraj that he could exploit. "Yes, we both know Hamara cheated on my dead father and used some wicked excuse to get away with it. Her actions hurt me. And I think if Hamara was still alive, she would feel the same way about you. Look, the real reason why I made this painting wasn't to humiliate my grandfather. It was to make you an offer you can't refuse."

"Huh? Do you plan to double-cross me, brother? Because you know the price."

"Oh, but what I offer you is much more valuable than punishing Jamen. I have reached an agreement with Lord Jarahad and the elves want to offer you their frozen seed for posterity."

"What?"

A snicker embellished Tioja's lip because he was winning this round. "Think about it. If you bully Jamen into having children, your 500 mortal halflings will eventually die from old age or in the battlefield. How long will they live? 300 years? 500 years? We still don't know the average lifespan of a halfling. If we eliminate the mage, the pureblood elves will continue to live in Almjarhad. You are honor bound to respect the friendship pact between both clans that was first enforced by your father. Don't forget I was present when Jarahad and Hurrujat shook hands and made an oath of assistance whenever our clans were in need."

Gulraj lifted in eyebrow with incredulity. "What are you getting with all of this?"

"I am no fool. My mother insisted I learned about harlequin society from the best tutors, and I understand the laws. Our clans agreed to come for aid at a time of need, but they never stated they had to assist each other more than once. If you don't accept this valuable counteroffer and keep on wasting our time even further, the remaining refugees in Almjarhad could either be murdered by the mage or the Eirmite guard. Now, imagine if your poor actions had Jamarnid killed. That act of clumsiness would reflect poorly upon you with the other harlequin clans. Your clan would be known as one that doesn't stand true to your promises and only try to exploit loopholes that are unfavorable to your supposed allies. Don't forget this city no longer has a sword master. Once the knights die, you will be the only initiated left. You can boast about your prowess using two swords all you want, but you will appear weak among the other clans. They could cease to offer you söma as well. How many of these 500 children will be unable to summon a demonic beast? 200? 100? You know from personal experience that some promising candidates may need söma to awaken their beast. Accept my counteroffer while you still can or risk ruining the clan. Your choice."

Gulraj thought about his limited prospects. He finally spoke after studying the beguiled expression on Jamen's face. "I would like to learn more about this offer of yours."

"Look, once these elves return to Almjarhad, they will no longer be under any moral grounds to help your clan a second time. While your clan gains 500 mages, we will only get a possible method to defeat the mage with zero guarantees it will work. Your clan is getting the better side of the deal. Even if we defeat the mage and save Almjarhad, Jarahad will have no reason to set foot in this city ever again."

"So, are you threatening me to risk my scant knights to fight against a pathetic human mage? When we have our own problems keeping the nearby human enclaves under control?"

"Now we are on the same page. Almjarhad needs pureblood elves to supply mana. You need your own mages to ward off invaders while trying to maintain friendly alliances with the other clans. Since I doubt Jarahad and the others will visit this city in the future, this leaves you back to square one. I want you to respect Jamen's vows. In exchange, we will give you vials of frozen seed that you can inseminate into your servant's bodies whenever you want. I am certain your sorcery can keep that seed preserved for centuries."

"When you talk about seed… how much are we talking about?"

"A generous 100 extra vials from Sharad, Imano, Kukuro and Gumi. Given my grandfather hasn't impregnated anyone; he will be expected to give you 200 vials. Don't you think this deal is acceptable?"

It took Gulraj a long time to process the information. He then stared at Jamen's eager face whose eyes glittered in agreement.

After pondering for a while, Gulraj spoke. "Yes, I like this idea. So, this is the reason why you made that painting. You planned on cornering me to a wall and predicted your grandfather would jack off to his heart's delight in front of this work of art. I suppose I could do that. But given we have zero guarantees inseminating my servants will work, I will only do it under two conditions."

"As long as I am allowed to become the recipient of your beast, I believe we have a deal."

Gulraj grinned because Tioja gave him a free pass to issue a beneficial demand. "Jamen must give me 400 vials to compensate for his failure. I want him drowning in those virility potions. And… I want 200 vials from you and Nurran. Both of you have demonic beasts and your seed will serve me well."

Tioja gulped at once and stared at an equally disconcerted Nurran.

Nurran was quick to answer. "Why would you choose me? I am just an ordinary peasant, and my phantom beast isn't really all that exciting. It is sort of gross."

"Let's just say I want to keep some cards in my hand in case you wish to return to my city sometime in the future."

While Nurran seemed agreeable enough as he shook Gulraj's hand, Tioja pondered for a moment. He knew his hopes of being initiated were ruined forever, and there were no guarantees he would survive Gulraj's magic. Despite the somewhat ridiculous counteroffer, Tioja stared at his grandfather who was already gulping the virility potions. From the expression on Jamen's face, it was obvious he wanted to return to Almjarhad before the mage killed anyone else. Even though Tioja knew he would regret this decision, he swallowed his pride, approached Gulraj, and hugged him.

Dismayed from Tioja's rare act of outwardly emotions, Gulraj only patted his shoulder with a frown. "You know I always honor my promises, dear brother. I just hope you don't regret this someday."

CHAPTER 21 ♦ JARAHAD

Feeling helpless was one of Jarahad's biggest pet peeves. Call it survivor's guilt or shame if you want. Wealth, respect, he didn't care about any of those things. It felt even more demeaning to know the brilliant plan that enticed Jamen to cooperate and keep Gulraj happy was devised by Sharad instead of him. None of this mattered in the long run. Imano finished impregnating his allotted women, the vials with seed were stored somewhere in Gulraj's castle and everyone was packing their belongings.

If anyone had told Jarahad what Gulraj planned to do before brandishing his demonic beast inside of Tioja, he would have called it heresy.

Jarahad and Tioja were accompanying a determined Gulraj through a disorientating series of hallways of his palace for some unexplained reason. There was something that vibed Jarahad the wrong way about Gulraj this evening. Ever since Tioja pinned Gulraj to a wall, Gulraj's behavior changed. Every evening, Jarahad was invited to have dinner in Gulraj's palace alongside the liberated pureblood elves. While Sharad innocently presumed Gulraj's hospitality harbored good intentions, something felt wrong. Gulraj was a capable actor and could feign laughter, but the ruse didn't work on him. Maybe being raised by an Äimite guard taught Jarahad a thing or two about reading the body language of your peers. Gulraj would sometimes pull his eating utensils away and furrow his brows in between bouts of rehearsed politeness. While Jarahad avoided speaking to Tioja in private about his suspicions, there were signs Tioja remained unconvinced by the charade as well.

Presuming this mysterious meeting was for an innocuous purpose, both siblings were engaged in a menial conversation that offered zero hints about Gulraj's motives. Just when Jarahad started to relax, Gulraj took an unexpected turn to the left. He then descended a nondescript staircase. For some reason, Tioja's voice stuttered and thus began a nonstop series of pleadings in Harlequin that went ignored.

Was Gulraj bringing them to a dungeon? Nonsense. Tioja seemed confident Gulraj was honor bound to respect Hurrujat's pact. As far as

Jarahad knew, Sharad remained in the lounge room along with the remainder of his entourage. Even Nurran was free to return home. Chances are, Gulraj only offered Nurran to become a knight for his own personal entertainment, knowing the halfling would decline his offer all along. Jamen ceased to remain under speaking terms with Kashin and it was poor Nurran who had to relay messages. Linda would frequently coax Jamen to forgive his son's actions to no avail. This was not Jarahad's business and so he tried to avoid getting involved. The only thing he knew was that Kashin's bell had chimed approximately 50 times. His only hopes of seeing Svetlana one last time would require her to travel to Murdorhiolan. This prospect sounded unlikely given Jamen's ordeal.

Tioja's jitters increased a notch with each step into the underground levels of the palace. Before Jarahad realized it, a few drops of sweat beaded from his temples. Was it nervousness? No… it was heat. For some reason, the series of locked metallic doors gave way into an increasingly heated and malodorous section of the palace. This intrigued Jarahad because he knew Murdorhiolan's sewage system was impeccable. Soon enough, Tioja began a pitiable display of tugging Gulraj's robes in vain while the harlequin continued berating him and marching on.

Whenever Tioja turned in Jarahad's direction, Jarahad espoused a brief smile to cheer him up, only to increase Tioja's despair. For what reason, Jarahad was soon to find out.

Gulraj finally stopped in front of a final door and turned around with a sinister grin on his face. "You have been a wonderful guest. I feel honored to have spent some time with you, Lord Jarahad. As you know, I have pleaded with my brother for countless days to reject being the sacrifice. He is adamant in accepting the risk. I am indeed most jealous of you."

"Why would you feel jealous of an exiled hybrid elf like me? Your father never wanted me to become his heir," Jarahad said.

The grin on Gulraj's face increased a notch. "Nonsense. You indeed have many talents, but wit is not one of them. You see, I have offered my beloved brother everything he could ever want. Yet, he prefers to live with the elves that exiled him. I don't know what kind of mind control you possess to command such a degree of loyalty from my own blood. But I dare say it is admirable. I will presume you know a little bit about my phantom beast."

Despite the commotion, Jarahad remained unfazed. "Before the seer passed away from her wounds, she told me her demonic beast is named the Giltemarraj and it caused her great agony."

"Oh, I find this tidbit of knowledge to be most interesting. So that explains why I have... sightseeing capabilities." Gulraj's sneer creased to the fullness of his handsome face.

Tioja continued pulling Gulraj's sleeves and screeched even louder. "Brother, I have not betrayed your clan! They need our help! I gave you my seed, for crying out loud!"

Jarahad ignored the spectacle as he spoke. "I would believe your beast works differently. Talgel couldn't select her target or demand useful predictions at will. She seldom ever saw my future for some odd reason."

"Or perhaps she withheld it to make your life even more miserable than it already is," Gulraj seethed with pleasure.

Jarahad evaded Gulraj's latest failed gaslighting attempt by answering with a coarser tone of voice. "Perhaps. Or chances are informing me about my future ahead of time would be pointless. She sometimes did this to plenty of targets because the most desirable outcome would happen anyways. For whatever reason, she chose her final client to be Tioja. You have no idea how much she suffered to stay alive and offer him his fortune. And therefore, Tioja is here tonight to accept your beast."

"Even if he knows he could be dead in just a few weeks?"

Tioja's hands let go with a tremble. "Or become insane. Brother, stop this madness! You have my seed. My bloodline is now your property, and you can raise those children to become what I will never be. I love you so much, but I need to defeat the mage. Please, let's go upstairs and let the gods decide whether I live or die."

After hearing Tioja's heartfelt confession, Gulraj's hand nestled on the doorknob to the mysterious door and stood still for a moment. Much to Tioja's dismay, it twisted and creaked open. "I need mana."

"Wait! Brother!" Tioja tried to chase after Gulraj, but it was fruitless.

Before Jarahad knew it, they were inside a gigantic cavern that was imbued with a potent stench of human filth and the clattering of metal. Chains? Was Gulraj going to imprison him for some twisted reason? His own nephew?

"Brother, I'll give you my mana! Don't show it to him!" Tioja pleaded.

Gulraj spoke with a sinister tone. "In case you are wondering Jarahad, you are not going to be arrested. Lord Sharad and the other volunteers are free to leave as well. I will presume you know that my brother failed his initiation."

A shocking revelation that intrigued Jarahad. It always seemed rather odd Tioja did not inherit his deceased mother's sword. On the contrary, Gulraj was the very first initiate he ever met that carried two harlequin weapons at the same time. "Tioja was initiated? He is no bloodthirsty murderer like…"

It was the first time Gulraj cackled in Jarahad's presence, and the sound made his body freeze from terror. Up until now, Jarahad found Tioja's brother to be accommodating albeit somewhat brash, whereas this hidden aspect of the man was revolting. It was no wonder why Tioja ran back to Almjarhad when he had the chance.

Gulraj unsheathed Hamara's sword and it glowed into a light cyan hue. There was zero doubt Gulraj successfully bonded to the weapon. As soon as he proved his point, Gulraj guarded his weapon while ignoring Tioja's relentless pleas. "I made a foolish mistake a few years ago. I thought Tioja was mentally ready. His fencing skills were always pathetic, and I begged Lazarius to make an exception in the hopes his clan's sword master could unearth his nascent talent. While Tioja became good at hand combat and never flinched during his inking sessions, he proved to be unteachable in the sword. My brother then miserably failed to murder the sniveling slave child during his final test."

Upon hearing this announcement, Tioja ceased to tug Gulraj's robes and slumped his shoulders while tears welled into his eyes.

Jarahad remained adamant as he heard the bad news. "This would mean he has been inked. Can't he repeat the final test?"

Despite the well-intentioned comment, Tioja's eyes remained subdued while Gulraj laughed even harder. "My brother would have to bond with another weapon and get inked from the start, which would make zero sense because he could risk burning into pieces. Magical tattooing ink cannot be removed, and I doubt another sword would ever accept him. I was very lucky to find a way to conserve our alliance after Lazarius stormed into my palace alongside my brother. To compensate for losing face, I had to pay a hefty price in retribution."

Somehow, Jarahad started to understand the whole purpose of this visit and heard moans emanating from the holes in the ground. This was also the first time he noticed the entire cavern was covered from the floor to ceiling in metal sheets. A part of him wanted to run away from the madness upon realizing the purpose of this room. Gulraj grabbed his wrist and yanked him towards one of the holes. To say Jarahad expected to see the depravity of Tioja's brother beforehand was an understatement. Here he was: staring at an eight foot deep hole with a drain to wash away soiled human waste, taut chains dangling from the ceiling and a mutilated human child whimpering inside. A part of Jarahad knew this human was the embodiment of Tioja's failure and he collapsed on the ground as all remaining figment of hope for humanity washed away at the pitiable sight.

With a clever movement, Gulraj yanked a metal lever to the side and heat emanated from below. Knowing the signal, the child wailed incoherent noises of pain which hinted his tongue had been chopped off alongside his eyes and forearms. Mana invaded his body and a small air beast floated into the air. Gulraj seemed indifferent as he absorbed the phantom beast while the poor human's feet were constantly shifting due to the heated metallic flooring. Relentless clinking of chains echoed from below.

Feeling satisfied by proving a point, Gulraj switched the lever. It only took a few moments for the imprisoned human to collapse on the ground and rub his scorched feet against the filth on the drain until he passed out.

Horrified, Jarahad didn't even realize tears were spewing from his eyelids and it was little surprise Tioja cried in shame. Jarahad wished he could unsee all of this, and felt self-hatred because Gulraj got what he wanted.

Gulraj aimed back towards the door. "Since our clan doesn't have any pureblood elves, we need a constant source of mana donors. I was forced to reach an honor pact with Lazarius to keep Tioja's slave alive until his natural death as a symbol of our clan's failure. The blundering idiot didn't realize I found a loophole to exploit and have created this little mana farm. If you want some mana, feel free to activate the heating levers and the slaves will give you all the mana you need. I will be waiting for you in the lounge room. If any of you try to set them free, your cousin Sharad will die." With his misdeed done, Gulraj marched off and Jarahad was left alone with Tioja to share their equal misery.

CHAPTER 22 ♦ TIOJA

Tioja knew Gulraj wanted avenge his bold behavior from the other day. He initially presumed he would get a beating in private. Gulraj opted to humiliate him in front of Jarahad instead, which felt far more painful. Tioja had to set the record straight before Jarahad hated him forever.

Much to his surprise, Jarahad spoke first as he tried to stay strong. "I forbid you to hate yourself, Tioja. You should not feel guilty for failing your initiation!"

"Look at him, Jarahad! I did this! Toby has been condemned to a life sentence of misery. And now Gulraj will do the same to countless innocent humans to obtain mana!"

From the look on Jarahad's face, it was obvious the halfling felt tempted to insult Gulraj. It must have required every fiber of his being to stay quiet. "I will not divulge the truth to anyone without your permission. Remember what I told you when you were first threatened with exile: I am not afraid of you and believe in you. The only person that has lingering self-doubt is yourself. Seeing you battle against the mage with so much perseverance only made me feel confident in your capabilities. Furthermore, we can't do anything regarding this city. Any false move and Sharad or any of the other pureblood elves could be the ones trapped in one of these cells."

Consonant dissonance from the gravity of the truth collided within Tioja at once with such brutal force, the feeling of self-doubt evaporated in an instant. Jarahad not only believed in him. He also knew Gulraj would stop at nothing to capture the pureblood elves and harm them forever. The only thing stopping Gulraj was Hurrujat's unpaid honor debt and Tioja was just too stupid to figure things out. "Gulraj knows I will survive his beast. And once he uses it on me, he will have free reign to enslave the pureblood elves. I…"

Jarahad stood up and patted Tioja's head. "I don't think this will happen. So, wipe off your tears. If Sharad sees you simpering into the lounge room looking like this, you will be forced to confess everything. And

Gulraj will win."

A small chuckle escaped Tioja's lips. Jarahad was a master in outsmarting Gulraj's little mind games and would not give him the satisfaction he desired.

When they reached the hallway and closed the door, Jarahad decided to take this brief respite to make an inquiry that itched him for ages. "Maybe it would be a good time to explain what really happened to Gulraj's parents. Would you feel comfortable enough to share?"

The screams, the sadness. This was a memory Tioja preferred to forget. Perhaps he would never find a better chance to tell the truth. At least Jarahad was reliable and would keep the secret to the grave. And so, Tioja nodded in defeat. "Some halflings with Gulraj's blood purity can summon demonic beasts using söma. They still prove to be valuable assets despite producing limited amounts of mana. My brother was unable to awaken his beast. Hurrujat was now permanently bedridden, and time was running out. If Gulraj failed to prove he was a worthy mage, the city could collapse by an invasion. My mother was aware of this and coaxed the truth from her mentor."

"What truth?"

"There is a fail-proof method to extract the latent magic from a harlequin mage because it can be passed by blood."

"Huh? That doesn't make any sense!"

"Foolish Jarahad! You can summon a phantom beast thanks to Jamarnid! He gave you a small part of his magic and you might potentially pass it down to your offspring. This is the reason why harlequin mages can only pass their own element to their children. It's all in the blood!"

A small figment of realization appeared on Jarahad's face. "What happened next?"

"Hamara returned to Murdorhiolan looking both terrified and excited. She found a method that could extract her own magic and pass it to Gulraj. Knowing there was very little time left, she dragged my unwitting brother into a room and whispered the method into his ears. He was adamantly against it. And that is when medics barged inside to inform them that Hurrujat was about to die."

"Do you mean…?"

"Jarahad, you have no idea how insane my mother was! She just stopped caring about me, her husband or even herself! It is like she was obsessed with her son's legacy or something of the sort. I don't know if Talgel fed some lies into her head, but Hamara knew the price and was willing to pay it." At this point, Tioja's body was trembling as he rummaged into his pocket and caressed the braided locks of hair, a small treasure Gulraj would never feel capable of taking away.

"Tioja! Please tell me! What happened?"

"Fine. I will tell it to you in the hopes you take this knowledge to the grave."

And so, Tioja spent the next few minutes explaining to Jarahad about Kashin's festering hatred for being unable to marry Linda and the disdain he felt towards Tioja.

Jarahad remained pensive as he heard Tioja's side of the story. It was possible either Kashin or Linda talked to Jarahad in private and Tioja was only confirming the story's veracity.

A sigh escaped Tioja's lips. Knowing Jarahad would never divulge their conversation, it was a good opportunity to speak. "I deserve to receive Gulraj's beast."

"Huh? Tioja, you… I respect you for failing your initiation. Don't blame yourself for what happened to the child."

"If I don't tell you the truth now, then my mind might become too lost, and I'll lose my chance to make a confession." Before Jarahad could argue further, Tioja shook his head. "When Gulraj broke the wine glass and injured my grandfather, we reached my brother's office alongside his knights. Gulraj barked his knights to assign prison guards and the concubines that would get pregnant. After following the command, the knights returned. I remained in Gulraj's office and asked him about the handkerchief."

Jarahad lifted his eyebrow. "Gulraj injured him on purpose to place a blood spell on that bell. Right?"

With a sigh, Tioja nodded. "I recall Sharad stopped you before you made a scene. You were wise to keep your mouth shut. Before I delve further, you need to know that Gulraj wanted to meet Jamen for a long time. But Kashin didn't want anyone to discover Linda's true identity."

This took Jarahad by surprise. "You know Linda is a hybrid elf?"

Tioja grinned. "I have used my Lehart and saw her shadow. People with elf ancestry exude different qualities in their shadows and I never divulged the truth. Just because I don't get along very well with Kashin doesn't mean Linda deserves to be punished. I never expected Hurrujat to wed off Kashin to those horrid women to obtain söma and can't undo my mistake."

"That sounds reasonable. But what does this confession you are withholding have to do with your mother's death?"

"Once you see the big picture, you'll realize everything makes sense. In a nutshell, Kashin lied to my brother that he didn't get along with Jamen in the hopes of maintaining Linda's identity a secret. When Gulraj saw my grandfather standing in the crowd, he snatched some blood and tossed the handkerchief at my face when we were alone. He was testing me. Knowing how I felt about Kashin's betrayal, I said some hurtful words and Gulraj felt compelled to enchant the bell."

Jarahad sighed. "So, you confess that you harbor resentment towards Kashin for assisting your mother. And Gulraj interpreted your feelings as a free reign to punish him."

"Yes, that is true."

"Well, why don't you confess it to him? Kashin deserves to see his mother!"

"I hate him! He helped Gulraj murder my mom!"

"What?!"

A spate of dizziness imbued Tioja as he confessed the truth that was burning itself into the deepest recesses of his soul. The halfling's fingers twitched, churned, and clawed the stone walls until his legs gave up. Tioja didn't care what Jarahad thought about him at this point. At first, Tioja didn't want to receive Gulraj's beast at all costs. He felt angry for being manipulated by Talgel and scared of dying. Over the past few weeks, guilt ravaged within. These feelings overcame the last remaining figments of self-doubt that lingered inside. Without mattering what he would lose by entering contact with Gulraj's beast, Tioja hoped Jarahad would convince Svetlana to visit Kashin and expiate some of his sins. His soul was already condemned to damnation for playing the victim, maybe he could expiate his guilt by saving Almjarhad. It was the least he could do.

Instead of showing anger, Jarahad sat by his side, rested his head on Tioja's shoulder and patted his hair. A gurgle tried to escape Tioja's throat from the tears that begged for release. With well practiced restraint after living under Gulraj's thumb for several decades, Tioja inhaled with all his might and calmed down.

Jarahad spoke with a softer voice. "I forgive you. If we save Almjarhad, I'll try to remain under friendly terms with Gulraj so that Linda can visit us. With your permission, I'll tell Svetlana about this and hope she considers visiting Kashin. For your peace of mind."

"Thank you, my friend. I never had the chance to thank you for your training. You always wanted me to master my beast."

Jarahad patted Tioja's messy hair once again in a sign of acknowledgement. "Now that you feel more relaxed, tell me what happened to your mother."

Tioja lifted his head and stared at the nondescript ceiling. "Brace yourself. And no matter what happens, I forbid you to tell this to anyone else for as long as you live."

"I promise."

***

Tioja's mind returned to that evening when his young brother returned to his side sobbing his heart away. To know this would be the last time Gulraj would still retain his last figments of innocence felt worse than seeing Hamara's untimely death.

"Impossible! Gulraj, why are you sobbing? You're going to awaken your phantom beast! You should celebrate!"

A teenage Gulraj stared at Tioja with so much vitriol, his penetrating gaze could dig into your soul and claw it into pieces. "You don't understand it? Don't you? Hamara is mad! Mad I say!"

"But… Don't you want magic?"

Before Gulraj could say his true thoughts out loud, the door slammed open, and Kashin stared at both siblings. His eyes burned fire and his fists remained clenched to the point of bleeding. Whatever Hamara told him, it left him emboldened to follow suit. "Hurry up, Master Gulraj. Time is running out. If you don't say goodbye to your father, it will all be for nothing."

Unsure of his vague words, Tioja dragged his legs alongside his distraught brother through the familiar hallways. For unexplained reasons, there were no servants or guards anywhere. Tioja would discover years later Kashin took advantage of his authority as a knight and Hurrujat's political cousin to order some privacy.

They reached the door to Hurrujat's bedroom. Kashin fumbled into his pocket and grabbed a key. Without turning around, he spoke with a flat voice. "Master Gulraj, from this day forward, I will remain as your faithful servant. I will never abuse my position as your blood relative to defy your authority. My entire bloodline only lives to serve you. You have my word that nobody will interrupt your initiation."

And so, Kashin finished his cryptic oath and allowed both siblings inside. The first thing Tioja noticed was the penetrating smell. Mixed along with the fetid odors of Hurrujat's growth were assortments of complex herbs and potions that imbued the room with a pungent odor. Tioja was about to step inside, until his feet stopped in the very last minute. Someone scribbled unusual harlequin symbols with glowing chalk that pulsated on the ground.

Gulraj's sobs heightened even more as he saw his mother writing the final symbols to complete the rune. During the minutes Tioja spoke with Gulraj, Kashin helped Hamara pull Hurrujat's bed into the middle of the incantation circle and opened vials with the potions. With each symbol that was drawn, the drawing pulsated more strongly, along with Gulraj's incoherent whimpers.

As expected, Hurrujat was so delirious from his disease that he barely stirred from the commotion. No wonder Hamara was in such a rush!

Tioja and Gulraj stood by the entrance without knowing what to do. Hamara eventually turned around and smiled with cruel glee. "Yes, my beloved children are here. My blood, my heirs, the saviors of our people!"

Something was not quite right. Hamara's face twisted and contorted with expressions that didn't show sorrow about her husband's imminent death or concern about the future. No, she was beyond ecstatic. Her hopes and dreams for Gulraj's success depended on this moment. She was unstoppable. "The spell is ready. Tioja, stand where you are. Okay sweetie?"

"Uh… yes."

Without saying another word, Gulraj lifted his foot and was about to step inside the circle when Tioja grabbed his wrist. He didn't even know why. Only that he felt he would forever regret it if he didn't say his thoughts out loud. "Don't do it, Gulraj."

Before Gulraj could answer, Hamara stood up. Her feet strode and whisked Gulraj away.

"Brother! Don't do it! You still have a chance!"

It was in this moment that something inside Gulraj snapped. A delirious fear of the unknown enveloped him and he fought and wailed from his mother's embrace. "Tio's right! I can't do it! I can't!"

"Yes, you will! Gulraj, stop it! Your father is about to die! Perform the ritual before it's too late!"

"No!"

The instant Gulraj tried using his weak air magic to shove Hamara away, Kashin slammed the door open. "Hamara! You must hurry! I can hear voices outside!"

Faced without any better alternatives, Hamara nodded and closed her eyes. Soon enough, mana invaded her body. This was it. The last time she would summon her demonic beast ever again. To use it against her son. To protect her son. To save the clan. To condemn the world.

"I summon thee my phantom beast, the Demonic Doll Pirrum!"

From this day forward, Tioja will never know if the circle fully activated because of Hamara's magic, or it was sheer coincidence. The only thing he knew was Hamara covered Gulraj's unwitting body in her clay phantom beast. He wailed, struggled, and tried using his magic to repel it. Any attempts to escape were worthless as the clay covered his body and placed both of his parent's swords on each hand. They instantly reacted to his magic and glowed a cyan blue that illuminated the room.

Hurrujat's eye opened, and he muttered a series of words in Harlequin that Tioja surmised were insults of some sort. Not that it mattered. His attempts to enter the circle were thwarted by Kashin who held him in a tight embrace.

Taking advantage of her beast, Hamara's voice resonated inside of Gulraj's covered body and spoke an incantation spell. There was no turning back now.

"Gods, emerge from the pits of death. Be heralded by my prayer! I am a worthy child of the depths and deserve my gift. Pass me the blood of my ancestors and let me inherit their magic. Two lives for one life, from here and from now on!"

Beneath the layers of clay, Tioja could hear faint screams from his poor brother as Hamara mentally controlled his body and let him pierce the swords into the chest of his two parents. While Hurrujat flayed during his final moments, Hamara clung on and even shoved her sword deeper into her chest, hoping to fill it with as much of her life force as possible. Soon enough, a flicker of fire ignited from both swords and enveloped both of Gulraj's parents in a dalliance of blueish flames.

From now and forever, Tioja would always become haunted by the nightmares of Hamara's pleased face as she stared at her two children. Two siblings forever bonded by blood and would now share the traumatic experience of seeing their mother kill herself.

As the life began to vanish from Hamara's body, a cacophony of pounding exerted from the door. Servants became aware someone was using mana and were trying to get in.

Kashin only cackled with amusement. "Can you hear that, Tio? They think I betrayed your parents. But there is nothing they can do. Once the magic bonds and Master Gulraj ends up triumphant, I will be heralded as a hero. He will forever be indebted to me for giving him the throne he deserves. And I'll use his honor debt to finally wed the one woman I have ever loved!"

Tioja wanted to hate Kashin for those words. He would forever harbor these feelings and hoped Linda eventually gave up on ever marrying him. She deserved better. Watching your own mother die from manipulating your brother's body like a puppet changes you. You start to feel numb to any kind of pain. Nothing and nobody will ever cause you worse suffering for as long as you live. Hamara's eyes shifted from crimson, to pink, and finally to a pale greyish blue, an announcement of imminent death among halflings. Soon enough, the flames consumed her body while the swords Gulraj held absorbed their life force. Mana ceased to exert from Hamara's corpse that evaporated into a pile of ash alongside poor Hurrujat who barely stirred during his unwarranted death.

Cracks multiplied on the clay covering Gulraj as someone pounded the door until it finally opened. Hordes of guards swarmed inside, but there was nothing they could do at this point. Instead of stopping the ceremony or tampering with the incantation circle, everyone stood dumbfounded as the last remaining trickles of blood from Hamara and Hurrujat were lured into the glowing swords.

The sight was too mesmerizing to make anyone stop it. Tioja remained unable to escape Kashin's grasp as he saw both swords redirect this energy into Gulraj's hands. Billowing smoke and the stench of charring flesh barged into Gulraj's hands as the clay crumbled further. Little by little, more portions of Gulraj's body pulsated with charred heat and the remaining fragments of Hamara's phantom beast crumbled off his body. Like a piece of pottery in a kiln, what remained inside of this braised cocoon was no longer the person that Tioja knew as his kind and gentle brother.

No, something heinous had indeed happened. As the swords finished redirecting the stolen life force inside of Gulraj's body, he lifted both swords in the air and grinned. Even though Gulraj was not yet an initiate, both swords seemed to accept him in a strange sort of way. When the swords eventually returned to their dormant state, Gulraj turned around.

Upon seeing his face, Tioja had realized his brother had just died, along with his mother and adoptive father. What remained was a monster.

***

When Tioja finished his story, Jarahad remained stupefied. In a way, Tioja hoped he would have reacted with anger. "Well? Aren't you going to say something? Like why I didn't summon my Lehart and kill my mother while I still had the chance?"

This prompted a jerking movement and Jarahad pulled away. Both halflings stared at each other with befuddled expressions.

Jarahad finally sighed. "I'm speechless, that is all. I suspected something went wrong. Was your mother's suicide worth it?"

"Well, considering my brother can now summon a demonic beast, she would have felt proud."

"Gulraj changed, didn't he?"

"Yes. I already told you. He was the sweetest person you could have ever met. Even your father would have liked him. I…" Before Tioja accused his brother of turning into a murderous monster, he shut his eyes and lowered his voice to a subdued whisper. "My beloved brother died that day. I think it is no coincidence he summoned the exact same demonic beast as the seer. Maybe the demon pulled the strings of fate from the very start and Talgel was used for its ulterior purposes. That is what I believe."

After Jarahad remained in stunned silence for a while, he rested his back against the wall and processed Tioja's haunting tale. "Your story explains a lot of things."

"What do you mean?" Tioja asked.

"Talgel was never the same after she summoned her demonic beast for the very first time. Her eyes rotted away and never grew back. I always presumed her change of personality was a consequence of ending up blind. After hearing your confession, I believe it was that demonic beast. The Giltemarraj or whatever you call it did something to her, much the way it changed your younger brother."

While Tioja didn't quite understand the full extent of Jarahad's point of view, it didn't allay his hurt feelings. "Gulraj murdered our mother right in front of me and doesn't seem to care. Can't he return to the way he was? I understand my mother sacrificed her life for a noble reason, but... I miss him."

Jarahad didn't know what to say about all of this and finished rubbing his eyes until the remaining figments of sadness vanished from his face. "Maybe we will find a way to save Gulraj from his madness, Tioja. The only thing we can do now is to defeat the mage. If Talgel believes you are the chosen one, then so be it. You know that she has played with your life from the very start. Yet, you still wish to become the sacrifice to save Almjarhad. If you continue to insist on fulfilling her prophecy, then help me save Almjarhad before it is too late."

And with his brief speech said, Jarahad marched off leaving Tioja alone. Knowing there was no other way; Tioja grabbed every figment of sadness into a small little ball, stuffed it into the deepest recess of his mind and walked away. While Tioja felt great sadness for being unable to save poor Toby, there was little he could do at this point. The refugees on

Almjarhad could get murdered anytime and Tioja was the only person that could save them.

By the time Tioja reached the lounge room, everyone rushed in his direction and bowed with effusive politeness. They knew it must take an insurmountable degree of self-restraint to accept the hefty price of Gulraj's magic, and Tioja appreciated their gratitude. Judging from the inert expression on Gulraj's face, he was a master in hiding his emotions like a perfectly devised mask. Any visible traces of trying to gaslight Jarahad had vanished and were replaced by overt indifference. Chances are Gulraj knew he had truly lost his brother's loyalty forever and started to regret it.

None of this mattered. After engaging in some menial small talk with the volunteers and Gulraj's knights, everyone marched into the throne room and Gulraj stood in front of his throne. "Members of Almjarhad. I hereby accept your generous payment for helping my clan. Your debt to my father has been paid and I must fulfil my side of the pact. My clan will not assist in your battle against the mage. In exchange, the doors of my home are always open. You have my word."

With solace in his face, both brothers saw each other for perhaps the very last time. Lingering sorrow filled Tioja's heart, but there was no turning back. Whatever goodness that remained in Gulraj was lost forever, and it was now replaced by an empty vessel that housed his body. After accepting this harsh truth, an emboldened Tioja accepted the dagger in Gulraj's hand. Some of the pureblood elves gasped when Tioja sliced his own hand. He then returned it to his brother. After Gulraj cut his own right hand, mana invaded his body. "I summon thee my phantom beast, the Demonic Mind Giltemarraj!"

Tioja had seen Gulraj use his phantom beast on unwitting human criminals a handful of times. The sacrifice would remain in a catatonic state for a few minutes and then collapse on the ground forever changed.

It felt rather strange for Tioja to experience the beast beforehand. The instant both siblings clasped their bloodied hands and closed their eyes, Tioja saw the Giltemarraj floating in front of him. Could this be the beast that ruined Talgel and Gulraj? It was hard to tell. On all accounts, the beast didn't physically look as repulsive as Tioja initially presumed.

The beast spoke with an echoing voice that surrounded the perpetual darkness of his inner subconscious. "I am the beast that knows it all. Tell me your most inner desire and I shall give it to you."

Tioja knew what he wanted immediately. "Give me the secret to destroy the calamity stone. There is a human mage named Anduvio who has conquered Almjarhad. I want to know how to defeat him."

"Oh, this is quite an amusing request. The secret was sitting in front of you the whole time. You never realized it is your Lehart?"

Feeling somewhat insulted, Tioja shook his head and grumbled. "I have already tried to use my beast on him. The stone remains intact! Don't double-cross me!"

Espoused by sharp teeth, the demon grinned. "I will give you the truth you desperately want, and you will be capable of defeating the stone. In exchange, I have chosen to keep your mind."

Heaps of knowledge both immaterial and illogical shoved inside of Tioja's subconscious. No wonder the demon laughed upon hearing his request! The truth was sitting right in front of him the whole time. Tioja never realized he only had to use his Lehart in fast succession to crack the stone. Jarahad's sword would be more than capable of doing the rest. After receiving what he wanted, something changed in Tioja. Thoughts, thousands upon thousands of conflicting anxious thoughts and feelings invaded every inch of his mind. No longer shielded by the respite of silence, Tioja could hear senseless repetitive droning in his head. Anxious feelings of Gulraj hurling threats and insults, both real and imaginary. Cries, hopelessness, and a carnal desire of self-mutilation Tioja always hid deep inside. All these conflicting thoughts and desires reached the surface of his mind with abhorrent force. Blood, destroy, and change the world. As his field of vision began to recover upon waking up, the collision of obsessive terrifying thoughts remained forever imprinted as relentless as the humming of mosquitos. Tioja soon came to realize his mind had been ruined forever.

CHAPTER 23 ♦ JAMARNID

Four months had passed since the volunteers left the city and Jamarnid's hopes of seeing Jarahad and Sharad alive ever again were vanishing with each passing day. Seated on a chair within the safe confines of Soremin's temple, Jamarnid spent his day staring at the hordes of human invaders pillaging with Anduvio's blessing.

With great effort, Jamarnid convinced Henrietta to return to her home city and forget about Almjarhad's woes. Given the dire news about the city's imminent downfall and Jarahad's forced departure, it was likely Henrietta's father would suspend their engagement and wed her off to another husband to save his clan.

While Talgel's death ignited mixed feelings, Henrietta's departure spurred a small degree of sorrow in Jamarnid. If Jarahad returned with the method to defeat the mage, Jamarnid would personally accompany his son to Henrietta's city and allow her to live in Almjarhad permanently as an honored guest. In exchange for her services as an initiated warrior, Jamarnid was willing to offer technological assistance to her family as fair payment because their blood wine had helped the halflings so much.

A weary Soremin strode to the patio and his eyes watered in tears when he saw the pitiable crimes in the distance. "Those ruthless humans are stealing yet another one of Sharad's precious wooden tables."

"Ignore them. I prefer seeing those humans tossing our city's wares into their ships instead of terrorizing the survivors that are camping inside of your temple."

"They will soon run out of things to plunder, my Lord. I cannot stop them from entering these sacred grounds forever."

"I am aware your ploy of threatening them with eternal damnation in hell will only work with the feeblest thugs. But we need more time. Anduvio doesn't know how to detect harlequin magic and your priests have done a fabulous job thwarting any human that is foolish enough to try to enter these sacred grounds and kidnap the women."

A strong echo soon reverberated within both of their minds. *"Have some hope. The Chosen One will return."*

It still felt strange to sense Tanato's strange phantom beast that he awakened with Gulraj's söma. After Tioja and the others departed, Tanato eagerly performed the fast. He obtained his phantom beast the very instant he swallowed the potion. Whether or not his claims were true that he could now talk to both elf and harlequin gods, Tanato had found a clever solution to his newfound handicap. Tanato's telepathic beast seemed to become stronger with each passing day.

Soremin's stunned expression hinted something quite terrifying about Tanato's demonic beast that he was unwilling to share with Jamarnid for some unknown reason. Upon noticing the constrained look on Jamarnid's face, Soremin offered a brief smile. "I am starting to wonder if this was another one of Talgel's predictions. She must have offered Tioja's brother his fortune and told him to give us a bottle of söma on purpose."

Jamarnid grumbled. "I don't understand. Why would Gulraj bother to help us? He has never come by for a visit."

"There is still enough söma left for at least one more halfling," Soremin replied.

"Keep it in a safe place. Our clan urgently needs mages to try to drive away these pitiful human thugs, but I prefer to avoid aggravating the situation."

"You feel regret you can't defeat the mage. I urge you to stop feeling guilt." Taking advantage they were alone as a drizzle of rain fell from above, Soremin discreetly approached Jamarnid and their lips interlocked into a passionate, albeit brief kiss.

Ashamed of himself, Jamarnid averted his gaze and rubbed his lips with his sleeve. "I already told you to stop doing those things. We separated when I became invited to the guard, and I plan to remain celibate."

"I know serving the kingdom was your greatest desire. That doesn't erase the feelings I always harbored for you."

"Find someone else that makes you happy. Everyone that comes close to me dies."

"Except for me. Never forget you chose to keep me alive when we were forced to flee Teryoura Palace."

"And doing so caused Chandrice to become beheaded the instant we passed the border."

Soremin smiled. "I summoned my Hiratori to save Jarahad on the brink of time. I never blamed you for cheating on me with a woman."

Jamarnid espoused a brief smile that he quickly extinguished to save face. "I never knew what you saw in me. Serumo would have snapped in hysteria if he ever found out we were a couple at one point of my life."

"I would prefer to believe we never separated and were destined to continue together… If that is what you want."

"No, I don't. My romantic antics are what ruined the clan and killed our families. The least I can do to expiate my sin is by ceasing to be tempted by earthly desires."

"Jamarnid, I don't find you to be unattractive in your current state."

"Stop it, you fool. Your whimpering doesn't help us solve the problem we have with this idiotic human."

A conniving grin appeared on Soremin's lip. "Would you have felt the same way if I had left my hair long and commenced a fling with Anduvio?"

It always puzzled Jamarnid the reason why Soremin cut his hair after speaking to Talgel. He soon recalled Anduvio felt unattracted to Soremin and barely even spoke to him. To this day, Anduvio left the refugees unmolested in the temple and it began to dawn on Jamarnid. A small laugh escaped his lips that he miserably failed to hide. "Was Anduvio part of your fortune? Did you know he would arrive?"

"Talgel probably knew the truth and sacrificed her life to send

Tioja off to his impossible mission. I only knew this human would set his eyes on me and I had to prove my loyalty to you by cutting off my hair without telling the truth to anyone. I offer you my humblest apology for lying. Who could have known Anduvio would use his calamity stone to ransack our city and kill Jamad?"

"Dammit! We must defeat him and I... I..."

A soft thump was audible nearby. Both elves turned around and gasped upon seeing Tanato hopping towards them with his new crutch. While it filled Jamarnid with great pleasure to know the maimed halfling was still able to walk without too much difficulty, it was unlikely his condition would improve much further. Not that Tanato seemed to mind. On all accounts, ever since he summoned his phantom beast, the halfling had become beyond intolerable. His overzealous preaching had worsened tenfold with his new beast.

Tanato felt like his new voice that directly spoke into a target's mind was a more than perfect solution to all his life's problems. Even worse, it seemed like his immense talent made his mana last for ages without wearing him down. His face was smeared with a grin that espoused every inch of his face. *"Good morning, dear Lord Jamarnid and Head Priest Soremin. Today is another wonderful day as a gift of the gods. The sun god Zazarikut is immensely happy today!"*

"Zazazriwhat? Foolish child! That is not an elf god!" Jamarnid mumbled while unsuccessfully pronouncing the tongue-twister.

Tanato beamed even more. *"I feel pleased you never tell a lie in my presence, Lord Jamarnid. Words may be painful, but deceit hurts the feelings of the gods far more."*

Outsmarted once again, Jamarnid slouched his shoulders in defeat and sighed. "Did you see us together a moment ago?"

"Kissing? Oh, the harlequin gods believe in free love if you are not bound by the bonds of marriage. So yes, I am pleased to see your blossoming love firsthand." Adding salt to Jamarnid's pride, Tanato's red eyes were twinkling. If Jamarnid still had legs, he would have run off due to the embarrassment of being caught kissing his former lover in front of a gawking audience. The fact the witness

was someone as obnoxious as Tanato only worsened everything.

Not that Soremin seemed to care. His seagreen eyes focused on Tanato's face as some sort of unheard message was shared between both priests. After a moment, Soremin nodded in agreement and stared at the badlands near the mountains. "My Lord, Tanato has good news. A friend is approaching us."

"Huh? Is it my son?!" Jamarnid's hopes evaporated when the visitor was Henrietta. He almost fell from his chair at the odd sight.

Soon enough, hordes of refugees exited the safe confines of the temple and offered parasols to the harlequin that landed in an open space and fastened her blue travel cloak. After offering her gratitude, Henrietta approached Jamarnid with her usual carefree attitude.

Jamarnid shook his head. "Why did you come here, Henrietta? Almjarhad's problems are not your burden."

"I know. My father was adamant that I no longer had any business meddling with any of you now that it had fallen to a human mage. I am fed up being used as his pawn."

While both Tanato and Soremin were gloating in silence, this only annoyed Jamarnid even further. "Stupid woman! You risk being executed if you defy your father! Go find somewhere else to live!"

"No! I will not lose hope! Talgel… she…" A blush invaded Henrietta's face and she resisted the urge to cry. "I am honor bound to keep Talgel's sessions a secret until my death. While I always rejected Talgel's offers to know my own fortune, I know this is the day the Chosen One would return a second time. I want to offer him my sword."

It soon dawned on Jamarnid that Tanato seemed awfully perky chattering with Soremin for an unknown reason. Could Tanato have developed a sightseeing ability like Talgel? Nonsense. The fact Henrietta was dressed in fine armor instead of her favored dresses hinted she was adamant to fight the mage. "Is it true? Will Jarahad and the others return to my side? Are you going to risk your life fighting the mage against your father's wishes?"

Soon enough Tanato's voice reverberated into Jamarnid's mind. *"That is correct. I am having difficulty communicating with Tioja. His mind seems to be blocked for some reason. Jarahad and Sharad are conversing with me from far away. They seem to feel quite surprised about my new beast."*

As expected, Jamarnid became ecstatic and urged Soremin with a pleading voice. "Soremin, summon your Hiratori and enter meditation! Please confirm my son has returned!"

With a nod, Soremin's body was soon invaded by mana and his firebird shot towards the northeast. Soremin remained idle as he focused all his mental energy in controlling his beast in real time.

The instant the Hiratori flew away, several refugees arrived to see the commotion. "Why is Priest Soremin using his phantom beast?" "Is something wrong?"

Tanato's voice reverberated within everyone's minds. *"All is well. Lord Jarahad and the other volunteers are walking our way."*

Without caring about the consequences, one of the pureblood elves squealed in delight, summoned his phantom beast, and zipped away before anyone could stop him.

"Don't do it! Dratted fool!" Jamarnid's pleas went unheard by the elf whose beast followed the path of the little red firebird flapping away in the sky. Jamarnid huffed with annoyance. "Stupid Dorin. Always too hot-headed to obey my orders. I hope the mage doesn't become alerted by his phantom beast."

Minutes passed by with no news. Soremin stood idle like a statue with closed eyes as his mind remained synchronized with his phantom beast. The only hints something was amiss was from the grimace on his face. This prompted several refugees to murmur amongst each other.

Henrietta was about to flap her wings when Jamarnid shook his head. "Stay here in hiding, Henrietta. If the mage sees you flying around dressed in armor, he might feel threatened and kill you."

A harrumph escaped her lips. "But my Lord! I flew towards this temple with my wings and could feel his stone. Anduvio has remained in the palace the whole time."

"I don't deny you have a keen ability to sense where that dratted calamity stone is. A weakness we must keep to ourselves for a tactical advantage. But Anduvio can sense Soremin and Dorin's phantom beasts. I'm not worried about Soremin. If Anduvio blasts his Hiratori into pieces, it won't harm his real body."

Henrietta's face turned grave. "Dorin's life might be at risk. He must have reached Jarahad by now. Oh my! Jarahad and the other's lives might be in danger!"

A troubling prospect that heightened the tension even further. A burly halfling approached Jamarnid. "My Lord, the temple still has one horse that we never sold. I could travel on it and extract Dorin. If the news about Tioja's return is true, the mage must not see his face. Tioja bartered an agreement he would depart Almjarhad. If Dorin's beast lures Anduvio towards Tioja, anything can happen!"

Everyone shared similar concerns. Even though Jamarnid agreed full heartedly with the halfling, he would not risk anyone's life unless Soremin or Tanato relayed any information. Much to his dismay, Soremin remained in meditation without offering any hints, whereas Tanato's disturbing smile hinted he was too busy speaking to imaginary voices to care about earthly matters.

Soon enough, Soremin gasped for air, screamed at the top of his lungs, and collapsed on the ground.

"Soremin!" Jamarnid's first instincts upon seeing his closest friend and former lover fall to the ground and writhe with pain was to jump off his chair and assist him.

The priest heaved and whittled from pain for a few moments until he rested on his elbows with an irate grimace. "Who told Dorin to come chase after me?"

"Huh?" Haunted from the sight of the priest trembling nonstop with an ashen face, Jamarnid lurked in every direction. From the way

Soremin woke up looking unusually agitated, chances are someone attacked his phantom beast. The instant Jamarnid stared at Henrietta's horrified face, he realized something. Even though he couldn't feel the stone, Jamarnid's ability to detect regular magic helped him surmise the obvious. "Anduvio… is no longer in the palace. Isn't he?"

Soremin nodded between gasps of air. As emotionally tolling it would be to have your phantom beast ripped apart while in meditation, the unpleasant experience would not cause permanent damage to Soremin. Jamarnid didn't need to worry about him. The temptation to ask the halfling volunteer to travel towards the commotion increased with every passing second.

"It's too late," Tanato's voice spoke to everyone.

A deepening pit of despair filled Jamarnid's heart at the prospect Dorin's foolishness would spell the inevitable death of Sharad… and his beloved son. Haunting, horrible thoughts invaded his mind, only further reinforcing the negative feelings that everyone he could ever love ended up dying because of his actions.

Henrietta meanwhile stared ahead and relaxed her posture. After flapping her wings for a moment, she tucked them as a cape and stared at a group of people that slowly approached the temple.

The desire to avoid seeing Jarahad's corpse was soon overcome by a greater urge to discover what happened. Soon enough, an irate Anduvio paraded right toward the main entrance of the temple. Just like the prior times Jamarnid had seen Anduvio, he was wearing yet another ridiculous jester costume. On this occasion, Anduvio wore a mustard yellow suit alternated by black with diamond motifs. He wore a mustard yellow hat with two conical edges with bells at the tips. His annoyed grimace increased even further as he tossed something in front of Jamarnid: Dorin's severed head. Worried about what he planned to do, Jamarnid realized Anduvio was dragging an unwitting but still unscathed Tioja with his other hand.

"Tell your filthy elves they should ask me for permission to summon their phantom beasts from now on. This stupid man got what he deserved."

Another innocent life had been lost, and it filled Jamarnid with great despair. The only shining ray of hope was seeing Jarahad and the other weary volunteers unscathed. From his vantage point, it seemed like Tioja was still alive, albeit he offered no resistance when Anduvio tossed him next to the severed head.

"I told him not to return to Almjarhad and he broke his promise. The only reason why I have pardoned his life is because he has become mute. Must have ended up insane when he saw me murder that stupid elf. But he remains unwelcome in my city. If I ever see him lurking around, I will kill him." With a sinister grin, Anduvio winked at a reclusive Jarahad and walked away.

As the refugees arrived to assist Jarahad and the others, Jamarnid could only stare at poor Tioja, who huddled in a fetal position and clawed the soil. All hopes to save the city were lost.

CHAPTER 24 ♦ JAMARNID

That evening, a small funeral for Dorin was performed amid the relentless rain that covered the temple's patio with piles of muddy water. A demure Jarahad used his harlequin earth magic to quickly entomb the new deceased and helped his widow plant a new olive tree.

Poor Jarahad remained so focused on moving like an automaton that he never even bothered to see the almond tree on top of Talgel's tomb. Henrietta stood by Jamarnid's side and constantly blew her nose in between bouts of crying. Chances are she shared a good friendship with Dorin over the years and his unexpected death hit her hard.

Other refugees were too busy moving their scant belongings on elevated stone platforms due to the surprise storm to give Dorin's funeral much importance. Given the recent turn of events, there didn't seem to be much to celebrate. While the pureblood elves were devoid of injuries after their dangerous voyage, every volunteer changed in some way. Sharad's demeanor had become less exuberant than usual, which offered zero hints about what truly happened in Gulraj's city. The elf that seemed the most changed was Jamen, who preferred to speak to his wife in private the instant he returned.

Dragged to a temple hallway was Tioja, who cowered in a ball without paying attention to his surroundings. The only hint he was still alive was from a relentless urge to scratch the wooden supporting beam. Was seeing Dorin's death sufficient to break his spirit? Given Tioja always lived a very coddled childhood, chances are this was the first time he had experienced a truly traumatic experience. When things settled down, Jamarnid would demand his son for much-needed answers.

Morning arrived and Jarahad's dour mood didn't improve as they had a meager breakfast in a crowded room. Everyone's voices were muffled by the nonstop pounding of rain that hit against the ceiling.

Feeling fed up with the nonstop silence, Jamarnid shoved the spoon from the priest that was feeding him today and spoke. "Jarahad, I swear I didn't authorize Dorin to come barging to his death like that."

After a moment, Jarahad sighed and stared at his father's face. A veil of concern embellished his once beautiful features. "I know you would never risk our men like that. We have also lost our element of surprise."

In between mouthfuls, Sharad spoke with his mouth open. "What's the point? Ever since Tioja accepted Gulraj's phantom beast, he has never said anything coherent. If it hadn't been for my insisting, Tioja would have starved to death weeks ago."

Upon hearing the surprising comment, Jamarnid's green eyes glistened at once. "Is it true? Did Tioja's half-brother help you? I thought none of you had any gold to pay him!"

Jarahad grimaced at once. "Gulraj accepted something else, and the debt had been paid in full."

"Really? What was it?"

Both Jarahad and Sharad averted his gaze without telling the truth. This prompted Jamarnid to study this bodies further for much-needed answers. On all accounts, neither one of his relatives showed visible wounds on their bodies and they looked well fed. Their evasive behavior hinted the task they did was denigrating and it was preferable to change the subject. There were far more pressing matters right now. "Tioja was already catatonic before Dorin got killed?"

Jarahad sighed. "Yes. The night before our departure to Murdorhiolan, he confessed to me in private that his brother's phantom beast... changes the recipient."

"What blasphemy! Why would Tioja accept harming himself? What happened to him?" Jamarnid hollered.

"Father, I know you wish to control the situation and I respect you for trying to keep things in order. But Talgel was adamant that Tioja had to become the sacrifice."

Sharad scooped a mouthful of soup and spoke. "I told Tio that I was willing to trade his place, and Gulraj told me a flat no. None of this makes any sense! I expected Tio to become more focused, and now he is just some whimpering mush that toils around. To make matters worse, we have been traveling under nonstop rainfall the whole trip."

Jarahad crossed his arms. "I think Tio is waiting for something."

"Like what? To become sane?" Jamarnid asked.

Sharad shook his head. His finger pointed at the ceiling. "Tioja needs sunlight. That's what's wrong."

Jarahad grumbled. "Father, we must get Tioja out of this city. If Anduvio sees him again, he will not pardon his life like the last time. If the monsoon season has barely begun, then we will not have decent weather for another two months."

"We are running out of food and can't remain here for much longer."

Soremin who was overhearing the conversation spoke. "Would Gulraj grant us safe refuge while we wait for the rains to stop?"

Jarahad grimaced. "I am never setting foot in that accursed city ever again. The decision is final."

Jamarnid and Soremin stared at each other and shrugged their shoulders. Jamarnid then studied an equally flummoxed Sharad.

Sharad set his spoon on the table. "Jarahad, you must be civil. Gulraj made a promise he would let the refugees live with him. Now that Dorin has died, we have lost one more mage. I know you think he is a jerk, but you should suck your pride and ask him to offer asylum to the refugees. There is no other option."

A straining pound echoed on the table as Jarahad's clenched fists trembled from anger. "No! Don't believe his empty promises! Gulraj is our enemy!"

"Huh?" Jamarnid realized this conversation would get him nowhere and then stared at Henrietta who remained pensive as she ate her meal. "Miss Henrietta, you might be our only hope. Would your father agree to help us?"

Henrietta's immediate response was a sigh, which didn't ally anyone's concerns. "The price would be too high for Jarahad. My father will want everyone to live under his rule and for Jarahad to become my husband. The second he discovers the pureblood elves could serve as mana donors; they will be expected to become his servants forever. Maybe when my father dies from old age, Jarahad can grant them their freedom and return to Almjarhad. But dearest Jarahad, are you willing to say goodbye to this city? Will you agree to become my husband and rule my birth city for the rest of your life?"

This was an answer that only Jarahad could answer, and it hurt every fiber of his being. Either option seemed terrible, yet Jamarnid didn't know why his son was so adamantly against asking for Gulraj's help. Did Talgel do this on purpose out of spite? Was causing Jarahad utter misery her true intention all along? Knowing what a wretched creature she was, Jamarnid would not be surprised Talgel wanted Tioja to become incapacitated and force Jarahad to choose the lesser of two evils.

Sharad and Soremin waited for Jarahad's answer with impatience, whereas Henrietta espoused a forlorn expression. Even though it was clear she liked Jarahad as a friend, neither one of them were interested in marrying each other.

With a heavy heart, Jarahad garnered sufficient composure to speak. "Thank you for your honesty, Henrietta. I knew from the start your father would issue a heinous demand as payback for not marrying you sooner. How long would the pureblood elves become indebted to your father's service?"

Henrietta stared ahead. "My father is still rather young. The elves might remain imprisoned in his city for at least fifty years."

"Fifty?!" Sharad screeched at the grim thought of living in an underground city for so long, whereas Soremin sighed in defeat.

Knowing he would regret the decision, Jamarnid straightened his back. "If you and my son agree to this political marriage, I will agree to serve under your father until our honor debt is paid."

"No! I will not agree to any of this! I oppose!" Everyone turned around and saw a surprising sight. While clutching his weeping wife with tense fingers, an irate Jamen shook his head. "I am staying put in this city! After what Gulraj did to me, I swear I am never setting foot in another harlequin cesspit for as long as I live!"

***

The following day, tensions remained high as Jamarnid sat in the hallway. The downpour continued during the night, forcing almost every inch and cranny of the temple to be inhabited by weary refugees. If the weather didn't improve soon, the overcrowding might provoke a disease outbreak and even more lives could be lost.

Jamen's outburst deeply troubled Jamarnid. The elf was always mild-mannered, and it seemed surprising such a peaceful person could escape both purges in the first place. In all respects, Jamen never deserved to suffer so much. It was selfish of him to manipulate the lives of his city's inhabitants like they were mindless pawns.

Another option was to count their losses and found yet another city somewhere. If they could build Almjarhad once, they could do it again. There was only one thing stopping them: nobody had any money or horses left. Worse, traveling in the open would render them vulnerable to any Äimite Guard lurking around. And then, Jamarnid turned around and saw someone walking outside. Who would be foolish enough to get drenched in this weather?

The person stepping on puddles happened to be Tioja. For the first time since their arrival, Tioja seemed moderately aware of his surroundings and was cruising around while his left hand rummaged in his pocket. His facial expression was characterized by complete madness and incoherent mumbling escaped his lips as he talked to himself. Whatever words were being said, the rain muffled the sounds and Jamarnid had no idea what troubled the poor halfling.

Instead of approaching Jamad's tomb, Tioja frittered in circles and occasionally hugged himself. The last time Jamarnid saw Tioja, he was in complete control of his emotions. What could have happened that left him in such a state of disarray? Jamarnid soon recalled Sharad mention he was supposed to become Gulraj's sacrifice, only for the topic to divert towards Henrietta's father. To this day, Jamarnid had no idea what happened in Gulraj's city, and it was unlikely anyone would be in the mood to share their experience when tensions remained so high. His only hints were Jamen's abrasiveness and Tioja's disdain for common sense. If this is what Gulraj did to his own family, then it was proof living in Henrietta's birth city was their last hope.

"Aprisiado! Why is this cockroach still wandering in my lands?"

As if their ruinous fortune couldn't become worse, the one person Jamarnid didn't want to see today was barging towards Tioja dressed in another gaudy costume. A wrathful expression adorned the mage's face as his ridiculous red circus shoes squelched against the muddy soil. Walking straight for poor Tioja who remained oblivious to his impending doom.

"Don't you dare touch him!" Chasing after him with sheer determination was Jarahad. Foolish child!

Despair filled Jamarnid as he searched for a staircase to crawl to stop the ensuing bloodbath. There was no way in hell the murderous mage was going to kill his son!

Before Anduvio reached Tioja, Jarahad grabbed the mage's shoulder, and turned him around with violent force. Assuming this would be Jarahad's downfall as mana filled inside of Anduvio's body, the halfling did something completely out of character. While sucking his pride, Jarahad stared into Anduvio's brown eyes with a grim demeanor, caressed his lower back, and kissed him as rain poured everywhere.

Jamarnid was dumbfounded as he saw such an irrational display of affection. Was his son bisexual like himself? From the terseness on Jarahad's face, there were no hints he was enjoying this. In fact, he seemed moderately repulsed as be rubbed the mage's buttocks and twiddled with the hair in the back of his neck. Meanwhile, Anduvio was melting in his embrace and enjoying every minute of it. Jamarnid hunkered against a wooden beam as refugees gawked at the odd spectacle and reached an impasse. This was the reason why Jarahad didn't want to return to Gulraj's city! He was forced to sell his body! A vile sense of self-hatred filled within

Jamarnid's heart upon reaching this painful conclusion. Chances are, Gulraj pimped every member of the entourage in exchange for his help. Knowing this, it made sense why Jamen was so adamant against being near Gulraj. But if Jarahad's romancing was just a ruse, what could they do? Would Jarahad opt for being Anduvio's plaything to appease Jamen? Even more nonsense. On all accounts, serving Henrietta's father was a far better option than risking certain death at the hands of the mercurial mage.

After kissing each other for a surprisingly long amount of time, Tioja had already wandered out of sight when Jarahad opened his eyes. With a certain degree of theatrics, Jarahad lifted Anduvio's chin to stare at his face. If Jamarnid had known any better, it seemed obvious Jarahad was a capable actor and his ruse had worked. Jarahad said some flowery words to Anduvio that were hard to decipher, and Anduvio soon left with a dreamy smile.

After sighing in relief, Jarahad approached his father with a forlorn expression. Feeling embarrassed that so many refugees saw what he did, Jarahad averted their gaze. "I had to fool him to save Tioja's life."

Knowing how hard it must have been for Jarahad, Jamarnid patted his shoulder for encouragement. "You don't have to apologize to anyone."

Jarahad nodded. "Anduvio is giving me one day. If he sees Tioja lingering here tomorrow, he will kill everyone. Unless…"

"Unless what, son? Tell me!"

The emotions bottled within Jarahad crumbled down and he collapsed on the mud and cried his heart out. Consoling him in this state would be impossible.

A voice pierced inside of Jamarnid's head. It was Tanato. *"Anduvio wants to marry Jarahad. Or more like, claim him as his sex toy. He plans to kill all the women and elderly and enslave the men. Especially you, Jamarnid. Breaking your will is his greatest desire."*

Jamarnid gasped in overt fear from the message that was heard by everyone in the temple. His face sharpened with determination. "We have to evacuate this city!"

***

A meeting was prepared that afternoon. Tanato clawed his fingers against the table in a feeble attempt to continue using more mana. Realizing he could no longer use his beast to communicate, Tanato slumped his shoulders in defeat.

Not that anything mattered. Jamarnid was busy watching the small pureblood elf named Daedoman stitching leather straps together. "How much longer?"

Daedoman was neither friendly nor approachable. As the elf that always built Talgel's masquerade masks, his abilities creating dolls made him an unlikely option for this specific duty. The elf turned around and sneered. "I'm sewing as many straps as possible. There isn't enough leather for what you plan to do."

Sharad meanwhile was hacking off slabs of wood that had been stripped from spare closet doors and flooring. Jamen and another pureblood elf were working together hammering nails into previously cut pieces of wood.

Jarahad soon entered the room carrying jars of some material alongside a weary Henrietta.

She was busy drying her hair with a towel. "Whew! We are so lucky I could find a store in the nearby human city that sold this!"

Jamarnid studied the can with curiosity. "Henrietta fetched that in the city?"

Jarahad nodded as his hands caressed the chair Sharad was constructing. "We need glue and varnish to finish the saddle. Are you sure your plan will work?"

Jamarnid grinned. "You forget something, my boy. Äimite guards must learn how to extract every viable usage of our phantom beasts. I have never traveled on my Lusenia after losing my legs, but I have seen other guards build saddles during our training. We had to learn how to extract injured civilians from dangerous areas. Can the halflings use magic to dry the varnish on time?"

Jarahad spun his fingers and made a small tornado float into the air. "I might be more attuned to earth magic, but I dare say I am not a shabby air mage."

Henrietta sat next to Jarahad and rested her head against his shoulder. "Are you afraid of dying, Jarahad? Why fight against the mage tomorrow?"

Jarahad sighed. "Anduvio wants to kill half of the refugees and enslave the rest. Our only hopes are to barge out of this city while my father distracts him. My father's beast is very fast and Anduvio will eventually stop chasing after him. By the time he realizes he was duped, we will all be halfway to your birth city. It's the only way."

The plan was suicidal, but Jamarnid's pride was the only remaining trump card they had left. Even though nobody could beat Anduvio, the mage would never dare enter a harlequin enclave. From the way a grim Jamen was helping build the saddle, it meant he too had agreed to live in Henrietta's city and serve her father.

The following day, the weather remained dreadful. With every able-bodied elf and halfling dressed in armor, they stood in a large circle awaiting the inevitable. Jamarnid was wearing a more austere black shirt with short sleeves and pants that were sewed shut at the height on his stumps. His hair was fastened in a ponytail. After spending the better portion of the evening in meditation to focus his mind, Jamarnid nodded at his son. "When I summon my phantom beast, fasten that saddle on the beast and help me get on it. If Anduvio is half as smart as I think he is, we will only have a few minutes before he gives me the biggest scare of my life."

Unlike everyone else, Jarahad opted to remain shirtless which allowed a feastful sight of his toned abs. Given Jarahad could summon an armor that protected his body perfectly well, he hoped the increased mobility and his physical attractiveness would come in handy to distract Anduvio during their escape. "If you end up wounded, there's no guarantees Henrietta will find you."

Jamarnid was undeterred. "Then leave me to die, son. I was always living on borrowed time ever since you were born. If my death helps give you and my loved ones a chance to continue living, then my honor as a disgraced guard will be restored." Jamarnid's heart thumped upon hearing Soremin whimper nearby. It was for the best. Their romance had no future and Soremin needed to continue living as Jarahad's advisor and inspire hope into his populace.

Without much ado, Jamarnid focused, and his greenish phantom beast clawed its way out of the soil, sat next to the saddle and rolled to the side. With extensive practice runs done late last night, Jarahad and several volunteers secured the belts of the saddle beneath the Lusenia's flat belly and placed the secondary straps against the beast's shoulders for increased stability. Jarahad then hauled his father and sat him on the saddle seat. His hands intuitively secured each belt and strap. The entire process must have taken a minute at the most.

Without bothering to say goodbye, Jamarnid launched straight towards the city while everyone grabbed whatever scant belonging they could carry in their arms and raced outside in the opposite direction. Knowing it would hurt him too much to say goodbye, Jamarnid focused his mind on his mission.

It didn't take long for the beast to reach the palace and spot Anduvio standing right at the door. For unexplained reasons, Anduvio was already up very early and dressed in a much more elegant jester costume than usual. With gold threaded seams and gloss blue silk, this suit embodied the perfect blend between gaudy trashiness and refined elegance.

With a twirl and an exaggerated curtsey, Anduvio spun around and clapped his hands. "Tada! Did you like my twirl, you mutilated elf swine?"

"Ah, looks like you rose early. Your nighttime lover ditched you before midnight?"

Anduvio cackled from the compliment and twiddled with his moustache. "I am no fool. Nobody in their sane mind would stay in my city after my threat. Just to let you know, my men have surrounded your home. Catch me if you can, my sweetest hearts!"

It never occurred to Jamarnid that Anduvio would be thinking far ahead and would double-cross him. How could he have underestimated him so much? And now, Jamarnid no longer felt remaining fear as he set his beast and chased after Anduvio who ran at an absurd speed. If he was going to die today, it will be fighting the bastard.

CHAPTER 25 ◆ JARAHAD

When Jamarnid departed to lure Anduvio away from the city, Jarahad assumed they would have a sufficient head start to reach the closest human enclave.

The refugees didn't even walk more than a few dozen feet away from the temple before being surrounded by dozens of armed humans with menacing glares. Jarahad and the others were so busy making Jamarnid's saddle in this miserable weather they never had sentries standing watch. "Curse our misfortune!"

Soremin glared at Jarahad's inappropriate language, but he couldn't blame him. Tanato was hobbling along and stared at the human thugs with a frustrated expression. If only he didn't run out of mana last night! Unable to summon his telepathic demonic beast, everyone stared at Jarahad with distress.

"There is no point in lamenting this mistake. We're going to have to move these people." Someone tightened Jarahad's wrist before he drew his sword. Assuming it was Soremin, Jarahad balked with a grunt. "Soremin, I know you don't want me to murder people, but this isn't the right time! These men are criminals that have looted our city. If they don't let us flee, then I have no moral qualms over stopping them by force."

The person's grip tightened and cleared their throat. "It isn't that."

When Jarahad heard the feminine voice, he turned around and gasped. "Henrietta! I thought you were…"

Aware of the humans surrounding them, Henrietta pointed her finger in another direction. Initially confused, it only took Jarahad a few seconds to realize something was wrong. "My father's phantom beast is turning back! Why?"

Before he knew it, pounding ripples from the puddles predated the arrival of a certain man. It only took Anduvio a few seconds to run towards the temple. Thugs grinned at the refugees as they exchanged a few words with the mage. From the way they returned to Almjarhad joking and fretting about their fate, it was obvious they were only ordered to surround the temple until Anduvio arrived.

Cornered to a wall, Jarahad stared at the startled refugees, many of whom were already crying as they returned to the temple. Much to his glee, Tioja wasn't among the crowd.

Anduvio studied the commotion while he giggled nonstop. Rail droplets soon drenched him, which didn't damper his mood. "Well, well, well. It seems like everyone tried to run away from me. I had a hunch you were up to something when my men spotted one of your strange friends flying in the sky. Naughty boy!"

Jarahad tensed his fist while he sensed his father's phantom beast fast approaching. "Give us safe passage, Magician Anduvio. The city is yours and we will never bother you again. This is your last chance."

"Ah, you are a good negotiator. But…" And Anduvio gloated even more as he saw Jamarnid's Lusenia arrive, which didn't seem to bother him much at all. "That little squirt, he's still here."

Jarahad cursed himself for not evacuating Tioja to the nearest city last night. Everyone was so busy finishing the saddle that nobody would have been able to care for him in his current state. "Tioja is incapable of hurting a fly. I beg of you to let us leave!"

Increasingly amused, Anduvio strode ahead, dallying his hips and leaning forward. His calamity stone vibrated ever more ferociously as his hand grabbed Jarahad's jaw and the other one touched his abs. "My, my. Your body is perfect. Have you agreed to marry me? I can only spare the men, but if you are especially obedient, I might let that scampering cockroach go. So, do we have a deal?"

Even more empty words that revolted Jarahad to no end. Jarahad knew in the bottom of his heart that bartering additional deals with this man would be fruitless. It would have been different if Anduvio let the women and infirm escape. But to kill and enslave everyone? Anduvio was a threat to this world, and he would rather die today than bend his knee. Knowing the risks, Jarahad filled his body with mana. "I summon thee my phantom beast, the Demonic Armor Rashid!"

As a shadow covered his body in the gelatinous green blob, Anduvio punched him hard in the stomach. While his body skidded a few feet backwards, he neither lost his balance nor felt considerable pain. Jarahad spoke in a commandeering voice. "Everyone! Change of plans! Pack your belongings and run for your lives while I fight this brute!"

"Don't you dare take my toys away from me, you scab!" Anduvio punched hard, but Jarahad blocked the punch with his sword. Several people began running while Jamarnid barked orders. But it was useless. "They are mine!"

With a roar, Anduvio clenched his right fist and pounded the ground. Much to everyone's dismay, explosions rattled all over the lands while potable water reservoirs sloshed in every direction, flooding the fields everywhere. Increased whimpers and groans erupted because the only exit to the nearest human city was covered in water and debris. They were trapped.

While terrifying, Jarahad wouldn't falter. His eyes burned in fury as he lifted his sword in the air and ushered a prayer in harlequin. "Give me flat earth!" The instant Jarahad shoved his sword into the ground, it glowed a brilliant light green and jolted strange energy aided by his harlequin earth magic. Water was being lured into underground tunnels. Gasps from the refugees soon ensued as sufficient trails of flattened earth appeared.

"Everyone! Now is our chance!"

"I won't let you!" Any attempts to lead the civilians to safety were constantly stopped by Anduvio, who either punched the ground making crevices appear, or previously cleared land became once again impassable from water. Jarahad swiped the man constant times, but the only damage he could do was tearing parts of Anduvio's blue costume.

"Son, let me help you!" Jamarnid charged in their direction, but Anduvio clenched his fist and punched the underbelly of the beast, making it jolt into the air.

"Father!" A keen sense of fury ebbed into Jarahad as he saw the grimace on Jamarnid's face turning a dizzying backflip high into the air. Hoping his father would survive the blow, Jarahad sneered at the mage.

"Ah, you devilish being! After all I did for you! You'd dare bring an army of scavengers to take what now belongs to me? Hrm..?" Anduvio's eyes glistened even further as he observed his surroundings. Initially bored from the rag-tag group of refugees still standing by his side, the mage's attention was focused on the Lusenia that safely landed nearby. "Maybe I should get rid of that pesky father of yours first."

Jarahad's hand pressed on his sword hilt and a feeling of vile hatred seeped from within. This only triggered the nascent blood lust of his cursed weapon. During his training, Jarahad was warned not to express overt negative emotions around the sword, because it could possess him. Not today. The only thing Jarahad could think of was how he could clavate his weapon into Anduvio's mouth and rip off that accursed stone that granted him so much power. He already lost the woman he could ever truly love, there was no way Anduvio was going to get away with killing his father as well.

With increased determination, Jarahad accelerated his pace and felt something within. Yes, anger, this was the feeling. This was what Charon warned him about during his training. If he had known that this emotion could be channeled into his sword that strengthened his phantom beast, Jarahad would have let go of these self-imposed prohibitions long ago. Each step that he took to avert Jamarnid's doom, his armor became lighter for him, and heavier at the same time. Jarahad could now feel it. His body wisped through the hurling crowds and leaped into the air.

Anduvio began a melee battle sending a series of rocks in Jamarnid's direction. After landing on the ground relatively unscathed, Jamarnid rubbed some mud off his face with his forearm to no avail. Stuck with no other options and an inherent need to counter Anduvio's attacks, the black-haired elf's body relaxed. Soon enough, the black eyes of Jamarnid's Lusenia glowed a copperish gold, and the beast accelerated its pace. Now that Jamarnid was in full control, his beast was fast enough to dodge every attack with increased precision.

Taking advantage of the distraction offered from his father, Jarahad drew his accursed sword and aimed for Anduvio's neck. Under normal circumstances, Anduvio would have been fast enough to dodge it. This time was different. With the increased acceleration offered by the sword, the blade collided against Anduvio's throat, and both men ricocheted into the air.

Confusion, dizziness, and a pang of pain from the impact hurled Jarahad with full force as he flew backward just like the time Talgel's house was bombarded. Only this time Jarahad was prepared. He bent his knees and curled his back. With the aid of his sword, Jarahad's feet crashed against the hard ground and tossed mud into the air.

After he fully landed, Jarahad stood up and looked around. His father's phantom beast seemed unscathed from the attacks and was circling a prone figure like a cat hunting for its prey. The claws of the beast scratched the ground, trying its best to control the urge to attack the mage knowing it would be fruitless.

Henrietta approached Jarahad at once. "Are you all right?"

This made Jarahad smile. "You should have told me sooner my sword could make my phantom beast stronger. It would have saved me plenty of problems over the years."

"Nonsense! You know that pureblood harlequins can't summon phantom beasts! How would I know…"

Jarahad's heart sunk. Just when he assumed his sword ideally decapitated or in the least, broke Anduvio's trachea, the vibration was fast approaching. "Get down, Henrietta!"

Whereas Henrietta's face was covered by the horror of impending death, an irate Anduvio was fast approaching with his right arm extended for the killer blow. Even if Jarahad's beast could become fast enough to dodge the mage, it was likely Henrietta would become his next victim.

A pounding heart. Seconds to go. It filled Jarahad with sorrow this might be the last time he saw Henrietta's face. Losing her would be too much for his shattered heart.

Just as Henrietta was closing her eyes to accept her impending death, warmth shone from above. The heavens were responding to everyone's prayers and the clouds skittered away, bombarding everyone with beams of sunlight.

In the very last instant before Anduvio's arm reached Henrietta's neck for the killing blow, a horrific, vibrating, voiding sensation was sensed all around Anduvio. It was a terror Jarahad knew all too well. Anduvio's body contorted for the briefest instant and he stumbled on the ground.

Knowing this was his chance, Jarahad grabbed Henrietta and pulled her to safety. His mind was too busy scanning the sky to worry about asking his friend the usual pleasantries. Soon enough, Jarahad spotted what he was looking for, and his heart filled with relentless joy.

Circling in the heavenly sky was a certain person Jarahad had long assumed to be lost forever from madness. An ally that was currently untouched by Gulraj's curse. Upon landing nearby, Tioja's face was emblazoned by the insanity that became a part of him since that fateful evening. But there was something different. No longer hindered by whatever malady kept his mind lost in its own thoughts, Tioja was focused on his mission. The savior on the zenith had just arrived.

CHAPTER 26 ◆ TIOJA

Ever since Tioja became cursed by the Giltemarraj, he wanted to fight. He needed to fight. It was the sole thing that maintained his focus. The night when he became cursed, he felt overwhelmed from his newfound disability more than anything. The voices, the screams. It was agony, but not too much worse than the suffering Gulraj inflicted on him after his failed initiation.

What truly aggravated Tioja was the thought he would fail everyone if he didn't defeat Anduvio. Tioja didn't even care about the man. In fact, he both despised yet respected Anduvio in equal measure. After being exposed to the knowledge of Gulraj's beast, he obtained a full panorama of the true power of the stone lodged on the mage's tongue. Its power was terrifyingly immense. Upon closer mental inspection, Tioja had hit the clown with 126 direct hits and another 43 indirect ones. It was barely enough to start damaging the stone.

Tioja spent his final night in Murdorhiolan tossing and turning in his bed. A part of him would have wished this frightful sleep was due to having nightmares. No, it was much worse. The pair of arms holding onto him and never wishing to let go was the monster that was once his brother.

Yes, in a final act of retaliation, Gulraj not only slept in his bedroom that evening, but they were also sharing the same bed. Memories of Hurrujat's festering skull, the smell, rot, pus, death, delicious. Oh, such delicious agony. Wretched man, rotten to the core, just like his vile son. These nonsensical thoughts ebbed and waned in Tioja's mind for nonstop hours as his hand fumbled into his pocket and touched for the briefest instant the braided piece of his parents' hair.

If Gulraj noticed this, he neither stopped him nor took his belongings away. If anything, it made him hug Tioja with increased firmness as he stared at the ceiling. "I have ruined you, brother. And to be honest, I am enjoying every minute of this. If you leave my city, the newest generations that will be born will never know I ever had a brother. You hear me? Your children will be orphans. And it was all for nothing."

Tioja mumbled. "Hamara failed. She thought we would be together."

Gulraj's hand trembled from this odd confession. For unexplained reasons, he didn't swat Tioja or do anything. Something jumped on the bed. It was soft and purred relentlessly. Despite its advanced age, Fluff still clung to life. As the oldest cat Tioja had ever heard of, Fluff decided to lay on top of his belly during his final night. Doing so did the trick and soothed Tioja's tempered mind. For the briefest instant, Tioja regained the peace he yearned from before.

The respite didn't last long. The instant the sun rose, Tioja's mind became bombarded once again by repetitive thoughts that impeded him to do even the most minimal of self-care. He didn't even remember saying goodbye to the city inhabitants or departing because his mind fretted over the bad omen that had become their ever-present accomplice: the rain.

Wet, mushy, cleany, coldy, windy, foggy, dampy, moldy, so much mold. Green, gooey, pestilent, fetid, putrid, death. Yes, so much death. Festering corpses. Bloated corpses. And this is what ringed in Tioja's mind on and on as the days passed as he rode in the back of a carriage he shared with Jamen and Sharad.

Ever since Tioja lost his mind, Sharad's general demeanor had changed. Long gone was their prior relationship as nobleman and peasant. Sharad held him in an embrace whenever thunder struck and hummed old nursery rhymes from his own childhood. These were songs Tioja had never heard before, but they were pleasant and soothed his mind.

Jamen helped share the burden of keeping him alive. Perhaps it was Jamen's way to apologize because he shunned Tioja when he awakened his Lehart. But there were still traces of the generous grandfather from Tioja's childhood. No matter how thoughtful both elves were, nothing replaced the dratted, darned, cursed, and horrendous nonstop rain. Moldy, rainy, dratted, drafty… Ugh, when will it stop?!

By the time Tioja returned to Almjarhad, he spent half his time muttering about the innate unwanted properties of rainy weather and telling a priest named Tanato to leave him alone. Who was this loser anyways?

Some weirdo that thought he had the right to probe into his mind and do something about it. No, the only thing that would allay Tioja's suffering was Anduvio. He would murder him and claim the man's corpse as his treasure. His precious. Yes, this is what Tioja wanted. And yet the rain continued pounding, pouring, dropping, falling, and never stopping.

There was a commotion one day when everyone started walking everywhere and someone yanked Tioja's shirt to make him walk. But his legs gave up and he plopped on the mud. Any efforts to make him move were fruitless. All Tioja could think about was the annoyed reflection of his face as the rain never wanted to stop.

More commotions, screaming and phantom beasts. Tioja was so out of it that he never realized Anduvio's men surrounded the temple and forced the events from the prior few minutes to take place. A dodge here, a shockwave there. Tioja was oblivious even to the blast Anduvio sent that damaged one of the buildings of the temple. Fortunately, nobody was inside at the time.

When all hopes were lost, something felt different. Warmth, caress, hope, life. A stir in Tioja's face prompted him to stare above and he smiled with wicked deviousness. The sun had returned, and now he could use his beast. The moment he had been anxiously waiting for was finally here, and he would stop at nothing to kill that disgusting man.

Without even thinking, Tioja removed his soggy shirt, stood up and grinned. "I summon thee my phantom beast, the Demonic Wing Lehart!" Within seconds, black harlequin wings grew on his back, and he ejected to the air with air magic. It only took a few flaps until he was circling above a muddy battlefield where terrified refugees stood at a safe distance alongside a few pureblood elves sitting on phantom beasts. Soremin's priestly robes were ripped apart and caked in mud as he held his Hiratori on his left hand. Disappointing. Tioja always assumed the priest would be capable of making his Hiratori large enough to ride the sky with it. Soremin was hunkering in a corner like a scolded puppy as he watched Jamarnid dodging blasts from the buffoon mage.

Ah, Jamarnid, the jerk that called him a cursed mongrel and a thousand other insults. Tioja had grown to detest him over the years he spent with Gulraj. Yes, now that Tioja's mind ran wild, he would never cure Jamarnid's body with his magic. Tioja lost his mother and mind, Jamarnid lost his honor and health. It was a fair tradeoff. Let Jamarnid rot forever as punishment for ruining his life. The only ruinous opinion Tioja would take back was calling Jamarnid a coward. While so many able-bodied elves and halflings hid in a corner, Jamarnid was seated on a saddle and trying his best to tire Anduvio without letting him steal his mana. It was commendable the jerk was capable of such a feat given he couldn't sense harlequin magic. Most impressive. And even more convenient. Jamarnid's unwanted presence in the battlefield will prove to be useful for his ulterior plan.

Tioja continued circling everyone as he studied the two people Anduvio was attacking: Jarahad and... Henrietta? Tioja was used to seeing Jarahad wearing his magical armor and had even traveled on it a few times. Given Anduvio's combat skills, Jarahad was wise in wearing his beast despite the risk Anduvio could absorb its mana. Much to Tioja's dismay, Jarahad was being careless by not stealing Anduvio's magic. His excessive honor would be his downfall! Fight like a harlequin, dammit!

Anduvio had finally noticed his presence and was shooting air blasts in his direction. Ah, so much fun, so worthless. While the crowds implored Tioja to dodge the attacks, he continued prancing in circles for a while without caring about the consequences. Whenever a blast was close enough to affect his chosen flight path, he'd absorb it. Ah, nice and warm. Good mana, fun mana. The day Tioja fought against the buffoon, he was too overconfident in absorbing the mage's mana in the throne room. No, that wasn't the right word. He was ignorant. This could be a forgivable mistake because he had never seen a calamity stone before. But looking back with the knowledge the Giltemarraj granted him, his plan was doomed to fail from the very beginning. He should have visited the clown at the break of dawn and summoned his demonic beast immediately. And...

Another blast was sent his way, but Tioja had changed course. Initially obsessed about killing Anduvio immediately, a few dratted clouds covered him, which reduced his shadow-reading ability. That wasn't too much of a problem. It was still the late summer and he had plenty of time to kill Anduvio. There are more urgent things in life at times.

Tioja flew to Almjarhad Castle where a few of Anduvio's human goons were busy pillaging the city. "Disgusting ants. Show me some blood!" Tioja's eyes shone in insanity as the cloudy sky offered sufficient sunlight to blow up every human foolish enough to stand outside. Guts, viscera, cracked bones and puddles of blood that preceded brief screams of pain embellished the stone paths of the city with glorious crimson. "So, beautiful, so much death. I want more!"

Another air blast shot in Tioja's way. Whether he absorbed Anduvio's mana or let it disperse, Tioja couldn't care less. His eyes continued marveling at the canvas he created as his demonic beast continued pounding the freshly deceased corpses into pudding. As expected, more humans ran outside thinking doing so would be their salvation. Most of them had come from the castle. All of them male and dressed in all sorts of revealing clothes with chokers and leather underwear. "How amusing! More gore! I want it! I need it!" Boom. Boom. Boom. If these stupid humans had known any better, they would have huddled inside and taken advantage of one of the unknown defects of his Lehart. He could destroy anything he saw while standing under the auric fire, but he was blind indoors. Anduvio would continue shooting air blasts at him every now and then, intertwined with screaming of some sort. "Aw… the mage didn't like my painting. But it is glorious! So much blood! So beautiful! And Anduvio will be next. But first…"

Convinced Tioja had murdered Anduvio's allies without using much mana, he obliterated one of the walls of Almjarhad palace. This was not a random display of violence. And he would apologize to Jarahad later for damaging his home. If he planned on killing Anduvio, he needed something tasty to drink. And his tastebuds were starving for something he sorely missed. Flapping his wings at an absurd speed, Tioja entered the hole he created, and reached a pantry hidden beneath a secret passageway Anduvio never even knew about. Tioja scooped something.

Bemused, Anduvio was panting as he stumbled on mortar. "You swine! My palace walls are damaged! And you killed them! Curse you!"

"I like to paint, and your friends have made my birth city beautiful! You will soon meet their fate!"

Tioja's back burned for a brief instant as one of two air blasts hit him. Not a problem in his opinion. He could heal himself perfectly fine as he continued stealing the clown's mana. Within a few seconds, Tioja was back in the air carrying his highly sought after prize: two bottles of blood wine. From the harvest before Hurrujat abandoned the city. Even better. That was a very good year, and the wine will taste even better than usual. Tioja's teeth dug in the cork, spat it out and gurgled in glee as he vacated the first bottle while dodging Anduvio's blasts. In a further display of his newly found chaotic nature, Tioja tossed the bottle and it somehow hit Anduvio in the head with a thump.

"Ow! You threw an embotellado at me! Curse you!"

Anduvio's complaints were like music to Tioja's ears. His teeth uncorked the second bottle. This time, Tioja took his time emptying the bottle and enjoying the flavor. Oh, such delicious sweetness. Carrier of life, destroyer of civilization. The perfect balance between blood and fruit that reached perfection after being stored for decades beneath the palace.

Satiated enough to fight with some seriousness, Tioja landed on the ground and continued slurping his wine as Anduvio heaved from the jog. Anduvio's jester hat was dangling behind his neck, his hair disheveled and his head was caked with tears and sweat. Oh, he smelled almost as delightful as he looked covered in grime. Too bad his stone protected his body and there weren't any traces of blood anywhere. A real bummer. At least the green glass shards sprinkled on his sweaty hair made him look funny. Feeling slightly tipsy, Tioja giggled as his mind swirled thinking about how pretty green was. Of course, Anduvio was busy whining about an insult of some sort. The man was a gifted mage, but he was far too easily aggravated to ever warrant Tioja's respect. What a waste.

By the time Jarahad, Jamarnid and Henrietta reached him, Tioja tossed the second bottle of wine on the ground and stomped on it. With his air magic and complete disdain for personal safety, the bottle crashed into thousands of pieces under the might of his bare foot. A giggle escaped Tioja's lips because he could feel pain on his foot. It was a most enjoyable sensation that he would remember to do more often from now on.

Jarahad and Anduvio were trying to speak to him, but Tioja was too entertained relishing the pain on his foot and the green shards Anduvio tried rustling from his hair to care. Feeling increased embodiment from inebriation, Tioja slurred something to Jarahad. "Stand over there Jarahad and protect me. I want to see an explosion!"

CHAPTER 27 ♦ JARAHAD

Who is this madman that stood next to Jarahad today? The quirky boy that served him vegetable soup one afternoon? The child that cried his heart away the evening his mother abandoned him? The confused teenager that didn't know why he was called the Cursed One? The warrior that failed to defeat Anduvio? The older brother of a monster? Or was this the simpering husk that soiled himself in the mud?

No, none of these possibilities were true. The halfling standing by his side was neither in control of his emotions or hiding from them. Proudly standing in front of their greatest enemy was a creature forever tainted by the veil of madness. Tioja had become a weapon of absolute destruction. Who did he plan to destroy today? Was it safe to be standing near him?

Jarahad shook his head as he stared at an equally disconcerted Henrietta and his father. Whatever thoughts cruised in Tioja's mind; nobody would know. Only that Anduvio was growing fed up with his nonsense and the vibration in his body increased with every passing moment. Jarahad drew his sword and stood in front of Tioja. "Do whatever you have to do, Tio. I'll protect you."

"Thank you, my beloved friend."

Jarahad's heart skipped a beat when he heard Tioja's soft voice. It was the first time he heard the confused halfling speak ever since he became cursed. Beneath endless layers of madness and irrational behavior was still the sweet and loyal elf he always knew. Soon enough, Jarahad felt the familiar voiding sensation whenever Tioja used his demonic beast. While most of the refugees had run inside of Soremin's temple to hide from Tioja's wrath, Jarahad was confident Tioja would be sufficiently in control of his beast to only attack his enemies. After feeling a tiny electric spark in Anduvio's stone while he and his allies remained unscathed was proof his suspicions were correct.

Anduvio would spend his time jerking his body whenever the Lehart pulsed against his body without showing any visible injuries.

Between these jerking movements, Anduvio sent blasts at Henrietta, his father, and occasionally himself. Thanks to his armor, the blasts only stung while his sword remained unharmed. Henrietta as the slowest of the three had to occasionally use spells from her own harlequin sword to dodge attacks. His father Jamarnid meanwhile entered meditation and his beast dodged every blast.

Occasionally, Jarahad would hear a mumble escaping Tioja's lips. "74, 75, 76…" It dawned on Jarahad that Tioja was counting the number of pulsations from his beast that hit the foolish mage. And yet he continued unscathed.

After a while, Jarahad felt something was starting to change. Anduvio's stone pulsated warmer, higher elevations of energy. While this filled him with hope, Tioja growled.

"What is wrong, Tio? You're starting to hurt him."

"We screwed up. The stone has already realized what I planned to do. I need someone to concentrate earth, fire, and air harlequin magic on the stone!"

"What? I thought…" As Jarahad stupidly turned around to stare at Tioja's maddened face that was equally smiling and horrified, a dizzying painful pulsation coursed through Jarahad's body that dazed him for a second.

Tioja was too busy fighting the stone to move, but Henrietta soon flew in front and slashed Anduvio's arm with her sword. "Jarahad, I can't believe you're still alive! The stone sent a black energy beam your way!"

Jamarnid's beast stood at a safe distance and spoke. "Son, how many times I told you never to keep your eyes off the enemy? I want to slap you right now for making such a careless mistake!"

Jarahad smiled after hearing Henrietta's concern and his father's encouragement hidden beneath his usual veneer of common sense. From now on, Jarahad would stare ahead. "Tioja told me something important. I need one of you to return to the temple and rally some halflings. We need fire, air, and earth mages to attack the stone. It's an order!"

Henrietta frowned as she lowered her sword. "I am a capable water mage. If the legends are true that calamity stones weaken with harlequin magic, then let's see if…" Henrietta blasted water particles at the stone and Anduvio thrashed. Instead of the usual vibration whenever Jarahad exposed his own harlequin magic to the stone, he felt a vile voiding sensation that sent bile up his stomach. While Jarahad keep his meal, Henrietta vacated her breakfast on the mud while Tioja gurgled for a moment.

After recovering from the onslaught, Tioja growled. "Fools! Follow my order and never do that stupid antic ever again! I need the other elements hitting the stone, dammit! Do it or else I'll murder you for getting on my nerves!"

Henrietta shuddered from the threat and jettisoned to the temple with her wings. Jarahad would have wanted to use his own magic, but his father anticipated his thoughts. "Protect Tio with your sword, my son. If the mage sends another black energy beam your way, your sword is the only thing keeping Tioja alive. Let our clan's mages take care of the rest."

"Aye, father."

Jamarnid's phantom beast continued dancing around Anduvio and taunting him with infantile insults. As everyone predicted, Anduvio's pride proved to be his greatest weakness as he continued focusing his attention on chasing Jamarnid. On rare occasions, Anduvio was fast enough to get sufficiently close to Jamarnid to steal some of his mana. Whenever that happened, Jarahad gritted his teeth because he was too busy protecting Tioja.

Tioja meanwhile continued mumbling numbers. "122, 123, 124…" Ever since Tioja awakened his demonic beast, Jarahad always surmised nothing would survive it. He even cast doubt on his own sword being able to outlive the Lehart. And yet Anduvio remained unharmed after being hit more than 100 times from the beast, still irritated and with no signs of running out of mana. "How much longer will this battle take?! Why doesn't he die?"

When no answer came from Tioja, Jarahad became increasingly discouraged. When they first left Gulraj's city, Jarahad felt their ordeal had been a complete waste of time. His mind flew with endless thoughts about whether it would have made more sense to vacate the temple and have a fully rested Tioja attack him with dozens of halflings stealing the mage's mana together. After seeing the way Anduvio continued fighting with occasional black energy blasts that shot through his open maw, Jarahad soon felt convinced. He now accepted the agony his entourage suffered in Murdorhiolan was a small price to pay in exchange for Gulraj's curse.

That didn't mean Jarahad would ever trust the shifty bastard. Only that they would forge an armistice now that both siblings had attained an equal footing regarding their combative skills. After a while, several halflings with the correct tuning elements arrived alongside Soremin and disconcertingly, Sharad.

Before Jarahad could protest, Sharad stood near Tioja. "Tio, I want to help you. What do you need?"

"Give me mana to blow up that stone into smithereens!"

Both pureblood elves summoned their phantom beasts and Jarahad felt Tioja absorbing their mana that invigorated his Lehart. This would cause Anduvio to stumble even more often as Henrietta would occasionally swoop from the sky and slash his arms with her enchanted sword to further distract him.

"Halflings, Tioja wants all of you to send harlequin magic to that stone. Whatever you do, don't send water magic!" Jarahad hollered.

"And mix both elements if you are dual mages of the elements I need," Tioja's soft voice echoed.

Without wasting time, the volunteers did as they were told, and it didn't take long before something new happened to Anduvio's stone: it pulsated warmer energy. Faster, higher, and increasingly dangerous.

"What is happening to me?" Was all Anduvio could muster before his mouth opened against his will and shot black energy beams in a circular fashion towards the halflings. Unlike Jarahad who was protected by his armor, whoever was incapable of blocking the beam with earth magic or leaping into the air became a victim of the beam and bellowed in pain from burning wounds. It filled Jarahad's heart with sorrow these brave citizens of his city would either end up permanently maimed or dead.

Tioja never paid any attention. He kept on counting numbers, stealing mana, and pounded Anduvio's body with faster pulsations. "465, 466, 467…"

Could they continue doing this forever? There was still enough sunlight left. But before they could claim victory, something terrible happened. Jamarnid squealed in pain as one of the black energy blasts pierced his phantom beast and he collapsed on the ground with a thud. "Father!"

"Focus, Jarahad! Protect Tioja and our city! If I die today, then so be it!"

Soremin whimpered upon hearing this, whereas Sharad gasped. Both elves wanted to drag Jamarnid to safety now that he was cowering on the ground while strapped to his saddle.

In between bouts of sending involuntary energy blasts everywhere from his mouth and crouching in pain, Anduvio pranced towards Jamarnid and pressed his pointy blue boot on Jamarnid's torso. The elf screeched from pain as his arms helplessly pounded the leather straps in the hopes of releasing himself from the saddle that fully restrained him.

Anduvio lifted his right index finger and swooshed it with cruelty. "No, no, no. A little worm like you will not die so quickly. I am going to stomp your genitals and kill you slowly!" Fearful and impotent. Jarahad wiped tears from his eyes as Anduvio's foot aimed for Jamarnid's crotch.

"Don't hurt him!" As Anduvio's foot nearly breached Jamarnid, Henrietta swiped her sword at Anduvio's neck, prompting his foot to stomp on the tip of Jamarnid's left stump instead.

"Awwwww!" Jamarnid screamed from pain, causing Jarahad to tremble envisioning the suffering his father was enduring at this moment.

The only consolation was seeing Anduvio twist his right ankle and screeched. "Ah! You rotten bitch!" Anduvio's fist wasted no time punching

Henrietta's cheek that was partially protected by her blade, and she was sent flying several feet against the muddy ground. Blood covered her mouth as the glow vanished from her sword and her body slumped.

Jarahad's heart pounded with anger and fear of potentially witnessing his dear friend die at the hands of this madman while his father agonized in pain.

Feeling satisfied with getting rid of the harlequin pest, Anduvio stared at Jamarnid and smiled with glee. "Yes, I love to hear your screams. Music to my ears. You know, I have changed my mind. After I kill your son and the rest of these vermin, I am claiming you as my consolation prize. You will be accompanying me to the remains of my birth city to become my toy for eternity!"

Anduvio then set his eyes on Jarahad, and they met face to face. Madness versus determination. Jarahad was left without options and did the one thing he could: he channeled all his anger into his sword, and it glowed fervently. As a vengeful Anduvio charged in his direction with his right fist clenched in a ball, blue mist enveloped the man like a fog.

"What is this? Henrietta? Is that you?"

Seconds felt like they had become agonizing hours as mysterious blue fumes started concentrating, circling, and turning into the ravenous teeth of a beast that would never stop until it claimed its prize. As Anduvio charged forward, Jarahad swooped his sword against the madman's jaw while accompanied by these godly blue spears. Henrietta's magic, his friend, his accomplice, and maybe the woman he would someday love to marry.

Endless thoughts cruised in Jarahad's mind as his sword clashed against the man and enveloped everything in a blinding light.

CHAPTER 28 ◆ TALGEL

"If this is death, then envelope me and never let go."

Talgel floated in darkness, naked and free from her binds that ruined her. Liberated from the Giltemarraj, her wish came true.

She was no heroine. But neither was she a villain. Talgel was a harbinger. Nobody but herself knew the true reason why she selected Tioja to become her final client. Ever since she obtained her demonic beast, it plagued her mind and tainted her soul.

Now that the Giltemarraj had bonded itself to a new host that enjoyed its company, the remaining figments of Talgel's spirit spurred through Tioja as a part of her became bonded to him. This was no accident. She only waited until the day Tioja savored söma for the first time to summon her demonic beast and had the absurdly good fortune she could alter reality that fateful day.

The echoes of the Giltemarraj reverberated into her mind. "It is not a waste. Nothing is, my beautiful and bitter Talgel."

"Ha! I was never yours. I am the wind, free to roam the world. I am the fire, emblazoned to destroy civilization until nothing is left. Go pollute the soul of Tioja's brother and let him steal the covenant from that great master. I couldn't care less."

This stroked the demon's fancy as it toiled around her body. "I am most impressed. You knew about him?"

"He is the creator of the Ominous Books, and your greatest prize as well. I hope Gulraj has the common sense of waiting until he opens his fortune that I personally wrote. He must wait until the sky turns daylight dark in the temple before he can go inside to train."

This amused the Giltemarraj as it floated in the air. "Whenever Gulraj summons me and steals a victim's sanity, I'll make him wiser and more like myself. He will be ready to meet that great master when the time comes. You'll see."

Talgel grinned as the beast began to vanish and released its tendrils from her soul forever. "We shall see each other one last time, my lovely demon. When Tioja asks for your wisdom at the eve of his life. Until then, I'll guide and protect him as penance for my sins."

The evening Tioja became cursed by his brother, that small figment of Talgel's remaining essence held him in a tight embrace. Liberated from her earthly shackles, Talgel's eyes would forever see far beyond what a mortal could. While it was most entertaining to confess to the Giltemarraj about her trickery, she was careful not to let it discover she used the rare window of absolute knowledge for a second motive: she stole a fragment of the demon's gift.

It was only fair given it stole her eyes, her humanity and eventually, her life. Given she suffered no divine punishment, it meant the demon owed her a magic debt, and Talgel took just enough to call it even.

From now on until Tioja died, she would soothe him when his mind felt troubled, inspire him to write and paint as his muse and grant him the focus to ensure his Lehart never harmed an innocent. And what was even better, channel his beast's power into a veil of Tioja's water magic whenever it reached its pinnacle to crack a calamity stone. It was a fair exchange now that Talgel had turned Tioja into a weapon of absolute destruction, just as she always wanted from the very start. Whenever Tioja entered contact with a calamity stone, she would entice and prod him nonstop until the stone was destroyed.

Anduvio's stone was gone, and there were only 12 stones missing. Unfortunately, Talgel only stole enough of the demon's gift to locate a stone that had already bonded to a mage. The remaining ones were still dormant. It was possible Tioja would not live long enough until the 13 stones vanished from this world, but she would help him destroy them whenever he had the good fortune of locating them along the way.

It was amusing to see the world from Tioja's eyes while Jarahad was busy tending to his injured father and Henrietta. Henrietta was very lucky to have survived that fall. As annoying as she was, Talgel hoped her former roommate lived a long and plentiful life. Maybe Henrietta will choose her path wisely.

Jamarnid was a whole other matter. He had become more mature and open minded after she died. For a while, Jamarnid would try to amend his relationship with Tioja. But Talgel knew deep in her heart Tioja would not forgive him. Any attempts to heal his body would fail. Jamarnid might even rekindle his romance with Soremin as the centuries marched on. In the greater scheme of things, Jamarnid played a very small role. The only thing that would forever grant Talgel some amusement was how his mind would slowly slip into insanity as the pureblood elves died one by one. The day Soremin dies, Jamarnid's soul would cloister in a shell, and his body would wither away. Jarahad should feel glad he would already be dead from old age and be spared from the anguish of witnessing his father's passing.

Talgel sighed thinking of her lover. She would always miss him. His caresses, his laughter, and the married life that would never happen. But it will be replaced by the friendship Jarahad would harbor for Tioja. Seeing him laugh and encourage Tioja would be a sufficient consolation prize until she vanished from this world completely. There was only one thing that truly saddened her: Jarahad was not yet aware of the price he paid when he obtained his demonic beast. Forever deprived of one source of joy in life that will cause him undue hardship. Knowing him, Jarahad would learn to accept this constraint and live a long & fulfilling life.

Tioja was now standing in front of Anduvio who wailed and whimpered as blood oozed from his severed jaw, compliments of Jarahad's sword. Talgel grinned almost as much as Tioja did as they both relished the man who had proven to be the most pitiable coward in his final moments.

Taking advantage Tioja's mind was too busy engraving this sight into his memory, Talgel spoke through him. "We meet again, Anduvio. Remember what Talgel told you the night you met her?"

Anduvio's brown eyes widened and stared at Tioja's wild expression. Any attempts to speak proved impossible due to the pain as life escaped from his body and stained the soil red.

"I told you I would kill you with my own hands. Your stone has been destroyed, and I have liberated you from your curse of eternal life." Talgel grinned as she enjoyed the astonishment in Anduvio's eyes. "Yes. After you murdered everyone in your birth city due to being corrupted by your stone, you became vengeful and insane. Even tried to remove the stone, but it became adhered to your body like a parasite. Go now, to the world of the dead, and be at peace."

Talgel's hands covered Anduvio's eyes shut as he expired with a peaceful demeanor on his face. Anduvio was not initially evil. He was just a victim to the stone. By using Tioja as her channeler, Talgel would help him destroy as many stones as possible. That didn't mean she would control his body. Only when it would prove necessary.

And one such moment had just arrived. With a smirk, the spirit of Talgel resting inside of Tioja saw his fingers clawing into Anduvio's corpse using his air magic and extracted his little prize: a part of the man's intestines.

It would take every fiber of Talgel's willpower to tell Tioja keeping such a disturbing memento of this battle was going to be a bad idea.

EPILOGUE

"Tioja couldn't have chosen a better place even if he tried." Sharad removed a heap of sweat from his brow under the relentless battering of the strongest sunlight he had ever experienced in his life. Standing by his side were an equally weary Jarahad and Nurran. The group was resting in a small oasis while their steeds were gulping the nourishing liquid in a valley surrounded by death.

Jarahad stared at the distant mountains while trace amounts of sand battered in every direction. "I hope we don't end up hit by a sandstorm while waiting for that elf."

Nurran meanwhile was busy sharpening Sharad's kilij sword with a pumice stone. "Trust him. Even though he lost a part of his persona forever, Tioja would never abandon us. His allegiance to Almjarhad is unbreakable."

Bubbles soon emerged from the nearby pond, startling the horses enough to stand back and whinny. The instant everyone turned around to look, a familiar female harlequin emerged from the water offering everyone present a rather awkward front-row view of her perfectly endowed naked body.

Jarahad was the first to rush to Henrietta's side and offer his travel cloak to avoid causing a scene. "Please cover yourself! This is so improper!"

Instead of showing offense, Henrietta giggled as she removed mud from her ears with harlequin water magic. "You are always so kind, my Lord. Perhaps we could honor Talgel's memory by once again proving her predictions never failed."

With blushed cheeks, Jarahad averted his gaze while still holding the cloak to provide Henrietta some privacy as she started to dress. "What do you mean?"

The instant Henrietta finished buttoning her shirt, she approached Jarahad, and her lips connected with his. Despite trembling from confusion and fear, he could still smell the lingering traces of the same scented perfumes Talgel wore and finally gave in to the lingering passion he tried his best to hide.

While Nurran gasped from experiencing the rare instance of Jarahad letting his true feelings surface, Sharad was effusively clapping. "Keep it up! I can't wait to see you two getting married!"

Jarahad turned away in utter shame whereas Henrietta smiled at her friends. Their hands remained firmly clasped. Her fingers caressed Jarahad's brand new nobleelf ring. Unlike the ring Sharad still didn't want to wear, Jarahad's new ring was black with a harlequin emblem as the new heraldic clan symbol.

Nurran continued sharpening Sharad's blade with a quizzical expression. "I guess it was inevitable that both of you would end up together. What do you plan to do, Henrietta? If you marry Jarahad, you will end up disowned."

This didn't deter her. "Almjarhad is my home. Maybe even Jamarnid will someday accept me."

Jarahad remained unconvinced as he stared at the traces of lesions appearing on her skin. "What will you do about the rotting disease? If you continue living in Almjarhad, you will inevitably suffer the same fate as Hurrujat."

"You are an earth mage. I am certain you can build me a few underground tunnels to reduce my sun exposure. Be creative!"

This comment perked Sharad's attention at once. "What a wonderful idea! Almjarhad fell so easily because we are vulnerable to attacks from the surrounding mountains."

"I perfectly understand the military advantage of building escape routes, but our city is located next to the ocean. One mistake and everyone could drown!" Jarahad stammered with a clenched fist.

Jarahad's overzealous concern for everyone's wellbeing was just one of the many things Henrietta always loved about him. "Didn't Murdorhiolan have special tunnels as well?"

The group stared at Nurran who shrugged his shoulders. "I didn't spend much time touring the city. Kashin… I think he mentioned there are some tunnels hidden somewhere. Maybe…" Nurran averted his gaze and wiped some tears from his eyes.

"Kashin made his choice, fear not." A familiar voice boomed from above. Before anyone had a chance to turn around, a dark shadow loomed overhead as Tioja circled a few instances and landed. He wrapped his black wings firmly together and stared at everyone with insanity. "Yes, Kashin chose to be a nobledemon and his blood will strengthen the sister clan. His descendants will forever be stained with blood. Beautiful, wonderful blood, and covered with a shadow of death as they finish swallowing the surrounding cities and rule those lands forever."

"Crazy Tio! Welcome back!" Ignoring the disturbing comment, Sharad rushed to the halfling's side and hugged him rather effusively. "You are always so poetic and I'm happy you are on our side!"

Tioja's cackling from Sharad's excessive act of companionship made everyone relax their shoulders.

Jarahad was the most relieved of the group. Even though he would always feel sorry about being unable to gain a lasting truce with Gulraj, Tioja's loyalty was still a far greater prize. He made a promise he would try to find a way to undo the curse that ruined his friend's mind. In the meantime, the trip to these lands was the first step into a carefully devised plan to ensure the safety of his clan. "Did you find a place, Tio?"

Sharad finally released his grip while Tio approached the pond and stared at the ripples with a grin on his face while his fingers twirled minuscule wind shafts in the air. "Yes, I have found what you need. This oasis is the final respite from the hottest place in the continent. I am certain it will cover your expectations, my Lord." A veil of increased insanity glistened in his eager eyes. "It is full of death and despair. I love it!"

The explication was more than enough to appease Nurran's lingering doubts of Jarahad's unusual plan and he sheathed Sharad's kilij into its beautiful beige scabbard. "I have finished removing the kinks. You should take better care of it if you ever plan on being even remotely capable with the sword."

Sharad took the warning without any insult as he fastened the belt on his waist. "How come Lord Jarahad's sword never needs any maintenance? It's so unfair!"

Before anyone had a chance to explain, Henrietta giggled as she drew her harlequin sword to admire the steel. "These weapons are imbued with a powerful spell. As long as the owner feeds it with a part of their life force, the sword will never fail the bearer in the battlefield."

While the explanation sort of convinced Sharad, Jarahad stared at her weapon with increased concern. "You know you can't conserve your sword, Henrietta. It was the agreement you reached."

Sharad turned around and frowned. "Why not? Henrietta is a free woman!"

Tioja approached the weapon with an eager grin. "The sword belongs to her clan. Henrietta is honor-bound to remain loyal to her masters. Harlequin swords are inherited from generations of nobledemons, and you cannot buy them. Even if you stole a sword from a corpse, the weapon would eventually rebel against the wielder because they are uninitiated, and they risk ending up devoured."

Jarahad lifted an eyebrow in disbelief. "You have seen that happen? I always believed it was a legend."

"My mother's sword told that to me when I failed my initiation."

Everyone fell silent as the wind blew in every direction, sending some dust particles into the otherwise completely light blue sky. Sharad then stared at Henrietta with concern. "Will you return your weapon? It seems so unfair."

Henrietta smiled nonetheless. "It is a cursed weapon and Hurrujat said Almjarhad is no longer a land of harlequins. Maybe it is time to find a place where my kind can truly embrace the elvish customs and flourish. Prove to the world we can evolve. If my family doesn't accept my decision, then I will gladly return this weapon! My father can give it to any of my younger siblings."

While Jarahad smiled from Henrietta's decision, a still skeptical Sharad turned around. "Hey Nurran, can you make a weapon that is stronger than anything in the world?"

"What do you mean?"

"It's like your phantom beast can change the property of metal. Maybe it isn't strong enough for the battlefield, but if you can continue your apprenticeship in metalworking, then…"

"I will assume this is precisely the reason why I am here today in this awful place. Right, Jarahad?" Nurran asked.

Everyone stared at Jarahad in the hopes for an answer, but he remained rather tightlipped. It only prompted Tioja to laugh. "Jarahad commanded a rule of silence until we reached the place I found. You will soon discover his plan." A cunning grin invaded Tioja's face as he hugged himself. "Yes, he is a great leader, and I will be loyal to him for the rest of my life. Yes, a leader must protect his people. So much bloodshed, and death, yes. It is beautiful indeed."

Jarahad sighed as he stretched his muscles. "Can you keep your wings for a while longer, Tio?"

Tioja nodded while he continued mumbling. "The shedding will not happen as long as I don't summon my beast. Yes, I can't wait to feel the pain of my wings being stripped very soon. Or the agony of the shedding, so much pain. I want to feel it again, but Lord Jarahad ordered me to control you, Lehart. Yes, I must obey him and Lord Sharad. I will always have a chance to kill an enemy."

Jarahad stared in every direction and sighed in relief. "Did you see anyone nearby, Tio?"

Tioja turned around and shook his head with a grin. "I could feel everything within this valley because the sun is so strong. We are completely alone in a 200-mile radius."

"Thank you. Sharad, can you summon your Artica?"

Sharad sighed as he turned around in both directions. "If I summon it using most of the water of this oasis, it might remain active for a while."

"Good to know. Tioja, can you carry me to the place you found?"

"Yes! I can fly very quickly, you will see." Tioja's face became pensive as he quietly cackled.

Henrietta was measuring Nurran's body and frowned. "You could spare to lose some weight, Nurran. I am in very good shape, but it's going to be annoying flying up there carrying such a heavy load."

"Let's go!"

Flying in Tioja's arms was an odd experience. It was both exhilarating and distressing due to Jarahad's newly found fear of heights. Or perhaps these concerns were because his life was in the hands of the clan's most dangerous mage. Tioja was in very good physical shape due to his incomplete training. Henrietta was meanwhile struggling a bit at times while a terrified Nurran was hugging her a tad bit too tightly. Jarahad even felt a pang of jealously Nurran's face was nestled in her bosom. He was certain Henrietta felt nothing for the blacksmith and decided it was best to avoid letting his insecurities make him say something he would regret. It was his fault he decided to travel by air to spare his horses from certain death. Sharad was meanwhile racing at a sufficient speed far below on his phantom beast. He regretted forcing the poor water mage to travel in the wretchedly hot and dry place during the summer. Despite being a mediocre swordsman, Sharad's sorcery was impressive. With proper training, he might someday garner the confidence to rule. There was plenty of time. With his plan set in motion, the safety of Almjarhad would be ensured for centuries to come.

They eventually reached a flat piece of land. After circling the place a few times, Tioja continued flying at a lower altitude and spoke. "Can you safely land, my Lord? I would prefer not to risk your life landing together too fast."

"Don't underestimate me!"

Tioja complied without thinking and Jarahad felt a void in his body accompanied by sudden acceleration to the ground. With a small amount of air magic, he landed safely. Soon enough, the other members of the group stood in the place right in the middle of the valley. With a relentless wind blowing heated air in every direction, the sun granting no respite, and the absolute absence of any life form, Jarahad soon felt convinced.

Even though Sharad removed ample amounts of sweat from his brow, his beast remained active.

While Henrietta stared in every direction, Nurran's boots felt the soil crunch with every step. He knelt and pressed his hand against the ground. He soon stood up and brushed the dirt from his hands.

Henrietta stared at Jarahad with a concerned face. "What is your plan?"

Jarahad smiled after observing his surroundings for a few moments. "We barely survived fighting that calamity stone with everyone's help. If I have learned anything, it is to be one step ahead of our enemies. Whether we end up attacked by the Elf Kingdom's army or another human wielding one of those malignant stones, we will never forfeit our city to an enemy ever again. We suffered for decades to bring our city to life, and I will never accept having our home taken away from us."

Jarahad then stared at Nurran. "Your phantom beast has a unique ability and I hope you will return soon from your apprenticeship. I want you forge us the strongest weapon we have ever known." A lingering concern distracted Jarahad for a brief instant. "We cannot depend on any harlequin clans. I mean them no ill and understand why they guard the secret to their steel so much." Jarahad then focused on Henrietta. "I am glad you are forfeiting your birthright to stay with us. If you have ever taught me anything, it is to learn how to rely on each other. We survived two purges, the calamity stone, and the elements themselves. I believe we can continue proving we will create the best elf city away from the kingdom's borders. Nurran will be able to create a weapon that can help us while I protect Tioja."

Tioja was the most excited of the group. "I can't wait to find those stones and destroy them! Fill the world with their screaming flashes of death!"

Even though Tioja's promise was encouraging, Jarahad remained concerned. "If you find any stones along the way, please inform me first. I would be more than glad to barter a deal with the owner. If we can avoid battling against mages that don't attack us first, that would be best for everyone. We have enough problems being enemies of the elves. Furthermore, we have another problem that must be addressed at once."

Sharad was the most curious of all. "What do you mean? I thought we had enough problems with the kingdom and the calamity stone mages."

"They are nuisances and a huge threat to our city, but we already have a far more dangerous enemy who could destroy the clan."

"Who?" Sharad asked.

Henrietta's face became grave as she stared at the ground. "Gulraj still wants your sword, right?"

Jarahad sighed. "I am afraid so. His minions pretty much raped my citizens for months while I could only helplessly watch. I was spared from the punishment because my human blood rendered me worthless in Gulraj's eyes. And I believe I know why."

Tioja, Sharad, and Nurran averted their gazes while trying to forget the vile things they did.

Sharad's face became covered in disgust. "If my children must remain in Murdorhiolan as a condition for the truce, I will forget they were mine. Gulraj is no friend of our people. I wished we could stop him."

Tioja shook his head and hugged himself. "My brother… he is an abomination. Fear his power and wrath. Gulraj's clan is honor-bound to submit to his will, and they will only become more powerful with the new halflings we gave in exchange for his assistance. I am not strong enough to defeat him. If only I hadn't failed my initiation, I might have had a chance."

Jarahad snarled at once. "Silence, Tioja! You should never feel ashamed of your failure. I am very proud of you for being brave enough to honor your morality. Even if you passed the test, Gulraj would have taken Hamara's sword anyways. This is also the reason why we are reunited today. I respect Gulraj's many qualities and pray for the freedom of his enslaved citizens. As long as I am alive, Gulraj is honor-bound to respect Hurrujat's truce." Jarahad then grasped his sword hilt. "I am far more concerned about what might happen the day I perish."

Everyone stared at him at once.

Henrietta covered her mouth with a cupped hand. "Don't break a verbal promise, my Lord! You must return the sword!"

Jarahad sighed because Henrietta spoke too much. It was a quality of hers that was equally endearing and distressing at times. "I made a promise to Hurrujat where technically I must return the sword. If I perish far away from Murdorhiolan and the sword can't be found, Gulraj will equally be honor-bound to assume there is no ill will between our clans and the truce will remain. I have realized I will never be strong enough to save the entire world from despotic rulers. King Salman and Gulraj are equally evil and there is nothing I can do about it. I must focus my energies on protecting my citizens from harm. If the secret of the missing sword dies with all of us, Gulraj will be unable to touch the clan."

Nurran was even more skeptical than Sharad. "Seriously? Gulraj can't kidnap one of us to torture for information?"

"I only know from my upbringing in Orsenmuray that honor promises can never be broken. In case anyone is wondering, this is the reason why we are here reunited in this horrible place today." After giving everyone ample time to observe the inhospitable badlands, Jarahad continued. "I promise I will do everything in my power to outlive all of you. Well, except Sharad of course." A wink from his eyes prompted Sharad to chuckle. Jarahad then stared at Nurran. "Learn everything you can to become a master swordsmith. If your phantom beast can make metal impervious to attacks, I want you to build reinforced tunnels beneath Almjarhad. I believe these tunnels will both benefit the city's pureblood harlequins and offer escape routes in case we are once again attacked. I will never let my citizens die due to a lack of planning."

Sharad rubbed his nose with a finger while a cunning grin invaded his face. "I like your plan very much. Your father is going to have a lot of fun applying his extensive military knowledge."

Tioja stared at Henrietta and nodded. "The harlequins should feel welcome in Almjarhad and never be treated like second class citizens ever again. If the tunnels existed from the start, the clan would have never split into two and he would have never been born."

Nurran shook his head. "Gulraj is a dangerous man. But he also helped you master your Lehart. Be thankful he helped us destroy the calamity stone and save our city." With a straighter back, Nurran seemed more commanding than usual. "You want me to hide the sword in this place, am I correct?"

Jarahad's face softened because he knew his allies would agree to the plan. "This is the last place a pureblood harlequin would ever visit. I want you to create a structure underground that will be capable of resisting any attack. When the secret location of my sword dies with us, Almjarhad will forever be safe from Gulraj's wrath."

While Tioja, Nurran, and Sharad seemed equally eager to abide, Henrietta remained somewhat skeptical. "My Lord, why risk the safety of the clan with such a strange plan? Gulraj has honor, albeit it is rather twisted. All harlequins pride themselves in proving to the world we are more civilized than we seem at first."

Jarahad sighed. "I saw the farm."

"Huh?"

It was Tioja's turn to speak with a stuttering voice while he hugged himself. "He is evil. Murdorhiolan has a secret pit filled with mutilated human mages that supply him mana only to be discarded once they serve their purpose. He doesn't kidnap enemies either. Gulraj lies to his human allies to offer him their children as sacrifices. My mother taught us to respect our human subjects and treat them like our friends. Gulraj only wishes to cause agony without completely breaking the harlequin rules. If he recovers Jarahad's sword, it would only be a matter of time before he conquers Almjarhad and kidnaps the pureblood elves. I will do everything I can to protect our people!" Tioja's eyes widened from excitement and insanity at the sheer thought. "I will cover these lands with the blood of a million souls and dance a ballad of death on top of their innards!"

Despite the comically disgusted expression on Henrietta's face, Jarahad couldn't have expected anything less from Tioja. "You sacrificed too many things. Yet, you harbor no grudges against any of us for abandoning you when you needed our help. I will forever be indebted and trust you will be able to safeguard the sword from harm."

Tioja beamed even more, and everyone stared at the sky as the sun was partially hidden from a meandering cloud. Henrietta grasped Jarahad's shoulder and tenderly kissed his cheek. He didn't correspond to her public display of affection. However, the interlocked hands offered sufficient proof there might be stronger feelings to develop over time. Even though they will face many challenges, being together with a common goal meant their dreams could become true.

Jarahad smiled even more as he observed the beautiful sky above. "It is an honor to have you as my friends."

THE END

A FEW WORDS FROM THE AUTHOR

(This text contains spoilers from the Ominous Book series. You have been
warned)

This is the conclusion to the Fragmented Fates duology, which has
been a real thrill to write. I would like to mention several events that
happen between the conclusion of this book and An Ominous Book, which
happens approximately 600 years after the conclusion of this story.

What is a calamity stone? As Henrietta explains, they are a legend
among harlequins that are malignant magic devices. They seem like ordinary
stones at first sight and remain inactive. Once they enter contact with mana,
the stones activate, and it forms a lifelong bond with the bearer. The person
wearing the device doesn't even need to be a mage for the bond to form, it
only requires to be activated with mana.

I leave most of the events affecting Almjarhad between this huge
time lapse unwritten, but a few things are discovered in the Ominous Book
series here and there.

Tioja grows used to his insanity and finds ways to cope with it. Just
as everyone feared, additional calamity stones exist in the world, and
Almjarhad becomes attacked only 30 years after the conclusion of this
novel. Since I have no plans to write the second battle, I will mention one
of my books spoil some tidbits about what happens. Nurran perfects his
demonic beast and creates weapons considered failed attempts to imitate
harlequin steel by using highly purified carbon. While they don't have magic
like true harlequin steel, they increase the power of harlequin earth mages
and can destroy calamity stones without breaking apart.

Now that everyone knows how to destroy calamity stones,
Almjarhad is better prepared to fight against the second mage.

After discovering Gulraj's cruelty firsthand, Jarahad opts to
maintain a neutral stance and avoid aggravating him in any way possible. I
never write what happens between both characters in my books. It would

be fun to believe Gulraj visits Almjarhad at least once to visit Tioja, recruit more inhabitants and stir trouble.

I also never write about what happens between Jarahad and Henrietta. Perhaps they get married, or maybe not. Jarahad does have children in the future, and I wish to mention he marries at least twice in his life.

In case anyone is wondering, Sharad eventually accepts his ring but never bothers to claim ownership of the clan. He marries a halfling named Rumirum and has two children, one of which becomes a prominent character in my books.

Tioja will also continue appearing in my books. It feels funny to explore Tioja's youth because I always met him as his mentally unstable self that has already mastered his magic. Many readers liked him in Fragmented Fates, but I like his adult persona much more. He's quirky, kind of disturbing, and fun as hell to write. Tioja plays a pivotal role in the book Quandary. Gulraj also appears in my later books, this time as a villain instead of a mere antagonist.

I have unfinished sequels where we meet other important members of Gulraj's city, including his children: the brutish Irfil, the obnoxious Arsenia, and his grandson Kocho. I haven't decided whether to publish Mortality. The draft was finished years ago, but I have never felt like publishing it. A draft for the 9th book also exists, expanding things even further. We meet a second, more assertive Kocho and my beloved Elias, the child Talgel could have birthed with Gulraj. I love Elias so much. His phantom beast ability is versatile yet devoid of the flashiness of other demonic beasts. At over 170,000 words, the 9th book seems unpublishable. I don't even know how it ended up so damn long. Editing such a monstruous book is too terrifying. I still feel the itch to write a draft for the 10th and possibly final novel of the Ominous Book series. Just to have the excuse of having Elias kicking some butt in his own unique way. Heads up: Elias would totally humiliate Lord Froylan. The battle would be so uneven it wouldn't be fair for Froylan's ego.

Well, I have finally gotten this information out of my head. If my books somehow become cult hits 50 years from now, I am offering some information within the story canon for fanfic writers.

Wow, someone has finished reading this ridiculously long foreword? And didn't mind sifting through these spoilers? Well, I… uh… hope you enjoyed it, dear reader. Have a nice day!

GLOSSARY

Pureblood Elves (Elf Kingdom)

Commander Ferhyr: The current commander of the Äimite guard at the beginning of Fragmented Fates. He is the last surviving founding member of the guard and has been the commander for at least several centuries. Strict and efficient, Jamarnid describes him to be a decent leader. Ferhyr's tuning element and phantom beast are unknown.

Linda's mother: A pureblood elf with liberal beliefs. Used to live among a human nomadic tribe and slept with various lovers until she birthed her daughter Linda. Currently resides in the Elf Kingdom paying off a hefty debt to lawyers for liberating Linda from prison.

Master Lord Salman: Current king of the Elf Kingdom who rules the country with an iron fist. Condemned the entire Grey Clan to death upon the bloodshed in his palace during Jamarnid's frantic rescue. Phantom beast is unknown, although it is proven in the series he is a mediocre air mage.

Senior Lord Froylan: A former criminal now serving a life sentence as a highly respected member of the Äimite guard. Was selected to become one of Jamarnid's two executioners and maimed part of his body. Froylan is a fire mage who summons a salamander with two tails named a Levanant.

Lord Tameer: A captain of the Äimite Guard and Froylan's closest ally. A very gifted and respected warrior, Salman never promotes him due to his abrasive personality. Tameer is an earth mage that summons an anteater phantom beast called a Yerjaha.

Pureblood Elves (Exiled elves of Almjarhad)

Boshi: A promiscuous elf with lilac hair, Boshi ends up being forced to marry 16 women as punishment for his infidelity.

Daedoman: An elf of very short stature, severe stocky face that wears an eyepatch. Works as a doll artisan for a living. Harbors resentment at Talgel because his son Egiel died rescuing her during Orsenmuray's downfall. Hostile towards the harlequins, Talgel tells him early in the first book that he will someday marry a human and have more children. Daedoman is a water mage.

Dorin: Another one of the exiled elves of Almjarhad. He is an earth mage.

Guma: One of the volunteers that accompanies Jarahad to Gulraj's city. Shorter than most elves with short white hair and crystalline light blue eyes. He resided in Teris's palace. His tuning element and phantom beast are unknown.

Imano: One of the five pureblood elves that visits Gulraj's city. Oshana slapped his face for disobedience, prompting Tioja's ire. His tuning element and phantom beast are unknown.

Jamad: Tioja's father and a depressed drunkard that still harbors hopes his former wife Hamara will return to his side. After attacking Sharad in the first book, Jamad is still serving a community service sentence several days a month. Sharad usually orders him to perform mundane activities such as polishing his boots or clean his bedroom. Jamad is a water mage.

Jamen: Tioja's grandfather who decided to remain in Almjarhad alongside his harlequin wife, Svetlana. Jamen is an earth mage that summons a phantom beast resembling a humanoid paper effigy with an unknown name.

Kukuro: One of the 5 pureblood elves that accompanies Tioja to Gulraj's city, that spends his time in Kibito's palace. Phantom beast and tuning element are unknown.

Lord Jamarnid: Former Äimite Guard and a member of the nobility class from the Grey Clan. The clan's former leader Serumo was his second cousin. Sentenced to death after impregnating a civilian with human and harlequin ancestry named Chandrice. Jamarnid is the current interim ruler of Almjarhad due to his distant blood claim while he waits for his nephew Sharad to become the ruler by birthright. Due to his disability after the botched execution, Jamarnid's son Jarahad covers for him. Jamarnid was once an immensely gifted swordsman which was the reason why he became invited to the guard. He is a capable earth mage who can summon a beast combining a humanoid face, wolf paws and a lizard body named Lusenia.

Lord Sharad: Lord Serumo's youngest son and thus the true heir of the Grey Clan. After escaping the Elf Kingdom at a very young age, Sharad suffered from relentless trauma witnessing the fall of Orsenmuray and the heart wrenching voyage to Almjarhad. Despite his childish demeanor, Sharad is a trustworthy person. Sharad is a water mage that summons a salamander shaped beast called an Artica.

Soremin: An ancient elf with wavy brown hair and seagreen eyes. His arms are covered in scars due to a secret reason that is never revealed in this series. Soremin currently resides in a temple in the mountainous outskirts of Almjarhad and trains his pupils to become priests. Soremin is a fire mage who can summon a fire bird known as a Hiratori.

Halflings (inhabitants of Almjarhad)

Jarahad: The illegitimate son of Jamarnid and a human-harlequin woman named Chandrice. Exiled from the Elf Kingdom as a newborn child, Jarahad spent his difficult childhood in the city ruled by Chandrice's grandfather Hurrujat. Brave and selfless, Jarahad keeps order in Almjarhad while always helping his peers. Hopeful of marrying his love interest Talgel, Jarahad tries to win her love by fulfilling his sword initiation. As an earth and air mage, Jarahad can also summon a demonic beast that envelops his body in a gelatinous armor called Rashid.

Nurran: Jamen's youngest son and Tioja's uncle. A boisterous young man who has awakened his demonic beast during some unspecified moment in the story. Nurran is a water and fire mage.

Talgel: Known as the seer of Almjarhad, her pureblood elf father and harlequin mother perished during the downfall of Orsenmuray. Once a vivacious person, her personality changed the day she awakened her phantom beast, a greenish monster bonded to her soul named Giltemarraj. Granted with the ability to see the future with absolute certainty in exchange for ending up blind, Talgel has moved every event of the first book in the hopes she can save Almjarhad from an unknown threat. Talgel is a fire and air mage.

Tanato: A priest apprentice who secretly wants to introduce harlequin religious rituals to the populace, Soremin enjoys his company as a friend and mentor. After ending up badly injured by Anduvio shortly after his arrival, Tanato will need to awaken his phantom beast if he ever wants to speak again. Tanato is a very gifted air mage. His second tuning element is unknown.

Halflings (inhabitants of Murdorhiolan)

Hamara: Tioja's mother who abandoned her husband Jamad at the end of book 1 to elope with Hurrujat. A selfish woman whose greatest desire is for her two sons to rule Murdorhiolan together. Her demonic beast covers her body in a clay armor for melee combat named Pirrum. She is a water and earth mage.

Mako: A young female halfling that lives in Murdorhiolan.

Pureblood Harlequins (inhabitants of Almjarhad)

Henrietta: Talgel's roommate with a mysterious past. She is boisterous, bubbly and very kind to everyone. She is not a member of Hurrujat's clan, albeit her identity and intentions are kept secret from everyone except

Jarahad. Henrietta is a water mage.

Svetlana: Jamen's wife and originally from Orsenmuray. They both have six children where only 3 of them are mentioned in the story (Kashin, Hamara, and Nurran). A kind person, Tioja frequently visits her home. Svetlana cannot use magic.

Pureblood Harlequins (inhabitants of Murdorhiolan or other harlequin cities)

Amaragaflantia: Kashin's fourth and final wife. Tioja had difficulty pronouncing her name when he first met her. Hurrujat forced Kashin to marry her instead of Linda as punishment for Gulraj's inability to awaken his phantom beast.

Baa: Tioja's mentor and the current sword master of Lazarius's clan. She is abrasive, very gifted in combat and believes Tioja will fail his initiation. Falsely believes the Elf Kingdom is a backwards patriarchy.

Golana: Kashin's second wife. Just like his other wives, she is cruel and proud of her arrangement. Her father was overthrown and murdered by another harlequin along with her entire family. Instead of showing appreciation for surviving the purge thanks to her marriage, she mistreats everyone instead.

Hurrujat: Ruler of the harlequin clan that forms an alliance with the exiled Grey Clan elves. He is also Jarahad's maternal great-grandfather. Abandons Almjarhad to create the new city of Murdorhiolan alongside his wife Hamara. Currently dying from skin cancer. Considered by most people to be a decent and jovial man, he becomes a crueler person in the second novel. Hurrujat is an air mage.

Iora: Nemoraj's daughter and now Kashin's first wife by arranged marriage. An arrogant woman who is proud of her current social position.

Lazarius: The dour leader of the clan where Tioja is sent for his initiation.

His tuning element is unknown.

Nemoraj: Leader of another clan. Agreed to become Hurrujat's ally by supplying him with söma and initiate some of his warriors. Forces Kashin to marry his daughter Iora and niece Yurivia.

Usana: One of Deshueila's two wives. She is shorter and stockier than most harlequins. Her tuning element is unknown.

Yurivia: Kashin's third wife and Iora's cousin. Her tuning element just like Kashin's other wives is unknown.

Knights of Murdorhiolan

Deshueila: The youngest of Hurrujat's 5 knights. He was still a child when his family abandoned Almjarhad and only recently finished his initiation. Currently married to two harlequins (one is never shown, the other named Usana). Unlike the other knights, Deshueila is reticent but polite to everyone.

Kashin: Tioja's uncle and one of Hamara's older brothers. Despite his father's concerns in book 1, Kashin proudly accompanies Hurrujat to his new city. In appreciation for building Murdorhiolan, Kashin is sent to another harlequin clan to train where he meets his love interest, a hybrid human-elf woman named Linda. Kashin is an earth and water mage like his sister. His demonic beast takes the form of an ink spewing from his blood that can leak into the soil.

Kibito: The weakest of the five knights, his lower elf ancestry forces him to overcome his shortcomings by being more brutish than his peers.

Oshana: The only female knight, she is described to have frizzy black hair and cross-eyes. Married to two male harlequins that are never shown in the story. Not much else is known about her.

Teris: A halfling that was born in Hurrujat's original city shortly before its downfall. Very skilled in combat, there are rumors his first murder was committed when he was only 12 years old.

Other inhabitants of Murdorhiolan:

Linda: Kashin's love interest and a human-elf hybrid. Linda can summon a phantom beast that is never revealed in the story.

Toby: The human slave that Tioja was morally against murdering. Toby is an air mage that summons a phantom beast resembling a balloon.

Other characters:

Anduvio: A human man from faraway lands who claims to be the most talented mage in the world. Dressed in gaudy jester costumes, Anduvio is equally campy and malicious. Anduvio is a gifted air mage that opts for close melee combat.

Fluff: A kitten Hamara gifted Tioja shortly after he arrived to Murdorhiolan as an apology for killing his pet in the first book. With fluffy fur and a flat face, Gulraj named it Fluff. The cat is more than 20 years old and still living thanks to Gulraj's healing magic.

Giltemarraj: The demon that has bonded to Talgel's soul, every event in the first book was planned by it to further its unknown personal agenda. The Giltemarraj has a masculine reptilian body that can float in the air. Its main ability is knowing the future and passing small amounts of knowledge at a time to its summoner.

OTHER WORKS FROM THE AUTHOR

Fragmented Fates Duology

1. Fragmented fates

2. Savior on the zenith

An Ominous Book series

1. An Ominous Book

2. Separation

3. Exile

4. Diaspora

5. A calamity

6. Quandary

7. Harlequins

8. Mortality (coming soon!)

Other works outside of the Ominous Book universe

Hyperian Monarch (coming soon!)

A romantic dystopic fantasy starring a clumsy (and very neurotic) heroine named Lydia. When the world's Dragon Emperor dies soon after she starts classes in a highly prestigious private magic school, Lydia along with another 99 students are randomly selected to compete for the throne. Quitting is not an option. Anyone who is eliminated in each round is erased from the world forever. To win, Lydia must overcome her fears, discover the whole purpose of this twisted game, and fall in love with one of several hot guys that are attracted to her for no apparent reason.

A curse of optical haptics (coming soon!)

One does not choose their family. But Leenx can still find the way of liberating himself from an ancient family curse. Is he willing to pay the price? A weird Sci-Fi/Fantasy adventure.

Sometimes dead is better (Coming soon!)

An upcoming collection of short horror stories with a Mexican twist. Written in English and Spanish.

ABOUT THE AUTHOR

Born in Minneapolis Minnesota and established in Mexico City when I started 4th grade without knowing a word of Spanish, and assumed my newly found country was going to be a tropical city covered with palm trees (boy was I wrong!). I grew up with the culture clash and economic crisis of the 1990's and a passion for Japanese animation, figure ice skating and cats.

When I'm not practicing medicine or fixing busted typewriters pro bono, I'm traveling to foreign countries to see spectacular nature, hard to reach pyramids and the occasional military museum. Who knows, perhaps you will bump into me in a youth hostel in Tokyo or a whale shark snorkeling tour.